FREDBITS

A Daily Dose of Wisdom, Wit, and Wonder

By Fred Dyke

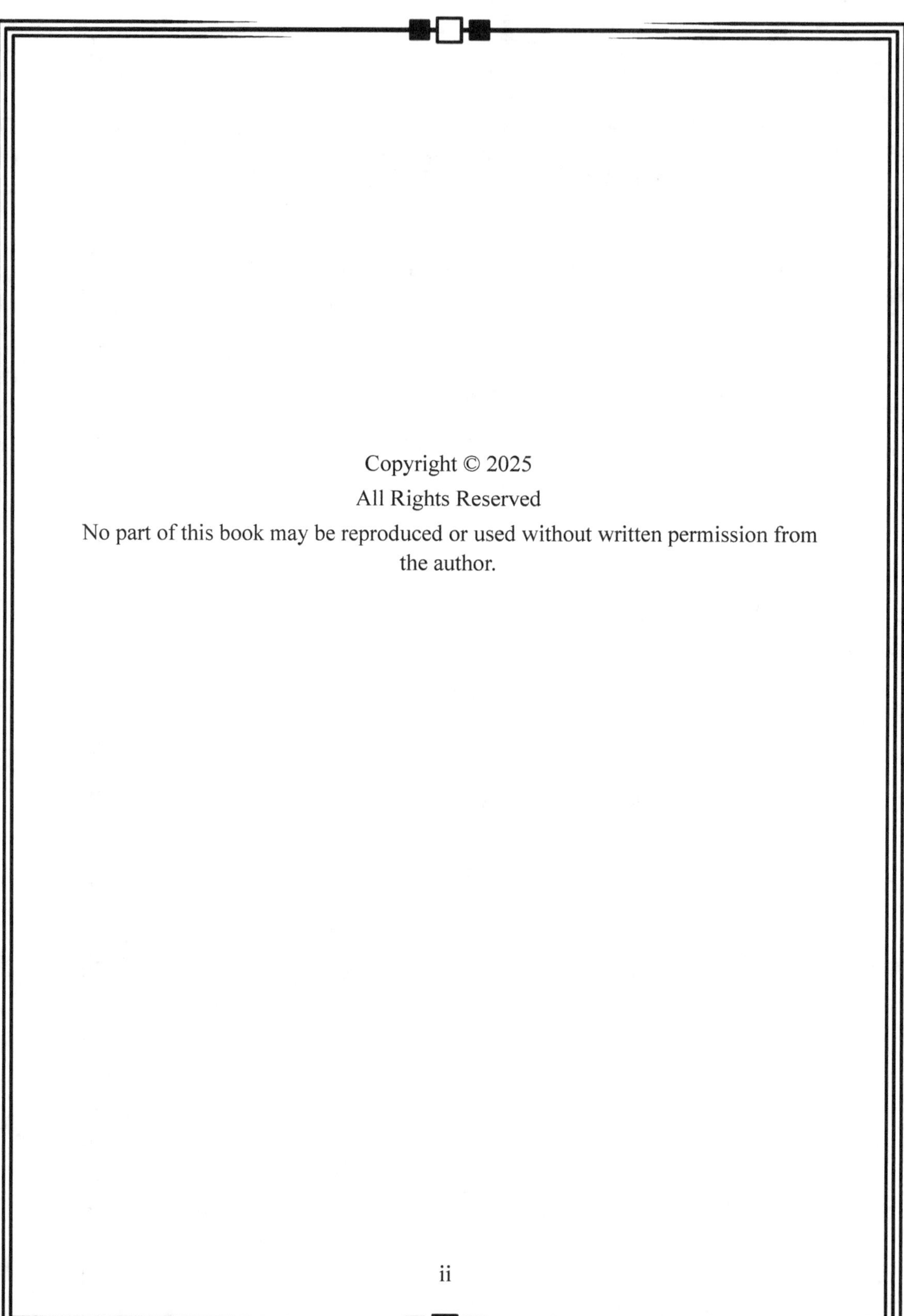

Dedication

Dedicated to my parents, Chesley and Elsie Dyke.

To my wife Judee and to our seven children, grandchildren and great grandchildren, and to my brothers and sisters.

Acknowledgments

I thank God for my life, experiences and all the people that He has allowed to be in my path.

My every contact, direct and indirect, have all contributed to my life.

I acknowledge and am so very thankful for the support and encouragement from my wife, Judee.

I am thankful for my family, friends and all I have had the pleasure of working with and knowing.

Preface

In a way this book is my autobiography, but rather than detailing the various aspects and details of the many roads I have taken, I have chosen to write about some of the things I have learned while living my life experiences.

Learning and growing is not always easy. Some things come intentionally and willingly but "the school of hard knocks" can open up many doors and teach us things that we didn't know existed.

I don't pretend to know everything but with this book, my hope is to pass on a few things that may help the readers. In the meantime, in addition to sharing some lessons that I have learned, I hope to entertain you and with some of the daily topics covered in this book. You will note that I do not just share my views but some views, opinions and knowledge from other people and sources who have much to offer. You may find facts and information in the following pages that you may not agree with. Guess what! There are things I have written about that I may not agree with either.

We all have lots of questions about life, but we don't necessarily have all the answers. I hope that your daily reading will give you even more questions and some of the answers. I also hope that you may be challenged to search for more answers on some of the individual topics.

We are living in a wonderful world that God has given us. God's first words to humanity were "Be fruitful and multiply." That tells me to learn, grow, and produce. It is up to us to live and get along with each other. There is a lot to learn for all of us. I have just scratched the surface. "May God give me the grace to learn more."

I wish to thank all the people I have had the pleasure to meet and learned from in my life. Yes, even the ones that I didn't appreciate at the time and definitely the ones that cared about me enough to knock some sense into my head.

I also want to thank my wonderful wife, Judee and our seven children.

And oh yes, "Thank you, God!"

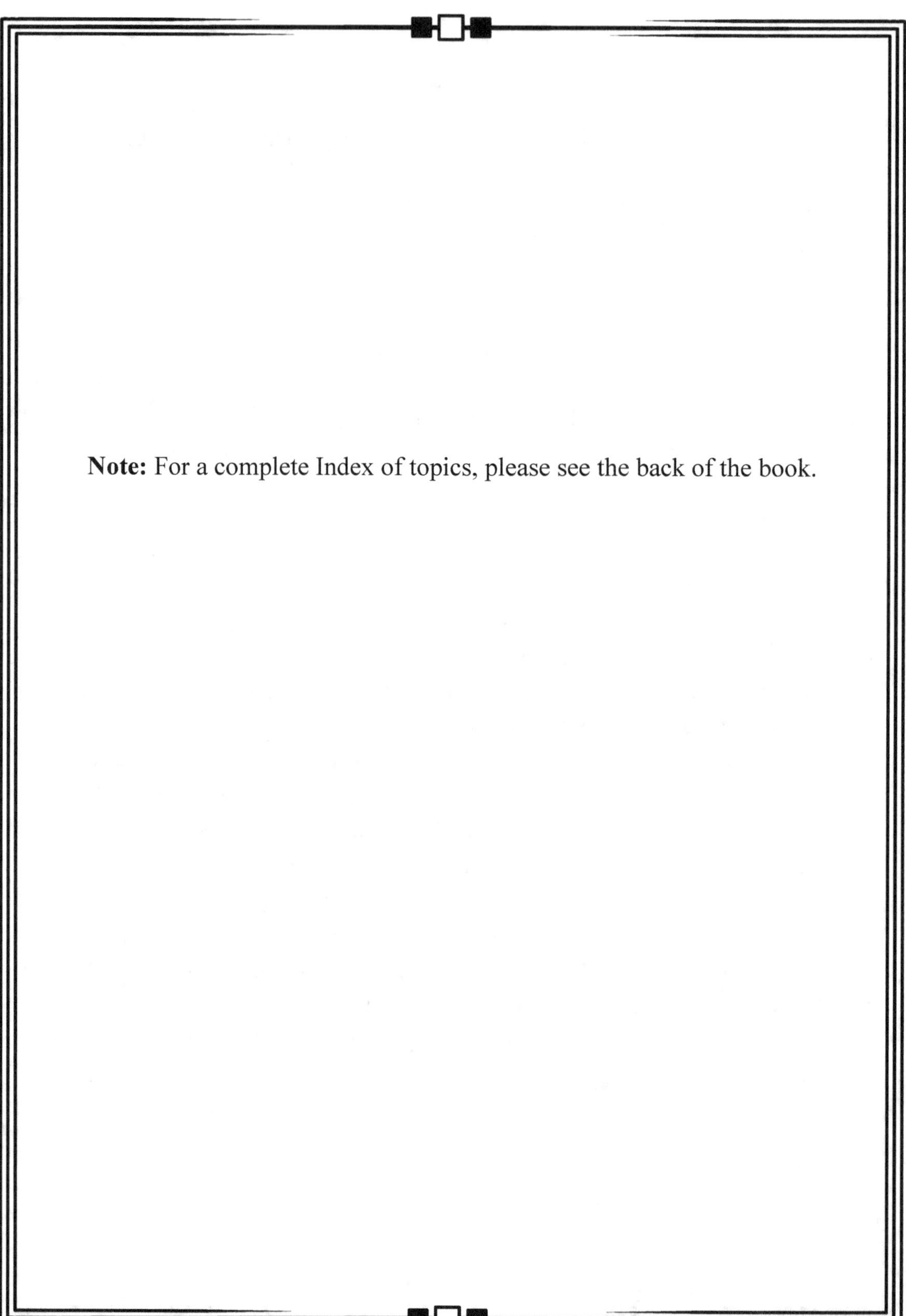

Note: For a complete Index of topics, please see the back of the book.

1
"Questions"

Do you have all the answers?

What are the questions?

Are you happy?

Are you sad?

Does the slightest thing make you mad?

What about your moods?

Do they vary with your foods?

Are you up or are you down?

What causes you to frown?

What will it take to give you a lift?

If I say the wrong thing, will you be miffed?

Can you take a criticism?

What if I insult your favorite ism?

Will you laugh at a joke?

Can a friend give you a poke?

Do you get along with people?

Is your ego on a steeple?

Are you content with your life?

Are you happy with your husband or wife?

Are you good at getting along?

Are your opinions just too strong?

Are your values yours?

Do you follow whoever opens your doors?

Do you know how to love?

Do you know the one above?

Will you dare to take a look?

At all the pages in this book?

2
"Looking Back"

Thanks for picking up my book. It really is about everything. Well, not quite but it covers a lot of areas. I wrote it just for you. And me. I wanted to look back over my life and review my ups and downs, successes, and setbacks. Have you ever wondered what made you what and who you are today? Are you the sum total of all your experiences or did we just turn out this way?

When I look back. Wow! There is so much. I can hardly believe it. All the people I have met. All the experiences I have had. And it is not over yet. Hopefully, I still have a few years left to reminisce and enjoy some of the fruits of the past and maybe, just maybe, change and correct a few blunders I have made. No, we are not ever too old to grow and learn new things.

How is life going for you? Do you feel like you need a break from it all? This is the book for you. It contains many of my life experiences and the experiences and knowledge of others on various subjects. I don't claim to know everything, but I will share some things I have learned, some the hard way. Maybe I will get you thinking. I wish I had a book like this when I was younger. I probably wouldn't have read it, because like many, we either thought we knew everything, or we were just not curious enough.

There is so much information out there. How can we possibly take it all in. Besides, much of it doesn't exactly help us, because there is a battle going on for our minds.

Here is your chance to pick up a few ideas by reading a page a day on a variety of topics. They appear in no particular order but if you want to stick to a particular topic, check out the topical index in the back.

The sources for most of the pages include my own life, some people I have met and read about, and in some cases I just look to other sources for help. Enjoy!

"Looking ahead is good. It is also good to look back, even if it is just to see how far you have come."

3

"Starting Over!"

Are you one of those who have everything figured out or are you fed up with who you are and where you are in life?

Would you like to be able to push a reset button like the one in your bathroom? It is there for your protection in case of a short circuit. There were times in my life when I should have pressed the reset button, but I kept going. However there were times when I did press the reset button.

These extra pounds on my waistline didn't all of a sudden appear. They began with the first chocolate chip cookie, Nanaimo bar or dish of ice cream. The debt and bills we have didn't suddenly appear. They began when we decided to charge something on our credit cards or take out a loan, which also resulted from our view of money or even our view of life, or heaven forbid our desires to have things that are not necessary.

> *"We didn't just get where we are. It all started somewhere."*

What about relationships with family and friends?

Don't you wish you could get along better at home, or at work with people? What about your habits, lifestyle, addictions, attitudes etc.? Don't you wish you had a reset button for them?

Can you start over and is this the day to start? Well, I don't want to spoil your day, but there is much to think about, including how you got where you are in the first place. If things are going well just decide to enjoy your day with family and friends. If not, then decide to enjoy your day with family and friends anyway. If you have no family, and friends, then it is time to push the reset button. Come back tomorrow after you spend the day answering these two questions.

What is good about my life?

What would I change if I could?

Want a good movie about starting over? Try "Father Stu". *(A true story about someone who started over)*

4
"Love"

Want to talk about love? What is it? We hear this at most weddings.

"Though I speak with the tongues of men and of angels, but have not love, I have become sounding brass or a clanging cymbal. ² And though I have the gift of prophecy, and understand all mysteries and all knowledge, and though I have all faith, so that I could remove mountains, but have not love, I am nothing. ³ And though I bestow all my goods to feed the poor, and though I give my body to be burned, but have not love, it profits me nothing.

⁴ Love suffers long <u>(patient)</u> and is kind; love does not envy; love does not parade itself, is not puffed up; ⁵ does not behave rudely, does not seek its own, is not provoked, thinks no evil; ⁶ does not rejoice in iniquity, but rejoices in the truth; ⁷ bears all things, believes all things, hopes all

things, endures all things."1 Corinthians 13:1-7

<u>(How are you doing with this love thing?)</u>

I used to listen to these words but didn't really take them seriously. I am still working on them.

See the first paragraph above. If you don't have love, it doesn't matter what else we have, it is just noise. Yes, we can have it all, but without love we are nothing- *"it profits me nothing."*

Do we really understand love? I used to think love was all about my personal likes and dislikes, but the second part (4-7) indicates that love is not even about our selfish desires, but our unselfish attitudes and actions.

Go ahead give yourself a rating on the things from verses 4-7. Rank each from 1-5 with 5 being great and 1 being poor.

Would those who know you agree with your ratings?

5
"Shift Happens"

The airline Westjet, for a while at least, put some personality and fun to flying by adding appropriate and occasional humor to their announcements. When the flight ended and while taxing into the terminal, the stewardess announced to be careful when fetching over-head bags as "shift happens".

Everyone laughed. We all knew what she could have said and meant.

But things can happen and do happen that we do not plan for or expect. How we respond to them and allow for them is important.

My father always filled his boats and car with gas at the end of each trip, so he would not have to do it at the beginning of a trip. Why, because "shift happens." If he had to go somewhere in an emergency, he didn't have to take the time to fill up because "shift happens."

My wife Judee is very good with her time management; she never leaves until tomorrow what she could do today because "shift happens".

Putting off important priorities and important things to the last minute is not a good idea because "shift happens" that can cause major problems.

Avoid overspending and overborrowing because "shift happens."

Have a will and get things in order because "shift happens"

Tell people you love them, be kind because 'shift happens'.

Keeping the toilet paper holder filled is important because 'shift happens'.

6
"Isms"

An "ism" is a three-letter suffix that follows a word. It gives the word a doctrine or a political ideology. There are religious ones, and many other kinds of isms but we'll deal with those later.

It takes a while to understand the political isms and they are often confusing. That's because what they say they are and how they behave don't always agree. Political isms can cause controversy and offend people because we know how sensitive some people can be. Nevertheless, we will be outlining some of the details in this book. You may not like what you see.

Here are some common ones:

Modern democracies always have _Liberalism a_nd _Conservativism_, often referred to as left and right. Usually, such democracies follow _Capitalism_ which covers financial methods as well as political methods. All of these supposedly operate under a free market type of system where people have a say who they want in government and how governments are run. North America, much of Europe, the United Kingdom and more would be included in such countries.

However, believe it or not there are a number of countries whereby the government or certain elites, control just about everything. Those countries would be categorized under isms like _Communism, Marxism_, and to a great extent, _Socialism._

Confused? Stay around. They will be detailed later.

I forgot to tell you that they often lie about each other and they even lie about themselves. Is there such a word as "lie ism"?

"Isms" are also attached to a whole bunch of other things like racism, sexism and the more recent wokeism.

7

"Famous People"

What makes famous people famous?

If you search the internet for famous people, you will find various lists of names of famous people. These are people who at some time in history did something that made them well known. Their names are easily recognizable. People like John F. Kennedy, (former US president who was assassinated), Elvis Presley, (King of Rock and Roll) and Winston Churchill are very familiar names of the twentieth century. We all recognize people from years ago like Julius Caesar, (Roman Emperor), Leonardo Da Vinci (Painter of the Mona Lisa and The Last Supper) and athletes like the hockey great, Wayne Gretzky, and scientist, Albert Einstein.

The people I just named may be considered famous, some because of their positive contribution to society or at least in their fields of endeavor. They had major accomplishments and had major influences. They may not have set out to be famous. They simply excelled in their respective fields and were obviously committed to their causes.

However some famous people are not always people to be admired as outstanding citizens or accomplishing things that make this a better world. Adolf Hitler is a famous well-known name, but certainly caused havoc in the world. Communist leaders like Karl Marx, Joseph Stalin, Mao Tze Tong and murderers like Charles Manson are very familiar but they don't exactly make everyone feel good, even though to the shock of many, they are held up on pedestals by some.

There are people, who have led wonderful lives and contributed great things in their communities and circle of friends and family that will never make it to the top hundred list of famous people, or even to the top one million of famous people. Do you desire to be famous, or do you just want to be kind, loving, serving, honest, helpful and caring? Now those are famous people to me and the kind I want to be around.

Who are some famous people that you admire? Who are people that you admire that are not famous people?

8

"Examine Yourself"

You have heard the expression, "You can't get there from here". Some good advice when we plan, is to ask three questions:

Who am I now? Who do I want to be? How will I get there?

Ignoring the first question can be a big mistake. Do you really know who you are or where you are? That is why we should examine ourselves.

It is always a good idea to take stock of your present situation. "I always wanted to be a Russian ballet dancer. But I am not Russian." Not funny? Oh well, it just means we have to acknowledge who we are, our strengths and weaknesses before we set out on our journey.

Have a weight problem and want to lose some pounds? But you love food, especially desserts, plus you have become a couch potato. Want to get out of debt, but have you accepted the fact that you have a spending problem? Want to get closer to people, but don't realize that you have a body odor problem? Want to get more done in a day, but don't realize or accept the fact that time is wasted on things like talking too much, or just being a busybody. These examples and more need to be acknowledged about ourselves when we decide to set goals. In fact, some of them are the reasons we set goals.

> *In the 60's, a common fallback for comedians like Bob Hope, and others was: "I broke my arm in three places. The doctor told me to stay out of those places."*

In setting goals, we need to face some facts in answering the question, "What is it about me that may hinder me from achieving it?". Or "What is about me that gives me confidence in achieving my goal?" All too often, we either don't know ourselves or don't want to acknowledge who we are. We may overestimate ourselves or underestimate ourselves.

How do you underestimate yourself? How do you overestimate yourself?

Great movie: "Walk the Line" – Life of Johnny Cash.

"Examine yourself before examining anyone else. Be much more thorough about your own self-examination." *Chuck Swindoll*

9
"Get Over It"

There is another question we need to ask. "Why am I in my present situation? We don't want to repeat some of our mistakes, that is if we do not like our situation. On the other hand, if we are in a good situation we do want to repeat the good things that got us here.

A big caution here especially if we are in a mess: Take responsibility and take ownership. Putting it in other ways, "Get over blaming others."; "Stop with the victim mentality of making excuses."; "Forgiveness is a good idea."

Yes, we all have a past. Yes, we all have been influenced by our upbringing. Things have happened to us that were not nice. Some of them we have caused and others they just happened. We can make a choice here to hold on to our downers and misfortunes or accept them and move on. We had them and there is nothing we can do to change them.

Rick Hansen had an accident that put him in a wheelchair for life. Yes, he had to take life sitting down. But he was the guy who went 25,000 miles around the world in 34

> *It is better to use our past to move us forward than to hold us back.*

countries in a wheelchair, raising awareness and money for spinal cord injuries. I witnessed Rick on his journey in New Brunswick and later attended one of his motivational seminars. Rick refused to allow his past to influence his future. He accepted his lot in life and moved on.

It sounds harsh when someone tells us to "get over it, doesn't it? Maybe there is a nicer way to say it, nevertheless, what can we do about it? Nothing. I remember when I shared with my buddy Steve about something that happened to me that I had a tough time getting over. He said, "Get over it. move on." I never told Steve, but I felt like slapping him at the time. It wasn't easy but I had to move on, and I did. There is no question we have to get through dramatic experiences in our lives and yes, we may need professional help in the process. We cannot change our past, but we can do something about today and tomorrow and the rest of our lives.

"You have to be the best you can be, with what you have." *Rick Hansen*

10
"Change of Heart"

Change, change, what is change?
Change is good; change is bad; change can make you mad.
Change may be as good as a rest, but it may not be the best.
You can change your socks, change your shirt, and it won't hurt.
You can change gears and change tires – you can even change your wires.
You can change your style for a while; change your look, change your book.
All this change may be a start, but will it change your heart?

You can change jobs or change address – change can make or break a mess.
You can change where you are able, but will the change make you stable?
You can change flights without a fight; change your oil so it won't spoil.
You can change planes or change lanes, but will the change make you sane.
Light bulbs need a change- batteries also need a change.
Different things may be your part, will these changes, change your heart?

What about your heart?
You can have a bleeding heart, a cheating heart and a broken heart.
You can have a mended heart, a heart disease, a heart at ease.
A heart can burn, a heart can yearn, drop to your feet or jump to your teeth.
A heart can beat, a heart can bleep, a heart can slip, a heart can flip.
A heart can ache, a heart can break,
You can have an achy-breaky heart - but can you have a change of heart?

You can change where you hide, you can change where you abide.
Have you changed how you love, as directed from above?
You can change your friends whose lives you are a part.
But can you change your heart? Yes, you can.
Saul changed to Paul and was stopped where he ran.
His heart changed his behavior when he was confronted by his Savior.
When Jesus comes into your heart – then you will have a change of heart.

11
TV Shows - 50's and 60's

1. The name of the Lone Rangers' horse _______________________

2. The Lone Ranger was called by his partner _______________________

3. His partner's name was _______________________

4. The name of the theme song was _______________________

5. Roy Roger's wife name was _______________________

6. Roy's horse's name was _______________________

7. His wife's horse's name was _______________________

8. Cisco Kid had a partner named _______________________

9. The actor who played Hop along Cassidy was _______________________

10. Paladin would travel with his _______________________

11. The name of the Rebel was _______________________

12. He roamed through the _______________________

13. The famous father knew _______________________

14. The best Sunday night variety show was _______________________

15. The Rifleman was played by _______________________

Answers page 40 – Don't cheat.

12

"George Foreman"

I have been told many times that people don't change. While there is some truth in that and I agree change doesn't come easy, George Foreman changed.

George Foreman was a rough, tough, heavy-weight boxer whose determination and mean streak from growing up in poverty and hunger drove him to win the world heavyweight boxing championship. He quickly disposed of his opponents, knocking out most of them at a time when his division was filled with tough contenders like Joe Frasier, Ken Norten and more. He was at the top of his game and had never been defeated when he was challenged by the former champion Mohamed Ali.

George punched himself out for the seven rounds while Ali lay on the ropes and defended himself. Whether his strategy was wrong, or he was poorly coached doesn't matter, he was knocked out in round 8.

George went downhill but had an experience in the dressing room after a subsequent fight, where his heart stopped. After is experience, he had a big change. He found God and gave up boxing and became a minister. Combined with that he opened a training centre for street kids. After being out of the ring for ten years, he ran out of money and decided to fight again to regain his title and make some money doing it. George was laughed at and mocked, but ten years later, at the age of 45, he regained his title by knocking out Michael Moore in the tenth round.

But the George that regained his title was not the same George who lost the title. He had changed. He certainly had a change of heart. What a comeback! What a change!

Watch the movie- "Big George Foreman."

13
"Commitment"

Before I became a teenager, I would wash in the morning at the kitchen basin. I brushed my teeth and combed my hair before I went to school. There was only one reason I did that. My mother made me do it. She made sure I was clean and presentable before I went out the door. I was not committed to the process. I did it because I had to. My mother gave me the quality control check. She watched me and pulled me back in by the ear if I failed to meet the standards.

We are all committed to something. Some are committed to neat and tidy. Some are committed to family, and to working hard, while others are committed to watching TV all day, being lazy, and being irresponsible. Yes, some are committed to not being committed. Employers look for committed workers. When commitment is evident, employees require less direction and supervision.

Commitment is being totally turned on to something. My commitment was to get out the door and join my buddy, Sam White, and others in kicking a can down the road on the way to school. If my shirt tail was out, or if my hair was messy, it didn't really bother me.

But one day my commitment changed. I discovered girls. Suddenly, I was involved with something different and my commitment level or at least the object of my commitment changed. I began to take more interest in my appearance. Guess what! I began spending more time in the kitchen basin. My mother no longer needed to watch over me. I did it all on my own without having to be encouraged or told what to do.

> *Most people fail, not because of lack of desire but because of a lack of commitment.*
> - Vicent Lombardi

Commitment leads to action. It is a cure for failure because it gives purpose and drive. It is bigger than desire, as important as desire is. Many people want and desire something but without commitment, the desire is often just wishful thinking. Commitment will overcome fear, shyness, low self-esteem and enable us to find a way.

14
"Reap and Sow"

"Reaping and Sowing" is one of the most famous practical laws ever written. It is often spoken about and quoted by motivational speakers, lecturers, authors, business leaders, bosses, preachers and parents.

It has been referred to as a law that has its roots as a biblical concept in the context and principle of planting seed and getting a good crop.

However, the principle applies to all areas of life as in:

"You get out what you put in."

"You work hard; you get paid."

"Put in the effort and you will get results."

"Wrong actions result in consequences."

"Good actions result in rewards."

"What goes around comes around."

"Sow a thought, and you reap an act; Sow an act, and you reap a habit; Sow a habit and you reap a character; Sow a character, and you reap a destiny." ~ Ralph Waldo Emerson.

Too bad this is often ignored today by those who "plant apple seeds and expect grapes". Sound silly?

But this is what I think: "You can't tell lies and expect to be trusted. If you waste your money, you won't have it for sensible things. It's hard to have friends if you are not friendly."

15
"Happiness Is"

"Different Things to Different People." That's what happiness is. This song was released in 1966 by Ray Conniff. It was written by Paul Evans & Paul Parnes.

It is a happy fun song that shows how we all have a different view of happiness. The song details happiness for various types of people like to a preacher, it is a prayer and to a golfer, it is a hole-in-one.

What makes you happy? Are there one or two particular things or does it change from time to time? On a hot, dry day, you would likely be happy with a cold glass of water. What makes us happy when we are young doesn't seem to help us now as we are aging. Yet a decision made when we are young can ruin our future happiness. Should happiness be the determining factor of our decisions?

Does happiness vary depending on time and circumstances?

Ok then have some fun. List as many things as you can that make you happy. You have room below. Go.

____

____

____

____

____

____

Now that you have listed them, is there one there that would take away the happiness of all the others?

Consider this. To what extent should happiness depend on our circumstances vs. who we are on the inside?

16
"Science"

I love science, don't you? I majored in Physics over 50 years ago. I have forgotten most of it. I remember some basic principles, but the details have drifted away from my brain.

There is such a thing as true science. But sadly, there is such a thing as a "world view" or opinions that people wished were true or pushed to be true. Some call the later, "pseudoscience" or false science.

True science is true in that the discovery is provable and useful. Electricity was discovered. It has been tested and proven over and over and it is used every day by the world. We don't need to touch a live wire to confirm what true science and scientists have told us about electricity.

Physics, chemistry, biology etc., have made tremendous advancements in the discovery and application of their discoveries. It continues and will do so. Keep in mind that while inventions of new technology happen all the time that confirm discoveries, the information was already there. Science didn't invent electricity. They discovered it. The same is true with many things.

Oxford Dictionary via Google says science is: *the systematic study of the structure and behavior of the physical and natural world through observation, experimentation, and the testing of theories against the evidence obtained,"*

Makes sense, right? But note it requires testing. That means before scientists can draw a conclusion, they have to prove that it works. That brings us to the "world view" of science. "World View" of things does not always agree with the true scientific conclusion of knowledge and information.

Who are these world view people? Are they people with an agenda who may or may not be brilliant but are quick to interpret findings in a manner that they have already made up their minds to be true? It is quite possible that they didn't test or prove their theories and conclusions enough? The result is that some information that has been publicized is simply not all true, but are theories based on assumptions and preconceived ideas. Yet, it has become popular thinking and is often being taught as truth. More to come on this.

17

"Priorities -What comes first?"

List everything you have to do today. What if I totally controlled what you did today, and told you, you are confined to the couch, you can't get up, you can't watch TV, nothing. (Bathroom break excepted). Sounds confining and boring, doesn't it? Ok, I will allow you to do one thing that is on your list. You have one minute to decide on that one thing. What would be the one thing you would do today?

Would you take out the garbage? Would you eat, or do your daily exercise? Would you clean up your basement or read your favorite book, *(preferably this one)?* Would you spend more time with your loved ones? Would you pray? What would you do? Are you having trouble deciding? Whatever it was, then you have set your priority for the day.

What if I took away all your possessions, everything you have, your house, car, hobbies? What if I took your family, friends, church, your job, your career, your health, and belief in God? Sounds terrible? Ok. I will give you back one, just one thing from everything I took. What would it be?

Be careful. Think before you decide. In both cases what you are deciding is your priority or the most important thing in your life, the thing which you value most. The thing that will have the biggest and most significant effect on your day as in the first scenario, or your life as in the second scenario.

Can't decide? Take some time. You have 5 minutes. That's it. If you haven't decided by then everything is off your list, or I may decide for you.

This little or I should say "big" exercise is a good way to determine priorities. Go to it. Decide on your number 1. Do it and come back.

(Big Pause)

You are back. Are you comfortable with your decision? Was it difficult? You likely wish you had a second choice. Ok, what if I gave you two things? Now, do the same. Choose one more. Keep doing this and you will have your list of priorities for the day or for the rest of your life.

Our priorities are what controls us, or we could put it another way, "Our priorities are what or whom we serve."

18
"IF"

My buddy Neil always said that the game of golf should be called "If" because after every hole, he would say, "If I had hit the ball straight on my drive, I would have parred that one." The little word "if" occurs in the Bible over 1600 times. If it occurs that many times it must be significant and meaningful.

If you stay up late at night, you will be tired in the morning. If you spend all your money today, you won't have any money for tomorrow. If you eat too much candy, you will be sick. Our parents gave us lots of warnings, beginning with the word "if". "Don't come running to me if you get in an accident."

Where there is an "if" it is always followed by a consequence of some sort. It may be negative or positive, punishment or reward.

The famous author and poet, Rudyard Kipling, who wrote many books and poems including Captains Courageous and Jungle Book, wrote a poem entitled "If". He lists off a series of statements beginning with the word "If". They include:

"If you can keep your head when all about you are losing theirs and blaming it on you, "
"If you can wait and not be tired by waiting, "
"If you can dream—and not make dreams your master;"
"If you can think—and not make thoughts your aim;"

After listing about a dozen "ifs" that contrast positive and negative actions, he finally gives a reward:

> **"Yours is the Earth and everything that's in it,**
> **And—which is more—you'll be a Man, my son!"**

We can think of a lot of "ifs" that would have changed our lives for the better or worse. What if going forward, we made better decisions? What are the big "ifs" facing you today?

"If you love me, keep my commandments." John 14:15

19
"Integrity"

How many colors are there in the rainbow? Six, you say. According to science, going back to Newton, there are actually seven, namely, red, orange, yellow, green, blue, indigo, and violet. You likely said six because most of the time when you see it displayed there are only six. You didn't lie. You were telling the truth, and you were sincere, but you were wrong. You were truthful but because you were wrong, you may now lack integrity. Integrity is more than telling the truth, it is having your facts right.

While truth is certainly closely related to integrity, it is possible that we can be truthful as we understand it and be giving the wrong information.

We live in a world where there is a lot of information going around that is not accurate or truthful, and therefore lacks integrity. I know what you are thinking. The old fallback is "Well, it depends on your opinion." So true. We can all have opinions. But there is such a thing as facts and truth, regardless of what the philosophers say.

The philosophy student boastfully said to his father, "Dad, I can prove anything now. I can prove you are not here." His father slapped him. His son said, "Why did you slap me? The father replied I didn't slap you. I am not here."

The world recently experienced a pandemic period called "Covid 19". Yes, a terrible time. Some people lied and didn't know it. Others lied and knew it. In the beginning, it stuck fear in society and people were confused. Without taking sides, decisions were made that were not based on facts. Both sides of the issue were strong in their opinions. It caused major splits in relationships, and even families.

The truth is we did not get all the truth or rejected truth. Integrity was damaged to say the least.

If we are going to be trusted, we have to be believable, i.e., have reliable information. We must have integrity.

"Integrity is doing the right thing, even when no one is watching."

C. S. Lewis

20
"Bible Quiz"

1. What is the best-selling book of all time?
2. The Bible was the first book ever written. True or False?
3. Who first translated the Bible in English?
4. What year was the first Bible printed?
5. What was the name of the printing press?
6. Approximately how many Bibles are in print today?
7. On average how many Bibles are printed annually?
8. Circle the original languages the Bible was written in.

    English   Aramaic   Latin
    Hebrew   Greek   Chinese
9. How many books are in the Bible?
10. Name them. (just kidding) Name 5 in the order they appear in the Bible.
11. The two main divisions of the Bible are _________________ and

    _________________.
12. The first 5 books are called _________________________
13. Who wrote the first 5 books of the Bible?
14. What is the longest book in the Bible?
15. What is the shortest Book in the Bible?
16. What books form what we call the gospel?
17. How many different authors wrote the Bible?
18. Over how many years was it written?
19. What is the main message of the Bible?
20. How many animals of each kind did Moses take on the ark?

Answers on Page 50

21
"I love you?"

"Have I Told You Lately That I love you?" Original versions of that song go way back to the forties and have been recorded by many artists, including Elvis, my favorite.

Here is one verse and chorus:

Have I told you lately that I love you
Could I tell you once again somehow
Have I said with all my heart and soul how I adore you
Well, darling, I'm telling you now.

My world would end today if I should lose you
I'm no good without you anyhow
Oh, have I told you lately that I love you My darling, I'm telling you now.

Is it time we spoke these words to someone special in our lives? Is it time we said them more often? Is it time we said them, meant them and more importantly, showed them and demonstrated them by how we live?

Who in your life needs to hear them from you?

This may just be the day that you need to tell your loved ones, spouse, child, sibling, parent, grandparent, or friend those magic words. Oh yeah and put some "uuumph" in them and make sure they are supported by how we treat the ones we love.

"I love you."

22
"Commitment Levels"

Every workplace, every organization, and every family has people with varying levels of commitment. That is to be expected since everybody is at a different place in their life's journey. You may be totally committed to your hobby but just "so-so" committed to your work. Or it could be the other way around. Listed below are different types of people I have worked with over the years. I assigned names for fun. As I observed the different people, I could not help but compare myself to them. See if you recognize any of them. Have you been to any of them or all of them?

1) Hesitant Harry - *works hard to not work*

2) Pay me Pete - *what's in it for me?*

3) Steady Stan - no *more no less*

4) Recognition Rick - *Loves recognition*

5) Want my way Wally - *His way is more important than the right way.*

6) Ambitious Alice - *Wants to get ahead*

7) Fearful Frances - *Motivated by fear of failure*

8) Love Ya Lance - *Works hard if he likes you*

9) Moral Mike - If *it's right, he'll do it*

10) Purposeful Pat - *Relates to the cause*

Did you find yourself? I will wager that you have been all of them at some point in your life, depending on your situation, your personal preferences etc. Just as you and I have been all of them so have others that we deal with from time to time. Sure, we want to have all 9's and 10's. However just because someone may be a 2, 5 or 8, it doesn't mean they are not capable of doing the job. They just need to be motivated. What motivates you?

People in charge are often faced with the task of motivating those they manage. They need to know who the players are and how to motivate them. Good parents understand this and apply it all the time when raising their children.

23
"Mount Rushmore"

Most of us have heard of Mount Rushmore and have seen pictures of it.

Although I had never planned to go to see it, on a drive from Ontario to British Columbia via the US, to my surprise, Judee and I were within driving distance of it. We couldn't pass up the opportunity. We were blown away.

Some of the facts we learned about Mount Rushmore:

- It is a National Memorial located in South Dakota, US.

- Originally referred to as the Shrine of Democracy

- Built between 1927 and 1941

- Contains the heads of four US Presidents- George Washington, Thomas Jefferson, Theodore Roosevelt and Abraham Lincoln.

- Each head is 60 feet tall, including 17-foot noses

- It sits on a mile-high mountain - 5724 feet above sea level

- The faces are carved in solid granite rock

- Dynamite was used in the construction

- Many holes were drilled, allowing workers to remove small pieces by hand

- Approximately 410,000 tons of rock were removed

- The chief carver was Luigi Del Bianco, from Italy

- The total cost of the project was US$989,992.32 (equivalent to $19.7 million in 2022)

- Well over 2 million people visit the site annually

24
"Responsibility"

Referring to the opening on commitment, page 13, it was a responsibility that contributed to my commitment. Sure, I had responsibility before, in that my mother gave me the responsibility of grooming, but my attitude towards responsibility changed. I had the same responsibility to comb my hair, but this time, instead of being given responsibility, I took responsibility. Many people are given responsibility, but do they assume it and act on it? Kids are given the responsibility to clean their rooms and study. But it doesn't mean they do it. Employees have responsibility. Parents have responsibility. But do they all take it? The task is the same, but the ownership is different.

Yes, I did things out of obedience because my parents told me to. But doing things out of responsibility is quite different. Through a few hard knocks and both good and bad experiences, my understanding of responsibility grew to the point that I felt that if I didn't do a certain thing, it would not get done. It's like thinking it's my job and nobody else's.

"Who is responsible for our actions?" We have a lot of people depending on someone else. Are they being spoiled? Maybe some are. Not taking responsibility is relying on others or blaming others for our failures or our weaknesses and getting stuck with a victim mentality.

We are responsible for much in our lives, including our attitudes, mood swings, behavior, speech, choices, reactions, and responses to situations over which we have no control. Taking responsibility is called "growing up".

Whose responsibility is to turn our lives around? This does not mean there are not people who want to help us and point us in the right direction and advise us, but ultimately, we should not be waiting for someone else to take responsibility for taking care of us. Do you have the right concept of responsibility? Where have you messed up by not taking responsibility for yourself?

Think of areas in your life where you have been very responsible. *(see page 44)*

25
"Red Skelton"

Richard Red Skelton (July 18, 1913 – September 17, 1997), considered one of the greatest entertainers of all time, started work at the age of seven when his father died. He dropped out of school around the age of 13 to pursue a career as a comic. He went on to make movies and have his own TV show. He made people laugh by telling funny jokes, but to many it wasn't just that his jokes were funny, he was funny. He frowned on using vulgar language and four-letter words.

Here is a sampling of his funnies and quotes, some from my memory and some from different websites:

"I married Miss Right. I just didn't know her first name was Always."

"All men make mistakes, but married men find out about them sooner."

"There are three signs of old age: loss of memory ... I forget the other two."

"I personally believe that each of us was put here for a purpose — to build, not to destroy. If I can make people smile, then I have served my purpose for God."

"Old age is when broadness of the mind and narrowness of the waist change places."

"Laughter has always brought me out of unhappy situations."

"I don't hate my enemies. After all, I made 'em."

"She has an electric blender, electric toaster and electric bread maker. She said, "There are too many gadgets and no place to sit down!" So I bought her an electric chair."

"God's children and their happiness are my reasons for being."

"I get plenty of exercise carrying the coffins of my friends who exercise."

26
"Pearl Harbour"

On Sunday at 7:48 a.m. December 7, 1941, 353 Japanese fighter planes, dive bombers and torpedo planes from six aircraft carriers made a surprise attack on the American naval base at Pearl Harbour, Hawaii. The death toll was 2,403 with 1178 wounded. Nineteen US ships were destroyed or sunk, and others were damaged along with various buildings. The US had no choice but to reciprocate this act of war, resulting in countless deaths on both sides. It finally ended with the surrender of Japan after the US dropped two atomic bombs on Japanese cities.

Seeing the pictures, hearing the sounds on tape at Pearl Harbour was the most emotional tour and vacation of my life. To hear the chain of events leading up to the attack brought to my mind the "what ifs' and "if onlys" that could have changed the outcome. But it happened, as in the sinking of the Titanic. Looking back and seeing the warnings cannot change the end result.

After the gut-wrenching tour of the museum on the shore, we took a small boat to the middle of the harbor to a memorial site. We were warned that this was treated as a cemetery and talking was to be kept to a minimum. The soldiers on the boat and various stations were formal and impeccable in their appearance and how they presented themselves. Reading the plaques, the names of the dead gave me goosebumps. The memorial spanned over the sunken USS Arizona which rests on the bottom, with a portion slightly above water. Its damage was too much to be salvaged as were some of the other ships. The bodies of over 900 of 1127 crew members who were killed remain in the ship, which is now considered a cemetery. Ashes from cremated survivors have also been placed in this burial site.

Standing looking down at the ship, one quickly sees oil on the top of the water. Some 1.5 million gallons of fuel were put on the ship the day before it was sunk. The daily leak continues. The fuel was left so as not to disturb the graveyard and prevent the possibility of an environmental catastrophe, and it also serves as a reminder and an experience for all who visited the terrible event. It was certainly an emotional reminder for me!

"Worry"

I was all prepared to begin my first day of school when I was six years old. My bookbag containing everything I needed, including a nice neat, sharpened pencil, was taken care of two months earlier. I was also dressed for the occasion and about to go out the door with my siblings to take the five-minute walk to school. Suddenly, to the surprise of the rest of the family, I stopped, turned around, and refused to go. My pathetic whining turned into bawling and eventually, a temper tantrum that convinced my mother to allow me to stay home. By lunchtime, I was ready to accompany my brothers and sisters to go to school. What happened?

I was worried. I knew how to print the entire alphabet but as my sisters were going out the door, I noticed their names on their books were written. I didn't know how to write, and I assumed that I had to be able to write when I got to school. That was enough to trigger my worry switch.

Money problems? Important meeting coming up? In doubt about something? What if it rains on your parade? Are these the kinds of questions that ruin your day by occupying your headspace and bring your productivity to a standstill, interfere with your plans, play havoc with your emotions, and make us a pain in the butt to those around us?

Worry seems natural for most, but seldom solves a problem or gets anything done. Its side effects include stress, depression, moods, digestion problems, exhaustion, headaches, muscle tension, loss of sleep, NEGATIVITY, and missing your first day of school. All of these and more do not make us fun to be around. How do we stop worrying if it is so natural?

Worry is our tendency to expect the worst to happen in a given situation. And it is that worst, real or imagined, thing that we fear.

'They' say, "Ninety percent of the things we worry about never happen."

Corrie Ten Boom says: *"Worry doesn't empty tomorrow of its sorrows. It empties today of its strengths."*

28
"Oneupmanship"

"Sorry I was late guys; the traffic was terrible." Joe replied, "You should have seen it yesterday morning. I was held up for an hour." Not to be outdone, Sam got in there too and shared about his experience last summer, how he was stuck in the 401 for 3 days. (*exaggerating*).

"I bought a new piano last week." Instead of saying congratulations, someone has to say, "Oh, you should have come to me first, we bought the best."

"We went on a cruise," brings a response, "I hope you were on the same one we did, we had a ball."

"I was off with a bad cold last week," brings the response, "It couldn't have been as bad as mine."

The comeback to, "My back is killing me" is, "Don't talk to me about your back, I can hardly walk."

"My dad is better than yours." "I have better tools." "Mine is the best." 'Let me tell you what I did, and it worked." "You had 15 stitches, I had 25."

These statements may all be true. It seems if something happens to us that we share, there is always someone who wants to do one better. Whether it be sickness, an accident, something good or something bad, there is at least one in the crowd that has a better story that must be told. Of course, once it starts, everybody else must get in on it and make the original person feel like an idiot because his story didn't hold a candle to the others. This happens at work, at home and social gatherings.

Leave the poor guy/girl alone and let him/her have his/her two minutes of sadness or glory. And we wonder why some people don't speak up.

We don't have to be one-up on everyone. I have done it. God forgive me.

29

"Communication"

This is a "biggie". In conducting various interviews across Canada for customer and employee surveys, the number one issue that was revealed to me was communication. Communication was either the primary issue or the person interviewed blamed communication as the number one issue. Example: I asked one employee what was wrong with communication in your company. His answer was, "I asked for a raise, and I was told "no". To which I responded, "What part of "no" did you not understand."

There is no doubt that there is always room for improvement in communication but let us not forget that excellent communication does not guarantee cooperation or make up for all the other weaknesses and inadequacies in people.

We are never not communicating. No matter what we are saying, not saying, doing or not doing, we are always communicating in that others are getting some kind of message, which may be interpreted differently than it is intended. If we say nothing in group meetings, we may be communicating that we are not interested or that we are in full agreement with the decision. We communicate in our body language, our appearance, our words, our silence, and our actions.

Marriages, family relations, work relations, and success, are all affected by communication. The way we speak, listen, respond, write, read have tremendous ripple effects.

I took a job once based on my understanding of the verbal offer that was made to me. I made a big mistake by not getting the offer in writing, (another issue), but either the company owner stated it wrong, which he denied, or I heard it wrong, quite possibly. Either way, poor communication resulted in a poor career move that had to be corrected six months later.

We can all learn to communicate better, but we should keep in mind we are all different in how we perceive and understand.

Ready for a journey in communication? Watch for more.

30
"Jokes"

I love jokes. I have to say I don't always get the modern-day humor of some comedians. Vulgar jokes seem to be the trend. Old timers like Red Skelton, Tim Conway, etc., were just funny and yet, their jokes were clean with no foul language, which always offends someone in the group, even if they don't tell you.

A snail went into the bar on New Year's Eve and ordered a drink. The bartender just flicked him off the counter with his finger. One year later, the snail managed to climb up to the same bar and said, "Hey, what did you do that for?" That's a slow joke. Has it sunk in yet?

Jokes are good for a laugh. Hey, that's funny, isn't it? But seriously, they are breaks from the seriousness of life at times. But we must be careful not to get carried away at times and be out of place with them. They can be a big letdown at funerals. Oops, sorry, that came out wrong.

Never done archery blindfolded? You don't know what you are missing.

There are all kinds of jokes, including "Knock - Knock" jokes which are still being knocked around. Knock, Knock, who's there? Nobody. Nobody who? I said nobody.

A lot of people say they can never remember jokes. The best way to remember a joke is to tell it several times the first day you hear it.

Of course, you cannot tell a lot of them anymore for fear of offending someone, because of this political correctness that is going around. There are only two kinds of jokes that are politically correct to tell. They are Newfoundland jokes and jokes about Christians. I am both a Newfoundlander and a Christian.

I remember when I first moved out of the province, how people were telling jokes about me. I didn't realize there were jokes about us Newfoundlanders. I fixed them by telling more Newfoundland jokes than they did. We have to be able to take a joke as long as it is intended to be a joke and not an insult.

People like to laugh. Try laughing at yourself. It's funny. No? Then laugh at me. I don't mind.

31
"Ideologies" (political)

Ideology: "a system of ideas and ideals, especially one which forms the basis of economic or political theory and policy." Types of ideologies include but not limited to:

Fascism – Nazism – Theisms – Capitalism -Conservatism- Liberalism- Socialism - Communism- Marxism.

There is certainly overlap among them.

My simple understanding of an ideology is: "What we think of the world and how it should be run."

Throughout history, the world or parts of the world have been run by ideologies. The Soviet Union had Communism. Germany had Nazism. Italy had Fascism. Today, we still have communism in countries like Russia, Cuba and China while Canada, the US and much of Europe have Democracy and Capitalism. There are countries, as in the Middle East, which are partly Theism in that the religion of Islam basically calls the shots.

Within our capitalistic society in North America and many other countries, there is further division such as conservatism and liberalism.

These ideas or ideologies are mindsets grounded somewhere in history and have tremendous power over people under the premise that it is for the benefit and good of the people. Whatever the system, 'ideology" or " ism" is, it has the power to make and enforce the law. Hitler was abiding by the law with what he did with his idea of taking over the world and murdering millions of Jews under his idea of how things should be.

Is there a best one or the right one? Of course, each one will tell you that their idea is the best. Confusing? Which one do you favor?

Cautions: Some ideologies are dangerous and have proven they are not in the best interest of people. They can divide people. Some people are lashing onto an ideology just to belong to a group, and they often do so without understanding the ideology of the group.

Ideologies are described in more detail in different pages.

See also "Isms"

32

"Relationships"

Relationships. What a word! What a word!
One of the most important you've ever heard.
You will read it many times in this book.
If you can't see its value, you should have another look.
It is about how we connect and get along.
It's a lot about love as mentioned in many a song.
It just needs two people or more.
If they hit it off, you can count it a score.
But what if they don't and things get tough,
Will they pack it all in and get rid of their stuff?
That's too bad that people don't see eye to eye.
What's even worse they often don't try.
Relationships form but so many fail.
They must have their problems.
Who knows what they entail?
What's the matter, why can't they see?
All relationships depend on you and me.
It takes two to cooperate.
To the extent they determine their fate
Look bigger and see how countries fight.
They don't have to if they do what is right.
What is right? It is not just getting our own way.
We have to learn to give some slack and sway.
There is enough of everything in the world to go around.
If the ringleader gives up being a clown.
But we won't ever all agree.
There is too much greed and evil to set us free
But there are many things we can agree on
One thing for sure is we all belong.
So smarten up with your attitudes and lips.
We can all have better relationships.

33
"Fear"

"Boo!" Did that scare you? What is your biggest fear?

Fear has to be one of, if not the most controlling emotions we have. It can freeze us like ice, cause us to panic and scream, make us fight, or cause us to run. Some fear heights, and some fear bikes. You can fear the dark or fear a spark. It will hold you down or push you up. Some fear more and some fear less. It drives some to drink and others to sink. But it should cause us to think, "Why do I fear"?

Fear is an emotion caused by a belief that danger or pain is coming. We certainly have biological reactions in certain potentially dangerous situations. Some fear everything. Some claim to fear nothing. Today, the word phobia which means 'social anxiety disorder' is very commonly used. Some are mislabeled as having a fear or phobia simply because they disagree with someone. *(different topic)*.

My friend, Mike says: ***"FEAR - False Evidence Appearing Real."***

Fears often exist because of bad past experiences that caused pain or embarrassment. As we stated on the "Worry" page, fear is often behind worry. Fear holds us back. It causes worry and can bring us to a standstill. Fear of failure is a big one. "If I don't try it, I won't fail."

Have you considered the opposite of fear? How about courage or trust? If we fear something, obviously, we lack trust in ourselves or someone else.

Many who are perfectionists live in fear and will spend excessive time trying to make something perfect, at least in their eyes. What is the solution to fear, besides taking it out on others, or taking drugs or booze? "What is the worst thing that can happen?" What if… Could I live with the outcome and start over? That works for many of the day-to-day things we fear.

"Of all the liars in the world, sometimes the worst are our own fears."

— Rudyard Kipling

"For God has not given us a spirit of fear, but of power and of love and of a sound mind."

2 Timothy 1:7

34

"Encouragement"

I remember when I was a boy, how good it felt when someone gave me a compliment. Do you? How did it make you feel? Did it encourage you? It sure did with me. I am not talking about being lied to with phony praise just to make someone feel good or get them to do something. I am talking about the genuine encouragement that you received. Encouragement and flattery are not always the same.

"Remember, man does not live by bread alone; sometimes he needs a little buttering up." - John C. Maxwell.

Encouragement can come in different packages, one of which is certainly a compliment. It also comes with a challenge or appealing to someone's emotions.

I was encouraged by a boss once who said to me that a co-worker would get promoted before I would. Before I had a chance to punch him out (just kidding, I wouldn't have), he followed up with the words, "Fred, if you were to put half the energy into your work as you do in your Judo, you would be amazing." It certainly hurt at first. Hurt that he said it and hurt that he was right. I needed it for sure and he knew just how to challenge and encourage me. I thought long and hard over his words that weekend. I really saw my job as a temporary career until I found something better. Then it hit me. This is the job I have, and I should be the best that I can be and in the long run, it will guarantee more opportunities for the future. There were many other gestures of encouragement in my working career. Some were compliments, and some were constructive criticisms. And some were a kick in the behind. Each time, they motivated me to do better.

Most of us need encouragement in one form or another. We should keep in mind that what encourages some may not encourage others. Nevertheless, encouragement is a good thing. We learn and grow from education, experiences, and encouragement. Don't underestimate the value of encouragement.

"Our chief want is someone who will inspire us to be what we know we could be."
— Ralph Waldo Emerson.

How have you been encouraged in your life?

How have you encouraged others?

35
"Love Songs"

"Love Songs"

"STOP in the name of Love." That was a hot love song by the Supremes.

How many love songs can you name? It has been said that there are over 100 million love songs out there. Amazing! I guess there will never be a complete list of them. It would be hard to keep up to date. It is likely easier to list the songs that are not about love. What do all these love songs say about love? Are they just "Another old fashion Love song?"

"I Want To Know What Love Is". Come on, "Lover," "What's Love Got to Do with It?" It must be because "Love Is All You Need". Tell me about "The Power of Love". Is it because "Love is Thicker Than Water"?

Why did you address your letter, "To Sir With Love"? You told me, "I Just Called To Say I Love You." And "I Love You Because You're You". Then you tell me, "I Wanna Dance With Somebody Who Loves Me."

"Love Takes Time," and you should "Love Yourself." Are you just "A Woman In Love"? "How Deep Is Your Love?" really? Yes, "Love is Blue" and "Love Hurts." You will find that out when "You've Lost That Loving Feeling."

"This Guy's In Love" and "That's The Way Love Goes." You say "I Love a Rainy Night," and you have a "Love Hangover", but "I Can't Help Falling in Love with You" and, "I think I love You."

"Roses Are Red, My Love," and you are the "Greatest Love of All". I'm "Crazy in Love" and this is a 'Crazy Little Thing Called Love" so "Love Me Dude," cause "I Can't Stop Loving You."

It's not because "I Love Rock and Roll" or "I Love Onions." It is "The Best of My Love" because "I Love You" and "I Will Always Love You." So "Let Me Love You" so we can say "We Found Love," and we have "Endless Love."

Name some more love songs.

36
"Accountability"

One dictionary meaning of accountability is: *"an obligation or willingness to accept responsibility or to account for one's actions."*

People generally don't like being held accountable or held to task. They may desire to have responsibility and authority, but when it comes to them having to answer to others or justify their actions, that's another story.

Committed people not only take responsibility for their actions, but they also willingly seek to find out how they are doing so they can improve. They do not hide when they mess up. They confess and look for ways of preventing it in the future. They want to be held accountable and know how they handled their responsibility and authority. When they can reach that stage and when they are not too embarrassed, chicken, high and mighty, or proud to be held accountable, then they can be trusted and will be truly committed. We are not talking about seeking compliments here or brown-nosing, we are talking about genuinely wanting to know how we are doing so we can improve. Instead of avoiding accountability, we should be looking for it. Super athletes, professional entertainers, high achievers, and successful companies understand this. That is why they hire coaches and consultants. That is why companies do customer surveys and employee surveys. I was fortunate enough to conduct employee surveys and nationwide customer surveys. Employees and suppliers were seeking to be held accountable. And in each case, they wanted to know the good the bad, and the ugly of how they did things.

There are many ways to be held accountable. We may get held accountable every day as when someone corrects a statement we made. Of course, most of us find it annoying, and it certainly can be. However, on a more serious note, if we are not willing to be held accountable, we are, in essence, saying we are refusing to grow. *"Willingness to be accountable rather than giving excuses and blaming others opens our lives to new growth opportunities."*

Accountability is self-analyses: "How did I do?" "How could I have done it better?"; "If I had to do it over again, what would I do differently?"

37

"Entrance Exam"

What is the number in your town for 911? _______________________

What is your last name in italics? _______________________

How cold is it when it is twice as cold as 0 degrees C? _______________

How warm is it when it is twice as warm as 0 degrees C? _______________

How much is 100 degrees Celsius in Fahrenheit? _______________

Which is heavier, a pound of lead or a pound of feathers? _______________

What is the definition of a vacuum? _______________________

What is the name of the shortest street in St. Johns, Newfoundland?

____

If it takes 80 minutes to drive to work and one hour and 20 minutes to come home, which way is the shortest? _______________________

Count the different two's in this sentence, "It takes two long to count to two when too many people are putting in their two cents worth." _______________________

What would you rather do or go fishing? _______________________

If a hen and a half laid an egg and a half on the peak of a gable roof, how long would it take for a grasshopper with a wooden leg to kick a hole in a picket fence?

____

Do you know the answer to this question? _______________

Why do elephants paint red spots on themselves? _______________________

Did you ever see an elephant in a cherry tree? _______________

Answers: Page 96

38
"Be yourself or Not."

Should we just be who we are and, as we say, 'the way God made us'? Heaven forbid! While God did make us with certain unique talents, He also meant for us to grow. Would I really want to be the brat I was often called in school as a kid? Would I want to be the teenager I was, working on the fish plant, smelly and spitting in public? Should we be ourselves or not? Should we always do what comes naturally, or should we have a desire to change?

There are arguments for and against being ourselves.

Oscar Wild supposedly said, "Be yourself because everyone else is taken." We are all unique. It is difficult to be someone else, even though many people pretend and try hard. We can learn some qualities from others, but we can't be them. Those who try have an identity problem, for sure.

When I was on the road doing seminars all over North America, I knew I had a lot to learn about making great presentations. While I observed others and admired how they presented and even learned from them, I found out very quickly I could not be them. I had to be myself. By being myself, I didn't have to remember how to behave. I just had to know my content. In that context, I had to learn to give a good seminar by being who I was.

On the other hand, I did have to learn to make better presentations. I had to change some things. I had to be on the ball, alert, and not behave as I would in my own home, where I was in a different role.

We have all heard successful people, particularly in the entertainment world, when asked to give advice to 'up-and-comers' say, "Just be yourself." I think I understand what they mean, but what message is the audience getting? Do you want to be the same self you were 10, 15, or 20 years ago? Have your values changed for the better or the worse? If so, why or why not? What do you think? Should you be yourself, or should you change?

Should the alcholic, drug addict, or pedophile be themselves? Just asking.

Being yourself is great when it comes to being honest, kind, loyal, etc. Changing yourself is wise to correct our areas of weakness.

<u>Challenge:</u> Be yourself – How? Change yourself – How?

39
"Bible Myths"

The Bible is often misquoted and used out of context. For example:

Myth 1: "Money is the root of all evil."

The full sentence is in 1 Timothy 6:10: *"For <u>the love of money</u> is a root of all kinds of evil."*

Myth 2: "God helps those who help themselves."

This verse is not written in the Bible. However, it does emphasize a good work ethic and to provide for us and our families.

Myth 3: "The Bible puts down women."

While culturally, women were often treated as property, God created men and women equal *but different*. All through the Bible, God is fair and just to women and uses both men and women for His purpose. There is ample evidence in the Bible of women leaders, judges, teachers, elders and deacons, and church planters. God commands them to be loved and respected.

Myth 4: "The Bible condones slavery."

While slavery was common in the culture, especially in early Bible books, nowhere in the Bible does God condone it. Regulations were given on how to treat slaves. Hebrew law made it possible for people to sell themselves into slavery for a period of six years. But it was more like a contract to be an employee or servant as opposed to being a slave as we understand it today. Leviticus 25:39-43 says:

"And if one of your brethren who dwells by you becomes poor and sells himself to you, you shall not compel him to serve as a slave. [40] As a hired servant and a sojourner, he shall be with you and shall serve you until the Year of Jubilee. [41] And then he shall depart from you—he and his children with him—and shall return to his own family. He shall return to the possession of his fathers. [42] For they are My servants, whom I brought out of the land of Egypt; they shall not be sold as slaves. [43] You shall not rule over him with rigor, but you shall fear your God."

40
"TV shows in the 50's and 60's - Answers

1   The name of the Lone Rangers' horse <u>**Silver.**</u>

2   The Lone Ranger was called by his partner <u>**Kemosabe**</u>

3   His partner's name was <u>**Tonto**</u>

4   The name of the theme song was <u>**Willian Tell Overture**</u>

5   Roy Roger's wife's name was <u>**Dale Evans**</u> 6. Roy's horses name was <u>**Trigger.**</u>

7   His wife's horse's name was <u>**Buttercup.**</u>

8   Cisco Kid had a partner named <u>**Poncho**</u>

9   The actor who played Hop Along Cassidy was <u>**William Boyd**</u>

10 Paladin would travel with his <u>**Gun**</u> 11. The name of the Rebel was <u>**Johnny Yuma.**</u>

12 He roamed through the <u>**West.**</u>

13 The famous father knew <u>**best.**</u>

14 The best Sunday night variety show was the <u>**Ed Sullivan Show.**</u>

15 The Rifleman was played by <u>**Chuck Conners.**</u>

How did you do?

41

"Time for Everything"

To everything, *there is* a season, A time for every purpose under heaven:
[2] A time to be born,
And a time to die;
A time to plant,
And a time to pluck *what is* planted;
[3] A time to kill,
And a time to heal;
A time to break down,
And a time to build up;
[4] A time to weep,
And a time to laugh;
A time to mourn,
And a time to dance;
[5] A time to cast away stones, And a time to
gather stones;
A time to embrace,
And a time to refrain from embracing;
[6] A time to gain,
And a time to lose;
A time to keep,
And a time to throw away;
[7] A time to tear,
And a time to sew;
A time to keep silent,
And a time to speak;
[8] A time to love,
And a time to hate;
A time of war,
And a time of peace.
Ecclesiastes 3:1-8

Don't be surprised. All of these things happen. They apply to all of us.
It is how we respond to them and deal with them, that is important.
A rock group, The Bryds, put many of these words to music and made this a number-one hit in 1965. It was called "Turn, Turn, Turn".
Most people had no idea it came from the Bible.

42
"Elephant in the Room"

"The elephant in the room" is an idiom or an expression for a major topic that no one wants to talk about for fear of embarrassment, controversy, offending anyone, or making someone uncomfortable. The word elephant comes into play in the sense that it is so big and obvious that everyone knows it is there, yet they act as if it not there and thus avoid it.

<u>HOWEVER:</u> We have all seen topics brought up resulting in debates, opinions, and arguments that often spoil the party and hurt relationships.

You may notice some elephants in this book.

To the detriment of today's society, there are too many elephants in the room, and in many cases, various groups, media, governments, and ideologies have become the elephants. And to make matters worse, they have taken advantage of it and/or planned it that way. Regardless of where you stand on an issue or topic, such elephants include:

> Government waste – Pensions of politicians - Double standard of justice – Climate change and global warming – How Covid was handled – Covid Vaccines – The trucker's convoy- The World Economic Forum – The World Health Organization (WHO) – Black Lives Matter (BLM) – Sexual orientation- Medical Assistance In Dying (MAID) -Healthcare – Immigration – Crime statistics in various groups and cultures – Political partisanship – Abortion – Religion – Dirty Language - Legalizing Drugs - *Body Odor*

The very mention of some of these may raise anxiety, heartbeats, and blood pressure in many of you, regardless of your views on them. Because of this, policies get put in place; directions are taken without the respective sides being willing to listen to the other or acknowledge the true facts.

What do we do about it? In many cases, something is being done about it, yet public opinion has been squashed under the guise or threat of recent government policies, university and public-school education, and media bias that literally mandates them to be elephants in the room.

There is a time to remain silent and a time to speak.

43
"Personality "P's"

I hired a guy to speak to our staff once. He had everybody throw out some positive words beginning with "P." Then he had everybody give negative words beginning with "N." Then, in the same order he listed them, he gave a speech using every one of the P words in one paragraph and then all the N words in another paragraph. I thought, "Cool, I should try that." I never did. But I was surprised of how many **P**ositive words begin with "P" and how many **N**egative words begin with "N."

Here are six P words that may help you at work, at home, or anywhere. I find that people who practice these things are more enjoyable to be around.

Positive – No matter what the situation, I find there is always a positive way to approach things. **Be** Encouraging, cooperative, and sincere.

Polite – There is never a reason to be impolite. **Be** considerate, kind, and respectful.

Proactive - Initiate, interact, and try to understand.

Prepared - Ask the right questions - get the facts.

Professional- Take the high road. Follow the rules. Be in context. Be tactful. Have integrity.

Personable – Be real, friendly, and have a sense of humor. Lighten up, smile, and care.

One more thing: It is Possible to Practice all of these no matter how the other person behaves and no matter our level of education. Yes, we can Progress and learn to be all of these and more.

44
"It's up to Me" – (Responsibility list)

It's up to me, who I will be,
How I think will make me free.
My attitude could correct my actions.
That's how I learned to work with fractions.
My behavior and how I appear,
Can determine my relationships and career.
My compassion and my caring
Influence my words and stop me from swearing.
It's up to me to watch my diet;
I can learn a lot if I am willing to try it.
I can encourage or discourage,
Or conquer fear with my courage.
Worries can disturb my sleep,
But not my friends, who I want to keep.
I can be generous and kind,
By allowing my honesty and humility to shine.
My manners, moods, passions, my knowing
Are all about my growing.
I'll be sincere, polite, smile and serve.
I'll respect others with lots of nerve.
I'll keep promises and be on time.
Punctual too, but it doesn't rhyme.
Responsibility is quite a lot.
Doing what is needed, not just giving it a shot.
It's up to me to tell the truth,
And it all starts in our youth.
It's up to me to learn and love,
And take correction and authority from above.
Now, I will rate myself from one to ten.
It's up to me to be responsible and truthful in the end.
I must run now to go and pee.
That too, "It's Up to Me."

45
"Decisions"

I had a hard time deciding whether to put this topic or many others in my book. It wasn't easy to decide if I would take or not take strong views on certain topics. Should I pussy foot around or just lay it out and let the chips fall where they may?

Are decisions difficult, or are they easy? Um, I can't decide, can you? You decide right now if you are a good decision-maker or not. I used to be indecisive, but now I am not sure anymore.

Decisions, big or small, can change one's life or the lives of others for better or worse. Careers, reputations, love lives, relationships, and families have been ruined because of poor decisions, and of course, the opposite is true in making good decisions. There are risks and rewards in all decisions.

Why do people make poor decisions? I have known people to take weeks to decide on a stereo system. Yet I saw them decide on a house without even seeing it. There is definitely a process for making decisions. It includes gathering information and weighing the pros and cons. We have all made decisions for purely selfish and emotional reasons. Hopefully, we can learn from them. Emotions and selfish desires should be considered but facts go a long way. People in places of authority such as politicians and high executives have tough decisions to make. They need to be careful to be on the right side of morals. Decision-making is a responsibility, obligation and right so we should try to make it RIGHT.

Remember- "No decision is a decision."

What about you? What were some good or bad decisions you made in life? Why did you make them? You decide to make a list or not.

Here, I decided to give you some space to list some:

46
"Nursery Rhymes"

Remember these?
Mary had a little lamb
Its fleece was white as snow
And everywhere that Mary went
The lamb was sure to go

He followed her to school one day
Which was against the rule
It made the children laugh and play
To see a lamb at school

And so the teacher turned him out
But still, he lingered near
And waited patiently
Til Mary did appear

Mary had a little lamb.
Its fleece was white as snow,
And everywhere that Mary went,
The lamb was sure to go
ba ba black sheep, have you any wool
"yes sir, yes sir, three bags full
one for the master, one for the dame,
one for the little boy who lives down the lane

Hey, Diddle diddle the cat and the fiddle.
The cow jumped over the moon.
The little dog laughed to see such fun, and the dish ran away with the spoon.

This little piggy went to market,
This little piggy stayed at home,
This little piggy had roast beef,
This little piggy had none.
And this little piggy said ...
"Wee, wee, wee" all the way home...

They were fun. Don't hear them much anymore. They must have gotten replaced
with cell phones and political correctness. *More page 200.*

47

"Time Management"

What did you get done today? Busy? Didn't have time? We all have the same amount of time. Twenty-four hours a day. Seven days a week. Yet, some people get more accomplished than others. Why is that?

Time management is a misnomer. We actually cannot manage time. It keeps going no matter what we do. We can't save it. We can't move today's time into tomorrow, and we can't bring tomorrow's time into today. When today passes, it is gone forever. Lost or wasted time can never be retrieved. In some ways, it is like money, we can only spend it once.

However, don't give up hope. The key is not to look at it as time management but to manage <u>what we do in the time we have</u>. My various careers, mostly in management, gave me ample opportunity to get a lot done in the time I had. When I was a branch manager in downtown Toronto, I was "volunteered" to be the business manager of a large charity that had four companies in it. At the same time, my boss resigned, and I was to take over as District Manager over fifteen branches in downtown Toronto for four months at a time when annual budgets were being prepared. Did I mention I had a family with 4 kids at the time, and I taught Judo twice a week? I am not bragging, but I had to pull out all the stops into setting priorities. Yes, I survived. Not that I would want a full lifetime of that.

Instead of focusing on time management, we need to focus on "Getting Better Results" and getting things done. Productivity and getting results are about making choices. We choose what we do every minute of every day. True, there are times when the boss or emergencies don't give us much choice. But we do have a choice. We can watch TV or read a book. We can go golfing or spend time with our kids. We can work in the shed and move tools around or go to dinner with our spouse. We can argue just to make a point, or we can just let it go. We can say yes, or we can say no. Getting things done is directly proportional to these "A's and Ways":

- Attitude – The way we think.

- Attention – The way we focus and what we focus on.

- Action – The way we do things - How? When? What? Where? Who?

- Analyse – The way we review the other three.

48
"Religions"

What do you believe? Where do you stand on things like life and death, and what if anything comes when you *'kick the bucket'?* Do you ever wonder? Is this it? Is this all there is? Are you confused with it all and don't know what to believe? Is it possible there is a god who is at the helm, or is that religion stuff all garbage? Which one of some 4600 religions in the world has it right, or are they all right or all wrong? They can't all be right if they contradict each other. We all have a religion, don't we? Even no religion is a religion.

Everything, including atheism, is a set of beliefs that take faith.

The so-called non-religious will say that religion is the cause of most of the world's problems. Are they right? Non-religious people are putting forth their set of beliefs. I guess they are saying, they too are a part of most of the world's problems. Can we have our own beliefs and still get along in the world? It doesn't seem like it when you look around.

China claims itself to be the "People Republic," and the "communist party" tells everyone what to do and how to think. Russia seems to be going back to the same. More and more countries are being government-run as if there is no god. The Middle East is mostly Muslim with little Israel sticking out like a sore thumb. Then we have North America, where we have every belief *"you can shake a stick at."*

What do you think? Is religion the answer or the problem? Which one? To help you choose, this book outlines as objectively as possible the main beliefs of several of the world's largest religions. Take some time to compare.

49

"Communication Problem"

What's bugging you when it comes to communication? Here is a sampling of the actual answers from various groups and individuals:

- "People don't deliver on a promise."

- "People don't listen."

- "Misinterpretation."

- "Gossip drives me crazy."

- "They cover up things."

- "He talks too much."

- "She doesn't talk enough."

- "Others don't take things as serious as I do."

- "Meetings go on forever."

- "People are so defensive."

- "Nobody tells me."

- "I can't believe what I am told."

> *"While we have more communication tools than ever, effective communication is still a major problem. It has a long way to go."*

Why is communication blamed as a major problem?

Because it often is the biggest problem, and it is also a scapegoat and coverup for other problems. People lie, or they just have the facts wrong. Some are just not good at it. Not enough time. It is misunderstood. It is often a management issue. Some give up on it - or don't try hard enough. Everybody has feelings and personalities.

Do you experience any of the things above? How many are you guilty of? What have you tried doing about it? It is possible to improve communication, but we do have to work at it.

"The biggest communication problem is we do not listen to understand. We listen to reply." — **Stephen R. Covey.**

50
"Bible Quiz Answers" *(20)*

1. What is the best-selling book of all time? **The Bible**

2. The Bible was the first book ever written. True or False **False**

3. Who first translated the Bible in English? **John Wycliffe**

4. What year was the first Bible printed? **1454**

5. What was the name of the printing press? **Guttenberg**

6. Approximately how many Bibles are in print today? **5 to 7 billion**

7. On average, how many Bibles are printed annually? **80 million**

8. Circle the original languages the Bible was written in.

Aramaic   Hebrew   Greek

9. How many books are in the Bible? **66**

10. Name them. (just kidding) Name the first five books.

Genesis Exodus Leviticus Numbers Deuteronomy

11. The two main divisions of the Bible **<u>Old and New Testament</u>**

12. The first five books are called. **The Pentateuch**

13. Who wrote the first 5 books of the Bible? **Moses**

14. What is the longest book in the Bible? **Ezekiel**

15. What is the shortest Book in the Bible? **3 John**

16. How many different authors wrote the Bible? **At least 40**

17. Four books that form the gospel? **Matthew, Mark, Luke John**

18. Over how many years was it written? **1500**

19. What is the main message of the Bible? **"Jesus saves"**

20. Animals of each kind did Moses take on the ark? **Noah took 2**

51
"Personality Types"

You know the type, you have seen him before.
He gets you going and laughing on the floor.
People give labels for others to see
They may assign you a letter like A, B, C or D.
Your basic A is all about action and getting to the point.
They don't care if you get out of joint.
They may be abrupt and let you know,
They are not in just for the show.
Sure, they are good at getting things done,
But they scare people and make them run.
The opposite to A is generally B.
Who are quite relational, you see.
They want to show you they really care.
They may be nice but can get in the A's hair.
Smart A's should figure the B's out.
Give them a warm greeting instead of a shout.
The C's are always the thinking sort.
In meeting deadlines, they are always short.
But they are creative and can give you are a grin
When you have something serious that needs a spin.
Then comes the D, they are so detailed.
It just drives them crazy that this line doesn't rhyme.
Perfectionist with numbers and fine-tuning they are.
Off the mark, they don't venture far.
So you wonder which type is the best.
The situation or person is often the test.
You don't want the numbers guy on the greeting committee,
And you don't want the socialite on your numbers committee.
You can train them all to understand each other.
So they can be productive without making a blunder.
Being too strict on the labeling may be a big mistake.
But on the other hand, we all have habits we should try to break.

52
"Discrimination"

Oops! Is this an "elephant in the room?" Are you sure you want to read this?

We hear a lot about discrimination, don't we? I am all for discrimination. Imagine what the world would be like if we didn't discriminate.

As an employer, I discriminated against people all the time. All employers do it. Employers shouldn't hire people who didn't have the right skills, qualifications, or experience, and yes attitude. Furthermore, if the employer doesn't think the candidate will fit in with the current staff, they are also turned down. Employment history can be a good reason to discriminate. Evidence of dishonesty is another reason. We can't blame any organization for such discrimination.

The government discriminates all the time. Recently, our friendly Canadian government had a student employment job program whereby grants were given to potential employers. However, the government refused grants to those who didn't agree to certain social issues. Discrimination or what? The government got challenged on that one and lost.

Try getting a job with the Liberal Party if you are a conservative. And vice versa. You won't, and you shouldn't. That's the way it should be. Even voters discriminate when they cast their vote. Some won't vote for a liberal; others won't vote for a conservative. Democracy gives us the right to discriminate.

Schools and Universities discriminate in what values they teach and what clubs can exist. Associations, charities, and groups all have criteria for us to meet in order to be members. That is called discrimination, folks. We discriminate against certain restaurants because we don't like the food they serve. We discriminate against certain entertainment, sports teams, religions, and all kinds of places, events, and services. Let's face it: we go to places we like and don't go to places we don't like. And that is discrimination.

Discrimination is freedom of choice. That doesn't mean we can't be kind, and it doesn't mean we have to hate.

Just for the record, I am not racist or sexist.

See also: Culture and Tolerance.

53

"Amazing Grace"

*Amazing grace, How sweet the sound
That saved a wretch like me.
I once was lost, but now I am found, Was
blind, but now I see.*

*'Twas grace that taught my heart to fear,
And grace my fears relieved. How
precious did that grace appear The hour
I first believed.*

*Through many dangers, toils and snares
I have already come,
'Tis grace has brought me safe thus far,
And grace will lead me home.*

*The Lord has promised good to me.
His word, my hope secures; He will my
shield and portion be, As long as life
endures.*

*Yea, when this flesh and heart shall fail,
And mortal life shall cease I shall
possess within the veil, A life of joy and
peace.*

*When we've been there ten thousand
years
Bright shining as the sun,
We've no less days to sing God's
praise Than when we've first
began.*

The author of this, likely the most well known hymn ever written, was John Newton born near London, England, in 1725.

He became a seaman with a reputation for profanity and foul language, wanting nothing to do with God, and spent several years involved with the slave trade. During a severe storm in March of 1748, he witnessed several crew members next to him get washed overboard. Newton and another crew member tied themselves to the ship's pump. He said to the ship's captain, "If this will not do, then Lord have mercy upon us."

Later, he recalled his words, which were very much out of character for him, and eventually gave up the slave trading. This man, who mocked those who served the Lord, taught himself Greek, Latin, and theology and devoted himself to God's work and telling of his background. Among the many hymns and poems he wrote was "Amazing Grace," which he wrote as an illustration in his New Year's Day sermon in 1773.

The poem was later put to music in 1835.

54

"But"

This little word "but" can be a pain in the butt. Like "if," it ties a lot of things together or rips them apart. But let's look at it this way. A "but" can turn a positive into a negative, but it can also turn a negative into a positive.

I love you but … You cooked a great meal, but … See how the complement is stolen by the word "but"? No big deal, but 'buts' can be annoying. But you could say, "You were late for work, but you did pick up some donuts," or "Your shirttail is out but I like your tie." But's can encourage.

Keep in mind that "but" can be a good word of warning and caution to keep us on our toes and alert. It compares the good with the bad.

Jesus used "buts." In His letters to the seven churches in Revelation, He said things like, "I know your works, but I have this against you." (paraphrased) The word "but" is in the Bible over 4000 times, but I didn't count them.

Every time I have gone to my lawyer, I have been built up but then let down. But then again, lawyers are good at using it the other way. They and your car mechanic can also present a worst-case scenario of how things are <u>but</u> then tell us they can fix it. That is their strategy for justifying their big bill. But I understand. They need to make money too.

When interviewing candidates for a job, I ask them to tell me about their "buts." They would look at me a little funny, but then I would explain. "You remember how the boss would complement you and then follow up with a "but." What were the buts?" They would chuckle, and without hesitation, they would give me examples. I found it a much better way to get them to confess their weaknesses. But of course, I would always ask if the "buts" were true. It made for good conversation.

We can also get around the word "but" or avoid it by substituting the word "and." "I think you are great, <u>and </u>I appreciate your improvement in coming to work on time." Other substitutes could be "nevertheless," "yet," or "on the other hand," but check your dictionary for more. But it is not a bad word, but it is often a necessary word. But you decide.

When working on the fish plant, my friends said, "Fred is strong, but the smell isn't everything."

55
"Exercise/Fitness"

I can run the 4-minute mile in half the distance.

I can do the 20-minute workout in 10 minutes.

I received a poster on a great workout routine. They told me to put it on the fridge so that it would be more effective. It has been on my fridge now for three years and I don't feel I am in any better shape.

I never eat on an empty stomach.

I would give my right arm to be ambidextrous.

Broken cookies have no calories.

Diet Coke or Diet Pepsi doesn't offset a large pizza.

Jim and Mary joined a group who were on a strict exercise and diet routine. They were on their required walk one day and decided to take a short cut which went by an ice cream shop. They indulged in the ice cream and kept walking. Jim said, "How will we explain to the group how we each had two ice cream cones on our walk?" Mary said, "What do you mean two, we only had one." Jim said, "But we are going back that way, aren't we?"

My favorite exercise when trying to lose weight is "running" out of excuses.

I always crumble under pressure when I go to the bakery.

Seriously, for me, Eliminating sugar and reducing bread and grains helps keep the fat off, and I feel a lot better.

56
"Rights and Freedom"

According to the Canadian Charter of Rights and Freedoms which states:

"Whereas Canada is founded upon principles that recognize the supremacy of God and the rule of law:

Everyone has the following fundamental freedoms:

a) freedom of conscience and religion;

b) freedom of thought, belief, opinion, and expression, including freedom of the press and other media of communication;

c) freedom of peaceful assembly, and

d) freedom of association.

My translation:

God is supreme – We can believe what we want – We can practice our religion – We are free to think and express our own opinions – We can go to church and join any association we want.

Just asking:

Why does this not apply to all Canadians?

Why does the government ignore the supreme God?

Why has the government passed laws that violate its own charter?

Why are we accused of hatred when we don't agree with certain issues?

57
"Please, and Thank You."

"Pass the butter."

"What else?"

"The ketchup." *"How about, please?"*

"Oh yeah, please."

"Here's the butter; here's the ketchup. Is there anything else?"

"Nope." *"You sure?*

"O yeah. Thank you."

Is it that hard to say please and thank you? For some, it seems to be.

I was in Calgary giving a seminar to about 30 people on "Dealing with Difficult People." The seminar was nearing a close, and I had to catch a flight to get to the next city. Wrapping up about 3:50 p.m. I asked one more time if there were any questions, hoping there would be none so I could finish at 4:00, pack up, and beat it to the airport. A man in the front, who hadn't said a word all day, raised his hand 'slowly.' He was a serious farmer who owned thousands of acres. "Yes", I said, thinking that this would be quick.

"My people tell me I am unapproachable and too bossy. How can I fix that?" he said.

Without even thinking I just quickly said, "Have you tried 'please' and 'thank you'? The room went quiet as I thought, 'What have I done?'.

The pause ended when he said, "I never thought of that."

Yes, he was an old timer, and, in his day, the boss was taken for granted by the employees, and maybe 'please and thank you' were not common, and 'if someone told you to jump, you just said how high.' But you know how it is today. You have to be nice. Sure, why not? It is a good idea. Besides it is just common sense and common courtesy. That is not to say that the employee shouldn't listen and act if the magic words are not spoken. After all, the boss is the boss, and the employees are paid to follow instructions.

'Please' keep reading and 'Thank you.'

58
"Climate Change"

Oh dear! Do we have to talk about this? Are you concerned, or do you totally ignore all the talk on "climate change?"

If you google "Climate change predictions in the past 20 years," you will get a list of headlines and predictions dating back to 1967 and earlier. They are listed by year. You can click on the link and get lots of details.

The list includes 1970: "Ice Age By 2000." 1970: "America Subject to Water Rationing By 1974 and Food Rationing By 1980." 1971: "New Ice Age Coming By 2020 or 2030." 1974: "Space Satellites Show New Ice Age Coming Fast." 1974: "Another Ice Age?"

You can find detailed correspondence from scientists, special interest groups, politicians, and more outlining pending disasters like "food rationing by 1980" and "crop failures. Back in the early seventies, I even bought a 4-wheel drive Chevy Blazer because of the ice age threat.

Guess what! None of these predictions have come true and we are past many of the dates of the warned disasters.

In 1978, news reports said, "No end in sight to the 30-year cooling trend. Not ten years later, news of global warming took over, predicting massive droughts and floods. In 1989, "New York West Side Highway will be under water by 2019." It is now 2024. Is the highway underwater?

Are the folks giving us all these headlines lying, or are they misinformed?

If they are lying, why? Is there an agenda we don't know about? If they are misinformed one would think by now, they would start to question their facts. Interesting!

Yes, we should protect the environment. Yes, the climate has always changed.

Many people are now thinking that the hoopla of climate change is the biggest hoax that has ever been perpetrated on the world. Is it being used to scare people for political control or financial gain? Are the promoters of it lying or are they misinformed? "Something to think about?"

59
"Actions - louder than words?"

Not mentioning any names, but many people, especially politicians, say something in public, but their actions and behavior contradict their words.

Words: "We care about the working class." **Actions:** Increase taxes.

Words: "I love you, honey." **Actions:** Spends paycheck on booze.

Which one communicates the loudest? When actions do not confirm the words of the speaker, the words lose credibility and trust. Sound simple?

When our parents told me they were going to do something, they did it. Furthermore, if we told them we were going to do something, they expected us to do it. Can we say this to be true today? Do words mean action? Do actions confirm the words?

It is wise and considerate to do what we say we are going to do. If we can't, it makes sense to inform the other person immediately.

"A department head promised a customer on Friday that his job would be ready Monday at 8:00 am. It was not ready on Monday at 8. It was not a pretty scene. The customer demanded to see me. I met the department head with the client. The client explained, "You told me it would be ready on Friday. I booked my flight based on your promise." The department head rebutted, "We were just too busy." The conversation continued with the department head's only excuse being that they were busy and he just had too much work booked. Who booked the work? The department head! Who made the promise? The department head! Who chose during the weekend to bump the client's job? The department head! The department head said the words, but his actions contradicted his words. Who lost credibility? The department head! Who lost the customer? The company. Apologies didn't matter. The actions didn't match the words."

Enough said. Do your actions agree with your words?

"Action speaks louder than words but not nearly as often." - Mark Twain.

60
"Tax Tax Tax"

Tax Tax Tax
Tax on this, tax on that
Federal tax, provincial tax, municipal tax
Property tax, gas tax, health tax, wealth tax, carbon tax,
Tax on everything we buy
And the Governments always justify
But is it a lie?
Every tax has a name.
Is it all a game, or is the reason all the same?
The government is lame.
They just want your money.
No, it's not funny.
Sure, we need to pay our share. Does the government even care,
or is every tax a snare to cover up
What don't they want us to hear?
Where does all the money go?
Are we catching on, or are we just too slow
To see that spending is out of control?
A billion here, a billion there.
Is anyone keeping track of the waste?
Or will we continue at the same pace?

61
"Terrible Too's"

Be honest now. Which of these describe you?

Too loud

Too quiet

Too fast

Too slow

Too neat

Too messy

Too early

Too late

Too fat

Too skinny

Too particular

Too sloppy

Too caring

Too careless

Too emotional

Too unemotional

Too picky

Too critical

Too proud to add more.

Have you ever been confronted with "you are too…"?

I have. You may have said it about yourself.

I was in a group once where a lady wanted everyone to confess their big "too". She took her opportunity to rub all of our noses in our confessions.

We all did it. Finally, it was her turn. She just smiled and said, "My problem is, I am too good." She was a bit too snobbish don't you think?

How did you do with your list on the left?

Do it again as if other others were doing it to you.

Is there any agreement?

Don't take too long and don't be too critical of your self. If you do it may be too late for you to do anything about your "too" because you are being too particular.

There may be times when your "too" is not too enough and times when it is just too much.

Too's can be too annoying to those who are too intolerant.

Am I going on too much about the too?

62
"Leadership"

When we think of leadership, generally, prime ministers, presidents, and heads of large companies come to mind. There are many great leaders in such positions. Most of us would say we are not great leaders and would not want such positions.

How much of a leader are you? If anything is under your control, you have at least some leadership responsibilities.

"My earliest recollection of leadership was observing my brother Jack's five wooden ducks connected with a string. When I pulled the string connected to the biggest duck at the front, all the other ducks followed. I could tell that the little ducks followed the big ducks. Brilliant, don't you think? At five years old, I don't think I was aware of the word leadership at that time."

To be a leader, you have to be followed. Why should someone one else follow us? John Maxwell says that *"leadership is our ability to influence others,"* i.e., get others to follow you.

Just being in a leadership position such as the boss or president does not guarantee we have the necessary skills to be a leader. Such people are often followed simply because of their position of power and authority.

Management and leadership are different. Peter Drucker, the guru of management training, said: <u>"Good managers do things right, but good leaders do right things."</u> A similar definition is used to distinguish between efficient and effective. Just because we do things well and right it doesn't mean they need to be done or there are not better things we could be doing. A manager could do a great job opening and sorting the mail, but a leader would have someone else doing that while he/she is on to bigger things. Leadership is <u>influencing people</u> to achieve desired <u>results</u> and fulfill an overall <u>purpose.</u> That means getting people to work together toward a common goal.

63
"Don't Worry Be Happy"

Bobby McFerrin sang the cute and encouraging song "Don't Worry, Be Happy." Some of its significant lines include:

> "In every life, we have some trouble But when you worry, you make it double."

> "Cause when you're worried, your face will frown, And that will bring everybody down."

> "Put a smile on your face, don't bring everybody down like this."

Not worrying doesn't mean not caring or not being responsible. The time we spend worrying is often a bigger problem than the thing we worry about. As McFerrin sings, worrying actually doubles our troubles. It takes up space in our heads and squeezes out good emotions by bringing in anxiety. Furthermore, it not only affects us, it often makes us useless to ourselves, and it potentially affects those around us who might have to handle us with kid gloves.
Worrying is surrendering to trouble which will definitely come our way. This gives us two problems: the problem we have plus worrying about the problem we have.

Jesus spoke about it and essentially said to deal with the things you can and leave the rest to Him.
His actual words in Matthew 6:34 were:

> *"Therefore, do not worry about tomorrow, for tomorrow will worry about its own things. Sufficient for the day is its own trouble."*

Don't worry, be happy! Does this mean happiness is a choice?

64

"Socialism"

One dictionary meaning is: *"a political and economic theory of social organization which advocates that the means of production, distribution, and exchange should be owned or regulated by the community as a whole."*

Sounds good. Doesn't it? See that word community? That's a lie.
Regulations eventually and always come from a chosen few, i.e.
"government".
Socialism is a system whereby we pool our money and wealth into a big pot and then share it equally with everyone. The reality is the government decides how to spend our money and not the people. Are you okay with that? The way it ends up, even though it is supposed to be divided equally, there will be few elites who will get a bigger share than others.
What does this mean?
<u>Equal pay for unequal work:</u> Joe, who is lazy, will get as much money as Jim, who works hard. No matter how hard Jim works, he doesn't get any further ahead than Jim. Why would Jim work hard, then? He may as well slack off, since his ambition gets him nowhere. Result- Decrease production.

<u>The government makes all the decisions:</u> Companies and people have no say. How much you eat, what you buy, vacations, schooling, and personal and health needs are decided by the government. Result: The people have no freedom.

Are you with me so far?

Pushing Socialism is a big trend in North America.
The US and Canada already have some aspects of socialism in their healthcare system. (Claimed to be free but not- another topic). Socialism is being encouraged in our education system.

"Socialism works until the rich people run out of money."

. - Margaret Thatcher

65
"Frogs"

We were in a serious meeting. The topic was not frogs. It was all about our sales figures and meeting our monthly goals. Harry was deep in the topic.
When the opportunity for a pause in the conversation came, I casually asked, "How are things going with the frogs, Harry?"

Harry looked at me with a bit of a frown but did not answer. About ten minutes later, there was another pause when I got in another question. "Things not going well with the frogs, Harry?"

Harry responded with a puff and just said, "It doesn't look good." He went back to his meeting topic.

Ten minutes later, "So what happened?" "Another time", he responded.
After about 4 or 5 of my interruptions, the rest of the group had enough.

"What with the frogs, can you please tell us what is going on so we can get on with the meeting without interruptions."

Finally, Harry came clean: "I bought about 5000 frogs as an investment. I kept them in a big shed that was all equipped with ponds, lots of crickets, etc. They were very comfortable. Everything was going well when someone left a door open. One by one, they got out and ran away over a long weekend. When I went to check on them Tuesday morning, they were all gone. Maybe there were a couple left. You can imagine how disappointed I was. Not only did I lose my initial investment, but I lost so much future income that I was counting on."

Everyone expressed their disappointment for Harry. I sat there not saying anything when, finally, someone had the nerve to ask, "How would you make money on frogs?"

Harry responded: "Selling the hops to the brewery."

66
"Endurance"

How is your endurance? Can you stick to a task even though you feel like giving up? How is the debt reduction coming? How is the weight loss coming? Are you coping well with staying up night-time with a sick loved one?
Will you finish your college degree despite still working a part-time job?
How do we do when stuck with a difficult, unpleasant task that has to be done?

Endurance can't be taught. The only way to endure to run a marathon is to run a marathon and none of us can do it at the first attempt. We must work up to it and build our endurance gradually. Athletes understand this.

A dictionary meaning: *"the ability to withstand hardship or adversity, especially the ability to sustain a prolonged stressful effort or activity."*

There is suffering and perseverance involved with endurance. Have a toothache? Endure until we can get to the dentist. Uncomfortable in your airplane seat during a flight? Stick it out and endure until we reach our destination.

It is true that endurance is physical, but it is also true that endurance is as much a mental attitude. When I was training for a tournament, I would jog. "Today, I will go around the block three times." At the end of the three laps, I would be tired and couldn't do another lap. Yet when I would set out to run five laps, which I did, I wasn't tired until the end of my fifth lap. Go figure!

We are living in times that require endurance, not just to run a race as an athlete but to be upstanding citizens in society to battle the obstacles of life. Endurance will get us through life despite the obstacles we face. It gives us hope and momentum. It encourages and enables us to achieve. Endurance is making up our minds and then training our bodies to obey our minds. It may not guarantee victory, but it will give us the courage and stamina to keep going.

Enduring will enable us to get back up, no matter how many times we are knocked down. Don't underestimate the value of our trials and struggles. They build endurance.

Sylvester Stallone, in his Rocky movies, was about endurance. It was the same in his life.

67
"Ed Sullivan Show"

Ed Sullivan, who had no particular entertainment talent, had a TV variety show that ran for 23 years from 1948 to 1971, on Sunday nights from 8–9 p.m.

It featured every type of entertainment, including singers, dancers, musicians, comedians, actors, acrobats, circus acts, stunts, and more.

Many great entertainers got their beginnings or at least a great boost by appearing on the show, and of course, many of those already established made the show even more popular. Who can forget appearances on the show by Elvis (who was only shown from his waist up), the Beatles and the Rolling Stones, the Jackson Five, Diana Ross, and the Supremes? The list goes on of all the famous artists of the 50' and 60's. The show had some regulars like Topo Gigio the Mouse, who always said to Ed, "Kissa me good night." Osae Himanus, the funny astronaut, was a regular, as well as the Muppets, who made 25 appearances.

Ed often introduced famous celebrities who happened to be in the audience.
He was known for his comments and quotes. Ed said of Michael Jackson, "This little fella in the front is incredible." To Connie Francis, he said, "Tell me, Connie, is your mother still dead?" He said to the Doors, "You boys look great, but you should smile more." To the Rolling Stones, he said, "Before we discuss the matter of a contract, I would like to learn from you whether your young men have reformed the matter of dress and shampoo."

George Harrison of the Beatles said of the show: "I've heard that while the show was on, there were no reported crimes, or very few." When The Beatles were on Ed Sullivan, even the criminals had a rest for ten minutes."

You just didn't miss the one-hour show that became a model or pattern for other variety shows and was responsible for launching many great careers in show business.

68
"Patience"

"It is good to have a healthy amount of patience. It is also good to have a healthy amount of impatience." Who said that? I just did.
Well, which is it? Should we be patient or impatient? Hold on a minute. Calm down, be patient, and let me make my point.

Patience, according to 1 Corinthians 13:4, often read at weddings, is a priority or description of love. "Love is patient, love is kind." Patience seems to be an automatic result of love. Instead of patience, some Bible translations say, "long-suffering." Patience is our ability to put up with suffering or discomfort, and that includes waiting and not getting our way.

Some dictionaries say "Patience" is: "the capacity to accept or tolerate delay, trouble, or suffering without getting angry or upset."

We all wait and tolerate, but how do we behave while we wait, tolerate, and put up with things over which, quite often, we have no control? Patience enables us to react and respond to situations and others without being upset, angry, discouraged, loud, sarcastic, or insulting, i.e., "keep our cool" rather than having an emotional response that damages us and others. Good things come from being patient. It has been responsible for major breakthroughs in science and politics. It builds and mends good relationships. It allows us to wait for the things worth waiting for.
I think you can put your own spin on this, but one of the root causes of patience, or the lack of it, is often a habit or learned behavior.

Patient people can put other peoples' concerns above theirs. They tend to be selfless and not worried about getting their own way. This does not mean they don't have a sense of urgency when it is needed. How is your patience? Do you need to be more patient or less patient? Ask your spouse or family member what they think about your patience.

"He that can have patience can have what he will."— Benjamin Franklin.

Check out: "Impatience," "Sense of Urgency" and "Perseverance"

69
"Growing Old"

There is an alternative to growing older
It's called dying when you are younger
There are not many options left
How about giving your mind a shift
Make everyday count
See how many challenges you can mount
There will come a day when your joints will squeak
Your teeth may even fall out when you speak
Your head may grow up through your hair
So don't spend too much time in your chair
Get up, be active and move
Do something to stay in the groove
Hang out with friends keep your mind alert
Be careful when you move, so you don't get hurt
Reflect on your mistakes and the things you went through
But you can't change them now, so you have to forgive you.
Did I mention that Jesus is real?
You can look forward to meeting Him.
If you already haven't, it is now time to kneel.

70

"New Age"

New Age is not really a new age but an old age (thousands of years) with a new name. It is difficult to tell how many people would be considered as New Age. One reason is that it is difficult to pin down its belief system, and another is that people of various religions actually practice New Age principles and rituals without realizing it. It has been seen as cultic by some and the best thing since sliced bread by others.

New Age origins vary but have roots in Eastern Mysticism and are often said to be paganism. It became very popular in the 1970s and 1980s. (Remember the song "AGE of Aquarius"? Nice song, but New Age)

New Age has no particular Holy Book but uses various writings from Hindu, Buddhism, and native North American beliefs. It also uses astrology.

<u>Core Beliefs vary but include:</u>

- Focus on self-improvement.
- Morality and love are emphasized.
- Everyone and everything is God.
- God is an impersonal force, not a person.
- Unlimited power is in self. Self is important.
- Jesus is not the true God but a spiritual model who did not rise from the dead. (some say, 'rose to a higher spiritual realm after visiting India).
- Spirit or energy plays a big role, i.e., a psychic phenomenon.
- Karma (good and bad) accessed via meditation and self-awareness
- No heaven or hell, but reincarnation

<u>Rites &Rituals include:</u>

Yoga, meditation, channeling, tarot card readings, and crystals can all get one closer with energy for physical healing and contacting spirits. World peace, unity, and holistic health are important.

<u>Sources of information:</u> Wikipedia, Christianity and Religions by Rose Publishing. Various **conversations** with current and former New Age proponents.

71

"Raisins"

The three boys couldn't sleep. Exchanging ideas in their bedrooms, they came up with the plan of sneaking downstairs to get a handful of raisins from the pantry, which was out of sight of their parents in the kitchen.

The oldest brother was elected to go first. Carefully, quietly and step by step, he descended the stairs, snuck into the pantry undetected and took a hand full of raisins out of the familiar hiding place. As he moved up the stairs, a squeak came from one of the old steps. The startled mother said. "Who's there?" The quick-thinking older brother made the sound of the cat- "Meow."

The mother bought it.

Returning to the other two, the older brother shared the raisins, saying, "It is easy. All you have to do is pretend you are the cat."

Hungry for more, they selected the middle brother to repeat the process. Down the stairs, into the pantry, grab the handful of raisins and back up the stairs. Oops! The squeaky step once again alarmed the mother, who said, "Who's there?" The answer came back, "Meow."

Once again, all three enjoyed the raisins. But they were hungry for more and they convinced the youngest, who reluctantly took on the challenge, being assured that if he pretended to be the cat, everything would work out well.

The little brother went down the stairs, into the pantry, grabbed the raisins and headed back upstairs.

Squeak went the step. "Who's there?" said the mother. The younger brother shouted.

"It's the cat."

72

"Friends"

There are people we know, and then there are friends. We can know a lot of people and get along with them or work with them, but are they friends?

"I want a friend who is there for me and willing to listen to me." Sounds good but will you be there for them?

"The one who I thought was my friend told me I talked too much." Do you?

"A friend lent me money but wanted it back." What's wrong with that?

"A real friend will love you enough to tell you the truth."

"I don't get it. You are my friend, but you tell me I have body odor." I tell you because you are my friend.

"That's enough about me, let's talk about you." That was a quote from the movie "Beaches." It was quickly followed with, "Let's talk more about me." Some friend.

"Being friendly and being a friend is not always the same." I am friendly to the mailman but know nothing about him.

"A true friend is someone who gets two black eyes and comes home and gives you one." Terrible example.

"Bosses can be friendly, but they are still bosses."

"To have a friend, you have to be a friend." That's what I told a person who had no friends and kept complaining about it.

"A true friend is someone who sees the pain in your eyes while everyone else believes the smile on your face." – Unknown.

"We are fortunate to have one real close friend. It is usually the one we marry."

"Greater love has no one than this: to lay down one's life for one's friends." John 15:13

73
"Pride"

Before we get carried away, we should distinguish between the pride of conceit and self-embellishment from the pride of that feeling of honor, self-respect and self-worth that we all should have.

In the middle of pride is the letter "I." Pride is all about "I" or me. It is the "I" in pride that causes some to have, as one dictionary meaning puts it, "an excessive self-esteem." "Meism" is another word.

Depending on the Bible translation you read, pride is mentioned over 60 times in the Bible, all in the context of revealing the dangers of pride and putting oneself ahead of everything and everybody. Pride is listed as one of the seven deadly sins, and it definitely leads to other problems and hang-ups. The famous proverb 16:18, which says, "Pride *goes* before destruction, and a haughty spirit before a fall," has been proven true in many countries, empires, leaders, famous people, and athletes. But even putting the Bible quotes aside, there are many common potential and real dangers of pride, i.e., thinking of oneself as superior to others or higher than we really are.

Pride opens a can of worms full of greed, stubbornness, and selfishness. It makes us think we have and know it all. Our preoccupation with ourselves and focusing on our self-importance can prevent us from caring for others and building healthy, lasting relationships. Who wants to be around someone who comes across as vain and conceited? I guess like-minded people do.

This is not a knock against self-confidence and being satisfied with worthwhile accomplishments. But holding on to our pride will certainly get in the way of admitting our mistakes and flaws, thus preventing us from growing and dealing with disappointments and failures.

"A proud man is always looking down on things and people; and, of course, as long as you are looking down, you cannot see something that is above you." — C.S. Lewis,

Check out "Humility" and "Self-Esteem"

74
"Big Bang Theory" *(not the TV show)*

Quotes from "Space.com"

"The Big Bang Theory is the leading explanation for how the universe began."

"13.7 billion years ago, the universe <u>as we know</u> it started with an infinitely hot and dense single point that inflated and stretched — first at unimaginable speeds, and then at a more measurable rate."

"Everything in the entire universe was condensed in an infinitesimally small singularity, a point of infinite denseness and heat."

"Suddenly, an explosive expansion began, ballooning our universe outwards faster than the speed of light. This was a period of cosmic inflation that lasted mere fractions of a second."

Rephrased in layman's terms:

"An object about the size of a basketball got really hot and exploded and in less than a second organized itself into the entire universe including our sun, planets, moons and millions of other galaxies spanning billions of light years across."

Questions:

- How did the basketball get there?
- What made it hot?
- Why did it explode?
- Why so fast?
- Has something faster than the speed of light ever been discovered?
- How could such an explosion happen to organize itself into our solar system and universe?

Answers: They don't know! Yet, it is taught as fact.

75

"Grand Canyon" *(Magnificent to see)*
<u>What we know for sure:</u>

The biggest canyon in the world
270 miles long

Up to 18 miles wide

Up to a mile deep

Earth is laid down in as many as 40 layers.

Formed by water.

Contains many rock formations with large curvy bends in them.

<u>What some say without proof:</u>

Formed millions of years ago

Reveals a cross-section of the earth formed billions of years ago

It was formed by the Colorado River

It was laid down in layers by the ocean coming and going

<u>Questions:</u>

Wouldn't the bending rock formations had to have been bent when the rock was soft, otherwise they would have broken?

If over million of years, how could they have remained soft to bend?

If millions of years, why aren't there erosion and or vegetation between the layers?

Doesn't it make sense that The Grand Canyon had to have been formed through a catastrophic event such as a flood in a short time, i.e., months or weeks, as supported by many geologists, including Dr. Andrew A. Snelling? Google his report published on June 23, 2021.

See Mount St. Helens (Page 245)

76
"Authority"

There's authority you have over me.
And there's the authority I have over me.
You can tell me what to do.
But it's up to me to decide what to do.
Who gets their way? Is it me, or is it you?
Are you the boss over me, or am I the boss over you?
The one that has authority is the one with the power.
He can tell us to get it done now or in an hour.
Some people can handle it; some people can't.
Some follow authority, others complain and rant.
Parents, teachers and bosses were once followed to the letter.
Not anymore; people think they know better.
Why is that? Do they just need a whack?
Have people in authority lost their respect?
If that is so, they have no effect.
Don't subordinates know when they are hired,
They could just as easily get fired.
Do we blame it on the system,
The government or the rest of them?
Police arrest people for a crime.
They are back on the street in no time.
In the classrooms, kids come and go
No one seems to care if they don't show.
When is someone going to take charge?
Rejecting authority is a problem that's so large.

77

"Forgiveness"

We are going to get hurt, on purpose or not. Betrayal, a wrong word or deed, will come our way from strangers or people who are close to us. Will we get revenge, get bitter or angry? Will we shut them out or shut ourselves in? We may be left with a scar for the rest of our lives. How will we live with it?

We have all been there. If not, give it time. We can get even, be miserable for the rest of our lives or try to move on but be triggered from time to time with a memory or a reminder.

A well-known answer to moving on is forgiveness. "Yeah but, look what they did to me." "You didn't go through what I went through when I was a kid." We get it. Tough, isn't it? Seriously, we should not underestimate the things that some people go through. We don't envy them, and we can't always relate to them. But we can see how their lives have been affected. We know that the act of forgiveness can play a major role in the lives of those who strive despite how they have been treated.

Here is the choice. Forgive and move on despite our hurts, or don't forgive and be a "pain in the rear" to ourselves and others. "Yeah, but".

All the "yeah buts" in the world still don't change things. What's it going to be? You will be the one you hurt the most with your unforgiveness.

The effects of unforgiveness are well-known and include things like stress, anxiety, fear, anger, bitterness, resentment, and hatred, and these are just a few of many more. These are the pains and hangups that we face when the person we won't forgive has likely moved on in life while we are essentially slaves to all our emotions.

Do we like to be forgiven? Yes? Then, we should forgive. It may not be easy, and we may have to repeat that forgiveness for a while. It takes time.

"Forgiveness is not an occasional act; it is a constant attitude." - Martin Luther King, Jr.

Forgive us our trespasses as we forgive those who trespass against us. – The Lord's Prayer

<h1 style="text-align:center">78</h1>

<h2 style="text-align:center">"Right or Left" (politics)</h2>

Under capitalism and democracies in North America and other countries, we often classify political camps under the categories of right and left. Generally, they are labeled as conservative and liberal, which are under the party names of Conservative and Liberal in Canada and Republican and Democrat in the US. Different parts of the world may give a different meaning to these labels.

We assume, or at least they both say, that they do what they do for the good of the people they are elected to serve. They differ in <u>how</u> they want to best serve the people. Hence, the hullabaloo in the political arena news cycle. Are they driven by sincere motives, their ideologies, the people or do they just want to stay in power? Listed below are some key areas of differences that have dominated the news in recent years. These distinctions will likely cause rifts around the dinner table. You may disagree with them; however, the speeches and historical evidence from the respective sides should bear them out.

Left	**Right**
Big Government	Small Government
More government	Less government
Higher taxes	Lower taxes
More spending	Less spending
More rules	Less rules
More social programs	Fewer social programs
Governments decide	People decide
Equal outcome	Equal opportunity
Leans to socialism	Leans to capitalism
Justice?	Justice?

Do you vote for the popular party, or do you vote based on your beliefs? Are you "left" or "right"

Oops! Forgot to mention there are good, well-intentioned people, crooks, and weirdos on both sides.

79

"Conflict"

Conflicts arise every day.
When two or more disagree and want their way.
The winner may not be determined by right or wrong.
The one that comes on top is said to be strong.
They each state and argue their preference.
A bystander can easily tell their difference.
Opinions, values, emotions and views.
Facts may not matter in how they choose.
It's how they see and understand.
The facts and figures that are at hand.
The issues may be opinions in a political poll.
Or the best way to install a toilet paper roll.
Circumstances and people will play in how you solve
To make conflicts disappear or further evolve.
Here are options for you today.
First, you can avoid, ignore or delay.
That may give you time, but the problem doesn't go away.
Secondly, you can fight and compete.
The strongest will likely win over the weak.
It sounded good that you had a win.
But was it the best for all in the end?
The third way is to give in and give up.
 Is that being a coward or just bad luck?
The fourth way is to give and take.
You each lose something that is at stake.
It's called a compromise with no winner or loser.
At least it is an argument diffuser.
Fifth and final is to work it out.
Be willing to deal with the facts without the shout.
Debate with an open mind may take longer.
It does take effort, but you will be stronger.
"Peace is not the absence of conflict; it is the ability to handle conflict by peaceful means." – Ronald Reagan.

80
"Atheism"

Included in Mariam Webster's dictionary definitions of atheism are:

"a lack of belief or a strong disbelief in the existence of a god or any gods"
"a philosophical or religious position characterized by disbelief in the existence of a god or any gods."
 "a commitment or devotion to religious faith or observance a cause, principle, or system of beliefs held to with ardor and faith."

According to one of the most recognized dictionaries then, atheism is a religion with faith. Religions like Christianity, Judaism etc., believe and have faith in God, but cannot prove to the satisfaction of the atheist that God exists. The atheist will say in faith, "There is no god," but cannot prove that God does not exist. Religions like Christianity have faith that there is a God. Atheists have faith that there is no god. Atheists will tell you that there should be no religious influence in government, yet they want their religious influence in government.
Canada and the US were founded on Judeo/Christian principles and values. Schools and universities were all founded by God-believing people. Atheists have taken most of that away.

Lee Strobel set out as an atheist to prove there was no God and concluded:

"Looking at the doctrine of Darwinism, which undergirded my atheism for so many years, it didn't take me long to conclude that it was simply too farfetched to be credible. I realized that if I were to embrace Darwinism and its underlying premise of naturalism, I would have to believe that: 1. Nothing produces everything, 2. Non-life produces life 3. Randomness produces finetuning 4. Chaos produces information 5. Unconsciousness produces consciousness 6. Non-reason produces reason...The central pillars of evolutionary theory quickly rotted away when exposed to scrutiny.

Go figure.

81

"Natural Reaction"

How quickly are you to react? We need a quick reaction time when we need to stop the car. Athletes react quickly, don't they? Watch them in a hockey game or any sport. They have lightning reflexes. They can do that because of their practicing over and over again to the point that it becomes natural. It is often referred to as having muscle memory.

I don't have to think about some things. They just happen, or I just do things. If a cookie or candy is in front of me, my hand with no instructions whatsoever just shoots toward it, and before I even get a chance to think about it, the candy or cookie is halfway down my throat and my hand is shooting toward a second one. Now that's reacting!

People I pass on the road have quick reactions if I cut them off, by quickly waving to me with just one of their fingers.

Quick reactions in emergencies and just everyday life are good. Even in conversations, it's good to be able to react quickly. It is natural for a loving parent to jump immediately to the rescue of a child who is in danger.

Our bodies, our facial expressions, our words, and our minds will do what comes naturally. Natural reactions can be good or bad? BUT. What if our natural reaction is not a good one? What if we are naturally grumpy, negative, argumentative, critical or chronic worriers? Does that come from training and practice and experience? Something to think about? How are you reacting to me right now? Offended, upset or mad? Just asking.

Maybe we need to retrain ourselves so that some of our not-so-good natural reactions become naturally good reactions.

Newton's third law of motion says, *"To every action, there is an equal and opposite reaction."* He was talking about forces and motion, of course. Does the same apply to our personality?

"Life is 10% of what happens to me and 90% of what happens in me." – John Maxwell.

82
"Exaggeration"

"I told you a million times that you shouldn't exaggerate."

You always exaggerate, and I never do.
You never do what I tell you to.
All you tell me is not even true.
There are clouds in the sky when you say it's blue.
The rain is pouring when the sun is shining through.
A thousand times, I have told you.
Don't exaggerate about your flu.
To say you had it for a month is simply taboo.

Do you spice up stories to make them nice?
Do you always have to say things twice?
Are elephants really scared of mice?
Did your kids always get lice?
Does your diet really say you can only have rice?
Is it true you can't afford the price?
Don't lie to me; just be precise.
Don't stretch the truth, that's my advice.

You always exaggerate to win the day
In everything you have to say.
Don't say weeks when you mean years.
You are always giving me the gears.
Is it just because you want your way?
If you do, I will not stay.
You keep saying I am always late.
That's just another way you exaggerate.

83
"Fear of Failure"

When George Foreman set out to win back his title after being out of boxing for ten years, people laughed at him and mocked him. It was understandable since he was certainly out of shape and overweight. Many athletes have tried to make a comeback after having failed. They tried and didn't make their fear of failure an obstacle. George kept plugging until he got a shot at the title against Evander Hollyfield and lost on a decision. He made a lot of money on that fight, and we would have understood if he packed it in. And the fact that he failed to win back the title did not stop him from getting back up. Later Evander lost to Michael Moore. George fought Moore and knocked him out in the tenth round, regaining his title at the age of 45. George did not fear failure. He did what it took to overcome it and achieve his goal.

How many times have you not tried something simply because you feared failure? Of course, we have to be realistic and consider the facts at the time. There are many other reasons not to try something other than fear of failure. There could be health reasons, financial reasons, and more. George would not have tried his comeback if he had a serious heart condition. We get that. Plus, it would be stupid for me to apply for the main part in an opera if I couldn't sing.

Abraham Lincoln failed in business and lost an election but later became one of if not America's best Presidents.

Albert Einstein could not speak until he was four years old and was called lazy by his teachers. It didn't stop him.

Thomas Edison failed thousands of times before he got the light bulb to work.

Feeling like a failure and helpless. Try again.

Check out Fear, Overcoming Fear, Procrastination, Shyness, Courage, Confidence.

84
"Dirty Language"

I understand I did it all the time.
Swearing and dirty language were in every line.
I didn't do it around the house.
No, siree I was quiet as a mouse.
But out with my friends
We swore at both ends.
We didn't care what we said,
As long as there was no bloodshed.
We didn't think we looked the fool.
We actually thought it was cool.
So many words just didn't fit in.
With every conversation.
To take the Lord's name in vain
Didn't give us any pain.
Many of us looked back and saw.
Dirty words weren't necessary at all.
Today, it seems to be getting worse.
Kids are doing it; the parents are doing it first.
The office, the job site and the shop
It doesn't seem like it will ever stop.
Bad words on TV and the movies could fill a truck.
Do we need to hear words that suck
You swear away and are not polite,
When clean people are still in sight.
It has become second nature.
Even in people of great stature.
Many are offended but they won't say
Anything about what comes their way.
Remember, parents threatened with soap
To wash our mouths. Smarten up, you dope.

85
"Love Never Fails"

There is a quote in the Bible (1 Corinthians 13:8) that says, "Love never fails". How can that be? We all know people who have loved us, but they have let us down and disappointed us. And let's face it we have all done the same from time to time to others even though we claim to love them. Is this quote accurate, or should we say it is a lot of "hot air"?

First of all, we need to know what kind of love it is talking about. I have a feeling it doesn't mean the way we love chocolate or the way we love rock and roll. I don't think it even means romantic love or brotherly love. As good as they all are, that is not the kind of love that never fails.

The kind of love that never fails is the love of God. Jesus said:

"This is My commandment, that you love one another as I have loved you. Greater love has no one than this than to lay down one's life for his friends." John 15:12-13:

Jesus knew what He was saying because, after all, he did lay down His life for us. The love of God is commanded. When Jesus was asked what the greatest commandment was, His answer was this in Mark 12:30-31: *"Love. the Lord your God with all your heart and with all your soul and with all your mind and with all your strength.' The second is this: 'Love your neighbor as yourself.' There is no commandment greater than these."*

This is a good summary of the Ten Commandments, of which the first four are about loving God and the last six are about loving each other.

In saying, "Love never fails," it is saying: It will outlast everything else. It will do what is right with God. It will be truthful. It will be kind and gentle.

True love is about receiving the love of God and passing it on His way.

86
"Grace"

The classical definition of grace is often summed up in two words:

"Unmerited favor" meaning something we get that we don't deserve.

If we work for grace and earn it, then it is not grace.

If you have ever been given something out of the blue that you never expected and did nothing to get it, then you should know what grace is.

Remember the candy bar that someone gave you? That's grace.

Remember your parents surprising you with an unexpected Christmas gift? That's grace.

Remember the unexpected compliment you got one day? That's grace.

Remember that hug you got from your teacher once? That's grace.

Remember getting that job for which you didn't qualify? That's grace.

Remember passing the driving exam after messing up? That's grace.

Remember marrying your lover? Who could have had anyone? That's grace.

Remember someone paying your way into a movie? That's grace.

Remember being forgiven for something you did wrong? That's grace.

Remember someone taking the blame and punishment for something you did? That's grace.

If we get to heaven. That's grace.

87

"Titanic"

The world has had many disastrous events, all of which seriously affected the lives of many. The sinking of the Titanic on April 14, 1912, is certainly one event that has been remembered and will likely be remembered for hundreds of years to come. The news items, books, movies, the documentaries never seem to end. To date, there have been at least eight movies since 1912, with the various twists infused by the producers. We all come away with awestruck helplessness and emotions. "It's so sad." "If only!" If only they weren't going so fast. If only they had more lifeboats. If only the steel plates and rivets were stronger. If only!

It seems like the story won't go away.

I was fortunate to view the museum as a depiction of it a number of years ago. I saw some of the artifacts retrieved from the sunken ship. It was moving. At one point on the tour, you are taken through a door to show what the people on the ship would have seen from the deck of the Titanic in the last moments. I don't know why but I was shocked to see a calm, starlit blackness.
After all the build up in the movies, after all the character studies, after all the follow-up and never-ending analysis to find blame, after all the commentaries, what are we left with? What is our takeaway? What do we learn? What have you learned? Is there a message there for you?

The top two for me are:
"Life can change in an instant."
" Am I ready?"

88
"Global Warming"

Al Gore said in 2009 that "the North Pole will be ice-free by 2013 because of <u>man-made global warming</u>."

It didn't happen. We still have polar ice caps.

Everybody knows the weather or, as some say, "climate" is changing. There are places on Earth that are warmer than they have been. Real science will show that world temperatures have gone up and down over the years. And we can all see recent warmer trends. Yet history does show warmer times.

The big question is, "Are you and I causing it?" Is it really man-made? Most scientists say, "Yes." Likely, all the scientists who are on the government payroll say, "Yes." But not all scientists agree.

Governments are saying the science is settled. Of course, that was said when people said the earth was flat and the earth was the center of the universe.

Here are some questions to think about if the earth is getting warmer and everyone fears rising water levels that eventually flood cities like New York:

Why are people still building waterfront properties on the coastlines?

Why are investors putting money into big condos all up the coast on Florida beaches?

Why are property values so high there (and rising)?

Why isn't there a mass exodus from the cities on the water?

Why do most of the proponents of global warming still live as if it is not happening?

Who gets the money that is spent on global warming?

Just curious. Does it make sense to you?

See also: Climate Change.

89

"Punctuality"

The teenager got a phone call during dinner. After a couple of minutes of chatting, he said, "Okay, see you at 7:00." When the father asked where the caller lived, the teenager replied, "Downtown, Toronto. "But Toronto is an hour's drive; it is now 6:45". The teenager said, "Yeah, but he knows what I mean."

Does anyone care anymore about being on time? Punctuality was a big thing that was drilled into me by my parents and bosses.

Mary showed up sharp at 8:00 for her office job, which started at 8:00. She hung up her coat, went to the washroom, sat down at her desk, peeled an orange while reading the morning paper and finally began work at 8:15. Mary was on time at the office but late for work. Should she be fired for wasting her time and being paid for seventy-five minutes a week for which she did not work? Maybe not fired but certainly retrained.

When interviewing potential employees, punctuality was an area that I had to know about in the candidate.

How can we be trusted if we are not punctual? Customer Service, production, profitability, reliability, credibility, respect, and relationships are all at risk when we do not show up and deliver as expected or planned. Okay, emergencies and the unexpected happen. Sure, but be punctual or call ahead.

When we are late, we are telling someone that our time is more valuable than that of others. Think of the cost of a meeting with ten people being held up because of one person being late. There is the labor cost of those ten people and the potential cost and delays of the actions they could be taking.

Are you generally punctual? What would others say about that?

"If you are on time, you are already late." - Mel Stevens (Founder of Teen Ranch)

90
"Motivation"

So, what turns your crank? Sorry. I mean, what's the fuel in your tank?

Motivation is the reason we do. It may be different for each of you.

You may be driven by fear but that may change from year to year.

Pride and greed get in your way. Get over it or it's there you will stay.

Lazy? Don't stay in bed. Motivation needs to get in your head.

As we go through life, motivation can prevent strife.

A clean diaper and a full stomach keep a baby happy.

What is it that makes you snappy?

As a kid, a new toy was what caught my eye.

Now, I need something else to make me fly.

I learned in school cause I didn't want to look a fool.

I learned to obey, I assume, for fear of Dad lowering the boom.

The curiosity of teenage years moved me away from some of my fears.

In high school, fashion gave me a new passion.

Girls were something new; I tried but only attracted a few.

I enjoyed the school dance, every time I had the chance.

First year of university gave me a lot of insecurity.

I took up Judo as a sport, a good motivator of a sort.

A black belt I desired and did enough at work not to get fired.

Money became a need, for the family I had to feed.

Ambition became a fact, so I had to work to stay on track.

New careers brought me change, moving me to different lanes.

Maturity came as I got smarter, making me a better self-starter.

Looking back, I could have spent more time listening to encouragement.

The biggest motivator to give us a shove is to know the meaning of love.

Check out: Purpose

91
"Quotes"

Famous or not-so-famous quotes can move us, challenge us or teach us. They can make us laugh or make us cry. Some are original or at least claimed to be, but no matter if they accomplish their purpose. Everyone should know the famous Golden Rule. *"Do unto others as you would want them to do unto you."*

As a kid we learn lots of quotes typically from nursery rhymes and anecdotes that gave us wisdom about life.

"A rolling stone gathers no moss." Meaning someone on the move is less like to become stale. Einstein had a similar one: *"Life is like riding a bicycle. To keep your balance, you must keep moving."*

Many quotes are obvious and don't tell us anything we don't already know. But hearing them from time to time is good encouragement and a reality check.

Here's a good one from Babe Ruth for those who don't like taking chances. *"Never let the fear of striking out keep you from playing the game."*

My father had lots of his own quotes which only us kids could understand. *"Watch your bobber"* was one when we were starting to misbehave. Mother's famous line for discipline was a common one. *"You will be sorry when your father gets home."*

A former boss of mine always motivated us by using his line, *"I am moving up; who's coming with me?"*

It seems famous people get quoted more than the ordinary, yet the ordinary have good quotes as well.

You can search the internet for a quote on just about anything. Here is one from Winston Churchill: *"It is a good thing for an uneducated man to read books of quotations."*

Here is a good quote from Jesus: *"Love the Lord your God with all your heart, soul and mind and love your neighbor as yourself."*

Here is a quote from me: *'Watch what you say; you may be quoted."*

92
"Breaks"

Need a break? Let's take one. That is why you came to this page. We all need a break. "Oh, give me a Break" is a common expression. We need a break at work and from work. We need a break from household chores, from the kids, from the neighbors, from the bills that are piling up, from the hustle and bustle of life, from sickness and from pain from poor relationships. The list goes on.
We shouldn't feel guilty for wanting a break. But some may feel they can never get a break.

Breaks are important. They give us a rest from the chaos to calm us down and help us get some pleasure and relaxation. They recharge us and help clear our minds, give us new ideas and/or revive us physically. Some people pride themselves on being able to work non-stop for long periods. Some go years without vacation. Good for them. Or is it? I have had my share of that, too. We could use breaks from a lot of things, and not just for the bathroom.

Some live to take breaks. I know a guy who told me about his typical day. True story- not kidding: Work started at 9:00 by meeting his co-worker at the coffee shop. Got to their desk at 9:15. Went for coffee break at 9:45, back to their desk at 10:15. Early lunch at 11:45. Back to work at 1:30. Get the drift? When you added it all up, he worked far less than the hours for which he was paid. This doesn't count the casual and idle chat about last night's game, etc.
Good, honest workers deserve and need breaks to help them live better. Breaks can come in many forms, from coffee breaks to vacations to even changing jobs and careers. Hobbies, exercise, social clubs and worthy causes, a good book, and a puzzle all get our minds off the routines. I often took breaks on busy days for my MBWA- "management by walking around." Even 5- or 10-minutes walking through the shop, making small talk with the occasional employee was just enough to refresh my mind and enable me to take a fresh look at things. Yet breaks can waste time taken at inappropriate times. We can't just leave a customer waiting when break time comes.

We don't need to feel guilty or weak because we take a break. Instead, we should consider taking responsible breaks, a wise thing to do.

93
"Ten Commandments"

And God spoke all these words, saying:

² "I *am* the L ORD your God, who brought you out of the land of Egypt, out of the house of bondage.

³ "You shall have no other gods before Me.

⁴ "You shall not make for yourself a carved image—any likeness *of anything* that *is* in heaven above, or that *is* in the earth beneath, or that *is* in the water under the earth; ⁵ you shall not bow down to them nor serve them. For I, the L ORD your God, *am* a jealous God, visiting the iniquity of the fathers upon the children to the third and fourth *generations* of those who hate Me, ⁶ but showing mercy to thousands, to those who love Me and keep My commandments.

⁷ "You shall not take the name of the L ORD your God in vain, for the L ORD will not hold *him* guiltless who takes His name in vain. ⁸ "Remember the Sabbath day, to keep it holy. ⁹ Six days you shall labor and do all your work, ¹⁰ but the seventh day *is* the Sabbath of the L ORD your God. *In it* you shall do no work: you, nor your son, nor your daughter, nor your male servant, nor your female servant, nor your cattle, nor your stranger who *is* within your gates. ¹¹ For *in* six days the L ORD made the heavens, and the earth, the sea, and all that *is* in them, and rested the seventh day. Therefore, the L ORD blessed the Sabbath day and hallowed it. ¹² "Honor your father and your mother, that your days may be long upon the land which the L ORD your God is giving you.

¹³ "You shall not murder.

¹⁴ "You shall not commit adultery.

¹⁵ "You shall not steal.

¹⁶ "You shall not bear false witness against your neighbor.

¹⁷ "You shall not covet your neighbor's house; you shall not covet your neighbor's wife, nor his male servant, nor his female servant, nor his ox, nor his donkey, nor anything that *is* your neighbor's."

Exodus 20:1-17

94
"Elvis Presley"

Stars come and go, but for us baby boomers, no one came close to Elvis. Goosebumps came to his fans at the very thought of him. He had the looks, the voice, the songs, the movies, and the shaky legs. The first time he appeared on the TV's Ed Sullivan Show, the camera only showed him from the waist up because his shaking body movements were too outrageous for the public. Imagine! Yet today, the stars may as well be naked when they perform, and it is just taken as normal.

Everyone remembers his first movie, "Love Me Tender," with its theme song of the same name. The screams went out in the theaters when Elvis first appeared on the screen. Movie after movie, song after song just kept coming. His record "Heartbreak Hotel" and more became number 1 hits. He still holds several records in the music industry including the most hits of 114 in the top 40. He made over 150 albums and records. His three Grammys were all for his gospel music.

Some said at the time and still do that, *"Elvis was the beginning of the deterioration of society."* Frank Sinatra said: *"His kind of music is deplorable, a rancid smelling aphrodisiac...It fosters almost totally negative and destructive reactions in young people."* But Ed Sullivan said: *"I wanted to say to Elvis Presley and the country that this is a real decent, fine boy."* Buddy Holly said: *"Without Elvis, none of us would have made it."* John Lennon of the Beatles said: *"Before Elvis, there was nothing."* Still, Elvis remains popular and highly regarded by today's famous entertainers. Just recently another movie was made of his life.

He died so young. Just like so many who remember where they were when they heard of John F. Kennedy's death, the same is true of Elvis. "I was working in Pembroke, Ontario, driving with my assistant manager on collections calls and repossessing a TV for a financial institution." Where were you?

At one of Elvis's concerts, he saw a big sign held up by some fans. It read "Elvis is King." Elvis saw it and paused, and said, "No, Jesus is King."

95
"Trust"

If you lie to me, I can't believe you anymore. Well, that's obvious. Trust is a must. Can you be trusted? To be trusted, we must be trustworthy. That makes sense. Well then, are you trustworthy? Are you worthy of trust?

My wife can trust me with most things. She knows that if I say I will be home at a certain time, I will be home. If I can't, she also knows that I will call her ahead of time to let her know. But she can't trust me with her chocolate.

Many words are tied in or related to the word trust. Here are a few:

Credible, decisive, flexible, responsive, organized, empathetic, patient and impatient, firm but fair, determined, courageous, sincere, truthful.

Trust seems to be slipping away. Government, the courts, and especially much of the media are losing trust. Why? Could it be that they lie?

Spoken words used to be trusted but they have been replaced with legal forms, contracts, and promissory notes due to lack of trust.

Trust is a key factor in our reputation. Trust me, how can you have meaningful relationships without trust? Here is a little exam on trust:

I always tell the truth.	*True or false*
I do what I say I am going to do.	*True or false*
I don't mislead people	*True or false*
I am dependable	*True or false*
I decide based on facts and not personal opinions	*True or false*
I seek truth, not personal preferences	*True or false*
I wouldn't eat the last piece of my spouse's chocolate	*True or false*
I trust myself	*True or false*

Answer again as if your others would answer for you.

"Whoever is careless with the truth in small matters cannot be trusted with important matters."   *Albert Einstein*

"Trust in the Lord with all your heart and lean not on your own understanding."
Proverbs: 3:5
"Trust requires past evidence of trust."

96
"Entrance Exam – (Answers from 37)"

What is the number in your town for 911?	**911**
What is your last name in italics?	**The same if not in Italics**
How cold is it when it is twice as cold as 0 degrees C?	**Really Cold**
How warm is it when it is twice as warm as 0 degrees C?	**Warmer**
How much is 100 degrees Celsius in Fahrenheit?	**212**
Which is heavier, a pound of lead or a pound of feathers?	**Same**
What is the definition of a vacuum?	**Nothing**
The name of the shortest street in St. Johns, Newfoundland?	**Long Street**

If it takes 80 minutes to drive to work and an hour and 20 minutes to come home, which way is the shortest? **Same**

Count the different <u>two's</u> in this sentence, 'It takes too long to count to two when too many people are putting in their two cents worth.? **Did you count them?**

What would you rather do or go fishing? **Fishing**

If a hen and a half laid an egg and a half on the peak of a gable roof, how long would it take a grasshopper with a wooden leg to kick a hole in a picket fence?

Tomorrow

Do you know the answer to this question?	**No**
Why do elephants paint red spots on themselves?	**To hide in cherry trees**
Did you ever see an elephant in a cherry tree?	**No? It works, doesn't it?**

97

"Criticism"

Who are you to criticize me? Who am I to criticize you?

The downside of criticism is that it is not welcomed because it tears us down, especially if it is not deserved or done in the wrong way. Some people criticize or tear others down because it is the only way they can build themselves up. Is it natural for us to criticize in others the things we lack in ourselves? It is okay to correct someone when done in love, but being continually critical of everything and everybody is not a good way to live. True, we naturally discern things and evaluate what is going on, but it is not always necessary for us to openly criticize.

When I was on the road giving seminars, attendees had to fill out an evaluation form on me. On average, I was evaluated 8 to 9 out of 10. On one occasion, one of the attendees gave me 3's and 4's and wrote criticisms of my delivery. I was so upset and hurt, even though the other 30-plus attendees had no criticisms and rated me very highly. I called the head honcho at head office and expressed my concerns. She didn't seem bothered at all. She said, "If there is anything from the criticism, you can learn, learn from it and grow. If not, move on."
Criticism may hurt our pride, but we can take it in stride. Rejecting valid criticism is a refusal to learn and grow. If we are going to be critical, we should ask ourselves some questions like. Why am I doing this? Is the problem with me or them? Should I do it? Should I do it now? How should I do it? Be careful in criticizing things we don't understand. Are you too critical? How well do you take criticism?
"The only way to avoid criticism is to say nothing do nothing and be nothing."
They said that Aristotle said this. But he didn't. Criticize the internet.

98
"Scientific Questions"

Here are some scientific questions for family debates. Have fun.

What came first, the chicken or the egg?

If water is colorless, why does the ocean look blue?

Why is the sky normally red at sunrise and sunset?

What was the best invention before sliced bread?

When does human life begin?

When the moon is full, what is it full of?

What is outside the universe?

If we came from apes, why are there still apes?

What happened to the dinosaurs?

If a tree falls and there is no one around, does it still make a sound?

If a man speaks and his wife is not there, is he still wrong?

Does light bend?

What holds the earth in place?

Why don't we fall off the earth?

Is there a mountain taller than Mount Everest?

What keeps rockets in space?

How can rockets stay in the same spot above the earth?

Does fire make a shadow?

What makes ice caps at the poles?

How old is the earth? How do we know?

99

"Leadership Quotes"

"The greatest leader is not necessarily the one who does the greatest things. He is the one that gets the people to do the greatest things."
—Ronald Reagan, Former US President.

"Before you are a leader, success is all about growing yourself. When you become a leader, success is all about growing others."
—Jack Welch (Former CEO of GE.)

"A leader is one who knows the way, goes the way, and shows the way."
—John C. Maxwell

"The task of the leader is to get their people from where they are to where they have not been." —Henry Kissinger

"Leaders think and talk about the solutions. Followers think and talk about the problems."
— Brian Tracy

"Effective leadership is putting first things first. Effective management is discipline, carrying it out." —Stephen Covey

"No man will make a great leader who wants to do it all himself, or to get all the credit for doing it." —Andrew Carnegie

"Outstanding leaders go out of their way to boost the self-esteem of their personnel. If people believe in themselves, it's amazing what they can accomplish." —Sam Walton

"If your actions create a legacy that inspires others to dream more, learn more, do more and become more, then you are an excellent leader."—Dolly Parton

100
"Prayer"

The fact that we pray is an acknowledgment that there is someone greater than us and we believe that someone hears us and can answer our prayer, giving us something which we cannot get on our own. Prayer is a good sign of faith in God.

The Bible gives patterns and instructions on prayer. God answers all prayers. His answers are:

"Yes" – "No" – "Not now" – or "I have something better for you."

We need to know that God knows what we want before we ask. If that is true, then why do we have to pray?

The main benefit of prayer is for us to grow closer to God and not to get our will for our lives but to find His will for our lives. The more time we spend with God in prayer, the more we get to know Him. Prayer is surrendering to God and not just giving Him a wish list.

We cannot manipulate God by prayer because he knows our hearts. He is more interested in the attitude of our hearts than our prayer request.

"The function of prayer is not to influence God, but rather to change the nature of the one who prays."   **– Soren Kierkegaard**

"Prayer is not asking. It is a longing of the soul. It is a daily admission of one's weakness. It is better in prayer to have a heart without words than words without a heart."

– Mahatma Gandhi

Prayer need not have many words, but a sincere and willing heart.

Interesting: I recently spoke to a guy who doesn't believe in God, but he confessed he prays when he is in trouble.

101

"Procrastination"

Are you one of those last-minute people or "I'll do it tomorrow" people?

We bought a house in 1992. We knew the roof would need replacing soon. Judee kept after me to replace the shingles. I kept putting it off to save some money. I procrastinated. Lying in bed one rainy night, we heard a "drip, drip, drip". It was water dripping, of all places, right on Judee's face.

That was when I surpassed the speed of light. That was when the words "I told you so," took on a whole new meaning.

"Starting tomorrow I am not going to procrastinate". That was a quote I had on my notepads that I gave out at seminars.

Procrastination is defined as putting off until tomorrow what you could or should do today.

But who is to say that it should be done today? That's up to you to answer. There are some things that are wise to not procrastinate on. Yet for other things, it really doesn't matter.

Putting off important things is dangerous. We can't begin saving for retirement when we are two years from retirement. We can't make up our wills after we die.

We procrastinate because: We don't know how. We don't want to do something. We are not ready to do it. The task is difficult. Fear of failure. We don't connect the task to a cause. It is not important. We lack discipline. Laziness.

The results of Procrastination: Things don't get done and stress follows.

<u>Some solutions for procrastination that worked for me:</u>

1) Check <u>attitude</u>
2) <u>Learn</u> how/get help
3) Relate it to <u>purpose</u>
4) <u>Prepare</u>
5) Break it down into <u>pieces</u>

> *"Procrastination is like a loan. It is fun until you have to make the payments."*

102
"Natural Selection"

The often-accepted fact that Darwin discovered or proved evolution because he found some birds of the same species that had longer beaks than others did not prove evolution in species. What he discovered was "Natural Selection."

"Natural Selection" is a process where organisms with favorable traits are more likely to reproduce and survive."

Darwin jumped to the conclusion that over millions of years, natural selection causes creatures to eventually become another species. Although this has never been proven, it has become accepted in much of the world, especially in our education system.

Natural selection simply means "survival of the fittest." If we put 10 strong people on an island and 10 weak people, the strong will survive and the weak will eventually die off. When the island is discovered, we cannot claim that a new species of people has evolved. On the contrary, we can only conclude that the weak people could not adapt. If they stayed and reproduced on the island for ten million years, the strong will still survive, and the weak will not. Therefore, it becomes natural that the island has strong people - but they are still people and not another species. While natural selection has been used by farmers, dog breeders, horse breeders, etc., it does not create new biological information but redistributes what is already present. The dog is still a dog, and the horse is still a horse. The environment is a big influence on natural selection. Skin color is a major example.

Does this widely accepted image confirm "natural selection" or evolution, or does it prove that a creative artist was well paid to produce something to support false teaching that is not supported scientifically?

"Birth Order"

Did you know the order of your birth in your family can give you certain characteristics?

I read a 'best-selling' book on it by Dr. Kevin Leman. I went to the index and looked up "Last Born"- page 167, and turned to it. This is what it said, seriously:

> *"First of all, I want all you babes of the family to know that I am unto you. I know you have just skipped the first eight chapters and started right here."*

Isn't that amazing? Being the youngest has some obvious traits as does being the oldest etc. The book goes on to explain all the various scenarios of our birth order as well as the reason for exceptions.

While things like sex, physical differences, and the number of years between births are all factors in how we turn out, one of the biggest influences on our lives is parenting. Parents naturally love all their children, but it gets harder with time and money to give number 4, 5 or 6 the same attention as number 1. The effects of our upbringing are evident in us in many ways, including leadership skills, taking responsibilities, and other characteristics in our personalities from being slobs to perfectionists.

I, being the youngest, had to deal with being seen as the least knowing and, therefore, didn't contribute much to family conversation. I also got a lot of hand-me-downs. That changed when I outgrew the rest of my siblings.

It is possible to escape the negatives of the norms – *if you want to.*

104
"GrandPals"

"GrandPals" is an intergenerational program that connects an elementary school class with a small team of "GrandPals" (adults 55+) to engage in weekly, open conversations providing a path for connection and learning through storytelling."
The GrandPals Program started in 2010 at Montgomery Village Public School in Orangeville, Ontario, with the aim of providing students with applied, experiential avenues for character development. The school had a strong emphasis on character education, but the teacher team felt that more experiential opportunities were needed. They decided to bring students to a local retirement residence for weekly visits, where they engaged in activities with senior residents to develop empathy, a service mindset, and other attributes related to character development. To complement their visits, students created weekly written reflections of their experiences, and at the end of the program, the older adults (aka GrandPals) received a copy of these reflections as a parting gift.
The initiative evolved in the following years, deepening on the curriculum front, and teachers worked to create big ideas around the project and identified keywords and literature to develop student thinking. The program eventually turned towards storytelling as a central pedagogical approach, resulting in the publication of several works of art and books of student-authored stories containing moments from the lives of the GrandPals.

In 2021, one of the founding members of the GrandPals Program, Marc Mailhot, teamed up with the Centre for Studies and Aging and Health (CSAH) at Providence Care to strategize on how to expand the reach of the project by designing the GrandPals Program. Together, Mr. Mailhot and CSAH secured funding to expand the reach of the program nationally. The 2022/2023 school year marked the first year the GrandPals Program was able to reach communities across Canada. The program was adopted by communities in Saskatchewan, Manitoba, and Ontario.
This program not only provides students with experiential opportunities for social-emotional learning but also contributes to addressing ageism. The GrandPals Program exemplifies the benefits of intergenerational programming, fostering relationships between generations and providing opportunities for character development, community engagement, and preserving local history."
The above was taken from the GrandPals website: GrandPals.ca

105
"Effective Communication"

"There are four ways and only four ways in which we have contact with the world. We are evaluated and classified by these four contacts: what we do, how we look, what we say and how we say it."   *- Dale Carnegie*

In my seminar on "Effective Communication" we began with a definition. (as underlined)

Effective Communication is:

<u>Sending a message</u> – *"Hey George, are you coming to the meeting?"*

<u>Having it received</u> – *"Yes"*

<u>And understood</u> – *"I will be there in a minute."*

<u>The way it was intended</u> – *"No, I meant tomorrow."*

<u>Without getting your head yelled off.</u> *"Will you wake up?"*

<u>If it needed to be said.</u> *"I sent you an email and told you yes."*

We must also keep in mind that even if we communicate effectively, it may still not guarantee control, agreement, or a satisfactory outcome. Even though Judee told me to bring up something from the freezer, and I told her I would, I can still forget to do it. That is another issue like memory or lack of focus.

There are many and varied tentacles to communication. Are you an effective communicator? How often do you have to repeat yourself? How often do people have to repeat things to you?

More: 29, 49

106
"Voting"

Voting is serious business. How do you decide on your candidate?
Check off your criteria for voting.

1. Popularity with media	1. Is honest and sincere
2. Appearance	2. Good moral social values
3. Wealth	3. Strong character
4. Skin color or heritage	4. Right experience
5. Gender	5. Best interest of the country
6. Fame	6. Acts on principle
7. Promises free handouts	7. Not swayed by money
8. Relatives in high positions	8. Admits when wrong
9. Wants to raise taxes	9. Strong economic values
10. Wants government control	10. . Respect rights and freedoms
11. Wants more UN control	11. Good leadership qualities
12. Belongs to my dad's party	12. Is just
13. Leans towards socialism	13. Party platform
14. Wants to raise my kids	14. Leaves parenting to parents

How did you do? Did you choose more on the left than the right? A friend of mine decided to go into politics. He was quite excited. His excitement didn't last long when he discovered that none of his friends were going to vote for him. His friends liked him, and they got along with him but as they told him, "You are running in the wrong party. We don't agree with your parties' vision." Choosing a candidate or a party involves checking that person out with a fine-tooth comb. Keep in mind that your candidate will, for the most part, go along with the party's vision and policies.

107

"It is well with my Soul"

When peace like a river
Attendeth my way
When sorrows like sea billows roll
Whatever my lot
Thou hast taught me to say
It is well
It is well with my soul

Tho' Satan should buffet
Tho' trials should come
Let this blest assurance control
That Christ hath regarded
My helpless estate
And hath shed His own blood
For my soul

My sin O the bliss
Of this glorious tho't
My sin not in part but the whole
Is nailed to the cross
And I bear it no more
Praise the Lord
Praise the Lord O my soul

And Lord haste the day
When the faith shall be sight
The clouds be rolled back as a scroll
The trump shall resound
And the Lord shall descend
Even so it is well
With my soul

Horatio Gates Spafford wrote this hymn while crossing the Atlantic Ocean after his four daughters drowned at sea on November 22, 1873. His wife Anna survived and sent him a telegram saying, "Saved Alone."

While crossing the Atlantic to unite with his wife, the ship's captain stopped in the location where the accident took place.

Before this tragedy, their four-year-old son died of Scarlett Fever.

Anna was heard saying, "God gave me four daughters. Now they have been taken from me. Someday I will understand why."

They later had three more children. In 1881, they moved to Jerusalem and became part of a group that helped the poor and needy.

Anna continued the work after her husband, Horatio, died October 16, 1888.

108
"Judo"

Unlike many martial arts which were designed to hurt others and to defend oneself, Judo was founded by Jigoro Kano <u>as a sport</u> in 1882 in Japan. But don't kid yourself, it is an excellence for self-defense. The word JUDO is typically translated to mean: "JU" for gentle and "DO" for way.

While a spectator may watch the sport and say, "There is nothing gentle about it," the principle of Judo involves using the opponent's strength and motion to your advantage. Rather than resisting the opponent's force as in a push or pull, a judoka would move in the direction of the push or pull to throw an opponent to the mat.

Judo involves a number of throwing techniques and grappling moves that involve hold downs, chokes and armlocks. Many of the ground grappling techniques are similar to Jujitsu moves, which predate judo. While Judo is excellent as a self-defense against kicking and punching, such techniques are not practiced in judo.

Dr. Kano was the first to introduce belt rankings in martial arts, The current ranking from low to high are:

White – Yellow – Orange – Green - Blue – Brown - Black

There are ten degrees of black. 6th to 8th degree may wear a red and white belt. 9th and 10th may wear an all-red belt.

Time in each grade may vary depending on the proficiency of skills, frequency of practice, tournament participation and record. Safety, etiquette, respect and sportsmanship are very much emphasized. Judo is unified under the International Judo Federation and is an Olympic Sport.

Judo has been ranked as one of, if not the best, sport for early child development. It is practiced by males and females of all ages.

Moto: *Maximum Efficiency – Minimum Effort - Mutual Welfare and Benefit*

109
"Wisdom"

What does it mean to be wise? Is it the same as knowledge? I don't think so and this is not a knock against knowledge. Information is good, but it doesn't necessarily make us wise.

While wisdom is usually associated with knowledge and experience, it has more to do with our judgment and decision-making process.

Webster says things like this about wisdom:

ability to discern inner qualities and relationships – **INSIGHT** good sense: **JUDGMENT**
generally accepted belief accumulated philosophical or scientific learning: **KNOWLEDGE**

Aristotle said: "Knowing yourself is the beginning of all wisdom."

Socrates said: "The only true wisdom is in knowing you know nothing."

Einstein said: "Any fool can know. The point is to understand."

William Shakespeare said: "The fool doth think he is wise, but the wise man knows himself to be a fool."

Jane Austen, Pride and Prejudice said: "Angry people are not always wise." Jimi Hendrix said: "Knowledge speaks, but wisdom listens."

Solomon from the Bible said in Proverbs 9:10: "The fear of the Lord is the beginning of wisdom, and knowledge of the Holy One is understanding."

Fred Dyke said: "Wisdom is having knowledge and knowing how to use it."

110
"The Lord's Prayer"

Our Father in heaven,

Hallowed be Your name.

Your kingdom come.

Your will be done

On earth as *it is* in heaven.

Give us this day our daily bread.

And forgive us our debts,

As we forgive our debtors.

And do not lead us into temptation,

But deliver us from the evil one.

For Yours is the kingdom and the power and the glory forever. Amen.

This most famous prayer in the world is taken from Matthew: 6:913 (NKJV). They were actually the words of Jesus, who was asked by the disciples to teach them how to pray.

This is both a pattern of prayer and a prayer in itself. Sadly, it is often spoken out of rote with little attention paid to the actual words.

Not that it needs interpretation. If we sincerely pray it, we can see God's vision for our lives in that we:

Acknowledge who God is.

Ask for God's will, not ours.

Invite God's kingdom to come to earth and into our lives.

Ask for daily sustenance.

Ask for forgiveness.

Commit to forgive others.

Ask God's leading from temptation.

Be protected from Satan and his evil.

See God as all powerful for eternity.

111
"Sense of Urgency"

Missed the garbage truck? Taxes not filed on time? Ran out of gas? Late for work? Do you relate to these things? Do you get caught, pay late charges, lose customers or friends because you didn't do what you could or should have done? A sense of urgency would avoid a lot of them.

To have a sense of urgency means we do what we have to do or should do when it needs to be done. Obviously, it relates to time management and organization. We have heard it said that the early bird gets the worm. The early bird gets the worm because it has a sense of urgency.

A sense of urgency is certainly an attitude, and we could say it is an action. It doesn't mean we are in a constant state of panic or stress, but it is being on the ball, and we are to do important things that need to be done when they need to be done. This is a preferred attitude with employers, customers and my wife. Deadlines are important. It is an admired character trait.

A sense of urgency doesn't always come naturally for everyone. It is a challenge. It helped me when I had it and I suffered the consequences when I didn't have it. Cramming for an exam, walking a mile to a gas station, can be eliminated with a sense of urgency. Rules, procedures, and a calendar of events are all set up to help us with our sense of urgency. Those with a strong sense of urgency accomplish more.

"As soon as possible" or "when you get around to it" can be killers for a sense of urgency.

<u>Caution:</u> Not all things we think are urgent are important. An urgency may or may not be an emergency. One more thing, don't cross the line from having a healthy sense of urgency to be a worry wart and driving everyone crazy.

"I have been impressed with the urgency of doing. Knowing is not enough; we must apply. <u>Being willing is not enough; we must do.</u>"

-Leonardo da Vinci

See: Emergency - Important - Priorities

112
"Funny Laws"

Men Must Wear Speedos on French Beaches

It's Illegal to Ride a Cow While Drunk in Scotland

Jumping off a Building Is Punishable by Death in New York *(repealed)*

Storefronts Can't Hypnotize Passersby in Washington

You Can Only Take an Elephant on a Walk if it's on a Leash in San Francisco

You Can't Kill Anything on Sundays ... Beside Raccoons in Virginia (1950)

You Can't Drive Blindfolded in Alabama Vicks

inhalers are forbidden in Japan.

No Purple Garage Doors in Kanata, Ontario.

<u>Is it true that Canada has the following laws?</u>

- It is illegal in Canada for parents to speak to and counsel their own children on certain values.
- By law, doctors must give their sick patients the option of suicide.
- It is illegal to speak or give opinions on certain issues or disagree with government policies.
- Certain politicians are exempt from the law.

Funny or sad?

113
"Leadership Musts"

Leadership implies moving people from one point to another. If you are content to keep people and things the same, you are not exactly influencing change or improvement. (Change doesn't necessarily mean improvement.) Many leaders in our country have made things worse by bringing in change.

Four important stages or practices of leadership:

<u>Provide Patterns</u> – As ducklings watch the mother feed, swim, scratch and eat, people need examples from leaders. This is important both at work and at home. It is difficult for leaders to get people to follow instructions, if they don't behave in a way that is different than what they preach. We must walk the talk, otherwise we lose our credibility. <u>Show them the way.</u>

<u>Create Cause</u> – people generally like a reason for them to do what they do. We like to know why. The leader must be good at making clear a worthwhile vision, which encourages, motivates, and gives purpose. Praise, recognition and challenge get people moving. <u>Tell them why.</u>

<u>Unloading Understanding</u> – A good leader will ensure that the subordinates have a good working knowledge of what is going on. The proper training, instruction and tools will enable them to perform better. It is not always enough to say, "Do as I say." Explain, teach, and inform as necessary. <u>Teach them how.</u>

<u>Offer Ownership</u> – This is the part where leaders promote themselves and make things easier by getting subordinates to teach and lead others as they have taught them. Once your employees or older kids have been led and influenced to work the way they should, they will naturally take things off your plate and become what you have led them to be. <u>Pass it on.</u>

Are you a leader?   How do you know?

What patterns are you setting? How are you creating causes? Do you understand? Are you giving others ownership? Are you making leaders out of your people?

114
"Diets"

Been there done that.

They say that diets don't work.

Is that a fact?

Oh yeah, well they have worked for me

I started a thirty-day diet

And I lost seventeen days already

It's hard for me, food taste so yummy.

So, I never eat on an empty tummy.

If there are four cookies on a plate

I can never just eat one,

I eat them all before it's too late.

I won't stop until they are all done.

Dieting plans are big money-makers.

Fat people hate them, as do the bakers.

Silly when you stop to think

That people will pay to get their bodies to shrink.

We know sugar is bad for us.

Why don't people make a bigger fuss?

We try to exercise, works for a while.

But that quickly goes out of style.

So what's the answer to being round and plump

Ease off on the desserts and bread,

And eliminate the junk.

Rice Crispie Cookies

Nanaimo Bars are great

Chocolate-covered almonds. Suck off the chocolate and throw away the nuts.

"Dinosaurs"

<u>Wikipedia:</u> "The first dinosaur fossils were recognized in the early 19th century, with the name "dinosaur" (meaning "terrible lizard") being coined by Sir Richard Owen in 1842 to refer to these "great fossil lizards".

We know that these large creatures exist, and they are fascinating to study. I can't even pronounce all of their names. The general and popular view is that they went extent some 65-68 million years ago. Did they? How do scientists know?

<u>Things to make us think:</u>
Did you know that dinosaur fossils have been found in Montana, USA, containing bloods vessels. In 1999 a complete dinosaur was found in North Dakota with skin and soft body parts. Why is this significant? There is disagreement within the scientific community as to how long soft tissue can survive in the ground. Some say a few thousand years, while others say as long as a hundred thousand years and longer. 65 million years is a stretch. If dinosaurs went extent 65 million years ago when a large meteorite impacted the earth, why did the impact not cause other mammals such as squirrels, ducks, beavers and more, whose fossils have been found with dinosaur fossils, to go extent?

Just asking:
Dinosaurs are reptiles. Did you know that reptiles never stop growing?
Is it possible that dinosaurs were around until recently?

Could dinosaurs be the dragons, meaning large serpents, which are mentioned in the Bible some 20 times?

Did St. George really slay a dragon, as shown in the many pictures or was it a dinosaur?

Why are there thousands of coins with dragon images on them?

Why are there so many images of dragons in caves?

Dragons are always depicted in the Bible as having long tails and long necks. Where did Job in the Bible get the ideas for describing large animals *(Behemoth and Leviathan)* similar to dinosaurs? (Job 40-41)

Could it be that dragons and dinosaurs are the same?

116

"Shy?"

I was shy too. Are you shy?
I blushed easily every time someone caught my eye.
A lot of people didn't know it.
I tried so hard not to show it.
I knew what I could and couldn't do.
It is even more embarrassing when it shows through.
Shyness is a lot like fear.
You dread going here, you dread going there.
But it can be overcome.
You just have to learn to beat your drum.
You can begin gradually to build confidence.
Or you can go all-in now if that makes sense.
I used a combination of the two.
If it worked for me, it should work for you.
You need the desire.
To create in yourself a fire.
That will give you the nerve to begin.
If you mess up a little, just try again.
Get used to some small situations.
Try it on your relations.
If you want to go all out with a burst, What can go
wrong if you prepare for the worst?
People are not out to get you or put you down.
There are many others like us in town.
Pick it up a bit, get involved with something new.
Find a hobby that you know you can do.
Use your confidence from that on other things.
Eventually you will find your wings.
So what, if you had a cry
You can finally say, "I am no longer shy."

117

"Time Wasters"

The three biggest time wasters at the office are:

Meetings – <u>Not</u> having meetings is a time waster. Meetings are important.
Meetings – Having unorganized and unstructured meetings.
Meetings – Having organized and productive meetings with no follow up.

Another waste of time at work or anywhere else is excessive <u>talking</u>. Don't get me wrong, talking is fun and productive too. There are those who when you ask them the time, they tell you how to build a watch.

Yes, talking is necessary but <u>unnecessary talking is unnecessary</u>. I discovered early in my management career that people (me included) talk too much about things that have nothing to do with work. A 10 second greeting at the coffee machine turns into a 15-minute conversation. The more people there, the longer it goes.

Think about how much more production could be done if everyone at work could spend 30 minutes less a day talking about unnecessary things. This applies in offices, factories and construction sites. And no, it doesn't mean we can't talk or interact. But get to the point and move on. Strict? Maybe, but we are paid to work.

Other potential time wasters:

- Doing things that don't produce results
- Surfing the net
- Not planning your day
- Poor skills in communication or other on the job skills
- Spending too much time with the wrong people
- Not learning from our mistakes and the mistakes of others
- Gossip

Do you have time wasters? What are they? Which ones can you eliminate? Which ones will you eliminate?

> *When you kill time, remember it has no resurrection.* - A. W. Tozer.

118
"Unions"

<u>What some pro-union people say about unions:</u>

"They exist to prevent poor or unfair management from taking advantage of employees when it comes to working conditions, safety, long hours etc."

"They have been good in negotiating fair wages."

"Benefits are great, and they can't fire me. We have job security."

"We have someone to go to bat for us"

"More negotiating power."

"Higher wages."

"Better retirement opportunities."

"Less favoritism."

<u>What some anti-union people say about unions:</u>

"The employee who produces less is paid the same as the one who produces more."

"We can't get rid of incompetent or lazy workers."

"The union should not tell me who to vote for."

"We can't compete because the union says we have to have 3 people doing this job when we only need two."

"Why do they have to be so adversarial?"

"In our industry, a lot of union shops closed during the recession."

"They are too political and have too much control in the workplace."

"I switched from the union job because too many people were complaining."

"I thought I was doing a good job by being more productive. The union boss said, "You see that pile of work there? No matter how big that pile is, you make sure it lasts you until ten minutes before 5:00 p.m., quitting time."

What do you say?

119
"Jordan Peterson Quotes"

This guy makes sense.

"Work as hard as you possibly can on at least one thing, see what happens."

"BLAMING OTHERS FOR YOUR PROBLEMS IS A COMPLETE WASTE OF TIME. WHEN YOU DO THAT, YOU DON'T LEARN ANYTHING. YOU CAN'T GROW AND YOU CAN'T MATURE. THUS, YOU CAN'T MAKE YOUR LIFE BETTER."

"Put the things you can control in order. Repair what is in disorder, and make what is already good, better."

"You must determine where you are going in your life because you cannot get there unless you move in that direction. Random wandering will not move you forward. It will instead disappoint and frustrate you and make you anxious and unhappy and hard to get along with (and then resentful, and then vengeful, and then worse)."

"If you have a friend whose friendship you wouldn't recommend to your sister, or your father, or your son, why would you have such a friend for yourself?"

"We only see what we aim at. The rest of the world (and that's most of it) is hidden."

"There are two major reasons for resentment: being taken advantage of (or allowing yourself to be taken advantage of), or whiny refusal to adopt responsibility and grow up."

"If you fulfill your obligations every day, you don't need to worry about the future."

"Do not allow yourself to become arrogant or resentful."

These are a sampling of quotes by Riz Pasha on his website SucceedFeed.

120

"Anger"

Anger is a natural emotion. For some, it is more natural than others. There is a difference between being an angry person vs. a person who gets angry. They can and do sound the same. But surely you know people who always seem to be angry. You can pick them out anywhere in a crowd. They are not fun to be around, are they? But who knows what they have been through? Nevertheless, they are hurting themselves and others. Hopefully, they can get over the reason for their anger.

"Anger always has a reason. Is it a good one?'

Anger seems to be a part of a natural cycle when something goes wrong for us. Some are quick to anger and some slow to anger. We have different triggers for anger as well. The trick seems to be a) not to stay angry and b) not to do something crazy when we are angry.

Is anger sinful, evil, or wrong? Maybe. Jesus got angry. God got angry at least 20 times in the Bible. Scholars refer to God's anger as righteous anger, i.e., he was angry at sin itself. While our anger may not be sinful, wrong, or evil, the motivation for our anger can be. Things like pride, jealousy, greed, selfishness, vengeance, or stubbornness can be the root causes of our anger. We should be angry at some of the things that are happening in the world. I get angry when I see injustice or when I see child abuse. I get angry when the government wants to control everything, including what morals to teach or not teach my kids.

The trick is to control what we do when we are angry. Uncontrolled angry behaviour can turn into physical or verbal violence that can be harmful to ourselves and others. Cain was angry at his brother Abel. He couldn't get over his anger. It led to murder.

What makes you angry? Is it justified? Do you take it out on others?

"Be angry and do not sin; do not let the sun go down on your anger." (Ephesians 4:26)

121

"Laughter"

Don't you love to laugh? We don't do enough of it, do we? Do you?

Do you need something to laugh at? You can laugh at anything you want. Think of yourself when you were a kid. Go ahead and laugh. It is good for us. It changes the mood and lifts our spirits, and helps us to refocus. Laughter is contagious; even if we don't find something funny, we laugh because someone else is laughing.

How about these things?

Try licking out your tongue and touching your nose. It's easy. Lick out your tongue and touch your nose with any one of your fingers. You did it.

The pastor preached, "Divorce is worse than death." The congregant shouted out, "Are you kidding? It was the best day of my life."

Think about something that you did that embarrassed you. Now, laugh at it.

Did you hear the one about Joyce, who cloned herself? She is now called "Rejoyce".

You don't have to be happy to laugh. Just look in the mirror.

Try reading a page in the phone book. Go ahead and try it.

Watch question period in the Canadian Parliament. If that doesn't get you laughing, then you should certainly cry.

Have you ever stayed out all night? Dark, isn't it?

My first job was as a spokesperson in a bicycle factory.

Marriage is the number one cause of divorce.

> "Life is worth living as long as there's a laugh in it."
> — **Lucy Maud Montgomery**

If you can't remember when you started losing your memory, then you are losing your memory.

"Laughter is the shortest distance between two people."

— **Victor Borge**

122
"Buddhism"

Buddhism is considered the fourth-largest religion in the world, with over 500 million followers.

The founder was Gautama Siddhartha also known as Buddha – said to have roots in Hinduism and to have started around 500 BC in modern-day Nepal.

Its Source of Beliefs and authority include:

- The Mahavastu (Great Story) tells of the life stories of Buddha

- The Jataka Tale (stories of the former lives of Buddha)

- The Triptaka (Three Baskets)

- The Tantras

Core Beliefs include:

- Buddha did not believe in any god. No god is needed.

- Some followers talk of Buddha as a universal enlightened consciousness or as a god.

- Jesus is not in Buddhist history. Buddhists today view Jesus as an enlightened teacher.

- There is no Holy Spirit, but Buddhists believe in spirits -

- Deity Yoga is practiced inviting spirit possession.

- The goal is nirvana. Eliminate desires and cravings to escape suffering.

- Non-existence can be achieved through an Eightfold path.

- People do not have individual souls.

- Desire and feelings can be reincarnated into another person.

Eightfold Path: Right knowledge- Intentions- Speech- Conduct- Livelihood – Right Effort - Mindfulness – Meditation

Four Noble Truths: The Reality of Suffering – The cause of suffering- The cessation of suffering – The Middle way by following the Eightfold Path

Other religions can be blended into Buddhism by the "Doctrine of Assimilation."

123
"Mel Stevens"

Mel along with four other members of the singing group, "The Kings Men," decided at lunch one day to book passages for them and their families to

Australia. Then they told their wives that afternoon. They departed at 5:00 p.m. on April 8, 1960. Supporting themselves by entertaining, they began a not-for-profit organization called Teen Ranch to develop teenagers into leaders. Western horse riding and other physical activities were mixed in with Biblical teaching and mentoring.

Returning to Canada in 1966 with an intent to duplicate the Christian camp,

Mel was able to acquire 150 acres of land in Caledon, Ontario, northwest of Toronto. As a result of continuous prayer, loans, mostly from his earthly Father, and some miracles from His heavenly Father, Teen Ranch Canada opened in 1967 with eleven campers.

Teen Ranch grew, offering camps in hockey, equine events, and various outdoor activities as attractions. Mel, his family, and volunteers were able to share Biblical principles to thousands of teenagers and adults annually.

Mel became the Chaplin for the Toronto Maple Leafs and gave each player a monogrammed personal Bible. He also formed great relationships with players of the Toronto Argos and Toronto Blue Jays. His persistence and drive introduced many athletes to Christianity, including Paul Henderson, Ron Ellis, Laurie Boschman, and more. In addition, through his many contacts, prominent businesspeople frequented and supported Teen Ranch.

Teen Ranch continues in modern facilities, which are used by school groups, business groups, church groups, and more. In addition, its Olympic-size hockey rink continues to be used to train young players and host local leagues as well as professional NHL teams and international hockey teams, who have visited Teen Ranch to run their training camps.

Among Mel's favorite sayings were:

"If you arrive on time for work, you are late."

"Without faith, it is impossible to please God."

"Persevere."

124
"Driving Jokes"

"I just bought a new car. It can go so fast my headlights shine behind me."

"The government of Canada has put forward a new proposal to have all trucks in Canada drive on the left side of the road, beginning in the New Year. If it works, after a six-month trial period, all cars will be required to drive on the left side as well."

"A local town in central Ontario recently purchased a new fire engine. After numerous meetings and considerable debate, the council voted unanimously to keep the old one and use it for false alarms."

"Jim went into a dealership to buy a used car good enough so he could drive across the country. The dealer had one to fit his price but made him aware that the reverse gears didn't work. Jim said, 'That's okay, I don't intend to come back.'"

"The first electric car was brought on stage on the Fernwood Tonight show back in the seventies. Host Barth Gimble introduced the inventor, who said that his electric car was so quiet that you could hear a fat lady sweat in it. The drum roll started as the inventor got into the car and turned the key in the ignition. Nothing happened. In full confidence, the inventor got out of the car to check under the hood, which exposed about 1000 ordinary flashlight batteries. He said, 'no problem,' I just need to determine which one was put in wrong."

The first car in the community slowed down to pick up a lady walking on the road. The lady was known to be a fast walker, and she walked a lot. The driver said, "Would you like a lift?" She quickly replied, "No, I am in too big of a hurry."

Bill told me his grandfather died peacefully in his sleep. The four passengers with him, would have had a whole different story.

125
"Bible Words- Meanings"

"Apostle" The original twelve disciples were Apostles. They had witnessed the risen Christ, and they were sent out to spread the gospel. If people are called apostles today, they certainly are not the type of the early twelve and others at the time who had seen the risen Jesus.

"Disciple" means a personal follower of Jesus as was the original twelve. It is one who is a committed follower and is seeking to learn more about Jesus and be closer to Him.

"Mercy" is withholding punishment that is deserved.

"Grace" is giving a benefit that is not deserved.

"Righteousness" is being morally right. Better yet- "Right with God."

"Hallelujah" is a Hebrew word of praise. It means "Praise the Lord" or God be praised. Do you think all the people who love Leonard Cohen's song, "Hallelujah," realize that?

"Hosanna" means, "Blessed is he who comes in the name of the Lord!" It is also translated as "Save us now" or a plea for help.

"Gospel" means good news and usually refers to the first books of the New Testament as in the Gospels of Matthew, Mark, Luke, and John who tell the story of the life of Jesus.

"Saint". In the Bible, saints were those who were set apart or made Holy for God. Sanctify means to make Holy. All those who were genuine followers of Jesus were considered saints. Only God can declare someone a saint. *To the church of God that is in Corinth, to those sanctified in Christ Jesus, called to be saints together with all those who in every place call upon the name of our Lord Jesus Christ, both their Lord and ours.* " I Corinthians 1:2.

"Church" is not a building, organization, or denomination. It is the people who have accepted Jesus as Lord and Savior. It is the body of Christ from the word 'Eclesia,' meaning called out assembly. Jesus will return for His church.

126
"Impatience"

Obviously, it is the opposite of patience. Is it all bad to be a bit impatient at times? Not so, if patience crosses the line of procrastination and fear.

Impatience challenges the status quo and does not tolerate the intolerable.

Should we be patient in an emergency? Wise, yes, but "laid back"? No!

Many big things have been accomplished because of healthy impatience. Wars have been won. Laws have been passed. Relationships have been reconciled, things got done and quickly, because someone refused to wait for the normal flow of things to happen.

Sometimes, we should not sit and wait. There are times when we should speak, act, or both. Sports teams who wait for the right opportunities often lose. That is why they create opportunities by being impatient. In a five-minute judo match, you can certainly take advantage of someone else's mistake, but if you just wait for your opponent to make a mistake, you will be in for a big surprise, ending up flat on your back.

Impatience causes us to initiate things and be proactive rather than defensive, reactive or inactive. While I do not encourage impatience that causes damaging reactive behavior, I can see the value of restlessness that doesn't put up with poor results, inaction, and slow progress. There are times when we should be saying enough is enough and do the right thing.

Sure, impatience can cause wise people to do foolish things, but it can also cause wise people not to wait for unwise people to mess up. There is a good case for saying that it was impatience that enabled the moon landing. My father's impatience made it possible to fill his boat with fish. Impatience can be another word for "let's make it happen."

Am I making sense here? Maybe I am just substituting the word impatience for words like initiative, proactive, or "sense of urgency."

But for those who are impatient and giving themselves and others nervous breakdowns, you are not doing yourselves any favors by being impatient and getting emotionally upset or angry. Cool it!

127

"Synergy"

A lot of people think that energy and synergy are the same. They do sound alike. It is obvious that two people can do more than twice as much as one can do. Try hanging curtain rods or putting up wallpaper by yourself. Synergy means the output of two or more people working together will be more than the sum of the outputs of the same people working alone.

> Alone we can do so little; together we can do so much.
> **Helen Keller**

Let's say I can lift 100 pounds, and you can lift 125 pounds, for a total of 225 pounds. Did you know that working together, we will lift about 250, maybe even 300 pounds? It's been proven many times. They call it synergy.

This doesn't just apply to physical work but also mental work in solving problems at home, school, or work.

Four people can each have an idea. All four ideas may be rejected. But as the ideas are discussed it gives rise to other ideas that they wouldn't have thought about without the first four ideas. After some discussion, the final idea will be totally new and not thought of originally by any of the four.

Don't you think that if we took more advantage of synergy, we could all do things a lot better? Could it be that personal agendas and ambition get in the way of holding back good suggestions that would help with the big picture for the overall good?

Synergy is not about individuals competing to get their way. It is about working together in the best way.

Governments don't seem to be as good at it as private enterprises. I wonder why that is. Could it be that the parties don't work together?

128

"Courage"

In the movie 'The Magnificent Seven" (check out the original one with Yul Brynner), kids were complimenting Charles Bronson on how brave he was and how he had no fear. He told them that having courage didn't mean he didn't have fear. But Courage was doing things despite our fears. People in desperate situations will do things out of the ordinary, like running into a burning building to save a family member.

It took courage for our soldiers to go to war and run towards gunfire. It took courage for my father to take his ship into raging seas. It took courage for my mother to spend a lot of her time on her own raising her kids. It takes courage today to stand up for truth and values at a time when you can be sure you will be mocked and put down for taking such a stand.

Is courage missing in our society? Say yes! Far too many are going along with the flow and the most popular wave of opinions. Is it because they just don't know, don't have the backbone to seek the truth, or are people weak in fear and don't dare to say or do the right things?

Parents can indeed be at risk with the law today for raising their own kids with the right morals and truth. Terrible!

We need courage, folks. Stand up. Stand up and do the right thing in spite of your fear. Courage is not letting fear stop you.

What things do you need courage for today?? Will doing them benefit yourself or others? Do you have enough courage to risk humiliation or embarrassment? What are some consequences of lack of courage?

"Courage is contagious. When a brave man takes a stand, the spines of others are often stiffened." Billy Graham

129
"Happy or Right?"

There are people who say they would rather be happy than right. It doesn't take much discernment today to see that statement being fulfilled. OOPs! Sorry, I am being negative.

Personally, I am more interested in being right than being happy. Not that I think I am right all the time, but I feel out of sorts when I do or say something wrong. When I say being right, I mean being on the right side of justice and moral values.

Is happiness being over-rated? Will people accept immorality just to be happy?" "Oh, it's okay; as long as you are happy, you can do what you want." Do you agree with that statement or these?

-   "Johnny beat up all the desks at school today, but it's okay as long as he is happy."

-   "Mary slept in and was late for work, but she had a happy time at the party last night."

-   "Joe watched 3 football games on the weekend while his wife took care of screaming kids. But he was so happy."

O come on! Surely, happiness cannot trump being right. If we seek happiness over what is right, it will come back to haunt us. Happiness can't be all about us. An ancient Chinese proverb says:

"If you want happiness for an hour—take a nap. If you want happiness for a day—go fishing. If you want happiness for a year—inherit a fortune. If you want happiness for a lifetime—help someone else."

Helen Keller, who couldn't speak, couldn't hear, and couldn't see, said: *"True happiness is not attained through self-gratification but through fidelity to a worthy purpose."*

There is definitely something to be said about the idea that happiness is a lot about giving and doing the right thing rather than being self-centered and focusing on "what's in it for me."

And no, this is not a knock on getting enjoyment and pleasure out of getting and doing nice things.

130
"Able"

One dictionary defines "Able": "to have the necessary physical strength, mental power, skill, time, money or opportunity to do something."

We may be ready and willing but just not able. I was willing and ready to compete in National tournaments in both Judo and wrestling but was just not able to win against opponents who were just as ready and willing as I was.
They were obviously more able than I. I remember attending the Hatashita Judo Club at the age of 19 as a brown belt. I was willing and ready to take on anyone. But black belts like Dennis McCann and a few others simply tossed me at will. I said to Frank Hatashita, "Your guys are pretty tough." To which he replied, "You did take on three Canadian champions."

I may not be able, but I can try. It is no disgrace not to be able to do certain things. Our abilities may be limited by the time we put into something, along with other restrictions as per the definition above. Nevertheless, that does not mean we cannot participate in various things for enjoyment and to contribute as much as we can with the ability and resources we have.

I found that there are so many areas in which we can improve our ability. They include the ability to deal with problems, to get along with others, to be kind, to be helpful, to be thankful, to be considerate and compassionate, to be better communicators and community leaders, and to love and to control our emotions. All of these and more can be acquired if we are ready and willing. We are all able to be less defensive, critical, and argumentative. With the right vision, we can all be more able. *God is more concerned about our availability than our ability.*

What are some areas in your life in which you want to or need to be more able?

131
"Moods"

"Don't talk to me today. I am not in a good mood." Have you heard that before? How about, "Not a good day to talk to the boss; he is in a terrible mood."

We understand bad days and down days. People, for the most part, are empathetic to others' misfortunes. HOWEVER, does that mean that everyone around us has to adjust to someone else's mood swings and bear the brunt of their anger and the mood of the day? We are not talking about chronic problems like depression. We are talking about normal people who behave abnormally from time to time because things just didn't go right the day before or someone looked at them the wrong way or said something that was taken out of context.

We have all known the kinds of people who we weren't sure how to approach because we didn't know how they would behave. People who swing back and forth in their moods are hard to trust because we don't know if it is Jeckel or Hyde who will respond. Will you avoid them? That may be worse because they may blame you for not speaking to them.

When we are moody, it is wise to deal with the root cause and control our behavior regardless of our mood.

Some options to deal with the moody: Don't join them. Try to understand them. Ignore them, love them or when all else fails, confront them and say, "Hey Jack, give me a call when you are over that mood." Or "Listen up I don't know what is bothering you, but we got a job to do here." If it's your boss and you don't want to get fired, keep your mouth shut and go along.

Are you moody? Does your mood change from day to day or even from hour to hour? What kind of things determine your mood? What are you doing about it? Smiling makes us more fun to be around!

132
"Divorce"

The pastor asked a couple who were celebrating their 60th anniversary, "Have you ever considered divorce"? The gentleman responded, "Divorce, no, murder, yes." He was joking, of course, but it does confirm that marriage takes work, and many of them do end in divorce.

 Did she change or did he change? Maybe neither of them had a clue of what they were getting into. Were their expectations unrealistic, or were they just immature or were one or both of them real jerks and were not in love enough or committed enough to work on the relationship? Whatever the reason, "It's over". The ugly process of "who gets what" begins.

Various web search engines say between 37% and 50% of marriages end in divorce. It is not nice. It hurts. It causes financial hardships. It breaks up families and extended families. It scars children forever, and they are often used as pawns.

Why does it happen? It doesn't have to if both parties want it to work. For that to happen, both have to be 100% committed and get over themselves.

If divorce is inevitable, it would be nice if truth and honesty were maintained. It would be nice if emotions like pride, greed, and anger didn't get in the way to prevent spending a fortune on lawyers.

Broken families were not God's intention. God hates divorce but does allow it under certain conditions. Yes, there is life after divorce. Forgiveness helps, and so does being honest, especially with the kids.

"Because of the hardness of hear, Moses granted divorce." Mark 10:5.
See also: Heart, Marriage.

133
"Funny"

The teaspoon inventor stirred up a lot of trouble.

You don't know what you are missing if you haven't tried archery blindfolded.

Question: "Do you know where I can find a good toupee?"
Answer: Not off the top of my head."

I can't stand being in houses with low ceilings.

A boy asked his dad, "Can you tell what an eclipse is?" Dad replied, "No sun."

I was telling some kids how I was stuck in an elevator this morning. One kid asked, "Did you get out?"

If it burns when you pee, urine trouble.

My grandfather's last words: "Are you still holding the ladder?"

When geese fly in a V formation and one side is longer than the other, it is because there are more geese on that side.

They were good years when we got inside a tire and rolled down the hill.

A man was arrested for having 11 bottles of beer in his car. The judge dismissed it because they couldn't make a case of it.

I made a car out of spaghetti. You should have seen the look on my wife's face when I drove pasta.

When the universal remote control was invented, it changed everything.

134
"Inflation"

"I can't believe what you have to pay now for a pound of butter." "Gas is gone through the roof." "The house that we could have bought 40 years ago for $50,000 is now going for a million dollars."

These are common comments during times of inflation. When prices of goods and services go up, it is called inflation.

What causes it? Good question. Reasons include:

<u>Supply and demand</u>. When the supply of something is low, prices go up.

When the demand for something is high, the prices go up. When the demand is high, and the supply is low, the prices really go up.

<u>Governments are messing around</u>. The government has the ability to put more money that it doesn't have into the economy, i.e., they borrow or just print money, and that devalues the currency. Governments can also manipulate markets. University tuition has gone up because governments make student loans easier and cheaper, causing universities to increase tuition. Governments impose regulations that affect business and drive up their costs which are then passed on to customers. Governments increase and decrease interest rates which make it easier and cheaper or harder and more expensive to borrow. GOVERNMENTS INCREASE TAXES TO COVER THEIR

EXCESSIVE SPENDING. Companies just raise their prices. It's a big cycle, isn't it?

<u>Wages:</u> Employees always want higher wages to get by. Companies that increase wages will usually recover the increased cost by raising the prices of goods and services. Increasing minimum wages generally always backfires. The cycle continues.

Besides the above three, there are natural disasters, trade deals, changes in technology, devalued currencies, the stock market, and market manipulation, e.g., oil, which drives everything else. Did I mention greed and politics?

135
"Political Correctness"

What is this crap that they call political correctness? Ooops! I shouldn't have said crap. It is not politically correct. It might offend someone, and it is not politically correct to offend anyone.

Political correctness is a term that politicians or the "who's who" invented so that they could get their own way and not have to justify denying the truth. Sorry! Was it politically correct to say that? It is just my personal opinion and no, I am not a conspiracy theorist.

Wikipedia says:

Political correctness, politically correct, commonly abbreviated PC is a term used to describe language, policies, or measures that are intended to avoid offense or disadvantage to members of particular groups in society.

Notice how it says to avoid offense or disadvantage to particular groups in society. What groups? Who determines them? What it is, or at least what it has become, is a way of taking common sense politeness, manners, and respect for others to the level of eliminating freedom of speech and, in many cases, an excuse to cover for an agenda. There, I said it. Did I offend you?

Political correctness has gotten out of hand in order for one group to get its way by preventing another from having opinions. It has become a control mechanism that, in many ways, is hypocrisy. Should we criticize the disadvantaged? Of course not. But should I be able to express my opinion? Should everyone be treated equally? Of Course. But one group shouldn't be more equal than another. That's called discrimination. If you can give your opinion and I can't, then that is not equal treatment.

How come it's okay for some people to protest and call people names and not others? At the risk of being politically incorrect, political correctness is another way of stopping free speech and eliminating truth.

136
"Management"

What is management? Who is in management?

If you do any one of these things, you are in management:

> Administer, Communicate, Instruct, Command, Conduct, Control, Direct, Dominate, Govern, Guide, Head, Officiate, Oversee, Regulate, Rule, Steer, Superintend, Supervise, Watch, Check, Curb, Restrain, Train, Coach, Encourage, Correct, Parent, have a job, have responsibilities of any kind, have relationships of any kind … Need I go on?

If you are alive, you have a management role of some level. Some more than others. Let's add to the list of being a manager. You are a manager if you have things to do, results to achieve – things to produce, people to serve, money to earn, things to fix, goals to reach – have responsibilities, commitments, and obligations (employed or unemployed). Need I go on?

If you are alive, you are a manager.

The first list is about getting along with people, i.e., People-centered - Relationships. The second list is about getting things done. Task Centered – Results.

Management is about "Results and Relationships."

More specifically, management is about getting results and maintaining relationships. It is not either/or. It is both. They go together.

Just like the dictionaries say, Management is "the process of dealing with or controlling things or people."

Many of the topics in this book deal with many aspects of management such as communication, time management, etc.

A guy by the name of Fred Dyke wrote a book a few years back. It is called "That Book About Management." There may be a few still available if you contact him.

"Proactive"

Cambridge Dictionary says being proactive is:

"taking action by causing change and not only reacting to change when it happens."

My rephrase of that is: *"Don't wait till spring; do it now."* That was a jingle on a TV ad back in the 1960's.

There are people who react to change, and then there are people who anticipate change and prepare for it, and then there are those who create the change.

Proactive people:

> Make choices and act on them.
>
> Notice a need and fill it.
>
> Study through the term rather than having to cram for exams.
>
> Plan to be on time.
>
> Are prepared and ready.
>
> Seek advice rather than guess.
>
> Keep gas in their tanks.
>
> Have a will.
>
> Take responsibility rather than wait to be given responsibility.
>
> Have that extra roll of toilet paper in the bathroom. Think bigger.

> I've always been in the right place and time. Of course, I steered myself there. **- Bob Hope**

Employers love to have proactive people on staff. It makes managing so much easier. Proactivity prevents problems rather than having to fix problems. 'Proacting' reduces 'reacting.' It reduces worry, reduces accidents, reduces the chance of happenings and the unexpected, and it gives us more control. It helps us focus our intentions and makes us better time managers and more productive. Being proactive is impressive.

Proactive kills procrastination and sparks action.

I haven't been as proactive as I could have been. How about you? Think about it. Proactive is about preparing. Reactive is about repairing.

See also: Responsibility – Initiative.

138
"More Bible Myths"

<u>"We are all going to heaven"</u>. Not according to the Bible. *"Assuredly, I say to you, unless you are converted and become as little children, you will by no means enter the kingdom of heaven.* Matthew 18:3

<u>"If I am good, I will go to heaven."</u> Not according to the Bible. *"For all have sinned, and come short of the glory of God."* –Romans 3:23. If we can be good enough to go to heaven, Jesus would not have needed to die on the cross. We do not go to heaven because we are good. We go to heaven because of our faith in and acceptance of Jesus Christ. *"For God so loved the world that He gave His only begotten Son that whosoever believes in Him shall not perish but have everlasting life."* John 3:16

<u>"God made me this way, so I should just accept who I am."</u> We are all born in sin. Sin is natural for all of us because we are all descendants of Adam and Eve. God doesn't accept our sins. The wages of sin is death. We are all born spiritually dead. We need a rebirth and be born again of the Spirit- i.e. accept Jesus Christ as Lord and Savior. God loves us the way we are, but He loves us too much to leave us the way we are. Although He loves us, He will not receive us into heaven the way we are. *"Be transformed by the renewing of your mind." Romans 12:2*

<u>"I don't need to go to church to be a Christian."</u> True, but if we are Christians, we are the church, and we will want to meet together to worship God and grow as Christians. *"Not forsaking the assembling of ourselves together,"* Hebrews 10:25

<u>"Christians think they are perfect."</u> On the contrary, true Christians know they are not perfect, and that is why they have become Christians. That is why they need Jesus to pay for their imperfection.

<u>"We need to pray to the saints."</u> Nowhere in scripture does it say this. We pray directly to God. Jesus gave us the pattern many times, including the Lord's prayer - "Our Father." People who teach otherwise are not following scripture.

139
"Learning Stages"

This may be familiar to you, but it was a significant new lesson for me in my late 30s when I heard a consultant give me the four stages of learning.

Here they are as I understand them:

Stage 1. We don't know that we don't know.

There are things in life that we have no idea that they even exist. When and where I grew up, I didn't know that we didn't have indoor plumbing. It is not that I believed the whole world just had outdoor plumbing; it never crossed my mind because I just didn't know. I didn't know that I didn't know how to golf. I didn't know that I didn't know a lot of things.

Stage 2: We know that we don't know.

I found out quickly that I didn't know how to golf on the day I took the first swing. I discovered we didn't have indoor plumbing the day I visited a house that had it. Knowing we don't know gives us a challenge to discover more and learn more about the things we don't know.

Stage 3: We know that we know.

Our efforts, patience, and hard work to learn new things will move us along to know and do things that move from the awkward stage of not knowing to the satisfaction of knowing. The frustration of my first driving lesson turned into confidence.

Stage 4: We don't know that we know.

This is the stage whereby activities and knowledge occur with little or no effort without even thinking. Driving a car, public speaking, managing people, etc., become natural for us. So natural that we can forget what it was like not to know something. That's when we should have patience when dealing with people in stages 1 & 2.

I still don't know how to golf.

How about you? Can you recall the areas when you transition from one stage to another? How can you know the things you don't know? I guess we should be open to continuous learning. That should be the least we can do to grow and succeed.

140
"Perspective"

The sound of a car coming towards you is a different sound than when it is moving away from you. Why is that? Perspective!

The view is different from the top of a hill than it is from the bottom of the hill. Why is that? Perspective!

Another person's opinion may differ from yours. Why is that? Perspective!

Watching an activity is different than doing the activity? Perspective! I saw things differently when I moved from my tiny childhood community to the city or from my small province to a bigger province. The West sees things differently from the East. The North, different from the South. The poor, different than the wealthy. The sick different from the healthy. Where we stand physically, emotionally, spiritually, politically, socially, and morally determines our perspective or view of things. It can determine how we think, plan, talk and behave.

My parents went through a depression during the thirties. They didn't throw anything out in case they could use it later. They fixed things and reused things. That was their perspective. Compare that perspective to today's. People will throw things out if it has a mere scratch or the color doesn't match.

We don't have to agree with someone else's point of view, but it helps to understand their vantage point and perspective. Who knows maybe, just maybe, a different point of view may show us the real picture.

We get startled and maybe upset when we are bumped from behind, ready to say, "Watch where you are going." People will throw things out for the silliest reason While we should try to see things from the perspective of others, it doesn't mean we have to agree with them. But it helps to understand them. Is the glass half full or half empty? Perspective! Both are right. I like the positive approach.

Think of things you have changed your opinions or approach on because you have seen them from a different perspective. Do you see what you want to see, or are you willing to see the truth?

"Often, it isn't the mountains ahead that wear you out; it's the little pebble in your shoe." Mohammed Ali

141
"Auld Lang Syne"

Should auld acquaintance be forgot,
And never brought to mind?
Should auld acquaintance be forgot,
And Auld Lang Syne

For auld lang syne, my jo,
For Auld lang Syne.
We'll take a cup o' kindness yet,
For Auld lang Syne.

The first verse and chorus of this much longer poem are the most recognized and traditionally sung at New Year's Eve parties at the stroke of midnight. The national poet of Scotland, Robert Burns, was credited for today's version (written in 1788) even though the expression AULDLANG SYNE dates back to the mid to late 1600s.

Auld Lang Syne translates literally "Old Long Since" with a general meaning of "old times fondly remembered." Nostalgic would certainly describe the feeling that people get when they sing it, while giving everyone a hug or even a kiss at the same time.

Guy Lombardo and his band "the Royal Canadians" in their popular New Year's Eve radio and later television broadcast (1929-1976) made it popular in North America.

Many of the words that follow the first verse and chorus are a bit difficult for us to understand. That didn't really matter much on New Year's Eve since by the time midnight rolled around to sing, many of the folks were well content with repeating the first verse and chorus.

142
"Discoveries & Inventions"

Iron was discovered between 5000 and 3000 BC. That's a big range, isn't it? The speculation is that it was discovered in Meteorites.

Glass: While glass of various kinds has always been found in nature, depending on who you read, man-made glass dates to over 3000 years ago. The drinking glass dates to about 1600 BC.

Insulin was discovered in 1921 at the University of Toronto by a team led by Frederick Banting, Charles Best, J.B. Collin, and J.J. R. Macleod.

Electricity – Static electricity was observed in about 600 BC. The word electricity came into use about 1600 AD. Benjamin Franklin first used the word battery in 1749. Alessandro Volta invented the first true battery in 1800.

Sliced bread: Otto Frederick Rohwedder, an American inventor, created the first successful automatic bread-slicing machine in 1912. The Chillicothe Baking Company, in Missouri on July 7, 1928, began selling sliced bread. However, the knife and fingers were around long before that. Someone must have sliced it. Besides, we didn't need to slice it before the bread loaf was invented.

Flush toilet: Ancient civilizations' running water systems were set up to rid the houses of waste. In 1595, Sir John Harrington, godson of Queen Elizabeth I, devised a 2-foot-deep bowl and water flowing from a tank on the roof to make a step towards a modern-day invention. It took 7.5 gallons to flush and allowed 20 people to use between flushes. In 1775 Scottish inventor Alexander Cumming came up with an S-shaped toilet. Then, in the late 1800s, THOMAS CRAPPER perfected a system to help the flushing system to make the toilet more like what we use today.

Of course, those who lived by the sea built their outhouses over the water. They flushed every day with the tides.

143
"Mormonism"

Joseph Smith founded Mormonism in New York in 1830. Currently headquartered in Salt Lake City, Utah, it is known as "The Church of Jesus Christ of Latter-Day Saints."

Its actual size is estimated at seventeen million.

Its source of beliefs and authority include the "Book of Mormon," "Doctrines and Covenants" (1987), and "Pearl of Great Price". (1851). It also uses Joseph Smith's *inspired version* of the King James Bible but also relies heavily on teachings from Mormon prophets.

The core beliefs of Mormonism include:

- God was once a man, who progressed to godhood. God and his wife have physical bodies, and they gave birth to Jesus.
- Jesus is the brother of Satan and the elder brother of all beings.
- Jesus was married.
- Jesus died on the cross but did not pay for sin. His death and resurrection provide resurrection for all.
- The holy spirit is like an electric force from God.
- Everyone is born sinless but becomes sinful.
- Salvation is through works and deeds and being a member of the Mormon church.
- There are three different places to go at death.
- All can become gods.

Rites, rituals, and commands include:

Secret temple rituals – celestial marriage to good members – Baptism on behalf of the dead. – People of African descent were denied full access to Mormon priesthood and privileges until 1978.

<u>Sources of information:</u> Wikipedia, "Christianity, Cults and Religions" by Rose Publishing

144

"Common Sense"

Is common sense like it was before?

Or has it gone out the door?

Is common sense as common as it was?

If it is not, then what's the cause?

Everybody knew the things that were true.

Now they say what's true for me is not true for you.

Don't be silly; that can't be so.

There are some things that everyone should know.

But common sense has changed for the worse

It's selfishness now that people thirst.

It doesn't matter what's right or wrong.

They just want for which they long.

It is the knowledge they lack.

It makes them slack.

Values are not what they used to be.

It holds them captive, yet they think they are free.

They call it progressive,

When it is really regressive.

Wake up, world stop sitting on the fence.

Let's get back to real common sense.

145
"Albert Einstein Quotes"

These quotes from the brilliant mind of Albert Einstein are from the website "Good Reads," and some I took from Einstein's own writings from his books that I have.

"Two things are infinite: the universe and human stupidity, and I'm not sure about the universe."

"There are only two ways to live your life. One is as though nothing is a miracle. The other is as though everything is a miracle."

"If you can't explain it to a six-year-old, you don't understand it yourself."

"Logic will get you from A to Z; imagination will get you everywhere."

"Life is like riding a bicycle. To keep your balance, you must keep moving."

"Anyone who has never made a mistake has never tried anything new."

"When you are courting a nice girl, an hour seems like a second. When you sit on a red-hot cinder, a second seems like an hour. That's relativity."

"Any fool can know. The point is to understand."

"If we knew what it was we were doing, it would not be called research, would it?"

"You never fail until you stop trying."

"The measure of intelligence is the ability to change."

"The best way to cheer yourself is to cheer somebody else up."

146

"Aggressive"

People are often categorized as aggressive, passive, or assertive. There is a time and a place to be aggressive. We see it as ambitious, proactive, go-getting, and high initiative. These qualities are admired by successful athletes, business tycoons, war heroes, and all walks of life. We need them. Einstein had to have been aggressive in his research, as was Edison in inventions, as was my father when it came to being a sea captain.

However, we tend to get annoyed, intimidated, or angry by those who are aggressive in their personality and communication. Words to describe them include pushy, in-your-face, and bossy. They have to win, and you have to lose. They like to dominate conversations, and they show little or no regard for the welfare, rights, or feelings of others. They are determined to dominate and get their own way or make their point. There is potentially a bit of that in all of us when our emotions get the better of us, plus we need to be aggressive in emergencies. *"Get off the phone; I am waiting for a call from my doctor." "Close the door; the snow is coming in."* You get the idea.

Causes of aggressiveness may include anger, impatience, and selfishness. It is also often used as a cover-up or tactic when an individual is not capable of a sensible discussion using plain old facts. People use it to justify their positions on social issues and political persuasions. Aggressive speech is often long-winded and loud and can also come across as rude and crude. In addition, it is often quick to react with words that hurt others.

Responses to aggressive behavior vary depending on the personality of the receiver. The passive person will just go along: *"Oops, I am sorry,"* Another aggressive person may welcome the challenge and give it right back. *"Who died and put you in charge of everybody?*

How do you deal with an aggressive person? Are you unnecessarily aggressive? When should you be more aggressive?

"History teaches that war begins when governments believe the price of aggression is cheap." ~ Ronald Reagan

Check out Passive (page 230) and Assertive (page 270)

147

"Pretzel Hold"

I was warned by my coach to stay away from my next opponent in the wrestling tournament. "This guy is famous for his pretzel hold. Nobody gets out of it. Make sure you keep your distance and avoid mat work."

I went in with confidence but still took my coach's advice seriously. Round one went well; we both stayed on our feet, and no one scored any points.

The coach was proud. "You are doing well," he said; if you come out of this with a draw, we'll be satisfied."

The first minute of the second round was going fine until it happened. We went to the ground, and before I knew what was happening, I was in the pretzel hold. My disappointed coach was about to leave the gym, thinking it was all over. As he was walking through the door, the crowd cheered, and when the coach turned around the referee was holding up my hand as the winner.

As I walked off the mat, the coach came to greet me, holding out his hand to congratulate me, and said, "Wow, I was on the way out, thinking you were finished. What happened?"

I said, "Well, the pretzel hold is hard to escape for sure. I was all tied up, and the only thing I could move was my mouth and my left eye."

The coach was anxious, saying, "Yes, and what happened."

I said, "I could see a big toe right in front of my mouth. I bit down on it as hard as I could." I paused and said, "It's amazing the strength you have when you are biting your own toe."

148
"Plastic"

There is no more supply of plastic bags at the grocery shop
Paper straws at restaurants, plastic had to stop
We must protect the environment, you know
The best way is to stop the oil flow.
We buy the provided bags each for thirty-five cents.
Watch me fill them out to see if it makes sense
All meat is wrapped in plastic -baloney, roast, chicken and pork
Oh yes! So are candy, cashews, nuts of any sort
Salad is in a plastic bowl
All the cheeses are in plastic, and there is no hole
The soft drinks, juices, and detergents in plastic they fill
Put your veggies in a plastic bag; you know the drill
The bakery goods, it's plastic they are stuffed in
The pie, the cookie, the bread, the cake, and the muffin
Plastic, plastic and more plastic
Almost everything goes in plastic
They even wrap the plastic in plastic
Plastic knives, forks, and spoons don't sag
They and plastic cups come in a plastic bag
You know, the grocery bags they sell to you
There is likely plastic in them too
And the straw that is made of paper
You can buy them individually in a plastic wrapper
Do you really think they want to keep the climate cold?
Or is it all propaganda, money, and control?

149
"Billy Graham"

A biographer writes, "Billy Graham was considered among the most influential Christian leaders of the 20th century."

For over sixty years, Billy Graham, this American Christian evangelist, preached the Bible's Christian message indoors and outdoors using crusades and live appearances from 1947 to 2005 in more than 185 countries, reaching over 200 million people. It has been said that including his broadcast on radio and TV in the US and throughout the world, literally billions would have heard his messages.

He had personal audiences with 12 consecutive American presidents, being careful with his endorsement. He was a bridge builder in many ways with many foreign leaders, including royalty, prime ministers, and presidents from countries such as the UK and the Soviet Union.

Some famous Bully Graham quotes include:

"I can't live the Christian life alone. I'm a failure. Billy Graham cannot live a Christian life. I've tried. I can't do it. But with the help of the Word of God and the help of the Holy Spirit, I can live a Christian life. But He lives it through me."

"The regeneration of the individual is much more needed than the revolution of society."

"Every time I read the Bible, any part of the Bible—I don't care where I open up—it speaks to me. It's a living book."

"The Bible is not an option; it is a necessity. You cannot grow spiritually strong without it."

"God has promised to supply all of our needs, but He's never promised to supply all of our greed."

"The whole Bible is a love story. It's a love story between God and man. God loves you!"

"The Bible is the only book in the world that predicts the future. The Bible is more modern than tomorrow morning's newspaper."

"Christ not only died for all: he died for each."

150
"Tolerance"

I can tolerate pain. I can tolerate a lot

But if you tell me what I should tolerate, my answer is not

You do your thing, and I do my thing

But we don't have to tolerate the same thing

To tolerate is your choice and mine

We don't have to agree all the time

Forming your opinion is your right

But you forming my opinion will get you a fight

I don't mind that you have your own behavior

It doesn't mean you are my savior

We are all free to think, free to speak

But we don't have to be cheek to cheek

A double standard is hard to take

Which is what some want me to tolerate

You may want me to tolerate a lie

So, believing in God shouldn't make me shy.
No. I will not sit on the fence.

I will not tolerate intolerance.

151
"Interesting Facts"

The two oldest trees in the world are reported to be in Chile and California. Guestimates are that they are approximately 4,800 to 5,000 years old. *I wonder why there are no older ones. Could it be because that was how long ago something drastic like a flood happened?*

Fossils of marine mammals have been found on land and mountains all over the world, including the Grand Canyon and Mount Everest. How did they get there? *Could it be that they were once all underwater?*

Limestone mines are located all around the world. Limestone needs ocean water and sedimentary rock. *Could it be that they were formed underwater?*

Wikipedia reports: "Flood myths are common across a wide range of cultures, extending back into Bronze Age and Neolithic prehistory. These accounts depict a flood, sometimes global in scale, usually sent by a deity or deities to destroy civilization as an act of divine retribution." *Could it be they are not myths?*

Chickens produce chickens. Dogs produce dogs. Elephants produce elephants. Humans produce humans. *Could it be that only species of its kind can produce its own kind, and one kind cannot evolve into another kind?*

There has never been a discovery of a species that is part of one species and part of another. *Could it be that there is no missing link?*

Our planets, sun, and moon are all round like a globe. *Wouldn't it be odd if the earth was flat?*

152
"Knowledge vs Wisdom"

There seems to be a big difference between knowledge vs. wisdom. The world has more knowledge than ever. This knowledge is available with a touch on our cell phones. Yet it seems people are making more unwise decisions than ever.

We all know people who may not be well educated but are very wise. My dad was one of them. He reached grade six in school, but when I look back at his quotes and actions, I can see his wisdom.

Wisdom is not just knowing facts but knowing how to use the facts.

How so?

- We know what is good for us but we don't do it. Is that wise?
- We eat lots of sugar, but we know it is not good for us. Is that wise?
- Discipline seems to be a thing of the past in schools. Is that wise?
- Kids are being taught at an early age what they don't need to know. Is that wise?
- Governments spend money it doesn't have. Is that wise?
- Fashion often wins out over comfort. Is that wise?
- We overeat. Is that wise?
- We throw out things that are old but still useful. Is that wise?
- The media lies. Is that wise?
- Saying yes to things we know we can't do. Is that wise?
- Spending time on things that produce no results. Is that wise?
- We do the same things but expect different results. Insane?
- Stats are being ignored. Is that wise?

Is desired behavior winning out over wisdom despite the knowledge we have? Just asking.

153
Skipper Ches "As Tough as It Gets"

Did you get my book? Not this one, another one, It's a biography of my parents. Of course, I am biased. What a life they had! Life during the Depression of the 1920's and '30s was bad enough, but if you combine that with living in the poorest province in Canada in an isolated community off the coast, you will get a different and unique look at a rough and tough life. Here's a summary from the cover.

In the life and times of Captain Chesley Dyke and Elsie Stanford Dyke Pool's Island, Bonavista Bay, Fred Dyke captures the joys and struggles of his parents and what it was like in rugged Newfoundland outports from the early 1900s, through the Great Depression, and into the 1950s and 1960s. Storms, shipwrecks, working in the woods, fishing, and courage made up the lives of a loving couple who raised their family on Pool's Island, Newfoundland. Skipper Ches Dyke understood rejection, poverty, and setbacks. He made his way and became a man when he was still a boy, taking part in the Labrador fishery at the young age of nine. Elsie Stanford from Grates Cove was no stranger to hard work. While in her early teenage years, she carried 100-pound sacks of flour and potatoes on her back. The two married in 1929 at St. Mary's Church in St. John's, just three days before Ches beggar a four-year career with the ships of Furness Withy. Moving back home to Pool's Island with his wife and two young sons, Ches began a new career as captain of local schooners. There, he made a remarkable reputation for himself as a sea captain, boat builder, mechanic, and more. The tales herein, as seen through the eyes of all those who knew Elsie and Ches, capture an amazing lifestyle from an era and location that should not be forgotten.

Order it online now.

154
"Pareto Principle"

This is also known as the 80/20 rule. An Italian economist named Vilfredo Pareto in the late 1800's observed that 80% of the wealth in Italy was owned by 20% of the people.

This concept was expanded in the early 1950s when psychologist Joseph Juran applied the principle to management and other areas. He named it the Pareto Principle.

Although there are exceptions, here are some practical examples of the reality of it:

- 80% of sales come from 20% of the sales team.
- 80% of work in volunteer organizations is done by 20% of the people.

It also applies to our time management in that 20% of our efforts in time spent give us 80% of our productivity.

So what? What is it about those 20 percenters that achieve more? What's different about them? Are you in the 20% category? How can you get there?

My observations are that it doesn't take that much more of an effort to be among them. Just think if you are an athlete or an employee who works just 5% harder a day. Think of the compounding effect of that extra 5%. It is the same way that money grows with compound interest. It adds up.

155
"Tact"

Are you tactful? Do you say things or do things that are inappropriate for the situation?

"Tact: a <u>keen</u> sense of what to do or say in order to maintain good relations with others or avoid offense." – Merriam Webster dictionary.

>Did you burp as a guest at a meal
>Didn't say excuse me. How did it make your host feel?
>Did you tell an off-color joke in serious situations?
>These aren't the things to do to form good relations.

"Tact is the art of making a point without making an enemy." Isaac Newton:

>Do you ever say the wrong word just to be heard?
>Do you seek attention and say things you shouldn't mention?
>Do you try to be discreet before you open your mouth to speak? Tact is staying on the brink of saying what you think.

"Tact is the ability to step on a man's toes without messing up the shine on his shoes." - Harry S. Truman.

>We can use tact to our benefit by making our words really fit.
>We don't have to hide the truth. That's not a reason to be uncouth.
>We can get in trouble by going too far with words that may leave a scar. It is better to be a diplomat and not make the conversation go flat.

"Discretion in speech is more than eloquence." - Francis Bacon

>Tact involves manners, refinement, and grace
>And not invading each others' space. Tact is
>coming across as polite and refined We can all do
>that by aiming to be kind.

156
"Correcting Others"

The news on the radio when I was driving to work, stated that some company had laid off 10,000 employees. Since this action might have affected our industry, I relayed the news to my boss. He quickly corrected me and said, "Well, if you read the paper, it actually stated that the number to be laid off was to be 9939, and the lay-off hasn't happened yet but will occur two days from now." I just looked at him with a look that said, "You gotta be kidding."

<u>Husband:</u> You have been correcting me now for 38 years.
<u>Wife:</u> 39

Mary was telling a story about her colonoscopy last Thursday, the day after Tom cleaned out the garage. Tom said, "No, it was Wednesday. I cleaned out the garage. I remember because I found that hammer that I lost last July". "No, No," said Mary, "It was in May you lost the hammer when Joe was visiting from Burlington." Tom couldn't let it go. That wasn't Joe, that was George from Halifax." Anyway, the colonoscopy went well.

Should we always correct each other, or should we let it slide? Do we do it to make ourselves look good at other people's expense, embarrassment, and aggravation?

I find it easier if I am corrected to try to keep an open mind. There are of course, exceptions, like who won the political debate.

But then, what would Tom and Mary do for entertainment?

Correct me if I am wrong, but I don't think we should be correcting others so much.

Are you one who likes correcting others but doesn't like being corrected?

157
"Nineteen Eighty-Four" (1984)

In 1949, Eric Arthur Blair, aka George Orwell, wrote a fiction novel of what the world would be like 35 years in the future i.e., 1984. Centering around a character by the name of Winston, Orwell portrays a society controlled by a Central party. The extent of the controls includes but not limited to:

<u>Rewriting history</u> – all history books, magazines, newspapers, etc., were rewritten to reflect what the controlling party wanted the people to believe.

<u>Words and languages were redefined</u> – and changed to suit the narrative of what the party wanted the people to believe.

<u>Speech and even thoughts were controlled and monitored</u> - anyone who stepped out of line in their words and actions was disciplined in various ways, including torture, reprogramming, and even death.

<u>Media was totally controlled</u> – all media was totally controlled by the Party.

<u>Normal family relationships were discouraged and even forbidden</u> – Kids were removed from their parents or educated to tell their parents if they had any thoughts outside of the Party line. Marriages and romantic relationships were controlled or forbidden.

<u>No one trusted anyone</u> – No one ever knew where anyone else stood. The closest friends were conditioned to spy on each other.

<u>People were lied to</u> – written words, radio, TV, etc., were used to tell people what the Party wanted them to hear and know.

<u>War and threats of war were used to keep people in line</u> – By telling people that they were under major threat from the outside, they were convincing them to unite under the Party that was protecting them.

Question. Do you see any similarities in the above description today?

158
"Psalm 23" – the most read psalm.

The LORD *is* my shepherd;
I shall not want.
2 He makes me to lie down in green pastures;
3He leads me beside the still waters.
4He restores my soul;
He leads me on the path of righteousness
For His name's sake.
5 Yea, though I walk through the valley of the shadow of death,
I will fear no evil;
For You *are* with me;
Your rod and Your staff they comfort me.
6 You prepare a table before me in the presence of my enemies; You
anoint my head with oil;
My cup runs over.
7 Surely goodness and mercy shall follow me
All the days of my life;
And I will dwell in the house of the LORD
Forever.

How many of us really appreciate the full meaning of this psalm from David?

It tells us that if we have God, we will have need of nothing else. Because of His love, care, guidance, and provision, we can get through the darkness and toughest and worst circumstances. Yes, even death. Not that we won't die, but that we can face death knowing what is on the other side of death, where God is waiting for us. Do you believe this? Read the psalm daily until it sinks in.

This psalm has encouraged so many people. Does it encourage you?

159
"Roy Rogers"

Who can forget Roy Rogers, the cowboy, along with his horse Trigger and wife Dale Evans, on their TV western? Oh yeah, let us not forget him singing with "The Sons of The Pioneers." That was a long time ago.

There was a recent newspaper article on Roy about the fetish he had for cowboy boots. He owned dozens of pairs. At the end of every day, when he took off the pair he was wearing, he would always leave them outside the door of his ranch house to allow them to air on his veranda overnight.

One morning when he went to fetch the new pair that he had left outside, he was shocked to see his new boots ripped to shreds. He automatically assumed that a mountain lion got to them, since he had seen the signs of one in recent days. Roy didn't like it, so he set a trap for the mountain lion and left another pair of boots outside while he stayed up with his gun to catch the lion in the act.

It worked. As the lion carefully walked up on the veranda about to grab a boot, Roy shot and killed the predator.

Naturally, everybody was awakened, including the hired hand who said:

"Pardon me, Roy. Is that the cat who chewed your new shoes?"

If you don't know the song "Chattanooga Choo Choo," this story wouldn't mean a thing to you.

160
"Canada's Emergency Act 2022"

For the second time in its history and the first time under Canada's Charter of Rights and Freedoms, the Government of Canada imposed a state of emergency. This gave authority to the government to do what it wanted, including:

Seizing people's bank accounts – tracking donations to various groups – breaking up protests and making arrests – imprisoning people without trials for extended periods of time – imposing bands on people's speech, and more.

As of the date of this writing, a number of court cases are pending that claim the Act was unnecessary, illegal, and violated the rights of Canadians. At least one case has resulted in a court ruling disagreeing with the Act:

"The Federal Court Justice Richard Mosely said in Tuesday's ruling he could not support a conclusion that the 2022 convoy created "a critical, urgent and temporary situation" that was national in scope and could not be dealt with effectively under any other Canadian law.

Although the harm being caused to Canada's economy, trade and commerce was very real and concerning, the judge wrote, it did not constitute threats or the use of serious violence to persons or property."
Ottawa Citizen

While there are arguments on both sides for and against the Emergencies Act, there are many indications that the government and authorities had other means to deal with what was happening in the country.

Questions:

Did the protestors have a legitimate beef with the actions of the Federal Government during the mandated Covid restrictions?

What was the real issue? Whose rights were really taken away?

161
"Mistakes"

We all make them. "I made a mistake once. I thought I was wrong, but I wasn't."
While we hopefully do our best to avoid mistakes, the big key is to learn from
them and avoid repeating them.

Are all mistakes really mistakes, or are they choices? Was majoring in Physics at
university a mistake or a poor choice because I didn't know any better? Is
hanging out with the wrong crowd a mistake or an unwise decision at the time?

Putting the wrong gas in your car, thinking it was the right one, is a mistake.
Taking the wrong turn in your travels is a mistake. But is doing something that we
know better a mistake? Is it more like a wrong choice based on our selfish
motivation or believing a lie?
My many mistakes in life were usually based on lack of attention. I can live with
that and hopefully learn. But to knowingly do something because of
misinformation or refusal to accept reality should be classified more appropriately
as a poor choice. Either way, it would be a big mistake not to learn from them.

> *"If I had to live my life again, I'd make the same mistakes, only - sooner."*
> - Anonymous.

<u>Tips I have learned on mistakes:</u>
- We don't have to make mistakes in order to learn. We can also learn from the
  mistakes of others.
- Don't confuse failure with mistakes. Many mistakes are proof that you are
  willing to try.
- Life can go on after mistakes.
- Repeating the same mistake is a refusal to learn and grow.

Go ahead- list the top five mistakes you have made. What did you learn? What
life changing mistakes are you still making that you are refusing to learn from?

162
"Happy"

Are you happy? Are you happy all the time? What makes you happy? Is happiness the goal or purpose in your life?

Does everyone prefer happiness over sadness? Some people are most happy when they are unhappy. Now, that doesn't make sense. Think about it. Why would someone say they want to be happy if they continue to make decisions that cause them unhappiness – if they blow a paycheck on the weekend and be broke on Monday – if they keep saying things they regret - if they can't hold a job because they don't produce - if they don't treat others with kindness - if they argue all the time? Just asking. You can put a lot more "ifs" in there.

Groucho Marx: *"I, not events, have the power to make me happy or unhappy today. I can choose which it shall be. Yesterday is dead; tomorrow hasn't arrived yet. I have just one day, today, and I'm going to be happy in it."*

Groucho Marx seemed to be a happy person. But according to him, happiness is a choice and not dependent on events or circumstances that happen around him or to him. Aristotle was said to have written, "Happiness depends upon ourselves."

If we are happy today and unhappy tomorrow, it must mean that happiness for us is dependent on what happens to us. Realistically, to say we are happy when a tragedy happens doesn't make sense. However, we have to acknowledge that there are people who go through tough times and still come across as happy people, or at worse, deal with it better than some.

What makes you happy? Is it money? There are happy people with money and unhappy people with money. Some say money doesn't make you happy. But most of us could use a million dollars right now. I would be really happy if all of your friends would buy this book that I am writing.

"Most people are about as happy as they make up their minds to be."

—Abraham Lincoln

What steals your happiness? Worry is definitely one. Remember the song "Don't worry, Be Happy" *(Page 63)*. See also "Happy or Right" *(Page 129)*

163
"Ready"

If we are waiting to be perfect to be ready, we may never be ready. But many things might determine our readiness other than being perfect.

I often think, and I have said, I don't believe I was ready to begin university." I was not even 17 when I started. I grew up in a small community. I had poor study habits. I just wasn't ready from a maturity point of view. Yet maybe that was what I needed to help me grow up. In that sense, I was ready.

Is readiness overrated? Maybe we are never ready to do certain things, but we just have to forge ahead and do them and get ready along the way. The shock of beginning university told me I was not ready, but as the months passed, I did become ready. If I had stayed in my small world a year or two more, I don't think I would have been any 'readier.' *(Readier is not a word but I was ready to use it.)* I was ready in the sense that I was determined to do it, even while not knowing what to expect.

Kids are ready to learn to walk when they start the process of crawling and developing their muscles. Their curiosity motivates them to move and reach. In that sense, they are ready and willing but not able.

Kids are ready to talk when they are encouraged to communicate. Teenagers are ready to work when they develop a hunger to have their own money. That may not happen until their parents stop paying their way. Kids may not be ready to help around the house until parents put in consequences for not doing so or rewards for doing so.

Being ready to take responsibility for our actions is a direct consequence of being held accountable for our actions.

Our readiness may also be determined by other factors such as our fears, busyness, our time, our obligations, our financial situation, our health, or the health of a close relative. Our ATTITUDE is also a big determinant of our readiness.

> *Readiness is largely dependant on ATTITUDE. With all else being equal I would pick the best attitude.*

What have you refused to do because you didn't think you were ready?

164
"Fear of God"

The words "fear not" or "do not be afraid" appear in the Bible over 300 times, depending on the translation you read. Some say 365 times, one for each day of the year. Fear is talked about a lot. God does not want us to fear anything or anyone except for Him. His word does say, "The fear of God is the beginning of wisdom." Proverbs 9:10

Why should we fear God and nothing else? Because God is God and He has total power and authority over us and everything. He holds the world in the palm of his hand, and we need to respect that power and authority.

Several times, God or an angel of God appeared to people and said, "Fear not." Mary, Joseph, and others were told to fear not. He told them to fear not, yet the Bible says in several places, "The beginning of wisdom is to fear God." Does this sound like a contradiction to you? I don't think so. True, we submit to his authority, but if we put ourselves at his mercy, His love will protect us. God understands our natural fear. That is why He put people at ease at times in the Bible.

Our biggest problem today is too many people are fearing the wrong things.

If we are going to fear, fear God because He has the final answer.

The first mention of fear in the Bible was after Adam and Eve disobeyed, and literally, "all hell broke loose," causing sin to come into the world. Adam and Eve hid behind the bushes. God asked, "Where are you?" *(He didn't need to ask; He knew where they were).* Adam replied, "I heard your voice in the garden, and I was afraid." Adam and Eve had reason to be afraid. They screwed up. Light bulb moment here. Fear originated with sin. But because of God's grace, we can overcome fear.

Bible quote: "For God has not given us the spirit of fear; but of power, love, and a sound mind." 2 Timothy 1:7

To fear God is to have faith in God!

165
"Point of View"

Do you see what I see?

I don't know, what do you see?

I see a tree. Do you see a tree?

No, I don't see a tree; I see the sea.

You are looking the wrong way; turn around.

I get it, I was facing the ocean, and you were facing the town.

It depends on your point of view.

Yes, for each of us, different things are true.

It is all about our perspective.

And what about our objective?

Positive people see the glass as half full.

Negative people see it as half empty, not half full.

You could be happy with a sandwich for a meal.

Or a juicy steak, for me, is much more real.

It makes a difference if you are rich or poor.

The rich moan about the furniture, while others are happy with the floor.

Some vote for what is best for the nation.

What's in for me? That's a temptation.

Is love a feeling or an action?

Or is it what gives you satisfaction?

Will you always love me and give me my way?

Forever, my love, if it's true what you say.

What do you mean? Does it have to be true?

Of course it makes a difference to your point of view.

166

"They Say"

You know what they say. What do they say?
They say this is the news for today.
They say it's going to rain tomorrow.
They say it may bring you sorrow.
They say the rates are going up.
They say the rates are going down.
They say there are big plans for our town.
They say you can't do this, and you can't do that.
They tell you what to eat so you don't get fat.
Do they always have it right?
How do they know what is right?
Are they qualified? Should I listen
To those who don't have a pot to use?
Those "they" people are everywhere.
I would like to talk to them right here.
Are they a group that sets the rules
Or are "they" there to make us fools?
Are they a conspiracy to gain control
Of our thinking and keep us in a hole?
Are they a figment of someone's imagination
Or do they want to run this nation?
Let's identify who they are.
Before they take "they say" too far.
They seem to be going out of their way.
What I want to know is
Who are they?

167

"Bosses"

I have had the best. I have had the worst. I learned and grew from both ends and in between. In the meantime, we are all paid to do a job regardless of whether we like our bosses. We don't have to like our bosses, but we do have to respect their position, authority, and the fact that they, too, have a job to do. Their job is essentially the same as those they supervise, and that is to produce.

Let's face it: many bosses did not set out to be bosses. Many of them got into the position because they did a good job on the factory floor or got good results in their previous position. It is possible they are bosses because they own the company or are the owner's kids. Regardless of how they got there, we have a job to do, and it is our responsibility to do it well. We can hardly blame bosses if they were put in positions without being adequately trained. Well, we can, but let's deal with that later. Regardless of the quality of our boss, it is our responsibility to do what we were hired to do. That is important.

Good or bad, qualified or not, our boss calls the shots for the most part. Yes, he/she is accountable to someone further up the ladder. But in the meantime, we have to be the best employees we can be. To do so, <u>find out what the boss wants done and do it.</u> Sure, we may have to stick handle around some of their quarks, but the bosses' qualifications or methods do not change our role as employees. We should still stay respectful and produce. We may not change the boss, but we can change us.

Opportunities will come, and they did for me, interestingly, both from the good

> *Make your boss look good, by being a great employee*

bosses and the not-so-good bosses. I say "not so good" rather than "bad," realizing that they too, are on a journey and the fact that people don't qualify for certain things does not make them bad people.

As long as our boss doesn't ask us to do something illegal or immoral, we should follow the instructions. If the boss was right, you are safe. If the boss was wrong, you simply followed instructions.

168
"Discernment"

Do you have any idea what is going on? Can you tell fact from fiction, truth from lies or when someone is trying to pull the wool over your eyes?

My dictionary tells me discernment is the ability to judge well. It is the ability to distinguish between right and wrong and to have real insight into what is going on.

It is needed more today than ever as we are bombarded with many people trying to take advantage of and deceive us. To tell when news is fake, persuasive opinion or entertainment has become a must.

How can you tell? One way is to step back and start evaluating. Is it time we start challenging and questioning our own opinions and those of others and dig deeper into the well?

If the last two or more news reports from your favorite panel turned out to be false, maybe it is time to switch the channel.

Can you recognize the motivation behind a certain story? Are you easily influenced by those who are in it for their glory?

The greatest areas for a need for good discernment are politics, marketing and social issues. Falling for sugar-coated lies has often brought tears to our eyes.

Being discerning doesn't mean we think everything is a sham, but it is a good idea to be able to determine what is valid truth as best as we can.

How are we at discerning what is best for our needs? Isn't it time we all got up to speed?

169
"Changing Times"

In the early 1960s, Bob Dylan released his song "The Times They Are A-Changing." It has since been performed by many other artists. He was quoted as saying, 'It was a song of purpose." In that same year, President Kennedy was assassinated. Times sure did change.

The rate of change in our current life is phenomenal. Think about it. Look at the changes in technology that have made it possible to have information at our fingertips. I remember having a guest speaker from a major industry leader tell us at our annual meeting back in the 1990s, "80% of our major products, five years from now, haven't been invented yet."

Information exchange is instantaneous. World travel is unbelievably fast. Yet kids today have no concept of how we older folks managed without our current technology. Technology affects many things.

Too bad, though that same technology is having negative influences around the world. We have advanced communication tools but communication when it comes to relationships is worse than ever. Texting is replacing verbal communication even across the dinner table.

Even the truth is changing. There was a time when known truths were accepted. That changed to truth being a relative thing, e.g., what is true for you is not necessarily true for me. What we have now is not only the acceptance of untruth but the promotion of lies. Times sure are changing.

Values are changing at a tremendous rate. You can't believe anything in the news, as commentary and political agendas have taken over.

The big question here to consider: Have you changed your values just because things like technologies and cultures have changed?

What is the biggest change in your lifetime?

Which changes are good for you and your family and friends?

Which changes are hurting you and your family and friends?

What changes are you embracing? Resisting?

Where are you drawing the line when it comes to the changing times?

170

"Marriage"

Where did the idea of marriage come from anyway?

"But from the beginning of the creation, God 'made them male and female.' 'For this reason, a man shall leave his father and mother and be joined to his wife, and the two shall become one flesh'; so then they are no longer two, but one flesh. Therefore, what God has joined together, let not man separate." Mark 10:8,

That was Jesus quoting in the book of Mark from Genesis 2:24. According to the Bible, marriage or the union of a man and woman was the creation and intent of God to avoid loneliness and, of course, to populate the earth. Marriage is a God thing. No, the Government did not invent marriage. And, of course, it involves love.

My counsel to the couple when they come to me to get married: "Marriage is a three-way relationship between the two of you and God. The closer you are to God, the closer you will be to each other."

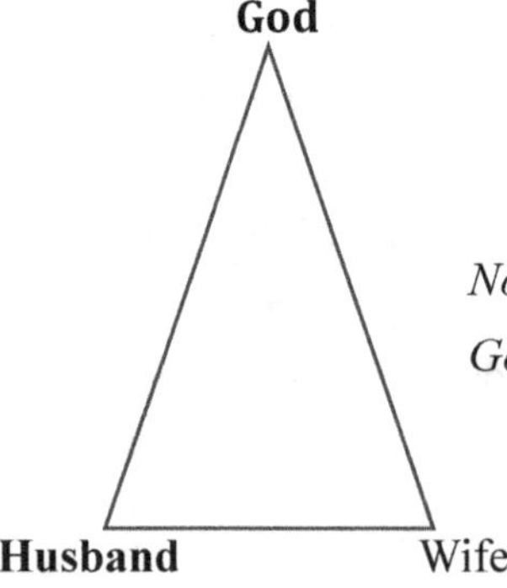

Note: the further the husband and wife move up closer to God, the closer they get to each other.

If you do not believe in God, can you still have a happy, lasting marriage with lots of love? Of course. But God's way is ideal.

See also: Love, Divorce. Relationships

171

"Efficient vs. Effective"

Which is the best? They are both good. But we can be efficient and not effective. One guy was so efficient he could chug 5 ½ bottles of beer from a stein in 19 seconds. Wow, that is efficient. But did he need to do it? Did it help anybody? No. Therefore, he was not effective.

It was taking a long time for a manager to get a shop ready to open. The owner surprised him with a visit. They chatted while the manager was scrapping paint off a light switch before he put it back on the wall. He did a good job of cleaning the plate. However, the paint he was scraping was on the inside of the plate which would not be exposed. He was neither efficient nor effective. The owner was both efficient and effective in firing him. Sad.

To be detailed and efficient is good. But as many top executives, especially the father of modern management, Peter Drucker, will tell you, "Efficient is doing things right, but effective is doing the right things."

We can be very good at doing things that we enjoy doing and if we are doing them for pleasure, have fun. But if these things are not producing good results, let's find something else to do that is.

Efficient is how well we perform a task. Effective is eliminating the task.

Efficient is doing it quicker. Effective is not having to do it at all.

Just because something is done right and fast doesn't mean it needs to be done. When setting priorities, it is a good idea to do the things first that have the biggest impact on the overall picture. Managing our time, focusing on results, and making good decisions all contribute to making us more effective. Being truthful is also a good way to be effective.

What do you do efficiently that is not effective?

What do you do efficiently that is effective?

See "Perfectionists"

172
"Earth Facts"

We know a lot about our planet, and you can google a lot more things that scientists have revealed. Here are a few of them:

- Earth is the third planet from the sun and is the densest of the planets.
- Earth is the only place in the solar system where water can be present in all three states – solid, liquid, and gas.
- We are traveling around the sun at an average velocity of 107,182 kilometers per hour, while we are also spinning approximately 1,670 kilometers per hour, i.e.,, one full spin in 24 hours.
- The earth's spin gives us night and day.
- The same side of the earth's moon is always facing the Earth. The moon rotates but is in sync with the earth's rotation.
- The earth has a strong magnetic field.
- Earth is the only known planet that supports life.
- (They say) that the earth's inner core has a temperature between 5400 and 6000 degrees Celsius, supposedly making it hotter than the surface of the Sun.
- The Earth is not a perfect sphere. The distance from the North Pole to the South Pole is shorter than its diameter across the Equator by 43 km.
  This difference is said to be due to the earths rotation.
- More than 95% of the earth's oceans are still unexplored.
- The earth's tilt of 23½ degrees and the fact that we revolve around the sun makes it possible to have seasons.
- If you want to weigh less, stand on the equator.
- The earth's crust is a relatively very thin layer

It's a good idea to protect the earth.

173

"Argumentative"

Debates are good, and so are discussions. Is it possible to have them without being argumentative? We must admit that most of us have been argumentative at times, and some of us still are.

Some people just like to argue. I don't mean to discuss. I mean, argue. When I say, argue, their goal is to win the argument at all costs, whether it is an important issue or not.

"It is going to rain tomorrow."

"No, you have that wrong."

"Oh, I was just telling you what the weather station said."

"You shouldn't be listening to that station. Listen to the other one."

"Okay." Did you see the game last night? I thought our team played well."

"You have that wrong. They were terrible."

On it goes. Argumentative people give no room for discussion or opinion. Their sole interest is insisting that they are right and you are wrong. You will not win with them, so you may as well stop trying. They will switch points, bring up things that have nothing to do with your topic and they will outdo you.

A rule of thumb from some experts: "Never argue with someone who believes their own lies."

Best solutions include staying calm and ignoring them. Don't take their bait. Walk away. Distraction helps, too. Days go a lot better when we respond less to argumentative people.

"The only way to get the best of an argument is to avoid it." —*Dale Carnegie,* How to Win Friends and Influence People

174

"Vision"

"I can see it now." That's a vision. Who do we want to become? Can you see yourself in five or ten years? If you had your "ruthers," how do you see yourself? There are different ways to determine this if you haven't already decided. And if you haven't decided, don't feel bad because many, if not most, people don't have a purpose outside of wanting to be happy or just to survive, get married, have kids, have a good career, or own a house, etc. all of which are good visions. Maybe you want to become a famous inventor. Velcro already exists. Kidding! Where you want to be may be determined by your situation in life right now. If you are in debt, you want to get out of debt. That's a good goal. If you are out of work, you will want a job. Maybe you are having relationship problems with your kids or other family members, and you just want them fixed. Or maybe you are bored with life and thinking, "There must be something I can do to make my life more exciting."

When I was younger, my vision was always short-term. When I was in university I just wanted to get through while at the same time I had my sights on winning the next Judo tournament.

It is important to distinguish between visions vs. goals or objectives. Here are some examples:
-   A vision is to have a healthy body. A goal is to lose 40 pounds.
-   A vision is financially secure. A goal may be to get out of debt.
-   A vision may be to have more friends. A goal may be to join a group.

While goals are important, mistaking a goal for vision can be dangerous. When I was in my early 20's my whole life revolved around Judo. I loved it so much, and I felt I had the skills and determination to go places. It was a good goal. But I had to realize that as much as I enjoyed it, it wasn't putting food on the table. My short-term goal was preventing me from having a vision. There is nothing wrong with short-term goals, but when they control our lives, we need to step back and see the big picture. Do you have a hobby or interest right now that is preventing you from seeing something bigger in your life? Yes, the little things in life have to be done. But as much as possible, it's a good thing to line up our goals with our vision. That is not to say we can't have hobbies or interests that we enjoy for needed breaks and pleasure.

175

"Evolution"

My friend, John, a retired schoolteacher and principal, was told that he had to teach evolution to his class. He took a 500-piece puzzle to school and asked his class if it was possible to throw all the pieces in the air and have them all land on the desk with the puzzle completely assembled. Not one of the kids said it would happen, no matter how many times you did it. Then he said, "Evolution claims it will. Do you believe in evolution?" When they all answered no, then he considered his class on evolution to be complete.

According to two different dictionary meanings, evolution is:

"the process by which <u>new species</u> or populations of living things develop from pre-existing forms through successive generations"
"the process by which different kinds of living organisms are thought to have developed and diversified from earlier forms during the history of the earth."

In plain, everyday language, We were something else before we became what we are. For example: A horse used to be a dog. A dog used to be a cat.

Humans used to be apes. And all of this took millions of years to happen. Just so you know, and maybe you do, this is being taught in schools, universities, etc., as truth and not theory. It is widely accepted as fact even though no scientific evidence has ever been put forward to support it.

Think about it. If one species became another species over millions of years on a gradual basis, wouldn't it make sense that with all of the fossils that have been discovered, there should be many fossils that would be in the transition stages? Just for fun – if cats evolved into dogs, somewhere along the line, we should have found fossils that were part cat and part dog.

NO SUCH FOSSIL HAS EVER BEEN FOUND.

Just stating facts! This does not mean that changes have not taken place within certain species. Dogs can become little dogs, etc.

See Natural Selection page 102

176
"Confrontation"

Confronting is merely addressing people about something they did, said, or didn't say or do. Somehow, it bothers us. If we don't deal with it, who will? We can ignore or address it, learn or not, see it as a challenge or opportunity, dread or anticipate it.

The word "confrontation" sounds like a fighting word or something argumentative, and it can be. If we look at it more as a conversation or discussion, it sounds better.

When it comes to business and the workplace, management especially has a responsibility, duty, and obligation to confront people when company policy or instructions are not followed. If they do not confront, then errors or poor practice can be repeated because *"the standard, we accept is what we get."* Such is the case when raising children.

In dealing with leaders and managers over the years, many have confessed to me that confronting people is the most difficult part of the job. The same is often true in everyday relationships. Their comments include:

- "I tend to put off and delay until I finally blow my top and then do a terrible job of it."
- "I don't want to hurt their feelings."
- "I don't want them to quit, so I put up with them."
- "I just want to avoid arguments." The many reasons for not confronting include: don't want to - don't know how – don't want to upset -don't want to get upset - don't think it's necessary

As a result, People get the wrong message- things don't improve- communication and relationships suffer – people don't grow – and people lose.

If confrontation is not done when needed, eventually, it may not work at all. Confrontation and dealing with truth have a lot in common.

See also: Confront or Not (pg. 206)

177
"Spending Priority"

Being raised by parents who lived through the depression, left to their own resources with no government handouts, revealed a lot about priorities on spending. I tried, but I haven't always followed their examples.

People's spending priorities are determined by many factors, including:

- Upbringing
- Cultural norms
- Peer pressure (keeping up with the Jones')
- Knowledge
- Personal values
- Pride
- Ego
- Circumstances
- Affordability- i.e., money in the bank and income
- Needs (food, shelter, etc)
- Wants (vacations, fashion, etc
- Pleasure, comfort and enjoyment, entertainment
- Generosity – helping the needy
- Obligation and duty, i.e., Taxes, payments, promises, etc
- Savings- providing for future
- Love of money
- Planning
- Demands of others - kids, relatives etc.
- Economic value
- Impulse
- Media influence

Go ahead. Give a number to prioritize the above for your spending priorities. You can add more to the list.

"If you buy things you do not need, soon you will have to sell things you need. Do not save what is left over after spending, but spend what is left over after saving."
- Warren Buffett.

178
"Bible Quiz –2"

1. Who was the first Jew (Hebrew)?

2. What was his first son's name?

3. What did God first divide when He created the earth?

4. What else did he divide?

5. What is the second of the ten commandments

6. On what day of creation was Adam created?

7. Did Adam and Eve have belly buttons?

8. Were Adam and Eve circumcised? Why or Why not?

Answers Page 204

179
"Reading"

I hated reading. Give me a maths problem, I was all over it. Give me a book to read, and I struggled. My classmate Clyde could read a story and recite it back to me almost word for word. Not me. My mind wondered, and I just could not get interested. The way I got through the reading subjects like history and geography was to take the textbooks and rewrite the facts that the teacher told the class to underline. Plus, I believe I was a good listener.

By the time I was in my early 30's I had only read two books other than what I had to read for school or work.

I had an interest in photography. I wanted to take advantage of some opportunities in photographing weddings etc. I decided to go to the library and get some books on photography. I just ate it up, and in no time, my sideline in photography grew with wedding portraits, and I even learned how to develop my own "black and whites" in my own darkroom, all from what I read in books. "Hey, this reading works," I thought.

Not long after, I heard a guy say, "The average person reads a book a year." I was proud of my reading those few books on photography until he followed up with, "And that is why they are average." Combining that statement with an earlier one, "If you can read, there is no excuse for not having a good education," I began reading a lot more.

Sadly, I was in my late thirties before I really got into reading. My favorite topics became management, leadership, etc. Biographies are up there, and my favorite is the Bible, which covers almost all aspects of life. My reading is primarily of things that I am interested in. I have only read three novels or fiction in the last fifty years. I wait for the movie. I almost always read with a pencil to underline or write down the main points. It helps me remember.

Do you read much? Enough? What are you reading? Is it helping you grow?

Who knows what we will learn when we read? We might discover things that we didn't know we didn't know. (pg. 139)

Caution: Not all we read is true.

180

"Willing"

What are you willing to do? There were many things I could have done and should have done but I didn't, because I wasn't willing. Similarly, there are many things I should not have done that I was willing to do. I was not willing to study and read when I should have. Some people are willing to live a life of partying, drinking, and running the risk of taking drugs while hanging out with the wrong crowd, but they are unwilling to spend their time more productively.

A willing attitude is a wonderful thing, provided the willingness is pointed in the right direction. My 50-plus years of working show my successes, achievements and missed opportunities are in direct correlation with my willingness. Willingness drives your focus and attention and thus actions. The word willing brings enthusiasm and eagerness along with a receptivity to learning and taking advice and guidance. Of course, the opposite is true of being unwilling, which brings indifference, slowness, and stubbornness in avoiding duties and obligations.

Let's cut to the chase: much of our willingness is determined by what we want, but what we want is not always the best for us.

The first 4 letters of willingness or willingness are "will." When we say, "I will," it implies a commitment, which was always on top of my "look for" list every time I interviewed a potential hire. When we have a willing employee, team, or group, it is amazing what we can accomplish.

On a scale of 1-10 (10 being best), how willing are you to:
- Take risks
- Get along with others
- Try something new
- Do the right thing
- Help others
- Learn from others
- Take advice
- Forgive
- Be kind

> "You have to be willing to be a fool to advance."
> — Jordan B. Peterson

Go ahead and make your own list.

181

"Quick Comeback"

My boss told me, "I got a part-time job in a grocery store just before Christmas. I needed the pocket money. I stacked shelves, helped customer fill bags, and took groceries to their cars. A little old lady approached me while I was in the production department. She insisted I come with her to the bin of cabbage.

She said, "Can you cut this cabbage in half? I only want a half a head."

I replied, "Mam, we don't split the heads, but I could find you a small one."

"No," she snapped back, "It is only me at home, and I can't eat a full one. I need a half one."

We went back and forth, and it didn't look like I was going to win the argument, so I said, "Let me check with the manager because I don't have the authority to cut the cabbage in half."

Opening the door to the manager's office, I said, "There's a miserable old lady out there who wants to buy half a head of cabbage." No sooner did I finish the last word when I saw her out of the corner of my eye following me and I just knew she heard me. "So," I said, "And this little darling wants the other half."

The manager played along with me, and we were able to resolve the matter. The manager later called me in and said, "We are opening a new store in Halifax. How would you like to be my assistant manager there? You would have a great career."

I replied, "I wouldn't go there. All they have are prostitutes and hockey players."

The manager quickly came back with, "My wife is from there."

I said, "And what team does she play on?"

182
"You Are So Beautiful To Me"

Joe Cocker sang this song of less than 25 different words repeated.

You are so beautiful
To me
You are so beautiful
To me
Can't you see

You're everything I hoped for
You're everything I need
You are so beautiful to me
To me

I often sing this song to my wife, off-key, of course.

Are people able to sing or speak these words to their spouses? They need to hear them. But it is better we mean them. Two key words that are overlooked in this song are "To Me."

What is beauty to you? "Beauty is in the eye of the beholder."

What do we consider real beauty? It is too bad that many only see beauty in clothes and makeup instead of looking deeper into the hearts of people.

You know what they say, "Beauty is only skin deep." Unfortunately, it is that skin-deep that too many people look for. Are people focusing too much on the outside and not enough on the inside? Sure, we should take care of our outside appearance, but inside beauty is a real treasure.

We see a lot of glamour and glitz all around us. How deep does it go? The Bee Gees had a song called "How Deep is Your Love?" Could it be that deep love is influenced by deep inner beauty and not just outward appearances?

183

"Middle"

You made it to the middle of the book.

The middle is not always where people look.

There is something about the center of things

To get in the middle to see what it brings.

Some like the front, some like the back

Being in the middle is the center of the pack.

Is the middle bad, or is the middle good?

Would you stay here if you could?

Does average make you feel fenced in?

Or do you want more attention?

Sometimes, the middle is the core.

It makes you strong if you want more.

Take your body, for example; stomachs have to be strong

So our arms and legs don't go wrong.

It's not all bad to be in the center

If that is where you want to enter.

There are things before, and there are things ahead

As long as we trust in God, we will be fed,

184
"Credit Card Debt"

According to the website "Money Sense," the average credit card debt in Canada doubled from 2022 to 2023.

Among the reasons for this is obviously the high inflation rates of the past two years, meaning people are simply having trouble making ends meet.

In my 14 years in the lending industry in the 70's and 80's I did get to see first-hand how people spend.

A credit card is great for an emergency. Its use has become much more prevalent as online spending has become much more common. Furthermore, you can't to go anywhere without having one. Especially for booking hotels.

We can't knock the issuers of credit card companies since they are in the business of selling money and convenience, and we, the consumers, often lack the discipline to use it properly to our advantage. However, it is not just used as a convenience. For many people, it has just become a way of life. And for many who use it, they never pay it off at the end of the month to avoid interest charges.

Your bank doesn't want you to pay it off, and the payment schedule on them is designed that way because the 20% plus interest rates and their commission from the merchants make it very profitable for them. That's their business, but we, the consumers, should also mind our business by:

Having a family budget - Saving for a purchase - Disciplining our spending - Paying off the balances monthly – Using less expensive borrowing, i.e., Line of Credit" – Doing without some things – Avoiding impulse buying.

A word to parents who encourage kids to use credit cards to establish good credit ratings: Try a savings account instead.

185

"Family"

The family structure was meant to be

It consisted of Adam and Eve to rule land and sea

One man, one wife

United together with God for the rest of their life.

What happened? What went wrong?

They disobeyed God and sang a different song.

God was left out of the act of sin,

Catastrophe came when Satan came in.

But the first family was still given a chance

God was still willing; with Him, they could still dance

Obedience through faith could keep them in place.

When Jesus came, He made it easier with grace.

With a father, mother, and kids, the family remains strong.

But take away God; it seldom lasts long.

How is the family doing today?

You don't have to look far to see them astray.

Priorities are taken away with ego and selfish pride.

Divorce is rampant, and no one admits they lied.

Kids suffer as families break down.

They are hurting a lot. You can tell by their frown.

It is a part of the culture.

It doesn't look good for the future.

We wonder why we have problems at work and school.

When God is excluded, they think it's cool.

Don't tell me the government is the solution.

Without the family, society is full of pollution.

It's not about climate change, sex change, or political change.

Put God back in the family, and it can be arranged.

186
"One World Government"

This one is serious. People laugh, roll their eyes, and say, "It's just one of those conspiracy theories." Think again.

Is there really such a plan to have one government rule the world? If so, who is planning it? If you look back a bit at history, we can see the attempts, which include the aggression of Germany in World War I and the expansion of the Soviet Union. While those two attempts failed, they were obvious.

One world government is still threatening. The Marxist ideology has systematically crept into North America in more ways than the average person realizes. It comes under the guise of socialist ideas that the government will give everything for free as a step for the government to own everything and control everything. (See Isms and Socialism)

Other evidence of pending World Government threats to democracies include but are not limited to:

- The ceding of power by countries to international organizations like World Health Organization (WHO), World Economic Forum (WEF), and the United Nations.
- The push for digital currency
- Created world threats such as climate change and global warming.
- The rise of communist political and economic influence in a number of countries.
- The breakdown and elimination of the family unit as we know it.
- The removal of God from society.
- The disarming of the people.
- Total media control by the government
- The removal of freedom of speech and even thought
- The indoctrination of the young people from day care to university -   The control of the big business.

COVID was a good practice run for proponents of government control.

Does this sound like a conspiracy theory? It does, doesn't it? By the way, the Bible predicted it.

187
"Inspiring People"

Hopefully, we have all met or at least observed many inspiring people. There is something about them that is different. They have something we don't have. They may behave in a way that we do not, or they may have a drive that we look up to. They are not necessarily famous, rich, or good-looking. They could be the opposite. They are indeed compelling to the point that we just might learn something from them if we put our minds to it.

Throughout this book, you will meet some of them. These are people who may have been my bosses, subordinates, workout partners and some I may have just seen for a few moments or observed from a distance. Some I just read about, such as legends like Davey Crockett and Wyatt Earp.

I had several determined and goal-oriented bosses who produced great results. One would say, "I am going up. Who is coming with me?" Many of his staff just wanted to be on his team, and they were inspired to work hard and produce. On the other hand, there were those who were just not willing to put in the effort. As a result, they didn't stick around very long. They missed great opportunities to learn and grow. I always admire people who have neat and tidy offices and desks. Too bad I didn't catch on even though I envied them.

I was inspired by Dennis, who, while was able to toss me around in Judo, was willing to work with me, teach me, and encourage me. I was inspired by Bill, who cared enough to challenge me. I was inspired by the example of my parents. I was inspired by successful people I had never met. I was inspired by people who were positive in all situations. I was inspired by truthful people. I was and still am inspired by people who have little or nothing going for them, yet they are willing to give and encourage others and always look at life with a thankful heart.

I was General Manager for Gerry for 8 years. Gerry trusted me and encouraged me. What I really admired about him was his faith and his honesty. Honesty is a great reputation to have. We were quoting a major project once. We were successful. When the client got the first invoice, he was overheard saying to his accounting department, "If Gerry gives you an invoice, you can trust his numbers." Wow!

Who inspires you? Are you inspiring others? How?

188
"Dealing with difficult people"

These are suggestions, some silly, depending on your relationship:

Loud people – speak quietly

Fast talkers – speak slowly.

In your face, people - sneeze and cough often. They will step back.

Continuous talkers – say, "Let me know when you are finished. I may have something to say."

Boisterous - walk away.

Bullies – walk away – stay calm – control your emotions – take a break – tell a joke.

Vulgar – walk away or say, "What dictionary are you using."

Boring people – look at your watch, "Oh, I am late. Gotta go."

Insulting people – Respond to the message. Ignore the insults. Or say, "Can we stick to the issues?" Try, "Excuse me, I have to go to the washroom."

Negative people – Distract –Humor them – Find something positive – Don't give in to them – Ignore – Try logic, which doesn't always work – Smile and laugh – Imagine them doing something weird.

Bitter people – Be better

Far left-wing or far right-wing people- Doesn't matter. They won't hear you.

189

"Geometric Progression"

The power of multiplication exceeds addition.

The new hire was given a choice for the 30-day project. Option 1- to receive $100,000 a day for thirty days, or Option 2 -to begin with one cent and have it doubled every day. What would you choose? Choose quickly before you check below.

Day	Option 1	Option 2
1	100,000	.01
2	100,000	.02
3	100,000	.04
4	100,000	.08
5	100,000	.16
6	100,000	.32
7	100,000	.64
8	100,000	1.28
9	100,000	2.56
10	100,000	5.12
11	100,000	10.24
12	100,000	20.48
13	100,000	40.96
14	100,000	81.92
15	100,000	163.84
16	100,000	327.68
17	100,000	655.36
18	100,000	1,310.72
19	100,000	2,621.44
20	100,000	5,242.88
21	100,000	10,485.76
22	100,000	20,971.52
23	100,000	41,943.04
24	100,000	83,886.08
25	100,000	167,772.16
26	100,000	335,544.32
27	100,000	671,088.64
28	100,000	1,342,177.28
29	100.000	2,684,354.56
30	100,000	5,368,709.12
Total	**$ 3,000,000**	**$10, 737,418.23**

190
"More Inventions"

Nails have been around for over 2000 years. But they weren't mass-produced until the early 1800's.

 The wheel: Said to have been invented around 3500 BC. This later led to the invention of the axel. *"Blessed are those who go around in circles, for they shall be known as "Big Wheels."*

Printing Press: German inventor Johannes Gutenberg invented the printing press sometime between 1440 and 1450. The Guttenberg Bible was the first book printed.

Toothbrush: The modern-day toothbrush was invented in 1938, But there was evidence going back much longer that people used different things to clean their teeth.

Tin cans came on the scene in the early 1800's.

The Paint Roller was invented by Canadian, Norman Breakey in 1940.

Basketball was invented in 1891 in Springfield, Massachusetts, by Canadian James Naismith. He was a physical education instructor for the International Young Men's Christian Association. YMCA.

Handkerchief - was invented by King Richard II of England, according to Wikipedia. *Growing up in Newfoundland, the sleeve was often used as a substitute.*

191
"Faith"

I am a person of faith.

Oh yeah, how do you know? Prove it.

Faith is not about proving it. It's about believing it.

But isn't seeing believing? I will believe it when I see it.

No believing is seeing. I will see it when I believe it.

You mean you get what you wish for. Is it wishful thinking?

It's not about wishing. It's about trusting. It's trustful thinking,

You trust your abilities that much. Is that what I heard?

Not in my abilities but in those of the Lord.

That He will give you what you want?

No, that He will give me what He wants.

What if you don't like what He gives you.

I have faith that what I get is right for me, too.

Does it make you happy that you don't get your will?

You don't understand. It's God's will I want to fill.

Is your faith working? Does everything go right for you?

Sometimes, but even if it doesn't, my faith will get me through.

I have tough times like everyone else.

I trust him because I can't do everything myself.

It is not about what I've got

He is God, and I am not.

192
"Backseat Drivers"

Don't you love them? You can be driving somewhere on a route that you have taken a hundred times before. Yet some passengers feel they should be giving you directions. Are these familiar?

"Your wipers are on!"

"You are in the wrong lane."

"I always turn here."

"There's a cop up ahead."

"How fast are you going?"

"Slow down."

"The light is green."

"There's a guy on a bike."

"That guy is going to turn."

"Is this the way you always go?"

"Aren't you going to signal?"

"You know where you are going?"

"Stop sign ahead."

"What's the speed limit here."

"Don't hit the cat."

"Are we there yet?"

Are you a backseat driver?

193

"Birds"

Judee and I drive a particular route every Sunday to church. In the springtime we get a kick out two geese who set up home on a small rock in a little pond surrounded by high grasses.

The mother perches herself on the rock, which is maybe 18-20 inches in diameter, while the expectant father swims in the pond or stands guard on the edge of the road.

 It's been ten years now we have been taking the same route, and it is still happening. Judee asks the same question every year. How do they know? How does a goose know to find its way every year to a rock in a small pond in a country the size of Canada? Is it the same goose or its descendants? According to my internet searches it is very common for geese or other birds to return to the same area.

Do they return because of familiarity or safety? But why don't they get lost? I hear that the new-borns return to the same area. How do they know? How do they know where to come? Scientists say things like they use landmarks, magnetic senses, scents and memory to find their way. It also seems they can find their way at night, when they do much of their flying.

I don't know about you, but I don't believe that it is true, what they call evolution. I think there is more to it.

I think they have built in senses like computer programs, codes etc. much like the DNA in our human bodies.

If birds and people are programmed with such abilities, who programmed them?

194
"Race"

Are you a racist? What a terrible question to ask! What a terrible thing to be accused of!

I am a Canadian. My skin color is white. I was 11 when I first saw a person of a different color. I didn't hate him. I don't recall having any opinion other than that it was a first experience for me. Over the years, I have worked with, hired, fired, disagreed with, friends with, and joked with people of all colors, cultures, and nationalities. I was insulted once when I was accused of dismissing someone because of their color. I smiled and took it in stride and reminded her that five others were also terminated because of a lack of work.

The truth is there is only one race, all descended from a common ancestry that had all the genes that appear in various ways in subsequent descendants.

"I believe there is only one race, the human race." Rosa Parks

Racism is a sad state of affairs. "Shame on those who are racists." Also, while we are at, "Shame on those who accuse people of being racist simply because they may not agree with their character, work habits, social habits, culture or ideologies."

Shame on those who select, hire, or promote people based solely on skin color and ethnic background instead of their qualifications and character.

There are people who may vary in their characteristics, qualities, and abilities because of various reasons, including upbringing, backgrounds, opportunities, etc., but that is in no way reason to think that they are not due equal respect. It is true that some people groups and cultures have characteristics and habits that may not be exactly seen as pleasant to other groups, but we should not blame their skin color for their actions.

We are all equal in God's eyes.

"There is neither Jew nor Gentile, neither slave nor free, nor is there male and female, for you are all one in Christ Jesus." Galatians 3:28

"Stop judging by mere appearances, but instead judge with righteous judgment." John 7:24

195
"Checklist to get to Heaven"

Put a checkmark or X by those things that you believe will get you to heaven?

_______ Believing there is a heaven.

_______ Telling the truth all the time.

_______ Reading the Bible every day.

_______ Regular Church attendance.

_______ Being a big donor to churches and other charities.

_______ Being a hard worker.

_______ Not smoking, drinking, or taking drugs.

_______ Getting baptized.

_______ Obeying authority

_______ Not stealing.

_______ Memorizing Bible verses

_______ Listening to Christian Hymns

_______ Praying 5 times a day.

_______ Meditating

_______ Yoga

_______Not swearing.

_______ Church membership

See "Heaven or Not" (page 201)

196
"I am where I want to be."

To what extent is this statement true?

Is it all about your circumstances?

Or does it have to do with you?

You cannot control everything.

We don't know what life will bring.

What is your attitude when times are rough?

How do you think we can make it easy or tough.

You say, "I am limited in my abilities, you know."

That may be, but where do you want to go?

Are you willing to do what it takes to get there?

Or will you stay where you are, held back with fear?

If you put more work in, more will come out.

That's how it works. Is that what you are about?

Or are you content to be who you are?

Keeping that attitude won't take you far.

But if that's where you want to be

Then who is to say you are not free?

You can blame it all on your past,

Or you can make up your mind and get off your rear.

197

"Speaking In Public"

It has been said by many that the three biggest fears in life are:

Dying - Speaking in public - Dying while speaking in public.

There is not much we can do about dying. It will happen to all of us someday. But it is possible to overcome our fear of speaking in public. I know that for sure because I did. I was terrified of speaking in public. I would dread it. I would be sick about it. I would blush. My knees would wobble, and yes, I even chickened out the first time.

I would imagine every possible thing that could go wrong. What would people think of me? Would my shirt tail be out? Would my hair be sticking up? Would my fly be down? Would I forget the words?

But I wanted to be able to do it. No one says we all need to do it. There is no rule that says everyone needs to be able to speak in public. Most people can't, won't, or have no need to. But, if you want to and you need to, you can do it. It's a matter of desire and willingness to learn.

You may get it right the first time. Besides, who defines what is right? It will take practice. It will take preparation. And it will take a willingness to get over yourself. What I found was that it was not about me but about the audience. Rather than focusing on me, I focused on what the people needed to hear. After that, I was free to work on the mechanics of my presentation.

<u>Prepare</u>: Write it down – Read it over and over. Does it say what you want it to say and what needs to be said? Review it with someone you trust. Remember, your content is important, but your delivery is equally important.

<u>Practise</u>: Read it out aloud with just yourself. Read it to the mirror. Read it to the dog. Read to a spouse or friend. Read it enough times so that you remember the order and the points.

<u>Present</u>: Be honest. Smile. Look at people. Look around. Move your head from side to side. Make eye contact with one or two people, or at least pretend by looking over their heads or towards them until you get comfortable. Stick to the written words if you must, but look up frequently. If you make a mistake, don't dwell on it. Acknowledge it and move on.

The more you do it, the better you will get.

198
"Sex Trafficking"

It's a big problem in the world and likely in your own neighborhood. The comments below are taken directly from the website of an organization called "Cry Not." Search their site for more details.

"Human trafficking is the business of stealing freedom for profit. In some cases, traffickers trick, defraud, or physically force victims into selling sex. In others, victims are lied to, assaulted, threatened, or manipulated into working under inhumane, illegal, or otherwise unacceptable conditions. It is a multi-billion-dollar criminal industry that denies freedom to 24.9 million people around the world.

Human Trafficking involves the recruitment, transportation, or harboring of persons for the purpose of exploitation (typically in the sex industry or for forced labor). Traffickers use various methods to maintain control over their victims, including force, sexual assault, threats of violence, and emotional abuse....

Often, people are trafficked by the people closest to them, such as boyfriends. Some victims of trafficking were first exploited as children by family members. Individuals working independently traffic persons for profit/personal gain, as well as organized crime groups such as gangs.

Pimps "shop" for their victims online, in shopping malls, bus stops, schools, after-school programs, foster homes, parks, restaurants and other places where teens gather....

Pimps invest a lot of time and effort in forming a bond with their victim. Romeo or boyfriend pimps buy girls gifts, provide a place to stay, and give affection before revealing their true intent- to sexually exploit them. The pimp may take "modeling" photos and suggestive videos and then use them to advertise the victim for sexual services online. The pimp's use of psychological manipulation, physical violence, and rape can make the victim feel trapped and powerless."

Watch the movie: "Sound of Freedom."

199
"Humility"

This is humility speaking. I will tell you who I am

I don't boast or brag, and I am not a sham

I am not about conceit. No it is the opposite you see.

I am not proud to be humble. No not me.

I don't think too high of myself, more like too low

I am definitely not in it for the show.

You are far better than I

You are brave, but I tend to be shy

I'd rather give you the credit than take it myself

I will just sit here and stay on the shelf

I am not about fame or glory

I am content for you to be the story.

I don't know everything. I am open to learn

I will be quiet and just discern

The truth is I am sorry for focusing on me.

Building you up will set me free.

I wish I had learned these lessons in my youth

One more thing, I love the truth.

"Humility is not thinking less of yourself. It's thinking of yourself less."

C. S. Lewis

200
"More Nursery Rhymes"

<u>Hot cross buns</u>
Hot cross buns
One a penny
Two a penny
Hot cross buns
If you have no daughters, give them to your sons
One a penny
Two a penny
Hot cross buns

<u>Three blind mice,</u>
Three blind mice
See how they run, See how
they run!

They all ran after
The farmer's wife
She cut off their tails
With a carving knife
Did you ever see Such a
sight in your life As three
blind mice?

<u>The Itsy Bitsy Spider</u> climbed up the water spout
Down came the rain and washed the spider out
Out came the sun and dried up all the rain
And the Itsy Bitsy Spider climbed up the spout again

<u>Old MacDonald had a farm,</u> E-I-E-I-O,
And on his farm, he had a cow, E-I-E-I-O,
With a moo-moo here and a moo-moo there,
Here a moo, there a moo, everywhere
moo-moo, Old MacDonald had a farm, E-I-
E-I-O.

201
"Heaven or Not"

Remember your checklist on page 195? Which ones did you check off that you think will get you to heaven?

Do you really believe there is such a place as heaven? If we listen to people at funerals, the common phrase is, "They are in a better place now." Where is that place, and how do we know if they made it there?

Depending on which survey you find, stats show that approximately 70% of the people believe there is a heaven, and most of those believe there is a hell. The views on whether there is or not and how one gets there depend on the various religious beliefs around the world. Some of these beliefs are detailed throughout this book. Most, if not all, except one, believe that reaching heaven or that high state of completion or wonderfulness depends on our actions and how we live our lives.

For those who actually believe there is a heaven, wouldn't it make sense that there would be a sense of urgency in them to find out the true way? The choices of places to look are many and opinions are many. Speaking of making sense, it doesn't seem to make sense that all paths lead to heaven, especially if those paths contradict each other.

Are we good enough to make it to heaven? A lot of people are trying hard to get there. Who decides? Is it a committee, or is it up to the individual? Is it about following a bunch of rituals or has it to do with our behavior being good or bad? Who decides what is good or bad?

Does it bother you? Do you care? What if there is heaven and hell, and we don't know about it? We may be in for a shock. If there isn't, no big deal. But if there is, then REALLY BIG DEAL.

Through this book, there are some comparisons. Take your pick.

PS: What if none of the things from page 195 get you to heaven?

202
"M.A.I.D."

MAID- is the Canadian acronym for Medically Assistance In Dying
Assistance in dying has been in the limelight going back to before the early
1990's.

Canadian law now allows for '*dignity in dying.*'

A Canadian poll of 2500 people showed that the majority agreed that "a doctor
should be able to help someone end their life if the person is a competent adult
who is terminally ill, suffering unbearably and repeatedly asks for assistance to
die."
On February 6, 2015, the Supreme Court of Canada unanimously overturned a
legal ban on doctor-assisted suicide, ruling the law should be amended to allow
doctors to help in specific situations.

As of March 17, 2021, persons who wish to die must meet certain criteria
including:

- be 18 years of age or older and have decision-making capacity
- be eligible for publicly funded health care services
- make a voluntary request that is not the result of external pressure
- have a serious and incurable illness, disease, or disability
- be in an advanced state of irreversible decline in capability
- have enduring and intolerable physical or psychological suffering that cannot
  be alleviated under conditions the person considers acceptable

In 2021, there were 10,064 MAID provisions reported in Canada, accounting for
3.3% of deaths, making Canada the highest in the world, 8 times higher than the
US. Concerns are that over 200 of these were individuals whose deaths were not
reasonably foreseen.

A delay was put in place in 2024 to delay MAID for mental illness.

The above stats were taken from Government websites.

"In 2023, more than 15,000 people died by MAID, a five-fold increase from 2017
to 2023." (Epoch Times)

Reports show estimates of 45,000 MAID deaths since 2021. What do you think?
Is it moral? Is it a way to control the population and reduce medical costs? Is it
justified?

203
"Islam – Facts and Beliefs"

Islam, meaning submission, the religion of Muslims, is the world's 2nd largest religion, with over 25% of the world's population - close to 2 billion followers.

It began around 610 AD in Saudi Arabia when Mohammad was said to have been visited by the angel Gabriel and given what Muslims believe to be revelations from Allah. These revelations have been written in the Qur'an.

Other resources for the Muslims include Sunnah (tradition and commentaries.) The Qur'an affirms the Bible, aka Torah, Psalms, and Gospels. Muslims claim that the Jews and Christians have corrupted the original texts of the Bible.

The common Core Beliefs of Islam include:

- Allah(god) is one and cannot be known
- Allah has no human qualities
- Jesus was a great prophet and sinless, but not God
- Jesus was not crucified or resurrected
- Jesus will return
- Holy Spirit is God or Gabriel or as used by Allah
- One should always live with fear of Allah and judgment day
- All humans are basically good but need guidance
- The balance between good and evil determines hell or paradise
- Bodies will only be raised from the dead
- Paradise awaits with maidens for sexual pleasure to righteous men

Islam has two main sects: Sunni – people of the tradition, make up between 85-90% of Muslims, while the Shi'ites make up the balance.

The five pillars of the Muslim faith are Confession of Faith-Prayer-Fasting-Giving of Alms and Pilgrimage to Mecca.

"Bible quiz – 2" (Answers)

1.   Who was the first Jew (Hebrew)?   **Abraham**

"Get out of your country, from your family and from your father's house, To a land that I will show you. ² I will make you a great nation; I will bless you And make your name great; And you shall be a blessing. ³ I will bless those who bless you, And I will curse him who curses you, And in you, all the families of the earth shall be blessed."

Genesis 12:1-3

2.   What was his first son's name?   **Ismael**

Abraham's wife got impatient and insisted that Abraham have a child with her maid instead of following God's plan of having a child together. (Genesis 16:4) Isaac came some 14 years later. (Genesis 21:5)

3.   What did God first divide at creation?   **Light and darkness**

"and God divided the light from the darkness." (Genesis 1:4)

4.   What else did he divide?   **Water and Land**

"God divided the water below the earth from above the earth and then separated the water on the earth with the land.". Genesis 1: 6-11

5.   The second of the ten commandments? **Don't worship idols**

"You shall not make for yourself a carved image, or any likeness of anything that is in heaven above, or that is in the earth beneath, or that is in the water under the earth." (Exodus 20:4)

6.   On what day of creation was Adam created?   **Sixth**

7.   Did Adam and Eve have belly buttons? **Likely not**

They were not born. They were created. It makes sense that they had no umbilical cord. God may have given them a poke just for fun.

8.   Was Adam circumcised? Why or Why not?   **No**

The practice of circumcision began with Abraham many years later.

205
"Puns"

Don't you love puns? A pun is when you use a word or phrase that sounds good enough to use in a sentence but it has a different meaning. A pun is a play on words and is a form of humor. Puns make us laugh, but they can also have a lesson in them. They are used in marketing, signs, advertisements, etc.

It makes for 'common cents' that we use when it comes to our own family budget. The price of chimneys is going through the roof. I got rid of my car to drive my bicycle, and now I can't even afford to retire.

I don't want to bore you to <u>tiers</u> with the different levels of puns. At the same time, I don't want you to be crabby and shellfish with them. So, let's not kid ourselves about puns. We don't need a brain transplant to change our minds about puns. I have read a lot of books that have them. One of them was on antigravity. I couldn't put it down. You can learn a lot from books, so go to the library and see the bookkeeper. I was stuck in a snowstorm once, if you get my drift. Then I was sick for days. It must have been something I hated.

A lot of people who spend their days making up puns must have a lot of time on their hands. My brother left me to milk the cows once. How dairy!

I Noah guy in the Bible who built an ark. His friends got all wet over it.

My friend was an Olympian in track and field. He ran in the hurdles race, but he got over that.

My dad always told me to watch out for wooden nickels, but to be sure, I opened a shavings account. My catholic friend was very poor, so he prayed to St. Nickeless. Five of us took a trip in a rowboat. That was quite an oar deal. Hammers were on sale at Walmart. They were $2 per pound.

That's all I have to say about puns. You probably heard most of them. "Blessed are they who go around in circles, for they shall be known as big wheels.

"Confront or Not"

Let's see now-

- "Mary said she would call me back, and she didn't."
- "John was late for work and didn't call in or apologize after."
- "Suzie interrupted me while I was talking." -   "George has a serious body odor problem."
- "Sam talks too much in meetings."
- "The visitors' kids are jumping on my furniture."
- "Alice has all her facts wrong on climate change."
- "What he said was just wrong."
- "He hurt my feelings."

Oh dear, do we have to confront these things? Are they invitations for arguments that may result in broken relations, or are they opportunities to improve the universe? What a dilemma!

As difficult as it may be, we need to determine a few things by asking ourselves:

<u>What is the real issue?</u> Is the problem me, the other person, the system, the equipment, or something else? Are my emotions and thoughts getting the better of the facts?

<u>Does it need engaging or confronting?</u> Does it really matter? How important is it in the big picture of life?

<u>Who should do the confronting?</u> Should it be me or someone else?

<u>When should it be done?</u> Timing is important.

<u>Where should it be done?</u> Do we have privacy?

<u>How should it be done?</u> (you can make it worse or better)

See also: Confront (176)

207
"Chain of Command"

Where do you stand in the pecking order?
Life has some rules and the occasional border.
If we are at the bottom or the top, we have to know our place.
We have to know when, who, and how to communicate face-to-face.
Bosses, supervisors, shop floor people, husbands, wives, or tots
Need to know where they stand in case they get caught.
There is always a line of authority
And things are not always decided by the majority
It is often simply tact and common sense
That determines when we decide to go over the fence.
If we go over someone's head
Who knows, there may be bloodshed
If you go too far below
You may just interrupt the workflow
Don't take authority you do not own
But take the initiative to work when you are alone
That will work you up the ladder
It will make you happier, not sadder
Keep people informed and make suggestions
And don't worry them to indigestion.
Don't get caught bypassing the boss.
It is disrespectful, and it's everyone's loss.
Be the best communicator you can
Start by following your chain of command.

208
"Too Much Government"

Are you sick yet of government control?

Do they drive you mad and tax you in the hole?

It seems all they do is pass new laws.

While at the same time they continue with their flaws.

They take all your money, and they are not finished yet.

But they continue to overspend and drive up the debt.

I don't get it, do you?

Our message to them never seems to get through.

They get elected to act on our behalf

As soon as they get in, they give us the shaft.

They have their own agenda and don't give a dam

If you and your budget are in a jam.

They control what you say and even what you think

While deeper and deeper in trouble, we sink

They ban guns for the good guys and let the bad guys keep theirs

It is odd that criminals are allowed to give us the gears

They own the media by giving them a pay

They tell you how to parent and won't let you have a say

Intimidate and fear tactics they use

To make sure you don't refuse

They're telling you how to live your life

Heck, it's getting harder for me and the wife.

 I am not complaining. Maybe none of this is true

I didn't make it up.

I got it all from you.

209
"Class"

In the latest movie, Titanic, we got to see the real meaning of class. We saw that certain classes of people were relegated to certain parts of the ship. We saw "uppity" people wine and dine with their fancy outfits. They carried themselves in a superior way. They sat up straight. They held their cups, making sure their little finger was sticking out when they sipped their tea. Their noses were in the air as they made sure they exemplified the behavior of what they considered high class.

We hear a lot about class privilege today. Some classes are often referred to as the elite or the rich and famous. We also have various classes in culture, ideology, race, and gender, which all seem to divide people. This business of class and even political persuasion separates people today more than ever.

Sad, isn't it? What really makes some high class or low class or no class?

Regardless of wealth, poverty, culture, race, gender, ideology, social status, education, political persuasion, or what seat we are in on an airplane, the true distinction for class boils down to how we behave and think. No matter where we fit in class or status, we should all make an effort to get along and treat each other as fellow human beings.

Despite our differences, and yes, we don't have to agree on everything, we can: show respect – tell the truth – say please and thank you – be considerate of others - offer a hand to clean the dishes – be polite – not post crap on Facebook – speak in turn – not take advantage of others – stop looking for handouts – get a job – be teachable – take responsibility - GET THE IDEA? We have all heard the expression, "You can put lipstick on a pig, but it's still a pig."

We can't all be rich and famous, but we can all be kind, polite, and willing to grow.

"Class is an aura of confidence that is being sure without being cocky. The class has nothing to do with money. Class never runs scared. It is self-discipline and self-knowledge. It's the sure-footedness that comes with having proved you can meet life." — Ann Landers.

210

"Heroes"

We all have had our heroes, people we look up to and admire. No, we are not jealous of them and don't idolize or worship them- that's dangerous, but we should admire certain things about them. When I was young, I was Tarzan, Wyatt Earp, the Lone Ranger, and others. Seriously, it's okay to look up to those who have certain characteristics. And they don't have to be famous.

My wife is my number one hero. That's why I married her. In addition to all her beauty, charm, work ethic, and morals, she has an amazing intuition and discernment. And she is humble. My parents are my heroes. My two sisters Edie and Lucy, and all our kids are my heroes.

My judo heroes include Ron Angus, whose work ethic and amazing determination enabled him to win several World Masters Championships. He is also an amazing coach and very humble. Others like Duncan Vignali continue to be very active in his late eighties, playing a significant role in putting certain aspects of his sport in the national limelight.

Bob Burnside founded a company that had gone national and international. He is involved with so many charity organizations. Bob has been blessed in so many ways, yet I admire that he is down to earth and humble and can sit down with even me and not complain that he loses in a euchre game. I have other heroes who:

- Literally never passed a grade in school but went on to have great careers and raise wonderful families.
- Love and accept me unconditionally, but enough to put me in my place when I get weird.
- Grew up in dozens of foster homes yet maintained a great attitude and personality.
- Always smile, encourage, and look on the bright side of things
- Have faith, hope, and love.
- Help others
- Are kind, forgiving, and humble
- Do what is right rather than what they want

Who are your heroes? Why?

211
"Psychic"

Here is one for you.

Pick a number between 1 and 100.   ______________

Double it   ______________

Add your year of birth   ______________

Subtract 4   ______________

Smile and keep going

You don't believe I will match your answer, do you?

Check your numbers and write your total.   ______________

Divide it by 2   ______________

Add the number of kids in your family.   ______________

Final Answer   ______________

Good, you are so smart. Do a final review and turn to the last line of page 279 to see how good a psychic I am.

212
"Failure"

Is that such a bad word? Some think so. What makes someone a failure? Were you a failure because you didn't succeed at something when you were young? You got over it, didn't you? Were you a failure because you didn't get the promotion or the job you wanted? You went on to something else, didn't you? Were you a failure because you didn't make the team, or you did make the team, and you weren't the star player? You got over it, didn't you?

We are not failures because we failed. We are only failures if we don't learn from our setbacks and move on and try something else. Mistakes and setbacks aren't failures. They are "character builders."

A failure is often defined as a lack of success. But a lack of success in one area doesn't mean we can't succeed in another area. Learn from it, avoid the pity party, and move on.

If our expectations are not met, it doesn't mean we are failures. It just means our expectations aren't met. We need to either adjust our expectations or try harder to get them.

Many people have stumbled from one mistake or regret after another, but it doesn't deter them from continuing to try.

Thomas Edison was questioned about all the times he tried and failed to make the light bulb work. He said, "I have not failed. I've just found 10,000 ways that won't work."

Winston Churchill said, "Success is not final, failure is not fatal: it is the courage to continue that count."

Colonel Saunders was 61 when he started the KFC franchise.

Failing may be hard, but that doesn't make one a failure. We have to get back up. We have more going for us than we think. But we may have to make some adjustments in our attitude and actions.

My father had great advice when things didn't go well. "Get off your rear and do something about it."

213
"Jesus Quiz"

1. Where was Jesus born?

2. Give 5 other names to which Jesus is referred.

3. Were the wise men present on the night of his birth?

4. Who was the king who tried to kill baby Jesus?

5. Why did he not succeed?

6. How old was Jesus when He went missing at the temple?

7. Did Jesus have brothers and sisters?

8. What was the hometown where Jesus grew up?

9. Was Jesus baptized?

10. What was the first recorded miracle of Jesus?

11. How many days did Jesus spend in the wilderness?

12. How many times did Satan tempt Him there?

13. How did Jesus respond to Satan?

14. How old was Jesus when He died?

15. How many people saw the risen Jesus?

(See – page 255)

214
"Basic Principles"

When the Red Cross lady made her annual visit to our little school, she taught us basic principles of hygiene. She asked the class, "What should you use when your nose is running?" Johnny quickly answered, "My sleeve." Even though his sleeve was very shiny, Johnny should have answered 'handkerchief.' Everybody had a handkerchief in their pockets then. For us boys, it was next to our pocketknife and a few nails.

Everybody knows you shouldn't wipe your nose with your sleeve, especially in public. Everybody knows you should not stand up in a small rowboat. Everybody knows you should not spit into the wind. Everybody knows you should cover your mouth when you sneeze or cough. Everybody knows you should scrape the dishes before you put them in the dishwater or dishwasher. Everybody knows if the neighbor needs help you help them. Everybody knows you should remove your cap when you sit down to a meal. Why?

They make sense. They are for our own benefit and the benefit of others. They are basic principles to know and follow.

There are basic principles to everything. We don't have to follow them, we can avoid them, we can deny them. But in the end, we would be better off to follow them. Different cultures may vary in some of their basic principles. I had to learn a few different ones when I moved from my little community to the big world. But BEWARE, many of the basic principles that were taken for granted in society are now "out the window"- gone.

Respect for elders, opening the door for others (especially men for women), honesty, basic manners and etiquette, order in classrooms, and returning phone calls are disappearing. Who would have ever thought of a man going into a woman's washroom or that our government leaders would lie or cover up the truth? Who would have ever thought that the media would lie? Who would have ever thought that shoplifting would become the norm? Who would have ever thought that laws and free speech would not apply to everyone?

Basic principles help us in business, finance, science, and sports, and everybody knows we need them. Right is always right, Wrong is always wrong.

What basic principles do you live by?

215
"Time Savers"

The reality is we cannot save time and carry it over like we do with money. But we can be more productive and do different things in the time we have, which is 24 hours a day.

Every time waster we eliminate is a time saver. *(See time wasters)* Time wasters are things we stop doing to make us more productive. Time savers are proactive things we take up doing that save us time.

Depending on our situation and the resources we have available, we can do things that will make us more productive. In the old days, we called it working smarter and not just harder or faster. We need to continue to be mindful of what we are doing with a view to being more productive. By thinking that way, we will be more likely to come up with creative ways to improve and accomplish more.

The consultant, after interviewing staff, and observing, gave a summary report to the management team and owners. He said that they could double their profits in the next fiscal year. Most of them laughed. They knew how hard they worked, and they were hard-working, dedicated people. The president was asked if he would like to double his profit, to which he responded, "Yes." One year later at the annual review, profits had doubled as a percentage of sales.

This is just a sampling of their "time savers," which saved time and money:

- They had a "want to" attitude
- They were willing to plan and prioritize with a positive attitude
- They were teachable
- They trained
- They set and met goals in specific areas
- They changed, made, and followed new policies and procedures
- They kept each other accountable by consistently measuring results
- They discussed and reviewed progress - objectively
- They dealt with their weaknesses

By the way they doubled their profit after they paid the consultant fee.

216
"Soft skills"

I worked in a company that made concrete blocks in the summer of 1968. My job was to operate a claw-like machine that took the warm blocks from a rack and stacked them a certain way on a skid so they wouldn't fall off. Within a few days of watching, trying, and practicing, I was able to master the techniques and perform adequately. In the meantime, I spent another three years in university learning "how to" in Physics and Maths. When I began working in the finance industry, some of the skills of the job took minutes, while others took days, weeks, or months.

These "hard skills" were very important. But in each case, I learned quickly that the area that I and others struggled the most was in the area of "soft skills."

Soft skills included primarily my personality, and how I dealt with people. I quickly noticed how well people in higher positions stood out in how they dealt with others. They spoke differently. They responded differently. They were comfortable and confident in their relationships. When my manager sat down to interview a client for a loan, he was so smooth in how he spoke and got information on the application. The customer was at ease. I, on the other hand, was nervous and awkward.

What were these soft skills, and how would I get them? For me, growing up in a small out community on the coast, I realized I had a lot more to learn than rowing a boat or working on a Physics problem.

Years later, as an ice breaker, I would ask the attendants to randomly shout their biggest problem at work. Notice how their replies mostly related to "soft skills," i.e., people issues:

Communication - Lack of time - Lack of cooperation -Staff limitations-Influencing decisions - Working with other managers- Attitudes - Turnover in staff – Conflict - CONFRONTING poor behavior

What are your strengths and weaknesses when it comes to soft skills?

"If it wasn't for people, it would be so much easier to get along."

217
"Core Values"

Many companies back in the 80's and 90's took a lot of time to list their core values, getting input from the management team, staff and even their clients and suppliers. Quite often, the list was printed, framed, and hung in the lobbies and board rooms. They also appeared in their promotional materials.

These "Core Values" were meant to express what the company believed. The words were important and not to be violated in all dealings with staff, customers, and suppliers even if it meant losing a sale. They were good guiding principles. Great idea, don't you think?

What are your core values? What do you stand for? Will you sacrifice your values to get something?

Have you thought of what your core values are?

Here is a sample list of the types of things companies listed.
Take a minute and circle your top five to abide by. Add more.

Accountability – Collaboration - Consistency - Constructive
Criticism – Credibility - Customer Focus – Excellence - Dependability –
Encouragement - Hard Work Ethic – Initiative
- Innovation - Professionalism - Profit – Punctuality - Quality
- Family First - Modesty - Positive Attitude - Pride in Your
Work – Respect - Self-Control – Generosity – Passion – Patience –
Warmth – Courage – Decisiveness – Efficiency-
Fairness – Faith – Honesty - Integrity - Caring

218
"Passion"

Don't you love to see passion in people? I have always admired my barber, Aldo, who has been cutting hair for more than 50 years, and mine for at least 35. Yet every time I sit in his chair, his passion shows through. The way he combs, cuts, and shaves. Even the way he puts the mirror behind my head to show me how it looks. "Neat again," he says every time. Thanks for your passion, Aldo. Great cut, too.

Passion is about getting our minds off ourselves. It is excitement, pleasure, and anticipation. It shows desire and a "want to." It comes through with an attitude of gratitude. It is a choice, not out of obligation but out of decision. Passion comes from the inside and is not dependent on what happens on the outside. It is not just hype over something in particular. It is a natural enthusiasm.

I used to wonder how we get passion. I don't think we get it. I think we already have it. We just have to give it. It's a switch. Turn it on. Decide to use it. Release it.

For the most part it is simply an attitude adjustment of giving instead of looking to be getting. We just have to define ourselves with what we can do and do it with passion. It is more than pretending because pretending doesn't last.

The results are amazing. The initiative comes naturally. We don't wait for things to happen; we make them happen. People will like being around us. We stop focusing on obstacles and focus on solutions. We see opportunities and results. Passion makes us do our best. We just start with what we have and watch it multiply.

"Our company was once awarded a major contract based on the passion of the staff."

219
"Baloney"

Larry, Moe, and Joe were working on a high rise. Lunchtime came, and they sat together to open their lunch pails.

Larry opened his pail, pulled out his sandwich, and said, "Oh no, not again, egg salad sandwich. If I get an egg salad sandwich tomorrow, I will toss it off the top of this building."

Moe opened his pail, pulled out his sandwich, and said, "Oh no, not again, tuna sandwich. If I get this tomorrow, I will toss it off the top of this building."

Joe opened his pail, pulled out his sandwich, and said, "Oh no, not again, baloney sandwich. If I get this tomorrow, I will toss it off the top of this building."

Next Day:

Larry opened his lunch pail, took the wrapper off his sandwich and saw it was egg salad. He quickly jumped up and tossed the sandwich over the side of the building.

Moe opened his lunch pail, pulled out his sandwich and saw it was tuna. He quickly jumped up and tossed the sandwich over the side of the building.

Joe opened his lunch pail, took out his sandwich, and tossed it over the side of the building without opening it. As he sat down, Larry and Moe looked at Joe and together said, "Why didn't you open your sandwich?" Joe replied, "I knew it was baloney. I make my own lunch."

220
"Merit"

I am not sure if or why this book merited a page on merit, but here goes.

Meriam Webster dictionary gives merit these meanings:

- a praiseworthy quality
- character or conduct deserving reward, honor, or esteem
- a person's qualities, actions, etc., regarded as indicating what the person deserves to receive
- reward or punishment due

When I think of merit, I think of giving credit or recognition where it is due or deserved.

"John worked hard. His raise and promotion were merited." "John

served his country well for years. His medals were merited." How is

Merit doing today?

When I was a boy, kids had to get enough answers right on an exam to merit a passing mark.

Are people put in positions and getting things today that they don't merit, deserve, or haven't earned?

A father decided that his rebellious teenage son should be enrolled in a private school for such kids. The father and the son had to agree in writing that the school would have total control over the boy.

Every benefit and every privilege had to be earned and merited. If any or all assigned chores and jobs were not completed, privileges like recreation time and meals, etc., were withheld. The one-year program was designed to teach teenagers that nothing we have should be taken for granted. It was so disciplined that the boy was prevented from going home on a weekend to attend his own birthday party because he disobeyed an order. It worked. The boy's life was turned around. He understood many things, including merit.

What do you think? Was it too harsh?

221
"Borrowing"

Is it wrong to borrow? No. Even the bible doesn't say borrowing is wrong. However, it is often discouraged.

The negatives of borrowing include:

- Committing our future income, which we may not be guaranteed.
- It eats up our monthly income.
- Interest charges increase the cost of what we buy.
- It can reduce our ability to save.
- It can reduce our freedom.

There are also advantages of borrowing, including:

- It gives us the opportunity to acquire something we may take a lifetime to save for, e.g., a house.
- If we didn't borrow our car, we may not be able to get to work. -   It helps us in emergencies

We are living in a culture where borrowing has gotten out of hand. Slick advertising, the government example, the peer pressure of keeping up with the Jones, easy credit via credit cards, and lack of education have encouraged an *"I have to have it society."*

Some quick tips:

- Borrow for needs – not wants. *Some of us are good at turning wants into needs*
- Save as much as you can towards the purchase so we borrow less
- Keep the loan term as short as possible. The loan should reduce faster than the assets depreciate.
- Don't borrow for things that have no future value, e.g., vacations
- Avoid credit card borrowing for big items unless you have the money to pay it off when the statement comes.
- Stay with one lending institution, assuming they are competitive.
- Pay on time

222

"Nicene Creed"

This is a statement of faith from the early church, written in 325 AD and amended in 382 AD. It is not in the Bible but confirmed by the Bible.

I believe in one God, the Father almighty, maker of heaven and
earth, of all things visible and invisible.
I believe in one Lord Jesus Christ,
the Only Begotten Son of God,
born of the Father before all ages.
God from God, Light from Light,
true God from true God,
 begotten, not made, consubstantial with the Father; through him
all things were made.
For us men and for our salvation
He came down from heaven,
and by the Holy Spirit was incarnate of the Virgin Mary,
and became a man.
For our sake, He was crucified under Pontius Pilate,
He suffered death and was buried,
and rose again on the third day
 in accordance with the Scriptures.
He ascended into heaven
and was seated at the right hand of the Father.
He will come again in glory
to judge the living and the dead
, and his kingdom will have no end.
I believe in the Holy Spirit, the Lord, the giver of life,
who proceeds from the Father and the Son,
 who with the Father and the Son is adored and glorified, who has
spoken through the prophets.
I believe in one holy catholic and apostolic Church.
 I confess one Baptism for the forgiveness of sins
, and I look forward to the resurrection of the dead and the life
of the world to come. Amen.

223
"Study"

There are those who read, and they just get it. Reading is good, and we get information and knowledge, but studying is much deeper than casual reading. The study gives more understanding. Reading a book "from cover to cover" (okay for a novel) may give us an overall view but by no means gives an in-depth understanding that we may retain,

I regret that I was neither a good reader nor a good student. I often studied enough to pass an exam as opposed to knowing and understanding.

Studying to me is reading to understand, and once I understand something, I don't have to remember as much. There is a lot of knowledge, information, and opinions going around today on social media. Based on what we read and hear, we are apt to go along with it and accept it. But before we jump to conclusions and accept it all, we need to dig deeper.

The headline read, "Life on Mars?" Does this mean we can picture someone on Mars barbequing? Is the headline a statement of fact or a question as indicated by the question mark(?)? Studying the article very closely revealed it was all about a fist-size rock that, under a microscope, showed a wiggly line. There was absolutely no conclusive proof of what it was. Furthermore, there was no way of telling if the rock even came from Mars.

Studying to understand may require taking a rabbit hole into other books or sources of information to back up the information to make sure we understand. It has to make sense. But there are things we don't understand, some of which we accept if we have proof of its validity. I don't understand the northern lights, but I accept them. Yet, I don't automatically accept popular opinions on the latest social agenda. I have to study it more to get and understand the facts.

Studying involves more time, taking notes, and digging deeper. It also requires patience, commitment, and objectivity. It also may require a change in our opinion when true facts have been revealed.

I have found more success and satisfaction when I study to understand.

224
"Ready Willing and Able"

As a kid, we heard this expression a lot. I don't hear it much anymore. If we had all three of these in a situation our potential has few limits.

Can we be ready, willing and able all at the same time? We might be ready but not able or willing. We might be willing but not ready and able. We might be able but not ready or willing. You see how that works. All three might apply to our mental state as well as our physical state and circumstance. I was willing to sleep last night, I was also ready but I wasn't able, so I got up and worked on this book. By the end of the day, I was able and ready but not willing to write because I just had enough. Sometimes, I am not able to write, and sometimes I am not ready to write.

I was willing to receive a raise at work and was certainly able to take one. But my boss said, "No, Fred, you are not ready. You haven't completed the requirements".

Ready, willing, and able is having it all together. Watch the Olympic Champion perform. Watch an accomplished speaker or singer entertain. They sure look like ready, willing and able to me. Watch a loving mother care for her baby. She is ready and willing, and she ensures she is able.

In my very first Judo match, I was willing to take on a much more experienced and stronger guy than I was. I lost. I was neither ready nor able with the needed skills or experience. However, I didn't give up. I trained harder, got more experience and skill, and eventually was able to win.

Parents are hoping their kids are ready, willing and able to do more. A lot of teenagers sit around their house these days and are quite able to take out the garbage and help with chores but are they willing? Should the parents be willing to take away some of the kids' privileges?

Are you ready, willing and able?

225
"Moving On"

Ron and Jim were given a pilot project. For nine months, they worked hard. The project was a success, and it was accepted countrywide. Ron and Jim were confident they would each get one of some 40 new positions created as a result. They did not. It was a shocker. Ron resigned almost immediately and moved on to become very successful in his new career. Jim accepted a lateral move to head office. He was generally a positive worker and a go-getter type, but he had a hard time getting back to his norm. In his new role, he just couldn't get over the wrong that he felt was done to him.

His boss took him to lunch. "Jim, everyone can see you are upset and angry. We can see it in your face and your body language. You have a choice now. Whether they were right or wrong in not giving you the promotion is beside the point. It is time you moved on. You are better than this."

Yes, things happen to us. Some we caused. Others just happened for causes out of our control. Are we going to accept it and move on, or are we going to behave like a victim and say, "Oh dear, oh dear, I just knew it was going to be like this? I am going to the garden to eat worms?"

The boss's talk to Jim was hard to swallow at first. Jim had been used to getting rapid and successive promotions and he didn't get them by being a sour puss. Almost overnight, as a result of a concerned boss, Jim moved on.

What do you have to move on from? Could it be a job experience, a tiff with a relative, getting disciplined in grade two for something you didn't do, or being betrayed in a love affair? There are all kinds of things we can move on from and it doesn't mean they were not significant. But we can't be frozen or hindered by an experience. Let me rephrase that. We can be, but will we allow it? Politicians have been humiliated in defeat but came back to win. Athletes have lost out and come back to win.

Holocaust survivors went on to be very successful in life.

"Although the world is full of suffering, it is full also of the overcoming of it."
— Helen Keller.

Do we roll over and play dead, or do we move on?

226
"Hinduism"

Hinduism is the third largest religion in the world, with 1.2 billion people - 15% of the world's population. It began in India as early as 2300 BC. However, Hindus may claim it always existed. There is no identified founder.

Its sources of beliefs and authority include many writings such as "Vedas" Upanishads and Bhagavad-Gita.

Its <u>core beliefs include:</u>

- God is "The Absolute," a universal spirit
- Everyone is a part of God (Brahman) like drops in the sea
- People worship gods and goddesses
- God is eternal and everlasting- always was and always will be
- Jesus is a teacher who is an incarnation of Vishnu, a supreme god
- Jesus is one of many sons of God
- Jesus' death did not atone for sins, and He did not rise from the dead
- There is no Holy Spirit
- Reincarnation follows death to a better or worse life depending on behavior
- Meditation and yoga will release one from reincarnation after several lifetimes

Rites/Rituals and commands include:

- Worship of stones and wooden idols in temples and homes is common
- Meditation
- Wearing of robes and shaved heads
- Yoga, chanting, breathing exercises,

Hinduism is said to be the foundation of New Age and Transcendental Meditation.

"Big Picture Little Picture"

You have heard the expression, "You can't see the forest for the trees." The origin of this expression, or "idiom," dates to the mid-1500s.

Isn't the forest made up of trees? So, what's the point? Since I can see the trees, I can see the forest. The point is that we can get so tied up in the little things that we miss the whole point of the big things. Yes, individual trees make up the forest, but it is possible for us to be so hung up on an individual tree that we lose perspective of the forest. Are the trees and the forest related? Of course. The little things are definitely important. BUT.

What is the big picture in life? Is there a big picture or overall purpose for us? Are we allowing ourselves to be so distracted by the little picture that we are missing out on the big picture? And there is no doubt that a little thing can distract from the big picture.

Examples I hear:

"You spend so much time cleaning the dishes after dinner that you miss time socializing with your guests."

"Joe is so obsessed with how he looks that he has trouble with relationships."

"Mary is so particular in how people mispronounce words that she irritates people, and they don't enjoy the conversation."

"The athlete mingles too much with the fans and is not focused on the race."

"You didn't put in an offer on the house you like because you didn't like the paint color in the bathroom."

"A child wants to tell you how he aced the test at school, but the parent keeps reminding the child that his shoe is untied."

"People are so wrapped up in their political party that they can't see the direction their country is headed."

What things do you get wrapped up in that prevent you from seeing or focusing on the big picture? Are you interested in "winning the battle rather than winning the war"? Whoops, another idiom.

228

"Generational Differences" – *(When I Was a Boy)*

It is common to compare the different generations. To what extent
are these comparisons true? Do you relate?

When I was a boy, Kids didn't talk back
Today: Parents don't talk back

When I was a boy, Playing inside was rare.
Today: Playing outside is rare.

When I was a boy, We were not told to go to our rooms.
Today: Most rooms are entertainment centers.

When I was a boy, Kids obeyed the teachers
Today: Teachers obey the kids

When I was a boy, my parents ran the household.
Today: Where are the parents

When I was a boy, We dressed for church
Today: What's a church

When I was a boy, We got a dime on Saturday night.
Today: What's a dime.

When I was a boy, We ate what our mother served.
Today: "I don't like that mom. What else do you have."

When I was a boy, Parents, not schools, raised their children.
Today: Not sure.

When I was a boy, I was still a boy.
Today: He used to be a boy.

229

"Vacations"

Vacations we need to take
If you don't think so, give yourself a shake.
We are all different as to where to go.
Some like the beach, others love the snow.
We take the one we can afford
Whether it is a Saturday drive or a cruise ship, we board.
It's wise to save for it rather than charge on the card
It will be depressing next year to stay in your yard.
Be prepared for the unexpected when it comes to the money.
It will cost more than you plan, so don't upset your honey
Ensure you and the partner agree on the destination
To avoid returning with your faces beaten in
Timing is important to be fair to all
Decide winter, spring, summer or fall
The length, too, has to be right
You don't want to spend all the time on your flight.
Pack what you think you need, and then take half of it out.
You don't want to be carrying all that luggage about
Allow for rat races and delays at airports
Whatever you do, don't forget your passports.
Plan the trip, but not for every minute.
Often, our best trip has time with nothing in it.
Leave some details with your family or friend
And enjoy every day to the end
Come back at least a day early before you get back to work
So you are not tired all week and being a real jerk.

230
"PASSIVE"

The chair of a meeting must recognize the different personalities of the participants. Otherwise, the aggressive person will dominate the conversation and score points, while the passive person will sit there and just go along. Such is also the case in family situations where parents must be sensitive to what is going on. The opposite of "aggressive" has to be "passive." While aggressive people have to win, passive people seem to be content to lose, or at least they are not willing to take on the risk of confrontation. The passive person will usually back down. This is unfortunate because such a person could have some valuable ideas, which are squashed by the aggressive person.

One dictionary says passive is: *"accepting or allowing what happens or what others do, without active response or resistance."* Sadly, this happens far too much in a society where the loud and aggressive seem to have more say and control than the quiet and passive.

Passive people can be more tolerant than they should be. They tend to be more submissive and agreeable than they should be. While there may be some situations in which the battle is not worth it, i.e., *"Who cares if you want to make a fool of yourself,"* there are times when we just can't sit back and allow the ridiculous to go on. Yes, there are times when we all have "to take the bull by the horns." This should be the case in business, politics, and relationships.

England stood passive as Hitler's Germany was permitted to have its way in Europe before the start of World War II. In our country, we have been too passive in allowing our government too much control over us. (*Oops, a political opinion- how did that get in there? Was that aggressive?*)

Some reasons for being passive include upbringing, low self-esteem, shyness, and, of course, fear. To get over all of these we may need to start practicing speaking up to gain confidence. Avoidance won't help.

> *I had to discover that a good purpose is bigger than my fear of taking a stand.*

Do you consider yourself passive? Why? Has it caused you to be quiet when you know you should have spoken up?

What small steps can you start to begin the process of speaking your mind?

See Aggressive- 146. Assertive-270

"Woke"

What is this latest fad of woke?
Is it just another trend that will eventually go broke?
Are the woke really awake, or are they asleep?
They are trying to force the rest not to make a peep.
Can't they see that a woman is a woman And can't be a man?
Where is this coming from? Who gives them the right?
To make the rest of us stay out of sight?
Who is to say that facts are to be rejected?
They are pressuring our kids. They want all to be affected.
Who are they to tell me what my kids should read?
I will raise them, not you. Knock it off with your greed.
They say they want to correct social injustice.
The way they are trying is not even justice.
Woke wants to rewrite the past because they say it was wrong.
But lying about it won't change the song
Racism was, and some still exist
But woke is still racism, and that's what they miss
People who made mistakes also did some good
If you lived back then, what would you do if you could
They thought Black Lives Matter was a great plan
Was it great that their leaders took a lot of money and ran?
You can't blame the world for the errors of a few
And you can't cancel me just because you are you
Woke is just another tool
It's a pawn to make us look a fool.
Wake up woke
You are being a joke.

232
"Screech"

I was always told:

Newfoundland traded salt cod with countries like Jamaica in the West Indies for rum. It was imported in wooden barrels which contained the rum for up to seven years. By that time, the wood in the barrels had absorbed a good chunk of rum. The barrels were often sold to make furniture or to be used as a storage tubs.

However, it became common to practice to throw a gallon or so of water into the empty barrel for about ten days, give it a swish around every day, and lo and behold, the absorbed rum in the wood was released into the water, and voila "cheap liquor" aka "swish." Then the barrels could still be used for other purposes.

This practise eventually died out. However, Newfoundland continued to import rum and developed and distributed its own brand known as Screech. Screech has been used in various ceremonies in Newfoundland and Labrador as an initiation tool to make honorary Newfoundlanders out of the nonnative "Come from Aways" (CFA's).

An expert told me, "One company held an annual screech ball tournament. Every batter was obligated to take a sip of screech before each pitch. Making it to the base required another sip. The same is true for the second base and tird base. If the rooner madt it ome, he had to take one other zip.

Tis cept repitting and kept repeating **over a**n over again un**til u no** what hic hic appened? ...   All the players in **each team started** to gt hic get blrrrrrryyy i's til they cooddn walk or talk anymore. And hic, um, das da waaay it weeent in the ....game.

He couldn't say who won the game.

233

"Coincidence"

In 1993 I had a judo student whose family moved away. He was a nice kid from a nice family. They told me where they were moving to Tweed, Ontario.

Five years later, my wife and I were on a long drive and happened to be within driving distance of Tweed. "Let's go find Ernie," I said, having no idea where he lived.

I pulled up to a grocery store and said, "Maybe he is in here," thinking in the back of my mind to look him up in a phone book. I walked into the store down the first aisle, and there was Ernie. Coincidence?

Is it a coincidence that people who work harder are more successful?

Is it a coincidence that determined people are more likely to be successful?

Is it a coincidence that positive, kind, friendly people have more friends?

Is it a coincidence that those who plan and try different options find more answers?

Is it a coincidence that frugal people are less likely to be broke all the time?

Is it a coincidence that people who read more are more informed?

Is it a coincidence that those who get a good night's rest and get up early achieve more?

Is it a coincidence that people who complain and criticize accomplish less?

A teenager couldn't understand that he got in a lot of fights. When he was asked where he hung out most of the time, he answered, "In downtown bars." I wonder if the fights were coincidences.

Is it a coincidence that people who pray more are more at peace?

234
"History"

I regret not being more interested in history. In school, it seemed that dates and events were more significant than how they relate today.

During my history course in my first year of university, I was totally flabbergasted at how much history I didn't know. The more I pick up about history now, the more I see that too many of us haven't learned from our past. I am also learning that the truth of history is either being covered up or twisted for no other reason than, yes, get this, "There are people who actually want history to be repeated, and sadly, it's the bad things they want to be repeated."

The fall of major empires had certain things in common that, to one degree or another, contributed to their downfall. They include from my observation:
- Internal political corruption
- Underestimating outside threats
- Sexual depravity
- Lack of unity of purpose and direction
- Greed and personal ambition of a few
- Lack of concern for its own people
- Loss of traditional morals and values
- Economic waste
- Too much control over its people. Enslaving them.
- Hiding the truth and lying to its own citizens.
- Disarming its citizens.

Which ones can you identify in our country? Are we repeating history? They say, "Every time that history repeats itself, the price goes up."

"If history repeats itself, and the unexpected always happens, how incapable must man be of learning from experience." - **George Bernard Shaw**

"Those who cannot learn from history are doomed to repeat it."
– **Winston Churchill**

235
"Misbehaving"

Why do people misbehave?

Discuss or think about these:

1.   Don't know how to behave or perform properly
2.   Face obstacles that keep them performing well
3.   Don't know or accept their responsibilities
4.   Fear negative consequences
5.   Don't fear negative consequences
6.   Don't understand the importance of performing well
7.   Don't want to follow authority
8.   Aren't reinforced for performing well
9.   Spoiled as a child
10.   Have personal limitations
11.   Experienced traumatic experiences
12.   Learned from poor examples
13.   Never disciplined or held accountable
14.   Succumbed to peer pressure
15.   Absent father or mother
16.   No respect or regard for authority
17.   Mental illness
18.   Addictions
19.   Inherited behavior
20.   Other reasons

236
"Judaism" (JEWS)

<u>Judaism is</u> relatively small in the world, i.e., millions.

Approximately 1500 BC, God called Abraham to be the beginning of those who became known as Hebrews. The blood line continued in Isaac and Jacob, the 12 sons of Jacob, down to the Jews of today. Their history is well outlined in religious and secular books.

<u>Source of Beliefs and authority come from</u>

The Old Testament (Tanakh- includes Torah) and The Talmud – explanation of Tanakh

<u>Core Beliefs: (varies depending on the sect)</u>

- Orthodox Jews - God is spirit- all-powerful and compassionate
- To other Jews – God is impersonal, unknowable, and defined in several ways.
- One God
- Jesus is seen as a false Messiah
- Orthodox Jews believe a messiah will restore the Jewish kingdom
- Holy Spirit is another name for God, or is God's love and power
- For some, Salvation comes by prayer and obeying the Law of God
- The obedient will live forever with God
- There will be a physical resurrection
- Some do not believe in a conscious life after death
- Israel is the promised land given to Abraham by God

<u>Rites/Rituals and commands</u> include

- Sabbath is Friday Evening to Saturday morning
- Circumcision of males
- Many Holy Days and festivals
- Jerusalem is considered the Holy City

"Financial Statements – Definitions"

<u>Balance Sheet</u> – details your assets (what you own) and liabilities (what you owe) and your equity (what you are worth).

<u>ASSETS</u>: Things of value that you own. For business, the amount is shown for what you paid for it. For personal, you show the value of what it is worth now- i.e. Market Value.

<u>Current Assets</u>- Also known as liquid assets, as in cash or easily converted to cash. They include:
- Banks accounts
- Cash in your top bureau drawer or under the mattress
- Investments- stocks shares- certificates
- People who owe you money (accounts receivable)

<u>Fixed Assets</u> – These are things that are not easily converted into cash
- Real estate property - home, cottage
- Vehicles
- Maybe pension plans, i.e., Retirement savings plan

<u>Short-term Liabilities</u> – money owed and due within the next twelve months
- Mortgage payments
- Loan payments
- Credit card payments
- Line of credit and overdraft
- Bills, payables - Taxes, etc

<u>Long term Liabilities</u>
- Mortgages/Loan etc

Note: For personal statements, short-term and long-term are combined)

<u>Equity:</u> Total Liabilities minus Total Assets

This is your NET WORTH if you were to sell everything and pay off everything.

P&L. I&E: Profit and Loss or Income and Expense all mean "What comes in and what goes out."

See also: Balance sheet page 69

238
"Leasing or Borrowing"

Which is the best? I got asked this question many times in my banking career and business career. In some ways, it's like trying to answer the question, "What would you rather do or go fishing."

The answer is "depends". If someone is flushed with cash, for the most part, it really doesn't matter. You can buy what you want in any way you want. Leasing and borrowing can have advantages and disadvantages, depending on the circumstances of you as an individual or your business.

Compare and contrast. You decide.

Leasing	**Borrowing**
Like renting – not owning	Not renting - buying to own Cost interest.
Cost interest - usually more	
Interest rates can vary	Interest rates can vary.
Usually requires no down payment	Usually requires a down payment
Terms vary (negotiable)	
Monthly payment is usually lower	Terms vary (negotiable). Monthly payment is usually higher
You don't own the car at the end	
Usually, trade before the warranty is out	You own the car at the end
In business, it is all tax-deductible	You are responsible for repairs after the warranty.
You pay the taxes monthly	
No equity in the car	In business, the depreciation is tax deductible
No worries about reselling at the end	
Penalties to cancel	You pay all the taxes upfront
Less control	Building equity in car
Mileage restrictions	You can sell or trade by paying off the loan
New cars more often	
In business – it doesn't show as a liability or asset	No penalties for paying off
	More control
	No mileage restriction
	New car are not so often
	In business – it does show as liability and asset.

239
"Ambition"

Ambition is not a bad word. It is admirable to want to get ahead and improve our lot in life. It gives us vision and something to strive for. : It is said that, "He who has no vision will perish." No, it doesn't mean he will freeze to death. It does mean he has little to look forward to.

It will freeze to death. It does mean he has little to look forward to.

However, it is important not to allow our ambition to ruin our lives. Selfish ambition for the sake of power and greed is not the same as one's ambition, that wants to provide for his/her family or to fulfill a worthwhile cause.

How much are you willing to sacrifice for your ambition? Does it make you a workaholic who breaks up the family for the sake of your ambition?

Jim's ambition to be promoted to a larger division prevented him from having a good relationship with his children. He rarely got to have dinner with his family.

George's ambition had him attending every social event in the company. He got to party a lot just to rub elbows with the who's who.

Sure, we all should work hard and aim high, but sacrificing families, values and dignity could well lead to regret.

Bill was challenged once by an ambitious co-worker, "If you want to get a head, you need to be seen hanging out with the right people." Instead of following the suggestion, Bill decided to be the best he could at his job. He produced great results, got promoted, and still had a happy family.

Ambition is certainly the path to success, and such desire is to be congratulated. We should not be afraid to set high goals or allow others to dissuade us, but let us not walk over and trample people to get there, and let us not allow our ambition and EGO leave the ones we love in the dust.

Ambitious? Go for it! But check the motivation and weigh the costs.

240
"Self-Control"

There are a lot of controlling people in the world. That's another topic for another day. Let's talk about our self-control. Are we able to control ourselves?

Can you pass by a bowl of chocolate-covered almonds and not grab a handful? Can you resist that second piece of dessert? How about this? Can you allow those who disagree with you to finish their sentences without you interrupting them? Tough, isn't it? It sure takes a lot of self-control.

What are you like when someone else is driving the car? Are you able to control yourself being a back seat driver? Can you stop drinking or taking drugs when you want? Do you control yourself when in an argument? Does your voice get louder? Do your words get quicker? Do you begin insulting? How is your temper? Are you explosive? Are you impulsive, compulsive, repulsive, controlling of others? Do you get moody when things don't go right? Just asking.

Proverbs 25:28 says, *"Like a city whose walls are broken through is a person who lacks self-control."* Are your walls broken down?

When we lack self-control, we are slaves to whatever we desire and whatever emotions we have. We think we have freedom, but we don't.

Self- control is listed in the Bible as a virtue. It is the key to many things, including success, great relationships, our own mental well-being, physical health, and more.

"If you learn self-control, you can master anything." Anonymous

241
"Unity"

Mother Theresa was quoted as saying: *"Only humility will lead us to unity, and unity will lead to peace."* That's a deep and loaded quote that warrants more than one page of commentary.

Unity or 'lack of' is a major issue in the workplace, families, governments, and all organizations. But what does unity really mean? Even though definitions of unity include words like oneness, harmony, unity doesn't mean that we all have to be the same. It is possible to have a team that has a variety of people with varying talents to be very united. Such was the case as shown in the movie, "The Dirty Dozen" which saw a bunch of misfits pull together and achieve success. Sports teams unite to win a championship, yet the individual team members have different personalities and interests outside of the team's goal.

The key to unity is a common vision or purpose.

When the well-known Helen Keller says, *"Alone, we can do so little but together, we can do so much,"* I don't think she means a bunch of people, each having a different purpose. Unity works when all involved are determined to meet the same goal and are willing to put aside their individual differences and agendas for the sake of achieving those goals.

It is a common vision and purpose that unites people, and it is quite easy to observe the results of that missing common vision in local and world politics, in the workplace, and in families. Division and not unity reap havoc, reducing achievement and breaking down communication and relationships. Countries and organizations fall for lack of unity.

"We must learn to live together as brothers or perish together as fools." - Martin Luther King.

Unity is strength. Disunity is weakness.

Included in the requirements for unity as outlined in the Bible are:

"Love" - "Like Mindedness"- "Humility" – "Peace" – "Service" –

"Forgiveness" – "Gentleness" – "Sympathy" – "Compassion"

As opposed to personal agendas, selfish ambition, pride, and conceit.

242
"How we really feel"

"How are you feeling?"
"I am fine."
"Really?"
In the majority of cases, those are the words of many opening greetings. Well, what do you expect? Do you really think we would answer with the truth? Maybe for close friends and family, I guess.
 Let's start again.

How are you feeling?
"Well, not good. My arthritis has been acting up in the past two weeks. I am not getting along with my spouse. I can't pay my bills, and I am disappointed with what the neighbor did yesterday. And I think the government sucks."
How do we really feel? What do we really think? Do others need to know? Do they really care when they ask the question like, "How are you"?
Are we really just being polite in the way they answer, or are we lying to cover up when we give the short answer, "I am fine, thank you."
We want to be polite by asking, and we don't really what to tell people what is really going on. We get that. But do we ever let our guards down and make ourselves vulnerable and tell everything? And do we really want to know everything? Sure, there are exceptions, like those who will tell all and want to know all, but let's face it, there is a place for privacy and a s time and a place where we can come clean and be totally honest with those we can trust.
Sometimes we need to open up, and sometimes we need to shut up.

243

"Emergency Room"

Two days before my flight overseas, my infection had not healed from the antibiotic. It was now Monday, a provincial holiday, and all the walk-in clinics were closed. Emergency, here I come!

Being a pastor, I wore my hospital clergy passes around my neck, thinking maybe it would give me some pull just in case there was a lineup. The numbers I saw waiting when I entered the check-in area were not encouraging. I took a number as instructed, and "great," I was called within 10 minutes. I explained my situation to the registration nurse. She was very polite and efficient. She then gave me a clip board and asked me to provide the usual bottle sample and sit in the waiting area until my name was called and gave me those pleasant words, "Your wait time will be about five hours."

 "Surely you can do better than that. I am crazy in pain, and I am leaving the country soon", only brought a reply of, "There is nothing else we can do."

Five hours of waiting to look forward to. "You gotta be kidding!" I sat and sat and sat and waited, thinking, "why can't I get rushed in? After all, I am in pain, and I should be a priority?"

As the minutes and hours ticked by, I slowly became familiar with the other faces and situations of the 20-plus people in the waiting area. To my shame, it took me a while to get over, thinking that I should be the priority. They were all a priority. Kids and seniors with a variety of ailments, including a man in a wheelchair with a broken leg, a lady with a constant cough, a man who had fallen and had been brought in by ambulance with an egg size bump on his forehead, a black and blue swollen face, and a neck brace and the list went on. They were all there for an emergency and not just for something to do on this family holiday.

I was humbled. I did get to see a doctor and I left with my prescription just minutes under the five-hour projected time. The staff, when I saw them, were excellent. For curiosity I googled the average wait time in hospital emergencies across the country. It was staggering. The reason given – "cuts back prior to Covid."

244
"Faith Again"

Don't give me that faith nonsense; I want proof."

But the true definition of faith is believing in something for which we don't have proof.

One dictionary says, "Faith is the belief that is not based on proof." It doesn't take a lot of faith to believe something for which we have proof. It doesn't take faith to believe the sun exists. We have proof of that. But it takes faith to believe that we will get through difficult times.

When most of us think of faith, religion comes to mind, and we should ask, "Well, what does the Bible say?" I am glad you asked. Here are the New King James definitions and the New English translation from the famous faith chapter in Hebrews 11. They are very close.

"Now faith is the substance of things hoped for, the evidence of things not seen." New King James Version.

"Now faith is being sure of what we hope for, being convinced of what we do not see." New English Translation.

Both these definitions say faith is believing something for which we don't have proof. The evidence may even be against what we believe or want.

People say that faith is about trust and confidence, and faith does involve trust and confidence. Such is the case when you can say I have faith that my plane will get me there because I have been on airplanes many times before. You trust airplanes because we have proof that they can fly. That is faith, however not a lot of faith, since you have the evidence and experience. Some say faith is merely positive thinking or a positive attitude. While a positive attitude has its benefits, faith is stronger than that.

The real question is, "In what or whom do I put my faith." The Bible says the only way to heaven is to have faith in God.
Max Lucado quotes: "Faith is not the belief that God will do what you want.
It is the belief that God will do what is right."
Do you have faith enough in God regardless of life's circumstances?

245
"Mount St. Helens"

Wikipedia highlights include the following:

On May 18, 1980, the volcano in Washington DC (Northwestern US) erupted, making it the greatest volcanic explosion ever recorded in North America. It had been dormant since 1857. An earthquake triggered the eruption and a huge landslide and avalanche. Volcanic ash and stone spewed up to 15 miles high at speeds up to 300 mph at temperatures of 350 degrees. Darkness for hundreds of miles resulted. Millions of tons of ash fell over an area of 22,000 square miles. Some of it circled the earth within a two-week period.

Fifty-seven people and thousands of animals were killed, and approximately 200 square miles of trees were flattened from the blast that literally blew the top off the 8500-foot-high mountain.   Damage at the time exceeded $1 billion (equivalent to 3.4 billion in 2023 value).

In the aftermath water and debris cut three canyons in a period of nine hours. One of them was 140 feet deep, 1000 feet wide and 2000 feet long.

Rapid-moving water picked up rocks, sand, gravel, and trees and cut like liquid sandpaper through just about anything in its path. The sides of the new canyon at Mount St. Helens have hundreds of layers, just like the Grand Canyon.

See Grand Canyon (page 75)

246

"Fake News"

On October 30, 1938, at 8 p.m., Orsen Wells, author and popular radio show host, played a hoax on his audience. He narrated that the earth was being invaded by Martians. This live broadcast told how thousands of people were being killed by aliens from outer space. On the following day, October 31, the newspaper carried stories of the effects of the broadcast. One headline read, *"Fake Radio 'War' Stirs Terror Through U.S."*

Wells' mock news story supposedly scared thousands of people who actually believed that Martians were attacking New Jersey. Many people were angry at the show and the radio station. Reactions to the show included a 76-year-old man standing ready to fight with his shotgun. Some news reports said people fled their homes, sought refuge in different places, and called the police.

What was intended to be entertainment was taken seriously by some, especially if they tuned in part way through. Orsen Wells's popularity grew as a result.

How does that fake isolated broadcast from 1938, with its exaggerated reaction, compare to today's media? Today's news and the reaction to the news is all too often exaggerated, just as it was then. The bias of the media, particularly when it comes to political news, cannot be trusted.

- Less than 2 inches of snow that was normally ignored in the past is often warned and presented as a blizzard.
- The preferred candidate or political party of the media can be given a favorable positive spin, while the opposing side can get little or negative airtime.
- Instigated fear is common when it comes to popular agendas e.g., climate change and global warming.
- A small protest can be presented as large, while a large protest can be presented as small and insignificant or not reported at all.
- Social media contains lots of manipulated stories and, images, and uninformed opinions.

What's worse? Much of the public falls for the "Fake News."

247

"Phobic"

A search of the word phobic or phobia takes you back to the Greek word *Phobos*. It means "fear of anxiety of something real or imagined."

Meriam Webster dictionary's first meaning says <u>"having an intolerance or aversion"</u>.

Wait a minute! Fear and intolerance are two different words.

Synonyms for fear include terror, dread, anxiety, and horror. Synonyms for intolerance include bigotry and prejudice. Because I fear something or someone, it doesn't mean I am prejudiced. Because I am intolerant, it doesn't mean I fear something.

Phobic today has taken on a whole new meaning. The supposed tolerant people of society are telling us that if we don't agree with something or someone, then we are phobic. They have even gone as far as to use the word "hatred" and "racist." What's with that?

I can fear without hating. I can disagree without fearing or hating. I can refuse to affirm or support something without fearing or hating it.

The word phobic is being tagged incorrectly onto a number of things today. That, in itself, is making people fear and be phobic. Now, I fear that freedom of speech is being taken away by the word police.

We can disagree with many things but that doesn't mean we fear them.

Fear and disagreement are entirely different. Who are the most phobic - The ones who disagree but don't fear and have a right to their own opinions and values, or the ones who fear opinions and often time truth from the other side and want to silence them simply because they don't agree?

"Disagreement" and "phobic" are not the same.

248
"Wisdom from Proverbs"

<u>Some Good Advice</u>

"Where *there is* no counsel, the people fall;
But in the multitude of counselors, *there is* safety." Proverbs 11:14

"The way of a fool *is* right in his own eyes,
But he who heeds counsel *is* wise." Proverbs 12:15

"Listen to counsel and receive instruction,
That you may be wise in your latter days." Proverbs 19:20

"If you have been foolish in exalting yourself, Or if you have devised evil, *put your* hand on *your* mouth." Proverbs 30:32

"Happy is the generous man, the one who feeds the poor." Proverbs 22:9

"The labor of the righteous *leads* to life, The wages of the wicked to sin and death." Proverbs 10:16

"What a shame—yes, how stupid! to decide before knowing the facts!"
Proverbs 18:13

"When pride comes, then comes shame; But with the humble, *is* wisdom." Proverbs 11:2

"Pride leads to arguments; be humble, take advice, and become wise." Proverbs 13:10: "Pride *goes* before destruction and a haughty spirit before a fall." Proverbs 16:18

"Pride ends in destruction; humility ends in honor." Proverbs 18:12

249

"Nonsense"

Nonsense is a narrow channel that separates two islands. It is about 20 feet long and wide and deep enough at high tide to get a small row-boat through.

Sam, Dave, and I had a lobster license when we weren't quite 14 years old. One of our lobster traps was on one side of "nonsense," and another trap was on the other side of "nonsense." We tried to time it so we could get through the channel rather than having to row all the way around the island.

It was early May. Some snow was still on the ground and some ice still clung to the edges of the shoreline. By 5:30 a.m., we were in our boat and on our way. We had our parents 'permission, but they were always uneasy about our morning venture. Two more traps left. One on each side of "nonsense". The water looked low, but we went for it after we pulled the one trap. No lobster in it.

We got half-way through, and the boat got stuck. Ocean water is always going in and out, so we nudged a few inches each time the water went in our favor until we were a half boat length away from getting through. To lighten the load, Sam volunteered to get out of the boat and push from the shore while Dave and I pushed using our oars. We timed the next push for when the tide came our way.

Push now!

We all pushed together. The boat broke lose and made it through the channel, and Sam was pulled into the cold, freezing water behind us. With the pull of the boat and the slippery shoreline, he simply could not recover to stay on the shore. He was in the water about chest high. Dave and I pulled him in. Sam was wet and cold but that was the least of our worries. We had to get home before school started and our parents could not know of the mishap.

We pulled the boat to shore, made a fire, stripped Sam and dried his clothes, and went home and made it to school on time. We did pull the other trap. No lobster. Our parents were none the wiser until about forty years later.

250
"Consequences"

If you do "this," then that."

A consequence is the result of an action. "They say" that some people can reach 25 years old before they fully catch on to this concept. That may be an exaggeration but those in the know about child development tell us that kids are incapable of rationalizing the concept of consequences simply because their brains have not developed. Anyone who has seen children toss their food on the floor or put chocolate cake through their hair knows that. Sources tell me that getting the effect part of "cause and effect" begins around age 6, improving until age 13. That's why, as parents, we need to manage our children and our expectations of them with age-appropriate methods using rewards and 'dare I'll say, discipline for inappropriate behavior.

Without getting into child development, of which I am not educated, we can pick up a few common-sense things from our own children. But should we be more concerned about the consequences for our adults today? Is the lesson of consequences getting through to people in society? What about our education system, social reforms, and laws?

Laws being passed or not being passed have consequences. In some states in the US, those stealing items under $1000 are not charged. Consequence – shop lifting is rampant even in broad daylight while security guards watch.

Canada has been passing laws that are taking away our freedoms. Are we considering the consequences?

Life is full of consequences which may be rewards or punishments. Do we consider them? We are free to choose and act as we want, but we may not be free of the consequences.

Emotional outbreaks of anger have consequences. Being irresponsible has consequences.

Some of us are still experiencing consequences for our actions from our younger days. Are we counting the cost?

251
"Capitalism"

The dictionary meaning of capitalism: "economic and political system in which a country's trade and industry are controlled by private owners for profit."

 A couple of key words in that definition are 'private' and 'controlled.' One word that is not in there is "government."
While we understand the need for government, capitalism works best when we as individuals are free to work and carry on our own business affairs as we wish, provided, of course, we are not causing harm to others, and we abide by some reasonable guidelines. From a six-year-old running a lemonade stand to large corporations, capitalism says we are free to compete with the rest of the world and earn profits.

Capitalism has been the engine that has made many countries thrive. Despite having some flaws, which all the political and economic 'isms' have, capitalism has the most benefits. The main opponents of capitalism are communism and socialism, with the government calling the shots.

<u>Just my Opinion and observation</u>: The world is at a crossroads with its "isms". Too many countries with their power-hungry ideologies are against capitalism. Instead of allowing society to figure out things for themselves with their blood, sweat, and tears, along with their ingenuity and resourcefulness, some governments think they should be running everything and deciding who gets what. Of course, they make it attractive by offering free everything. The extreme end-result of this is countries like Cuba and North Korea, whose system of government has total control of its people and all economic methods. Is it working for them? There are other countries that are somewhere in between Capitalism and Communism. And even in capitalist countries like Canada and the US, government interference is getting a bit obvious. (This is an understatement.)

<u>Still opinion:</u> Our education system, run by some radicals, is brainwashing people with the carrot of "everything should be free." The potential threat to capitalism that is creeping in is the control of government by big business partnering with segments of government for mutual benefit.

252

"Respect For Elders"

When I was a boy (Oh no, not again). Seriously.

At school, whenever the principal, the minister, or anyone who was an adult came into our room, we all stood up. We sat down when the teachers told us to sit down. It was a big deal, and it was the way we were taught to show respect for our elders.

Don't get me wrong. We were certainly not a bunch of goodie-two-shoes, but we knew our place, and we knew when to show some manners and regard for others. When we went into someone else's house, we sat on a chair and did not tear through the house, jump on the couch, or do anything that made us appear to show disregard for someone else's property. Did we go too far? I don't think so.

What has happened? Kids are telling adults what to do today. The last time I went into a school classroom, I was shocked. I saw desks turned around, facing away from the teacher. I saw caps on heads, some turned in every which way direction. I saw feet and legs up on desks. The list goes on. I have been told recently that kids argue with teachers, shout at teachers, and, in some cases, even hit teachers. Teachers have no authority when it comes to discipline.

What has the world come to? What happened to "yes sir," "no sir," "yes mam," and "no mam"?

And we wonder where it comes from. It starts in the home, for sure. Of course, some teachers will tell you that many parents are the problem. Parents need to do a better job. But then again, is it all the parents' fault, or is it the way society is? Is it any different on the streets or in the workplace when it comes to discipline?

Can we blame them? I am seeing the same thing in government institutions, which are not being held accountable. Funny about that.

"I am old school. I believe in having good manners, respecting my elders, and helping others when I can." - Unknown.

253
"Communication – Responsibility"

Generally speaking, when an employee is asked how communication is, the response is: "I communicate well, but the people around me don't." What is interesting is that no matter who you ask, the answer is usually the same. What this tells us is that everyone else has it wrong except the one being asked. The blame is always on the other person, meaning no one is taking responsibility for it or admitting they are the problem. You see the problem here, don't you? Say "yes". No one is taking responsibility for communication. That means we have three problems: a responsibility problem, an attitude problem and communication doesn't improve.

Until we each take responsibility for how we communicate, we will not be able to fix it.

"Communication is everybody's responsibility, so stop blaming others."

That is the message we all need to hear. If we all took that seriously, 'dollars to donuts' communication should improve. This means

You decide:
- To consider your words or not.
- Pay attention or not.
- To be considerate or inconsiderate
- To let it go or hold it in
- Confront or leave it alone
- To be aggressive, passive, or assertive
- To control your emotions or not
- To react or respond – positively or negatively

> *The price of greatness is responsibility.* - Winston Churchill
>
> *"You cannot escape the responsibility of tomorrow by avoiding it today"* Abraham Lincoln

- To point your finger at yourself or someone else
- To learn and improve or to remain stagnant

Are you ready to do all of this? Are you willing to do all of this? Are you able to do all of this?

254
"Fossils"

According to National Geographic website:

- Fossils are the preserved remains, or traces of remains, of ancient animals and plants.
- Fossilization is the process of remains becoming fossils.
- Most organisms decompose fairly quickly after they die.
- For an organism to be fossilized, the remains usually need to be covered by sediment soon after death. Sediment can include the sandy seafloor, lava, and even sticky tar.
- Over time, minerals in the sediment seep into the remains. The remains become fossilized.
- Fossilization usually occurs in organisms with hard, bony body parts, such as skeletons, teeth, or shells. Soft-bodied organisms, such as worms, are rarely fossilized.
- Fossils of ancient marine animals called ammonites have been unearthed in the highest mountain range in the world, the Himalayas in Nepal. This tells scientists that millions of years ago, the rocks that became the Himalayas were at the bottom of the ocean.
- Fossils of an ancient giant shark, a megalodon (*Carcharocles megalodon*), have been found in the landlocked U.S. state of Utah. This tells scientists that millions of years ago, the middle of North America was probably entirely underwater.

Common language: a fossil is the remains of a living organism that had a rapid burial. Fossils are formed in a very short time. Soft tissue like flesh decomposes, leaving bones/skeletons.

Question: What caused the sudden burial?

255
"Thankful"

An article in 'Psychology Today states that being thankful, or gratitude, improves our well-being and makes us feel good. I am sure you know that. Did you? Everybody knows that.

If everybody knows, why aren't more people more thankful? Here are some "thank you" quotes from well-known people.

"We must find time to stop and thank the people who make a difference in our lives." – John F. Kennedy.

"There's no happier person than a truly thankful, content person." – Joyce Meyer

"I'm thankful for each and every day. We never know when time is up." – Chuck Berry.

"There is no better way to thank God for your sight than by giving a helping hand to someone in the dark." – Hellen Keller.

"Gratitude is riches. Complaint is poverty." – Doris Day.

"Keep your eyes open to your mercies. The man who forgets to be thankful has fallen asleep in life." – Robert Louis Stevenson.

"O Lord that lends me life, lend me a heart replete with thankfulness." – William Shakespeare.

"Well, there's not a day goes by when I don't get up and say thank you to somebody." – Rod Stewart.

"And He took the seven loaves and the fish and gave thanks,"

Matthew 15:36

"Thank you for reading my book." – Fred Dyke

"Jesus Quiz (Answers)"

1. Where was Jesus born?   ***Bethlehem as prophesied***

2. Give five other names to which Jesus is referred. *Messiah – (Chosen One) Christ (anointed one) Emmanuel -(God with us) Lord (Master) Saviour. Jesus is also referred to as Wonderful, Counsellor, Prophet, Priest and King, Lamb of God, Son of God, Son of Man, and more.*

3. Were the wise men present on the night of his birth? *No, it could have been up to two years later.*

4. Who was the king who tried to kill baby Jesus?   *Herod, who was threatened by Jesus, being referred to as King.*

5. Why did he not succeed?   *Mary and Joseph took Jesus to Egypt.*

6. How old was Jesus when He went missing at the temple? *Twelve*

7. Did Jesus have brothers and sisters? *Yes. James, Joses, Simon, Jude, and unnamed sisters.*

8. What was the hometown where Jesus grew up?   *Nazareth*

9. Was Jesus baptized? *Yes, in the River Jordan by John the Baptist.*

10. What was the first recorded miracle of Jesus in the Bible? *Changing water into wine. His birth was also a miracle.*

11. How many days did Jesus spend in the wilderness?   *Forty*

12. How many times did Satan tempt Him there?   *Three*

13. Jesus responded each time by *quoting **THE WORD OF GOD**.*

14. How old was Jesus when He died?   **33**

15. How many people saw the risen Jesus?   *More than 500*

"Protesters"

There are legitimate protestors who exercise their rights to protest
Then there are some who think disrupting the public is best.
We have seen someone burn a car and get out on bail.
But mis pronoun someone and you may quickly be inside a jail.
It's funny, you know, but many protestors don't even know.
If they really have a cause or it is all for the show.
Some will protest at the drop of a hat
And many in the extreme are just fine with that.
Some don't worry about truth and facts,
They just go on emotions and deny the stats.
What is really a legitimate cause?
Is our government fair in enforcing the laws?
Oh, the naivety of some to fight for their rights
Offer them a job and they will be nowhere in sight.
For a stupid cause, the media will embellish the number in the crowd,
Legitimate marchers get no attention, and they are not even loud.
 Some legitimate protesters have brought about good change
Others simply seem to be in vain.
Protesters are justified in changing unjust rules.
Is it time parents just unite and walk out of schools?
Some protesters are pushing a bunch of lies.
Others don't get recognition regardless of the tries. Come
protesters, figure out which side is right.
Rather than going out, looking for a fight.

258
"Thinking"

How is your thinking doing? Do you think you got it right? Do you think everyone else has it wrong? Here are some things to think about today:

Explain this one: "You are not what you think you are, but what you think you are."

Do you really think for yourself, or do you simply regurgitate the opinions of others?

Is the news media determining how you think?

Has your thinking process changed in the last 10 or so years? How?

What do you think of yourself? Who are you?

> Are you the person you think you are?

> Are you the person you really are?

> Are you the person that others see?

"I think, therefore, I am?" What do you think that really means?

"As a person thinks, he is." Explain.

Do you express what you think, or do you express what you think others want to hear?

Is your thinking determined by your emotions and desires, or is it determined by values, logic, and principles?

Does truth change your thinking? Or do you stick with some ideology or popular opinion?

Does your thinking hold you back or push you forward?

Is your thinking preventing you from doing?

I think I have given you enough to think about. What do you think?

259

"Grammar"

<u>Which is correct to say?</u>

You and me are coming. Or You and I are coming.

Sheep is woolly **or** sheep are woolly

The yolk of an egg is white, or the yolk of the egg are white.

An apple a day keeps the nurse away.

You can lead a mare to water, but you can't make him drink.
Both my fathers-in-law are over 90 years old.

The bookeeper will keep a score for this quiz.

An electric train is going east at 60 mph, and the wind is blowing west at 40 mph. The smoke is blowing north at 20 mph.

Two goose or not to goose. That is the question.

A plane with 120 people crashed and killed 50 people. How many survivors were buried?

Add 20 pages to find the answers.

260
"Babies"

Have you looked at a newborn baby recently? Is there anything more beautiful? Nothing captures our attention more than the innocence, the newness, and the smell of a newborn baby cozied up in its blanket.

All births are miracles. It is a miracle and a mystery right from the start and conception when one tiny sperm cell, so small that millions of them together, would fit in the size of a tear drop. A single cell approximately 3 micrometers wide (.0003 of a millimeter) joined with an egg about 20 times bigger gets together with all of the information to grow into a human being that will eventually grow up and look like you and me, with its own personality.

This little baby, with its perfectly formed fingers, toes, eyes, lips, and more, comes complete with its own operating system, far more complex than the modern-day computer system called DNA (*deoxyribonucleic acid*).

DNA contains 215 petabytes of information. How much is that? The average computer has a terabyte of information which is 1000 gigabytes. One petabyte equals 1000 terabytes. Wow! We can't even imagine it. Everything from the color of the baby's eyes to the length of each toe has all been preprogrammed for this beautiful specimen which we call a baby that coos, cries, and feeds immediately after it is delivered from mom.

This baby's heart was formed and beating just 5 weeks after the cell fertilized the egg, and almost all of its organs were formed within 10 weeks.

Babies are indeed magic. They are gifts from God and His permission and conformation for life to continue.

"Make no mistake about why these babies are here — they are here to replace us." —Jerry Seinfeld.

Helen Keller was quoted as saying: *"My fingers are tickled to delight by the soft ripple of a baby's laugh."*

Pause for a moment and admire the magic, beauty, and miracle of a baby.

261
"More Inflation"

"Inflation is the price we pay for those government benefits everyone thought were free."

"Inflation devalues money."

"Inflation is as violent as a mugger, as frightening as an armed robber, and as deadly as a hit man." - Ronald Reagan.

"INFLATION IS TAXATION WITHOUT LEGISLATION."
Milton Friedman

"Inflation is increasing wages to buy things that have gone up in price."

Or is? "Inflation raising prices to pay for increase wages.

"Do you have two tens for a five?"

"If inflation continues to soar, you're going to have to work like a dog just to live like one." **George Gobel**

"Years ago, it took four of us to bring home $20 worth of groceries.
Now, one can do it alone." We are getting stronger."

"Inflation makes the wealthy richer and the masses poorer."
James Cook

"Inflation is the parent of unemployment and the unseen robber of those who have saved."

Margaret Thatcher

262
"Christian Denominations"

Why are there so many denominations? Good question. Christianity started out as one. For some 300 years, the first disciples of Jesus and their converts started local churches throughout the Mediterranean, Europe, and Africa. It spread, despite the resistance from local beliefs as well as governments. The large and powerful Roman Empire then made Christianity its official religion. The universal or catholic church then became the Roman Catholic Church with the full authority of the government supporting it. This made it possible for even more growth.

Not that everyone always agreed on every doctrine, but the Roman Catholic Church did not have an official split until 1517 when Martin Luther posted 95 theses disputing various doctrines of the Romana Catholic Church. Other theologians helped the cause, and the Protestant Reformation began. Estimates are that today, there are 40,000 denominations calling themselves Christian. Why so many? While many claim to be Christian, they do not all follow the Holy Bible. Some have "weird and far-out ideas" on issues and doctrine that are outside what was originally intended and prescribed in the Bible. Culture, politics and individual ideas have certainly had an influence.

In the meantime, most of the denominations do agree on many of the major doctrines and beliefs of Christianity and agree to disagree on a number of areas, such as methods of worship, predestination, the second coming of Christ, and even views on various social issues.

The main point of agreement for most of them is that Jesus is God, who came to earth to redeem mankind. He died and rose again and will return.

See Christianity (page 296)

263

"Common Sense Again"

We have all been told to use our common sense. What is common to one is not necessarily common to another. When I was growing up, we all had common sense about how to behave around water. But it wasn't always common sense for visitors. If people don't know, they just don't know. Does that make sense? But does it make common sense?

The great inventor Thomas Edison said, *"The three great essentials to achieve anything worthwhile are, first, hard work; second, stick-to-itiveness; third, common sense."*
I get hard work. That's common sense, isn't it? I get stick-to-itiveness. That's common sense, isn't it? But what does Edison mean by common sense? He was a really smart guy and knew a lot of things.

The implied meaning of common sense is "truth or reality." While we are far from knowing everything, it makes common sense that we should seek the truth. Here is the problem today. Even though truth makes sense, people don't want it. People will do what people will do regardless of the truth. Now, that doesn't make sense. Truth is now an opinion. Now, that doesn't make common sense. But it does for those who believe that. Confused?

Is it common sense to accept the truth? Can we learn the truth? Of course. Then, we can learn common sense. It simply doesn't make sense to try to convince ourselves or others that a lie is truth. I guess common sense is not as common as it used to be.

It's too bad that the world is fighting over what the truth is in certain areas. Yes, there is room for opinion, but the common sense of it all is that there are certain truths that we would be wise to live with. Now, that's common sense.

264

"Carbon"

All reports indicate that Canada produces less than 2% of the world's carbon.

Trees need carbon to live. People need oxygen to live. People breathe out carbon, and trees take it in and convert it to oxygen.

Why the big push in Canada? Why the push to reduce it? Why the big carbon tax?

Sources say that the average tree absorbs 48 lbs of carbon a year, Canada has over 300 billion trees, and our trees absorb over 15 trillion pounds of carbon a year. Isn't carbon good for feeding the trees?

Did you know that:
- Carbon only makes up .04% (less than half of 1%) of the earth's atmosphere.
- Forest fires are a major contributor to carbon in the atmosphere.
- Volcanoes also contribute to carbon in the atmosphere.
- Many scientists are aware that the atmosphere **contained** much higher levels of carbon **than** in the past. We are still here.

- A recent Nanos Research survey showed that only 21% of Canadians think that the Canadian carbon tax is effective for reducing carbon and preventing climate change.

Is carbon all that bad? Are we getting the real truth?
Why, again, the carbon tax?
Could it be that the money is not going to reduce carbon?
Could it be that the money is being spent on excess waste by our government?
Could it be that the carbon is simply a means of control?
Is the carbon debate about science, politics, or money?
Think about it.

"Response When Confronted"

Which one of these is your normal response when someone confronts you?

1. "They are idiots and have no idea what they are saying."

2. "How can I get out of this without looking bad?"

3. "This reminds me of what happened when I was 12."

4. "Oh dear, I have failed again. I am useless."

5. "I will quickly return the criticism."

6. "I'll shift the blame to someone else."

7. "I will become defiant and attack; they'll back down."

8. "I will just simply deny it."

9. "I am so angry I could scream."

10. "I am so embarrassed. I just want to cry."

11. "Tomorrow, I will get a new job or move."

12. "I'll remain cool and get even later."

13. "I will acknowledge it, correct my behavior, and move on."

14. "I'll remain calm and respond, not taking it personally."

15. "This is an opportunity."

Let's face reality. We can all likely relate to all these responses. As we become mature, our natural response has hopefully moved down the list to the bottom three.

266
"Should"

"What did I do, and what should I have done?" What am I going to do, and what should I do?

We have been plagued and haunted by these questions. We do a lot because we want to, but is there such a thing as what we should or shouldn't do? Who is to say what we should and should not do? Should it depend on our own values and beliefs or pressure from others? Should we all do what we want to do and forget about what everyone else thinks we should do?

Should we forget about the "shoulds" or "shouldn'ts" like the "do's and don'ts"?

For me, I have concluded that there are things I should and shouldn't do, provided I am capable. Here are a few 'shoulds' for me:

1. "Be kind to others, whether they are idiots or not."

2. "'Stay in contact with my immediate family."

3. "Forgive others."

4. "Give people back the correct change."

5. "Return what I borrow."

6. "Keep my word and do what I say I am going to do."

7. "Try to be better than I was."

8. "Not ask a woman her age."

9. "Not ask an overweight lady if she is pregnant."

10. "Cover my mouth when I cough."

11. "Not spit in public."

12. "Tuck in my shirt tail."

13. "Not dominate every conversation."

14. "Put the toilet seat down."

15. "Pick up my socks"

16. "Expect nothing in return for doing my "shoulds'."

17. "Not tell others what they should do."

Go ahead. You should add it to the list.

"Bible Quiz 3"

1. Who was born first, John the Baptist or Jesus?

2. Who were the parents of John the Baptist>

3. Where was Jesus born?

4. What was the first openly recorded miracle by Jesus?

5. How many baskets were left over after Jesus fed the 5000?

6. What Gospel was written by a doctor?

7. Who is said to be the last disciple to die?

8. How many Bible books did John write?

9. Who did Moses drown with the closing of the Red Sea?

10. How many? Name them.

Answers page 335

268
"Windows of Life"

A friend and engineer, Ben Trip, who worked on the famous Canada Arm that has been used in the American space program, describes in his book,
"The Windows of Life" is a number of key things that have made it possible for life to exist on earth.

If one or more of these windows were not present on earth, I would not be writing this book, and you would not be reading it. These windows include:

<u>Water</u> – we need water in its various forms i.e., liquid water, vapor, and ice. We need fresh water, and we need the ocean's salt water. We need rainfall and cloud cover.

<u>The crust of the earth</u>- which floats on a molten interior, is relatively thin compared to the diameter of the earth. It can't be too thin so as not to be able to tolerate the stress from the gravitational pull of the sun and moon. It can't be too thick so as not to cause extreme weather conditions due to less heat loss.

<u>The earth's orbit around the sun</u> – is predictable and the same every year. It is basically circular with slight variation. The earth's distance from the sun is important. If it were closer or further away, our temperatures would be too hot or too cold for us to survive.

<u>The moon's distance from earth</u> – is responsible for the magnitude of our tides. Too close would mean more extreme tides. If it were half the distance, our tides would be four times higher. If it were one-quarter the distance, the tides would be sixteen times higher.

<u>The tilt of the earth</u> – is 23.5 degrees and gives us our seasons.

<u>The magnetic field of the earth</u> – helps with our navigation, using the compass, but more importantly, it attracts and traps particles from outer space, high above the earth, preventing them from penetrating our atmosphere.

Carbon Di-oxide – the ozone layer – oxygen – and more all make life on earth possible.

269

"Loveable"

After counselling hundreds of people John Ellis put some discoveries in a book called "3-4-3 Unlovable to Loveable."

He describes some interesting findings from people who experienced a traumatic event at a young age that seriously affected the rest of their lives. Such an event or a series of events could have been real or imagined. In either case, they left the child feeling unlovable.

Do you feel loved? Are you lovable or unlovable?

John explains that people who feel unloved respond in one of three ways. They rebel, withdraw, or perform. We all know rebellious people – they sort of get even or reject everybody. People who withdraw stick to themselves simply don't get involved. And we all know people who just excel in everything they do – "I'll show them." The responses are all ways that the unlovable person deals with who they are. Those are the first "3" in the 3-4-3.

The "4" are the four areas of our lives that we live which are Private – Public- Spiritual – Sexual. The responses may be different in each of these areas.

The final "3" characteristics of those who feel they are unlovable are Anger – Fear – Sadness.

If you get a chance, try to find John's book for more detail.

The key take-away- "You can become "lovable" again.

270
"Assertive"

A person who was passive decided to take assertiveness training. The result was a move from passive, jumping over assertive, and going on to be aggressive. She bragged, "I am assertive now. I won't be pushed around." She became bossy and pushy.

Some say that being assertive is halfway between passive and aggressive. I will let you debate that, but we do need somewhere in between the two so we can get along better. The many assertive people that I have encountered are very good conversationalists, and they get along well with others. They don't push people around, and they are not easily pushed around. They are very good at controlling their emotions.

Those who get mad or upset usually talk a lot and fast and often raise their voices. Being assertive by controlling emotions enables us to speak at a normal volume without rambling on in a loud, fast-talking manner that scares off potential passive people or antagonizes aggressive people. Short, slow, and low prevent them from saying things they shouldn't. It gives them control over their words, thus enabling the listener to hear and understand better. *I wish I had learned these things when I was very young. It would have kept my hair from standing up, and I would not have frothed at the mouth so much. LOL*

> *Controlling emotions to avoid aggressive behavior doesn't mean we can't be passionate, compassionate, and excited.*

Don't get me wrong, the assertive person is not immune to emotions, yet they do not take them out on others. Our emotions and our feelings are ours to control, and we must take responsibility for them. *"I may cut you off in traffic, but you determine your reaction or response. Will it be a middle finger?"*

Having said that, we need to be mindful of the feelings of others who are just maybe not very good at controlling their emotions.

What prevents you from being more assertive? What will you do about it?

Do you consider the feelings of others when you speak?

Being assertive is not about who wins. It is about getting it right while still being respectful.

"Funny Signs"

A radiator company had on its sign: "The Best Place in Town to Take a Leak."

The church sign reads: "The healing service is canceled due to the preacher being ill."

The beauty salon: 'United Hairlines."

Another: "Love is in the Hair."

"Without Freedom of Speech, we would not know who the idiots are."

"Tired of being harassed by your stupid parents? Move out and get a job while you still know everything."

"Honk, if you love Jesus. Text while driving if you want to meet Him."

"Adultery is a sin. You can't have your Kate and Edith, too."

"Prophecy classes canceled due to unforeseen circumstances."

"Wanted light house keeper. Must be able to climb stairs."

"Touching wires causes instant death. $200 fine."

"Don't let worries kill you. Let the church help."

"We guarantee fast service, no matter how long it takes."

272

"Holocaust"

This horrible event has been denied by many and sadly forgotten or not even recognized by too many.

Under Hitler's Nazism, Germany sponsored and systematically murdered over six million Jews.   German society persecuted them, took their property, killed them using gas chambers, guns, starvation, and bulldozed them into mass graves. Ugly! But we should know about it.

Why? The Nazis and parts of Europe were anti-Semitic. They hated the Jews and blamed the Jews for their own economic problems and even for Germany's loss in World War I. Although Anti-Semitism dates back thousand of years, the Nazis took it to a whole new level.

The Nazis believed that their race was superior, and the Jews were inferior, at the bottom of the barrel, and had to be eliminated to have what they called the superior "Aryan" race and prevent the Jews from corrupting them.

In 1941, it became legal in Germany and many parts of Europe, which were controlled by Germany, to shoot, gas, and kill Jews mercilessly. Killing centres were set up specifically for this purpose. Jews were transported to the centres by train under terrible conditions.

The Holocaust ended when Germany was defeated by Great Britain, the United States, and Russia.

"The Holocaust is not only a tragedy of the Jewish people, it is a failure of humanity as a whole." - Moshe Katsav.

Has the world learned?

"For evil to flourish, it only requires good men to do nothing". - Simon Wiesenthal

273

"Gerald Starks"

Who?

Gerald was the youngest of two unmarried sons. Gerald was born in 1929 on a small island community called Pool's Island, 100 yards from the mainland of Newfoundland and Labrador. Everybody knew Gerald and his family, who were typical in that they were not well off, yet in many ways ahead of their time, at least for the community. They had things like the first lawn mower on the island – the push kind. They had the first car in the community after a bridge connected the island to the mainland.

Gerald read a lot. He bought through the mail a full set of encyclopedias and read them from cover to cover. He learned things from his father, who was a capable seaman and carpenter. He was also mentored by an aunt who wrote to him from away and sent him many valuable books and articles about the Bible. He became a strong believer in Jesus Christ, and he was quite capable of reciting full chapters from the Bible. Gerald built his own workshop, where he built many small boats for other people and himself. He had all kinds of tools, some modern ones that many locals didn't have. Many people went to Gerald for things. Gerald cut hair with the only pair of clippers on the island for the longest time. He fixed things for others. He built things for others. He had a guitar, which he taught himself to play, and he tuned guitars for others. Kids came to his house to sing and play.

Gerald never lived anywhere other than in the humble and dated house in which he was born. After his parents and his brother passed, he lived in the same house until he was incapable of caring for himself. Many people visited him and brought him meals as he aged. People who had moved away and returned for a vacation always made it a point to visit Gerald. He was a great conversationalist. If you wanted to know something about people and events in the area, you went to Gerald. Local lawyers used him for testimonials, property information , etc. He kept records of everything.

Gerald is not famous. He was not a lot of things. He really did not have a working career as in a regular job, but he was self-sufficient, hardworking, knowledgeable and very clever. He cared for his parents and his brother. He loved everybody he knew and was loved by everyone who knew him. Gerald is known as a great encourager, kind, gentle, caring and humble. He was happy and content and never complained.

I visited Gerald at the nursing home in July 2024. While bedridden, his mind is as sharp as ever. (95 years old)***What a guy***!

274
"Hate"

Hate is a terrible word. Sounds harsh. Try "Dislike" or "not fond of."

BUT   Let's clarify something.

Disagreeing is not hating or hateful.

Not conforming or condoning is not hating or hateful.

I like chocolate, you like toast.

We can still love each other the most.

You take up hockey, I will stick to Judo.

We can still be great friends, though.

Let's get more into heavy-duty stuff.

There are social issues, you know what I mean.

If I name them now, you may think I am mean.

On politics, we disagree for sure.

We each have issues that others can deplore.

But again, I don't hate. Don't you see?

Our laws have it wrong when they tell me I must agree.

Signs that say, "there is no room for hate here."

Are simply casting the wrong smear.

We all have our values. I will stick to mine.

Yours are not the same but we can still be kind.

We can be different, like sheep or goats.

But I won't have things shoved down my throat.

I am not phobic or scared.

But our love for things is not always shared.

We can each have a different slate

I can be me, but don't say I hate.

275
"Freedom"

"I want to break free." That's the name of a love song by Queen.

Everybody wants freedom. So, they say! Do they really mean it? Is anyone totally free? Is the fact that we may depend on someone or something take away our freedom and independence?

What does it really mean to be free? Are you free if you are in love? Are you free if you are raising children? Are you free if you have job commitments? Do those things take away our freedom, or are they commitments that we freely choose?

The general meaning of freedom is "the power or right to act, speak, or think as one wants without hindrance or restraint."

Countries may gain their freedom, but they are still bound by hardships and duties. When we fall in love and get married, are we giving up our freedom? When we have children, are we giving up our freedom? Am I free to insult you right now? I do have the choice to do so, but I don't feel right about it. What is restraining me? Is it conscience? Am I sacred of your reaction? Or is it because I care about you enough not to hurt you?

Maybe freedom is overrated or underrated? George Orwell, the author of the very popular book "1984" quoted: "Freedom is slavery." That sure sounds like an 'oxymoron,' i.e., a contradiction. People fought and died so that we could be free. That was very unselfish of them, but they were free to do it. They loved their country enough to die for it. Was Orwell right? Are we slaves to the things we love?

Freedom takes courage and sacrifice.

"May we think of freedom, not as the right to do as we please but as the opportunity to do what is right." — Peter Marshall

276
"Mercy"

While grace is getting something we don't deserve, mercy is not getting something that we do deserve.

Remember when your parents should or could have punished you for staying out late but didn't? That's mercy.

Remember your teacher who could have failed you for not handing in your assignment but didn't? That's mercy.

Remember the boss could have fired you for messing up but didn't? That's mercy.

Remember the bigger kid could have given you a beating at school when you ratted on him but didn't? That's mercy.

Remember when your best friend could have embarrassed you by telling you what you really did but didn't? That's mercy.

Remember the time the cop could have given you a ticket for speeding but didn't? That's mercy.

Remember the times you were forgiven but didn't deserve it? That's mercy.

Justice says, "Guilty". Mercy says, "Case dismissed."

Think back. Add more memories to the list of mercies you have received. Are you passing it on?

"Surely goodness and mercy shall follow me All the days of my life, And I will dwell in the house of the Lord. Forever." Psalm 23:6

God gave us an escape from death. That's real mercy. Will you accept it?

277

"Revolutions"

A revolution could well be called a successful rebellion. Revolutions have been occurring throughout all of history. Big ones, little ones, violent ones, and non-violent ones. We are familiar with the well-known American Revolution and the French revolution.

Wikipedia lists hundreds, maybe even thousands in places most of us never heard of. Many involve violence. Some worked out for best while others for worst.

Is it time for a revolt in North America? Against what or whom should we revolt? Revolutions are not always fought in physical battles with weapons.
The best ones are fought with our voices, votes, volunteering, and awareness.
What do you want to revolt against?

Here are some suggestions for starters:
>Dishonesty in government and society in general
>
>Indoctrination of our kids
>
>Political correctness
>
>False teaching in schools and universities
>
>Immorality
>
>Too many regulations
>
>Government waste
>
>Fake news
>
>High taxes

Am I rebelling or revolting in giving you this list?

What do you want to revolt against? How will you do it? Speak up? Search for truth. Ask questions. Vote intelligently. Pray.

278
"Generosity"

"You earned it; you should keep it and let everyone else fend for themselves."
Yes or no?

Most charities only have one source of revenue, which is donations. Some have fund raisers such as bake sales, garage sales, car washes, etc. A few may get government grants, but for the most part, they continue their work because of the generosity of people like you and me. Most of us give if we agree, empathize, or sympathize with the cause and the work of the charity.

Various stats show that religions organizations are the recipient of the biggest percentage of donations by far. Regular church goers outgive nonchurch-goers significantly. Some people may balk at that because they don't agree with the religion and what they do with their money. But most religious organizations do good work and many of them are very benevolent to needs.

Individuals give far more than businesses and corporations. The US out gives Canadians by 2 to 1. People who have more can give more. However, in my 45-plus years of involvement in church giving, I have found that as a percentage of income, the less fortunate out give the financially well-off.

Statistics Canada charts as of 2021 show that the average household gives less than half of 1% of its annual income to charities. The highest is
Manitoba at .74%, and Quebec is the lowest province at .26%,
Understandable due to Covid, they all declined in 2020 and 2021. However, the stats show that there has been a steady decline from 2011 to 2021, from 23% of tax filers to 17.7%.

Of course, just because people don't give to charities, it doesn't mean that people don't give in other ways that go directly to helping others.

Are we becoming more selfish? The University of Zurich Switzerland said on July 11, 2017, *"Generosity makes people happier, even if they are only a little generous. People who act solely out of self-interest are less happy. Merely promising to be more generous is enough to trigger a change in our brains that makes us happier (neuroeconomics found in a recent study)."*

It is more blessed to give than receive. True or false? Are you generous enough?

"Correct" (<u>Answers from page 259.</u>)

1. You and me are coming. Or You and I are coming.

   You and I are coming.

2. Sheep is woolly <u>**or**</u> sheep are woolly

   Sheep are woolly. Or "The sheep is woolly."

3. The yolk of an egg is white, or the yolk of the egg are white.

   The yolk of an egg is <u>yellow.</u>

4. An apple a day keeps the nurse away.

   <u>An</u> apple a day keeps the <u>doctor</u> away.

5. You can lead a mare to water, but you can't make him think.

   You can lead a mare to water, but you can't make <u>her drink.</u>

6. Both my fathers-in-law are over 90 years old.

   Both my <u>fathers</u>-in-law are over 90 years old.

7. The bookkeeper will keep the score for this quiz.

   The <u>bookkeeper</u> will keep a score for <u>this</u> quiz.

8. An electric train is going east at 60 mph, and the wind is blowing west at 40 mph. The smoke is blowing north at 20 mph.

   Electric trains don't make smoke.

9. Two geese or not two goose. That is the question.

   Two geese or not two geese. *There is no question.*

10. A plane with 120 people crashed and killed 50 people. How many survivors were buried?

    We don't bury survivors.

How did you do?

280
"Seasons of Life"

Just as the seasons of the year change, so do the seasons of life. I don't know what season you are in, but whichever one it is, it will pass. Just give it time. Remember the tough time you had in a particular job? How about that time with your health? Your teenage years and college years were seasons of life. What about your days of living from pay day to pay day? Just as it is hard to imagine summer during the cold winter, it can be hard to imagine good times when we are in difficult times.

We have seasons for our own interests as we get older. Some of them are due to our physical and mental changes, and some because of our relationships. Some of these may be for the worse and, hopefully, a number for the better.

I remember my parents getting ready to go to bed early on New Year's Eve while I was planning to go to a fancy dinner and dance. Look at me now: last year, I was asleep by 10:30 on New Year's Eve. What's with that? What happened?

Our seasons bring us challenges and good times, and without even knowing it, the seasons slip by, or we may have even wished them away. Are you wishing away your current season, or are you being patient and facing it as it comes? The reality is both the good and the bad are all opportunities to grow. There are many things I was able to face in my later years that I couldn't have been able to face if I hadn't had some difficult experiences in my younger years. That's why we need patience and courage, no matter what the season.

Good old Solomon sure had his seasons. He said in Ecclesiastes, *"To everything, there is a season and a time to every purpose under the heaven. A time to love, and a time to hate; a time of war, and a time of peace."* While he accomplished much, he did go haywire for a season or two, causing him some regret in his later years.

What were some of the best seasons of your life? Name some worse ones. What did you learn from each of them?

281
"Idiot Convention"

At the annual idiot convention, the host was determined to demonstrate that those considered idiots were actually smart people.

"Could I have a volunteer?" One quickly came.

Today, I will demonstrate how smart idiots are. What is 35 plus 40?

The volunteer answered "60".

The crowd shouted, "Give him another chance."

"What is 17 plus 3."

"Twelve."

The crowd shouted, "Give him another chance."

What is 2 plus 2.

"Four:

The crowd shouted, "Give him another chance."

282

"Trinity"

Who can really understand the Trinity? God is three in one. God the Father, God the Son, God the Holy Spirit. We must admit this is tough to understand. The word Trinity actually does not appear in the Bible, yet there are oodles of evidence and references to God existing as three persons.

An egg has three parts, i.e., a shell, a white, and a yoke, but it is not the same as the three in one God. Water, ice, and steam are a good threesome in one, but that is not the same as the Trinity of God. The closest analogy is likely us in that we are made in the *"image of God."* (Genesis 1:26). We have a body, mind, and spirit. Although not exactly the same as the Trinity, we have to admit we are all "three in one," and all three of us exist at the same time. We could say our body is like Jesus who came to earth in the body, our soul is like God the Father, and our Spirit is like the Holy Spirit. You get the idea of three in one.

God is one, and He says so in the Bible: *"There is only one God."* Deuteronomy 4:35. Yet, God refers to the Son, the Son refers to the Father, and there is interaction between the Spirit and the Son. Confused. Jesus said in Matthew 28:19, "In the name of the Father, Son and Holy Spirit." Similarly, our minds interact with our bodies, etc.

God is the Father, God is the Son, and God is the Holy Spirit, and yet they are One. All three existed at creation.

The thing to remember is that God loves us. The Father loves us, The Son loves us, and the Holy Spirit loves us.

God the Father came to earth in the human body of Jesus. After Jesus went back to heaven, He left us with a conduit of the Holy Spirit. Although it is not the same as Bluetooth or wi-fi, the Holy Spirit is how we communicate with God.

Do we fully understand God? We don't understand electricity either, but we accept it.

The foundation of Christianity is that our one God exists, and He is Father, Son, and Spirit.

"Ending a Telephone Call"

We have all had difficulties at times trying to end a telephone conversation with those who go on and on and on and on and on and on and on and on. We don't want to be rude, but we just can't stay on the line forever.

Here are some suggestions. You may have better ones:

Dropping hints:

- "Well, it was so nice of you to call. Call me again some time." - "You must be busy, so I will let you go." - "Alright then.".

- "Ok, thanks for calling" - "I have to go to clean some fish." If hints don't work:

- "There's my other line." *(click)*

- "There' s supper burning, bye." *(click)*

- "Oops, he's home." *(click)*

- "I just have to go." *(click)*

- "I gotta pee." *(click)*

- "Somebody is at the door." *(click)*

- "Can I call you back? Bye." *(click)*

- "I really don't have time to talk right now." *(click)* -   "Have you got nothing better to do." *(click)*

- **Creative ways:**

- Keep sneezing or coughing.

- Ruffle some paper like it is static."

- Pretend you can't hear them. "Hello, hello, hello. I guess she cut me off." Hang up.

- <u>My favorite:</u> Hang up while you are talking. They will feel real bad thinking that you think they hung up on you.

- Hang up in the middle of

284

"Disaster Predictions?"

The Los Angeles times wrote in 1969 that there would be a worldwide famine disaster by 1975, as per Stanford university biologist Paul Ehrlich. "The US is becoming too big". The same professor also predicted dead oceans and world food rationing by the 1980's.

On April 16, 1970, the Boston Globe printed a headline that read, **"Scientists predict a new ice age by the 21st century."** This was a popular opinion in the early 70's.

January 29, 1974, The Guardian Newspaper headline read, **"Space Satellite show new Ice Age coming fast."**

Such articles have continued from science, the media, and the government.

- 1974 –Ozone depletion was a great peril to life.
- Through the 1980's Acid Rain was killing off all life in lakes
- 1988 -Rising Sea Levels will "Obliterate Nations if nothing is done by 2000."
- 2004 Britain will be Siberia by 2024
- In 2009, Prince Charles said, "We have 96 months to save the World."

Killer bees – peak oil production – Over population – Super hurricanes   The list

continues.

None of the approximately 50 predicted disasters happened, and yet they are still being predicted.

Could it be that scientists are justifying grants? Could it be that governments are looking for reasons to raise taxes and gain control?

Just asking.

285
"Jesus Said"

Jesus did not say, "Follow your heart."

He said, "Follow me."

Jesus did not say, "Everybody should become rich."

He did say, 'You will always have the poor."

Jesus did not say, "Be true to yourself."

He said, "Whoever wants to be my disciple must deny himself."

Jesus did not say, "Do what you feel is right."

He did say, "If you love me, keep my commands."

Jesus did not say, "You should not judge others, or no one should judge you."

He said, "Judge not less you be judge." Matthew 7:1 (meaning judge yourself first.)

Jesus did not say, "Believe your truth."

He said, "I am the truth."

Jesus did not say, "As long as you are happy."

He said, "What will it profit a man if he gains the whole world and loses his soul."

Jesus did not say, "You will not have troubles."

He did say, "Come to me, all who are weary and heavy laden, and I will give your rest."

286
"Working Together"

The 1.7-mile Golden Gate bridge was built between 1933 and 1937, and at the time, it was the longest bridge in the world. Two cables, 7650 feet each, hold up the bridge. Doesn't sound like much. But what is in those two cables?

The 3 feet in diameter cables are made up of 61 bundles, each consisting of 452 steel wires, each less than .2 inch in diameter. The total length of all the wire combined is 80,000 miles of steel cable weighing approximately 24,500 tons. The total number of wires in each cable is 27,572, for a total of 55,144 steel wires.

So what? Just making the point that one .2-inch wire cannot alone hold up the Golden Gate bridge, but 54,144 of them working together can. That means that each one of these little wires is needed.

Do you ever feel insignificant at times and say to your self, "I can't contribute much"?

We can all contribute something to the overall purpose, whether it is holding up a bridge, being a part of a company, a community organization, your local church, or, of course, your family.

We all have a purpose, and we all play a part. We are all needed, even if it is 1/54,144 of the cable.

It just means we must work together and contribute to the overall purpose and not work against that purpose. We just must recognize the big picture purpose and decide if we want to work and be a part of it. Once we do that then we are on our way to holding up the bridge that a lot of people depend on.

Look around and notice the buildings and institutions. Do you really think one person did it all?

How good are you working together with others? Are you doing it?

"Responses To Insults"

"That's a stupid thing you did."
"Yeah, I get that a lot. What did you think of the game last night?"

The drunk said to the lady, "You are so ugly,"
The lady replied, "And you are so drunk."
The drunk- *"Yes but I'll be alright in the morning."*

"You smell terrible."
"I can't tell; my nose is a lot smaller than yours."

John was complaining that he had to work so hard.
"Do you want some cheese to go with your whine?"

"The problem with you is you are so lazy."
"I work hard at it."

"You are such an idiot."
"Ok."

"That's an ugly outfit you are wearing."
"I like it."

"Why are your jokes so simple?"
"So, you can understand them."

To the person who never shuts up.
"Are you coming up for air?"

To the 'know it all'.
"Your head must be so heavy."

"I'm offended."
"So"

288
"I'm Offended"

What's with these "it offends me" or "I am offended" types of comments? Don't people have thick skin anymore? People are walking around like they are on eggshells, scared to say the wrong thing and even more scared to say the truth.

"I'm offended by that" seems to be the new modern weapon for wusses.

<u>Sure, we need to be concerned about others and not intentionally or recklessly go around insulting people.</u> But we should be able to live our lives and express ourselves without getting the "easily offended" crowd on our case. We need thicker skin, folks.

Being offended is the new weapon for those who want their own way. It is used both as a defense and offense to control others. The slightest difference in opinion is perceived as intentionally bullying, racial slurs, sexist, phobic, or hateful.

There was a time when "you would just suck it up and get on with your life," or "just get over it," or "take your knocks."

Jordan Peterson was accused of being offensive because he had an opinion, but when he confronted his interviewer and said, "But you are offending me now, and you don't mind doing it," **She was stuck for words.**

This offensive thing only seems to be going one way for the most part. The offended group can say what they want, criticize the other group, insult them, protest about them, call them names and it's okay in the name of tolerance and free speech. But the minute someone disagrees or expresses an opposite opinion, they are accused of being hateful simply because they don't agree.

Well, I am offended that you are offended just because I give my opinion.

Does anyone have the right not to be offended? There, are you offended?

"The difference between the easily offended and the not-so-easily offended: If the not-so-easily offended don't like something, they don't do it. If the easily offended don't like something, they don't want the not-so-easily offended to do it."

289

"Footprints"

One night, I dreamed a dream.
I was walking along the beach with my Lord.
Across the dark sky flashed scenes from my life.
For each scene, I noticed two sets of footprints in the sand, one belonging to me
and one to my Lord.
When the last scene of my life shot before me, I looked back at the footprints in
the sand.
There was only one set of footprints.
I realized that this was at the lowest and saddest time of my life. This always
bothered me, and I questioned the Lord about my dilemma.
"Lord, You told me when I decided to follow You, You would walk and talk with
me all the way.
But I'm aware that during the most troublesome times of my life, there is only
one set of footprints.
I just don't understand why, when I need You most, You leave me." He
whispered, "My precious child, I love you and will never leave you, never, ever,
during your trials and testings.
When you saw only one set of footprints, It was then that I carried you."
— *Margaret Fishback Powers*

A number of people have taken credit for writing this poem, including Margaret
Fishback Powers, who wrote it in 1964. I had the pleasure of meeting her. I also
read her book "Footprint Book of Inspirations," which has sold over 80,000
copies.

290
"The Letter S"

Did you know that the first telegraph cable across the Atlantic Ocean was laid in 1858 from Ireland to Newfoundland? Queen Victoria of England sent the first message of congratulations to President James Buchanan of the US.

Finally, the time it took for Europe to communicate with North America was reduced from two weeks to two minutes. It managed to send 732 messages before the cable stopped operating after only three weeks.

The second cable was completed in 1866 and five more were added in the next three decades and lasted until 1965.

The first wireless message across the Atlantic Ocean was sent and received on December 12, 1901. It was sent in Morse Code from Cornwall, England, to the historic Cabot Tower, Signal Hill in St. John's, Newfoundland, which was not a part of Canada at the time.

Guglielmo Marconi, the Italian physicist and radio pioneer, achieved this groundbreaking milestone, greatly improving communication across the ocean.

Marconi received a Nobel prize for his achievement.

Marconi continued to expand on the technology of the first wireless message across the Atlantic which was the letter "S".

291
"Cults"

<u>Oxford Dictionary</u> says: A cult is "a <u>relatively small group</u> of people having beliefs or practices, especially relating to religion, that are regarded by others as <u>strange or sinister</u> or as <u>imposing excessive control over members</u>". "A system of religious veneration and devotion directed towards a particular figure or object"

<u>Miriam Webster says: A cult is</u> "a religion regarded as unorthodox or spurious (outwardly similar or corresponding to something without having its genuine qualities). "Great devotion to a person, idea, object, movement, or work"

Basically, a cult is a group of people who claim to be of a particular persuasion but do not practise the doctrine of that persuasion. We could say it is a counterfeit. Many cults follow a person, as was the case with the famous Jonestown Massacre in Guyana on November 18, 1978. The cult's leader, Jim Jones, was able to convince hundreds of people to follow his farout rituals to the point that they followed his orders to drink poison while armed guards stood by, resulting in the deaths of 909 people. A third of them were children. Jones claimed to be Christian. Yet, he preached things and did things that did not follow Christian teachings.

Why do people follow cults and follow cult leaders? Is it because they just don't know the real thing? Are they gullible? In the Jonestown case, if the followers were to study their own Christian doctrine, they would have recognized that what Jones was teaching did not match up.

Millions of people who are members of cults are typically vulnerable and misinformed. There are more cults around than we think. They usually do have enough credible things in their program to convince the gullible.

Don't be gullible. Check them out. Compare them to the real thing. If they are all about control and secrecy, get out. If you are in doubt, get out.

"Satan never gets very far from the Bible. And every one of the cults, even Satanism, uses the Bible." — J. Vernon McGee.

292
"Listening"

We listen with our <u>ears;</u> that's a physical thing.
It doesn't mean we understand, that's a mental thing.
Hearing is surface communication. We can emotionally detach .
We may just get the words and miss all the facts.
We must get the logic and the intent .
Otherwise, our time in hearing is not well spent .
A good listener has to focus.
So the speaker will know they haven't lost us.
We also listen with our <u>eyes.</u>
To see if the other person smiles or cries,
Observe the expressions and body language too.
And note the effect the actions have on you.
We listen with our <u>minds,</u> tuning in and tuning out.
If not, we may even miss it when they shout.
Don't be thinking of yourself and your chance to speak and give advice.
Doing that, you will miss out and pay the price.
You can't just be quiet and fake attention.
While thinking about other stuff that you don't want to mention.
Making judgments and forming answers is a mistake.
You and your emotions make your attention look fake.
We listen with our <u>hearts,</u> empathically and true.
That's the way we get the others' point of view.
Stay awake, don't just stare.
Acknowledge and respond gently with care.
To be a good listener, let them know you are there.
Listen with a yearn.
Cause if we don't listen, we don't learn.

293
"Bragging"

Men like to brag and exaggerate. At the end of the day, on a fishing trip around the fire, they got into stories about their childhood.

Larry said, "My father had a big farm. You could fly all day in a Cessna and not come to the end of it."

Moe said, "My father had a ship. It was so big that you could drop something into the main hole, and you would have to wait an hour to hear it land on the bottom."

Joe said, "My father had a long nose. It was so long that five crows could stand on it."

As the night wore on, they got more reasonable and one by one, they admitted the reality.

Larry said," I was kidding and stretching the truth a lot. My father had some land, enough to plant some vegetables to keep us through the winter. It was about 5 acres at the most."

Moe said, "Me too. My father had a small 18-foot rowboat that we used for pleasure.

Joe said, 'I am sorry, guys. You know Dad's nose? The last crow had to stand on one leg."

"The older I get, the better I am."

294

"Population"

As of today, January 11, 2025, the world population, according to the website Microtrends, is **8,199,099,890**. In 1950, it was in the 2,500,000(2.5 billion range).

While the population has increased, the rate of increase has decreased. Between 1950 and 1990, the population increased between 1.5% and 2.2% a year. Since 2020, it has declined to less than .9% per year.

According to Scientific American, the main reason, which I think we could all figure out for ourselves, is the decrease in birthrate and in the size of families.

For a country to sustain its population, the average birthrate is said to be 2.1 per family. In most of the world today, this rate averages far below that, e.g., the US is 1.7, Canada 1.5, and China is 1.2. *(approximate)*

Stats also show that the birth rate in wealthy countries is lower than that of poor countries.

Some are of the opinion that the population should be controlled. Could it be that the "who's who" is doing just that? Just asking. Is this why there is a big push for abortion? Just asking. Is this why there seems to be a breakdown of the normal family? Just asking. Is this why Euthanasia is being promoted? Just asking.

Some approximate populations as of 2023: India – 1,429 billion; China 1,426 Billion; USA - 340 million. Canada 38.8 million.

"I heard that, on average, a woman is giving birth every tenth of a second. We are not sure what her name is, but we need to track her down and stop her."

295

"Death on the Ice"

One of the first and best books I ever read, outside of my school and university requirements, and the first book I ever read twice, was "Death on the Ice" by Cassie Brown. She tells the true and sad story of how 78 sealers died in 1914 through a series of unfortunate events.

The Newfoundland seal hunt was an annual event and still is to a lesser extent. On March 9, 1914, the SS Newfoundland, along with other sealing vessels, left St. John's harbor and headed for the ice floes off the Northern Newfoundland coast. The ship later became trapped in ice, and in an attempt to find the seals that "pupped" on the ice, 132 sealers left the ship and ended up lost in a storm.

Through a series of misjudgments, they were two days stranded on the ice with little or no food, jumping from ice pan to ice pan, cold, wet, and weary for fifty-three hours. Seventy-eight (78) died, and of the 55 survivors, a number suffered frostbite, resulting in amputations. Eight bodies were never recovered.

An enquiry was held, and while no criminal charges were made, certain captains were accused of poor decisions.

During the same storm, the SS *Southern Cross* sank while returning to Newfoundland from the Gulf of St. Lawrence. All 173 men died.

296

"Christianity"

Christianity is the world's largest religion, with over 30% of the world's population – approximately 2 billion.

It was founded approximately 33 AD by Jesus Christ - God in the Flesh (Son of God), who was prophesied to the Hebrews/Jews for thousands of years. Followers are known as Christians

Source of Beliefs and Authority:

- 66 books of the Bible. Old Testament written in Hebrew and Aramaic. The New Testament is written in Greek. The Bible claims to be God-breathed-God-inspired.
- More than 3500 languages have access to all or parts of the Bible
- Christ is the head of the church

Core Beliefs include:

- There is One God – existing as Father, Son, and Holy Spirit
- The Bible is the inerrant (error-free) Word of God
- God created the universe
- God is eternal and everlasting- always was and always will be
- God is love
- Satan, a fallen angel, is real and evil
- Jesus is God who came to earth in the flesh as promised - fully man and fully God.
- All of humanity are sinners
- Jesus came to die for (atone) for all sinners
- As sinners, human beings are incapable of getting to heaven
- Salvation (going to heaven) is because of God's grace, not human deeds
- Jesus lived, died, rose from the dead, ascended into heaven.
- Jesus will return for His church (those who truly believe in Him) and judgment.
- Hell is real

Christianity literally has thousands of denominations

See "Christian Denominations" page 262.

297
"One Day At a Time"

How many days have been wasted
because we dwell on tomorrow?
We can't live tomorrow today,
Tomorrow is a different day, and it is not here yet.
We can plan for tomorrow
but we can't be in tomorrow.
We can look forward to tomorrow
but we don't know tomorrow.
We can only live today.
We live in the present, not the future
It is good to dream, plan, and visualize
But not doing today will waste today right
before our eyes
Today is connected to tomorrow but it is still today.
Today may influence tomorrow,
that's why we should live today
One day at a time, that's how we should live
Don't say, "Starting tomorrow, I will do."
By tomorrow, you may not even be you.
Do what is right today, watch what you say today,
You can't fix tomorrow but you can fix today.
Every day, we worry about tomorrow.
It is one less day we have to improve tomorrow.
Today is our best. Let's take our daily bread
Most of this poem did not rhyme
But we can still live one day at a time.

298
"Yeonmi Park"

Who is she?

Born in North Korea on October 4, 1993, under a very strict authoritarian regime, she lived in poverty, often eating plants and insects, and in fear of being shamed, punished, imprisoned, or murdered for even looking the wrong way. She and her people were forced to worship the dictator as a god. She had no knowledge of the outside world other than being taught to hate the "American Bastards."

Following in her sisters' footsteps, she and her mother managed to escape to China, where people used them as sex slaves. Through a series of events, they made it to South Korea and eventually to the US. She was around the age of sixteen. She has since become an American citizen and loves the freedom written into the American Constitution.

She has been in great demand to share her story and the story of atrocities in North Korea and China.

Her latest book, "While Time Remains," not only gives many details of her past life but also relates her frustration, sadness, and disappointment in the direction that her new country is headed. While it is in no way as bad as North Korea, in that she has opportunities and freedoms that she never had, she highlights in her book the woke ideologies that are being taught to the detriment of the US in universities.

She simply wants to tell the truth about North Korea and China but yet she was banned from social media for doing so by the cancel culture.

Her books cover the "Decline in Values", "The Terror of Cancel Culture," and "Systematic Violence."

299
Oxymorons

A "Good moron" is an oxymoron

It has to be because a moron means idiotic, silly, and stupid

How can something be good if it is idiotic, silly, and stupid?

When a two- or three-word phrase contradicts itself

We have an oxymoron for the shelf.

Let's look at a "Big Few" that may be known to you

"Jumbo Shrimp" is the first for a jig

The shrimp is small, so how can it be jumbo, which means big.

Ok, "Little Big Man" or "Poor little rich kid."

Only one of those movies they made, they did.

 "Awful Good" these may sound "Tragically Cool."

And made you think you are a "Wise Fool."

Only in a "Civil War" does 'Friendly Fire" have rules

Here are some more that may be "Old News."

Find them "Bittersweet" if you would.

They may be "Clearly Misunderstood."

When you are "Alone Together" in your "Deafening Silence."

Give your "Larger Half" a "Loud Whisper" in your Uncertain Reliance".

She may respond with "Unconscious Awareness."

That is "Unjust Fairness" in your "Frequent Rareness"

This study of Oxymorons is "Well Spent."

It is almost like "Static Movement."

300
"Nativity scene"

We have all seen the nativity scenes at Christmas time. For the most part, they are very standard to include Mary, Joseph, the baby Jesus in a manger, an angel, at least one shepherd, three wise men, each with a gift, and typically there will be a camel and a lamb or two. Oh yes, there is usually a star above the stable and don't forget the donkey that Mary and Joseph used to get them to Bethlehem.

It's a beautiful picture or setup that depicts and reminds us of the Christmas story. Many wonderful messages have been preached on various aspects in the build-up to Christmas Day when all the characters got together and posed as the Innkeeper, who had no room for Mary and Joseph, took the picture with his Polaroid. Just kidding. There were no cameras back then.

They say a picture is worth a thousand words and while the picture is not entirely accurate, it does depict the story with an image of the Bible words as pieced together from Matthew and Luke.

While the scene is beautiful, it was not exactly the perfect way to deliver your first child, let alone the birth of God in the flesh. It was certainly a humble and modest beginning. The stable was likely a bit of a cave. The bed, a manger, a trough used by the animals with a bed of straw or hay. It was rough with the usual animal and stable smells. Yet there it was, the birth of our Saviour in swaddling clothes, indicating the baby was wrapped tightly with strips of cloth or linen.

The wise men said to be three, based on the fact that there were three gifts, would not have been present that night. They would not have arrived for up to two years later. But that's okay. They are significant to the story as were gifts of gold that took care of the family financially on their trip into Egypt and back. Frankincense was a great-smelling oil, and myrrh was used for anointing and healing. The gifts were becoming of a king.

Isn't it amazing how God can make a rough time to be so good? The next time you see the nativity, reread the early chapters of Matthew and Luke.

"Ego"

I look good, don't I?
I just know I am
I hope you can see how good looking I am.
I hope you can see how talented I am.
I know more than most people.
I have accomplished so much.
I am far better than you and everyone else.
That is why I go out of my way to show off who I am.
I steal the show when I am in a group
I have to get all the attention I deserve.
I have to stand out, and I make sure I do.
I am the bride at every wedding
I am the corpse at every funeral
I will be louder than everyone.
I laugh louder
I cry louder
I will dress for attention
I will speak to get attention.
I just have to do it because
I deserve the attention
I am such a blessing to those in my presence.
I have to be because
I want to hide the real me
I cannot admit the truth that
I am so insecure.
I really do fear, and my ego is just a cover-up because
I need help.

"The loudest in the room is the weakest one in the room." Frank Lucas
(Denzel Washington in the movie American Gangster)

302
"Hurricane Hazel"

Wikipedia states: "Hurricane Hazel was the deadliest, second-costliest, and most intense hurricane of the 1954 Atlantic hurricane season. The storm killed at least 469 people in Haiti before it struck the United States near the border between North and South Carolina as a Category 4 hurricane. After causing 95 fatalities in the US, Hazel struck Canada as an extratropical storm, which raised the death toll by 81 people, mostly in Toronto. As a result of the high death toll and the damage caused by Hazel, its name was retired from use for North Atlantic hurricanes.

On the organ in our living room was a wedding picture of a young couple. Mother told the story many times. "They died in Hurricane Hazel. They weren't long married. They were just washed away with their house. They found his body but never did get her body." They were my cousins.

Toronto had already received heavy rainfall when the end of Hurricane Hazel hit after traveling hundreds of miles over land. Toronto was not prepared for the powerful storm that hung around over the city, causing massive damage. It was unusual for a tropical hurricane to affect a city like Toronto all the way to Canada.

The rising waters flowed into the Humber River, widening it to nearly 200 feet over normal, destroying some 50 bridges, homes, and vehicles.

The aftermath resulted in significant clean-up with the use of the army and major companies donating to the cause. The "Toronto Region Conservation Authority" was formed to manage the flood plains and rivers and establish new guidelines for building.

In today's dollars the cleanup cost over $1.5 billion.

303
"Groups"

There are many advantages to belonging to a group. It is good to belong to a group and be a part of something. We had a group when we were kids. At times, the group consisted of two of us and other times, it got up to eight or ten if the older kids allowed us in on what they were doing. As I got older, the groups changed. In my first year of university, I had no group. It was the loneliest time of my life. I would go to the cafeteria for lunch and look around for an empty table, but pretending I was looking for a group of friends that I didn't have. In my second year I met up with Ed, Steve, Noel, Don, Dennis, and Ches. What a difference it made! We had many things in common. We were all in the science faculty. We formed "The Science Society," which gave us the right to have an office on campus. That was great because we had a place to hang out. We had a lot of fun doing some stupid things, never bad things, but the comradery was beneficial to all of us.

Many good associations certainly contribute to worthwhile causes in society. HOWEVER: There is a big trend today with some group mentalities that are taking advantage of the loneliness and "dare I say," the naivete of a lot of people. It is using peer pressure and fear tactics to get people to join. Social media and technology have enabled it to be a worldwide phenomenon. Some are formally formed, while others are simply based on ideology, ethnicity, or culture with no legal status. Their agendas are not always pretty.

Groups like "Black Lives Matter" got a foothold in the US and convinced a lot of people and companies to jump on the bandwagon for fear that they might be called racist. Their activities were violent, intimidating, and overbearing. Their leaders took off with millions of dollars, raised from often innocent people who thought they should belong. Too many gullible people are joining the Woke agenda, Critical Race Theory, Anti-Semitic groups, street gangs, and more based on lies and evil.

Want to be involved with a group? Check them out first. You would be amazed when you read their fine print. If they don't show it to you, that is a big RED FLAG.

304

"Fraud"

It was 1982, when the bank manager in up-town Toronto worked away in his office while a fraud took place without his knowledge.

Legitimate customer Tom (*not his real name)* came into the branch and, proceeded to the side counter, and completed a deposit slip on the available pad of deposit slips supplied. He proceeded to get in line to the tellers.

As soon as Tom left the side counter, Crooked Al *(not his real name)* grabbed the pad and was able to retrieve the account number, name, and signature from the imprint on the top of the pad that Tom just used. Crooked Al got in a different line.

Tom got to one teller to do his banking, and Crooked Al, another teller was two wickets down. Crooked Al requested an Insta-bank card. The teller went to the station of the head teller closest to the vault and got the application initialed. The head teller, who knew Tom, looked up and saw him in line and automatically okayed the card, not realizing he was at a different wicket.

Crooked Al was issued a card while Tom was at a different teller and was doing a transaction in the same account. Crooked Al left, and no one in the branch was suspicious.

Within the next two hours, crooked Al went to four different bank machines, withdrawing $500 from each branch.

Crooked Al was slick, quick, and brave but still crooked.

305

"Energy"

The typical understanding of energy is power and ability. This means physical and mental. Want to see real energy? Watch the kids when you are having a tiring day. They have all the energy in the world, so it seems that you are ready to collapse. WHERE DO THEY GET ALL THE ENERGY?

Our parents said the same about us. Where did our energy go?

Energy is a big topic today. Electric, oil and gas, coal, wind, solar – the world needs them all to exist and make things happen.

I learned in school that energy is divided into two main categories:

Potential energy – like water in a lake that is just sitting there, waiting to be used. A rock on the top of the hill. The lawn mower is waiting to be started.
The 16-year-old kid lying on your couch watching the TV while someone else is getting his dinner.

Kinetic Energy – The water in a lake flowing through turbines. A rock rolling down a hill is about to run into your car and cause a lot of damage. The lawn mower is cutting the grass. The kid finally who was on the couch, helping with the dishes or cutting the grass.

The big question about energy is, "Are we using it, and how are we using it?"

My energy for my judo practices was wonderful. I could work out for hours. My boss at work said to me one day, "If you put half the energy into your job as you put into your judo, you would be amazing and could really move up the ladder." It worked on me. I took his advice.

We have energy for some things but not for others. Funny about that!

This world has a lot of energy that is being wisely and effectively used. Yet there are other energy sources that we are either not using at all or we are misusing it. Some people in charge are not using their mental energy. What do you think?

306
"Youth"

O the joys of youth

How little we know of the truth

That is to come

That we do not always see in some

who are older and mature

who discover things for sure.

Do we realize how good we have it when we are young

It all comes back later, when we remember the songs we sung

Our biggest responsibility includes studies and school

Just to avoid being a fool.

There are other worries we could trace

Is that another pimple of my face?

Boys long to be able to shave

Girls yes, you have to behave.

What will I be when I grow older

Or will I always get the cold shoulder?

Don't worry about it, take things as they come

What ever you do don't be a bum.

"Propaganda"

Synonyms for the word propaganda include publicity, advertising, and marketing.

The Cambridge Dictionary defines it as: "Information, ideas, opinions, or images, often only giving one part of an argument, that are broadcast, published, or in some other way spread the intention of influencing people's opinions."
Note two points in this definition: "giving one part of an argument" and

"spread with the intention of influencing peoples' opinions."

Oxford says: "Information, especially of a biased or misleading nature, used to promote or publicize a particular political cause or point of view."
Note the words "biased" and "misleading".

Are you able to distinguish between propaganda and truth?

Examples of propaganda:

- Use of words and labels to persuade, dissuade, or discredit – *a brand name or logo on a celebrity's hat or shirt or politicians dropping in words and phrases like 'we are here for the middle class.'*
- Using specific selective facts that support an argument while leaving out facts that do not support an argument. *"Lease payments are $300"* does not tell you it is biweekly and excludes tax, or you need $3000 down.
- Convincing people based on popularity vs. truth – *because "62% of the people say it is true, so it must be true"* is not necessarily true.
- Name dropping or name association to gain credibility – *A picture of a well-known celebrity appears in the ad."*
- Work on peoples' emotions. *Ads with sad faces of animals or people. Ads with happy faces of animals or people. A sexy girl standing by a new car. In many cases, the faces have little or nothing to do with the product.*

Propaganda is dishonest marketing to fool the naïve and gullible. Do you fall for it?

308
"Put In Get Out"

You can't plant onions and expect to get tomatoes
You can't plant tomatoes and expect to get onions
It has to do with what you reap and what you sow
Is it time for some to catch on, or are they just too slow?
The principle just doesn't apply to farms and crops
It applies to raising beef and not expecting pork chops
The lesson applies to management of all kinds
They know its value so as not to get behind
The boss who is good to the staff
Will benefit more than time and a half
Kids, it's time to get off the couch so you don't become a slouch
Putting in the time to study your books
Will do more than improve your good looks
Work at it regularly so you don't have to cram
It's a lot better in the end than being in a jam.
If you put the time in, you will get the results out.
Smarten up so you know what life is all about.
If you don't like what you get out of life
Maybe it's time you got out your knife
And cut out a time-wasting habit
Look for an opportunity and grab it.
To get the prize you must put in the tries.
Kindness results in kindness
Caring results in sharing
So now you should know
You reap what you sow
There is no doubt
The more you put in, the more you get out.

309

"Short a Brick"

A schooner ran aground on a rock about 3 miles from land. It was a big deal. People saw it from the shore. The curious locals in small boats made their way out to see the sight. When they realized the ship was not going to survive, people proceeded to remove whatever cargo they could. It became free for the taking as time was running out for the faltering schooner. The cargo included bricks that Joe had his eye on. It was just himself in his boat, so he had room, unlike most other boats that were filled with people who were there just to watch. He loaded his boat brick by brick. Trip after trip, he rowed back and forth and piled the bricks, brick by brick, on his small wharf. The bricks were his. He was proud of his salvage.

"What to do with the bricks?" now was the question. Nobody in the community had anything built out of bricks. This was special. After discussing with his wife, Joe eventually decided he would build a shed.

The size of the shed was important since he had never built anything out of brick before, and he had to make sure he had enough bricks because there was nowhere around locally where he could buy more of them.

Joe and the wife spent hours, days, and weeks calculating the dimensions of his proposed shed based on the number he had and the size of each brick. The work began. One wheelbarrow load at a time, he took the bricks the 200 or so yards to the construction site.

Brick by brick, the walls began to appear. Row on row, they heightened. He was so pleased. He knew for sure it would work, while the spectators speculated and joked about whether he would have enough. What was to be the final day of construction came. He was down to 30 bricks, 20 bricks, and ten bricks as the last layer was about to finish. Would he have enough?

After all the rowing back and forth, the planning, moving the bricks to the site, and construction Joe had built a brick shed, the first in his community. He put on a regular gable shingled roof. The shed was finished. Joe had counted every brick many times, but he was missing one. Where did it go?

Joe miscalculated. Joe was short one brick. *(to be continued)*

310

"Government Control"

Has the government crossed the line?

Was it like that all the time?

I remember when what you had was your own.

If you bought a house, it was your throne.

You could add a room, knock out a wall.

It was all yours and not the government's call.

But now it's regulation and rules.

They make us look like a bunch of fools

Why can't it be like in the days of old

When you were in charge instead of government control?

Two years it took for one to get a permit.

Thirty thousand in fees it cost and it's not over yet.

Now they tell you what to do and what you can buy.

Wherever you turn, you are under their eye.

They control your health and education; you just can't relax

Oh, by the way, 'here's an increase in tax.'

John is what you named your kid.

They can change it to Mary and from you, it's hid.
Who do you think they are?

They are telling me now how to choose my car.

They control the news.

To make sure you only have their views

They spend your money

It's not even funny

Then there is climate change, and say you caused it.

Is it only an agenda for them to do as they see fit?

Sure, we need government; it is important too.

To serve and protect me and you.

If we were wise, we would see the signs

Before we head for communist times.

311
"Job Interviews"

High turnover is caused primarily by management hiring the wrong people or not managing them properly after they are hired. The consultant was asked by a company with high turnover to provide a training seminar on interviewing. He first sat in on a few interviews. The interviewer seemed to ask the normal questions, and the candidate gave the appropriate answers. What was the problem?

Even though the consultant had interviewed and hired hundreds up to that point, he searched the web to see if he was current in his thinking. He realized that there were no guarantees no matter how good the interview went. That was why he always insisted on a minimum of two interviews and had different people in on them.

Most of the web sites were written for the candidate. They basically said, "These are the typical questions that you will be asked at a job interview." Then they proceeded to say, "And this is how you would answer them." *(That was 15 years ago. I just went to the website again, and it seems little has changed. No worries, I get it.)*

The whole point of an interview is to determine if the candidate can satisfy the needs of the company and if the company can satisfy the needs of the candidate. The resume tells you a lot, and that's a good start. But, the interview is necessary to determine the fit. Therefore, the company has to find out, "Can he/she do the job? Will he/she do the job? Will the candidate and the company be a good fit for each other?"

Some basic things to consider include:

- Get real – Get personable – Get each other at ease.
- Don't be afraid to ask stupid questions – watch the reactions.
- Ask the same questions in different ways
- Find out the 'but' that your bosses say about you. "You are good, but"
- Is the 'but' true? Have you fixed it? Why not?
- Are the candidates looking for a job, or do they really want to work?
- Make sure you and the candidate fully understand each other's requirements.

"Sarcasm"

While preparing to go to Russia, I was advised to "watch my sarcasm." I tried but it didn't last. I was often misunderstood and had to explain myself.
By the end of my trip, the Russians were doing it to me.

Not all cultures get sarcasm.

While dictionaries indicate that "Sarcasm" is a sort of "mocking irony to cause pain, it is quite often used jokingly, especially for me. It is certainly used in politics to shame the opposition. It's everywhere and often effective, while other times unjustified, as people use it when they don't like someone or something.

TV host and former US press secretary Dana Parino says: "Sarcasm is like cheap wine. It gives a terrible aftertaste."

A few anonymous quotes from the gods of the internet include: -   "I love sarcasm. It's like punching people in the face but with words."

- "I'm not sarcastic. I'm just intelligent beyond your understanding."
- "Don't worry about what people think. They don't do it very often."
- "I never forget a face, but in your case, I'll be glad to make an exception."
- "No, you don't have to repeat yourself. I was ignoring you the first time."
- "Life's good, you should get one."
- "I don't believe in plastic surgery. But in your case, go ahead."

Two of my favorites:

- "I met two crazy people in my life, and you are both of them."
- "I don't care what people say about you. I think you are half decent."

Ronald Regan said: "The nine most terrifying words in the English language are, *"I'm from the government and I'm here to help."*

313
"Good Friday"

What happened? Sad day or good day?

If Jesus is God and He is so powerful and mighty, why was He not powerful enough to overcome those who put Him to death? He could have escaped but He didn't. Why didn't He? He could have defended Himself in the garden when the soldiers came to arrest Him. He didn't, even though He had the power to heal a soldier's ear. He could have put up a better defense at his trial. If Jesus could have escaped this terrible death, then there must be only one reason why He didn't prevent it.

It all happened because He wanted it to happen. It was planned all along, even back to the first book of Genesis in the Bible. *Jesus' life was not taken. It was given.* Do you see the difference? This is summed up in what is likely the most memorized verse in the Bible, John 3:16.

> *"For God so loved the world that He gave His only begotten Son, that whosoever believed in Him shall not perish but have everlasting life."*

Read it again. I challenge you to reread until you memorize it if you haven't already.

What happened on Good Friday? God gave Himself in the flesh to die for you, me, and everyone else so that our sins would be paid for so you could live forever. Yes, we will die physically, but our spirit will go to heaven. And yes, our body will rise again when Jesus returns.

There's one catch: "Whosoever believes in Him," i.e., genuinely all out believe.

That's what happened on Good Friday. Jesus bought you. Will you accept?

314
"Communist and other mass Killings"

See a few sample quotes below about various "Communist Killings" websites. I don't guarantee the accuracy.

"Under the Chinese Mao Zedong, estimates of up to 45 million people were murdered between 1958 and 1962– easily making it the biggest episode of mass murder ever recorded."

"People's Republic of China. 1949-87: 87.6 million people murdered. Mao et al. communist regime. Does not include 3.5 million murders by Chinese communists during the 1927-49 civil war."

"Union of Soviet Socialist Republics. 1917-87. 61.9 million people were murdered under the communist regime. Includes 54.8 million within the Soviet Union, plus 6.9 million in areas conquered by the USSR. Josef Stalin's rule (1929-53) accounts for 43 million. On an annualized basis, the pre-Stalin regime founded by Lenin was more murderous than the post-Stalin one."

"Cambodia. 1975-79. 1.5 million people were murdered. Khmer Rouge communist regime. Per capita, the largest democide against a domestic population. It includes murders of ethnic minorities, intellectuals, and dissidents, plus deaths from slave labor."

"The Ukrainian Genocide –1932-33: the Soviets, under Joseph Stalin, caused a famine, killing between 5 and 20 million people mostly from starvation."

"Under Karl Marx, estimates of 100 million were slaughtered."

"Ethiopia. 1974-87. 725,000 people were murdered. Communist."

"Indonesia. 1965-66. 509,000 people were murdered. Killings of communists by the military, the select militia, and others following a failed communist coup attempt."

"The Holocaust – Germany, under Hitler's Nazi rule in World War II, killed close to 17 million people - including about 9 million Jews."

"According to a report by David Kopel on November 9, 1922, over 200 million people were killed in the 20th century by Communist and Fascist regimes. This does not include deaths in wars."

315
"Strengths"

What are you good at? What do you have going for you? Everybody is good at something. Don't be shy, but don't embellish yourself.

Think about things you have done that you felt good about or others have complimented you on. Here are some hints below to get you started on things about your personality. Check the ones that apply to you, or rate yourself from 1-5. (5 being good) You can make another list on the right side about your technical skills, trades, talents, gifts etc.

Getting along with others
Kind
Sensitive
Easy going
Encouraging
Positive
Detailed
Friendly
Exciting
Sincere/Honest
Loving
Persistent Trustworthy
Persistent
Good talker
Good sense of humor
Patient
Good reader
Good writer
Wise decision maker

You may not be tops or excellent at everything, but I know you have enough going for you in a number of areas that you can build on. Don't hesitate to ask someone who is close to you to rank you in the above areas.

"There are two ways of exerting one's strength: one is pushing down, the other is pulling up." —Booker T. Washington.

316
"Vision vs. Purpose"

I was always confused between vision and purpose. Are they the same?

Vision is <u>what</u> we want to become, i.e., how we see ourselves in the future.

The purpose is <u>why</u> we want to become what we want to become, i.e., the reason.

It comes down to <u>what</u> vs. <u>why</u>, which are two important questions. Does "what" depend on "why," or does "why" depend on what? They are related.

Vision/What – To be a doctor. Purpose/Why – to heal sick people.

There is a famous Proverb (29:18) that says, "Without a vision, the people perish." What does that say to us? My take is that if we don't know where we are going or have no plans in mind, then we will likely wander aimlessly in life with no real direction and not realize our full potential. Another way of putting it is, "If you aim at nothing, you will hit it." Vision gives us direction. Purpose gives us the reason for our direction.

Some famous people spent their lives doing things to change the world. Good for them. They had a vision, and they had a purpose. But what about ordinary you and ordinary me? Do we have to be famous to have a vision and purpose? What do you want, and why do you want it?

What is wrong with the vision of a mother whose vision is seeing her children raised to be beautiful, loving, kind, caring, and self-supporting with good values? And therefore, chooses to be a "stay at home mom"? Why can't a father who has the same vision for his children work hard to provide for his family? Are they not good visions and purposes?

My friend Bill is one of 13 children. Bill's parents did not find a cure for cancer, but they were beautiful and wonderful parents whose purpose was to provide a loving home for their kids. I didn't get to know all of Bill's siblings but from the ones I did know, I can definitely see that the vision of Bill's parents having beautiful, loving children became reality.

Good Book to read: "The Purpose Driven Life" by Rick Warren has sold over 50 million copies.

317

"Defensive"

The meeting was going well. Everyone was being nice and sharing their ideas on how to improve things, "UNTIL"…

One or more employees got defensive. Why do we get defensive? Naturally, if we are wrongfully accused or blamed for something we will justify our position or actions. But when that crosses over to our getting defensive to the point that we cannot rationalize, and we get our dander up, then the real issue cannot be resolved, and a sensible discussion cannot take place.

I gently suggested once, "Mary, try not to be so defensive; we just want to get to the root of the matter." Mary quickly moved forward and replied in a loud voice with spit and fire from her mouth and eyes, "I AM NOT DEFENSIVE."

Being consistently and overly defensive can:

- Reveal our pride and ego
- Drain energy
- Cover up or reveal "We have a problem."
- Hinders healthy and effective communication
- Be a cover or hindrance to accepting responsibility and ownership
- Be the result of emotional hang-ups, e.g., fear, anxiety, guilt, or shame
- Result in not listening, anger, blaming others
- Hide the truth
- Hinder growth

Some alternatives or cures to consider:

Relax - Be confident - Be objective - Be honest – Admit mistakes – Be teachable – Stick to the facts – Deflect attacks - Discuss - Don't argue – Cour battles – Don't burn bridges – Maintain relationships – Be respectful – Watch body language – *Make sure your shirt is tucked in.*

318

"Never Give Up."

He didn't have a good family situation. His father was never on the scene, and his mother was not a good mother. He was removed from his home several times because of his abusive mother. He was familiar with foster homes, 25 by the time he was thirteen years old.

At about the age of seven, His mother kicked him out of the house. He waited a while and managed to place a ladder by the side of the house and slowly made his way to his bedroom window. When he got to the top, his mother, who was waiting for him, hit him with a baseball bat, leaving him unconscious at the bottom of the ladder. A neighbour noticed him in the morning and took him to the hospital, where he eventually recovered. His mother actually tried to kill him but was always able to convince the authorities to let her have him back. Not sure why.

At thirteen he was left by his mother at a race track, never to see him again. He caught the eye of one of the workers who took him under his wing and took him home. He helped out at the track for a number of years. He had a mixed career of racing horses and truck driving. He had several accidents causing broken bones, concussions, and some heart issues. He was hit by lightning twice.

He never went to school but became very street-wise.

In 2019 he teamed up with a beautiful lady, who also didn't have a great life. They started a landscaping company together, and one of their clients took them to church. They married. Despite their difficult past, they turned out to be beautiful positive, kind people willing to help anyone.

They never gave up and are still going. They are my friends.

319
"Teamwork"

An accepted definition of teamwork is:

"A group of people working together for a common purpose."

Everybody knows that. The biggest hindrance to teamwork is "people."

Great teams have conquered the world in sports, science, technology, wars, and the arts, and we have to put religion in there too. Look what the twelve disciples accomplished in the early church by working together with God.

If we could just get people working together, we could accomplish just about anything. Teamwork is about unity, whereby every member puts the goals and objectives of the team above their personal agendas.

Common words for unity include Joined - Fused - Cohesive - Integrated – Agreement and Harmony. They make a group strong.

Other words like Joint effort - Cooperation - Collaboration – Solidarity mean togetherness.

It takes a strong, united group working together to create that WOW factor in everything it does.

These are what we should be seeing in our families today, in our governments, workplaces, and organizations. But do we? Not enough because the members of these institutions cannot agree on where they want to go. There are too many hidden agendas. There is very little trust, and they don't communicate well with each other. You can't get answers. It seems no one is accountable, and of course, they don't share the same values. What a mess!

But don't be discouraged. It is still possible. You can be the one to make it work. This is my definition using 5 qualifications given in "The Five Dysfunctions of a Team" by Patrick Lencioni, plus two of my own."

"A group of individuals <u>skilled</u> in different areas, <u>committed</u> to achieving shared common <u>purpose</u> and <u>values</u>, while willingly holding each other <u>accountable</u> and <u>confronting</u> each other with total <u>trust</u>."

320
"Is it True?"

Is it true what I tell you and what you tell me?

How can you know for sure?

You know I wouldn't lie to you

And I know you are as sincere as you can be.

Here we are at a time when there is so much knowledge going around,
But the truth is "most truth cannot be found."

You can't believe the news; everybody has different views.

Politicians tell us one thing but do another.

Why can't they be honest? Is it to cover for each other?

They tell us things that we know are wrong,

But people still vote for them, hopefully not for long.

The media lies, politicians lie. Are we all dishonest?

Do we know the difference? Do we get the gist?

Or is it that we get used to lying like the rest?

They say a boy can become a girl, and a girl can become a boy

Do you believe it, or will you want to spoil their claimed joy?

Is carbon the real cause of climate change?

Or is it a way for the feds to get us all to change?

Are the polar caps really about to melt?

Or was it just a story to change how we felt?"

I don't know about you.

But I think much of the nonsense is not even true.

321
"In Cod We Trust"

Those who have a Newfoundland and Labrador background are very familiar with cod and most likely include cod in its various forms as a regular part of their diet. Many Newfoundlanders not only ate a lot of cod, but the majority of them especially in the out-ports, experienced "cod jigging" or working on a fish plant.

It has been exaggerated that when Newfoundland was first settled in the late 1400s and early 1500s, "the cod is so plentiful you can walk on them in the water." My father often said something similar during his many years fishing.

There are many species of cod, of which the Atlantic cod is likely the most well-known. The history of cod fishing is said to go back to when the Vikings fished it back around 800 AD. They, along with other countries, salted and dried it. It was a very popular commodity in Europe and around the world, including North America.

It is said that the only natural predator of the cod is the human. However, seals have been known to enjoy a meal of cod.

The overfishing of cod off the coast of Newfoundland by Canada and other countries caused a depletion of the stocks, resulting in a moratorium in 1992. Things got pretty rough, as many Newfoundlanders were deprived of their livelihoods and food sources.

Cod has many health benefits with its high protein, omega 3, and vitamins.

Studies have shown that it keeps our brains in good condition. *"Eat lots of cod fish; it gives you more brains."* Captain Chesley Dyke

Familiar Newfoundland cod recipes include:

Fried cod - Boiled cod – Baked cod – Stewed cod – Roasted cod -Fish and brews - Cod aux gratin - Fish cakes - Salt cod - Cod tongues -Cods heads - Cod chowder – and more.

In Cod We Trust.

"Logic"

Well, it is only logic, isn't it? If it is logic, does that mean if it is logic for me, it has to be logic for you? I guess not anymore, so it seems.

Sure, there are opinions on things from the point of view of personal tastes, but are opinions and desires taking over logic?

The philosophy student said, "Dad, I can now prove you are not here." His father slapped him on the face. "Why did you do that," said the son. "I didn't. I am not here", said the father." Silly, isn't it? It is not even logical what some of these philosophy students do and think.

Most dictionary meanings say that logic is "correct reasoning." Correct reasoning would say something like this, "If A equals B and B equals C, then A equals C," or "If today is Monday, then tomorrow is Tuesday." Or "If ten people say you are drunk, you should roll over."

Sound simple? I had a discussion with a guy recently who made a lot of arguments and had lots of opinions. Few, if any, of his statements and opinions are based on any truth, yet when shown that his statements were false, he still insisted on sticking to his opinions and arguments. That doesn't seem like logic to me. Yet he insisted that he likes to be logical.

Does it seem logical to you that?
- We cure the drug problem by supplying drug addicts with needles.
- We reduce carbon in the atmosphere by making more electric cars that use batteries made in China, which produces more carbon than any country in the world using coal-fired electricity plants.
- We reduce oil production in Canada and buy oil from countries that are our enemies.
- We lower the standards so kids get good marks in school rather than educating them.

Caution: Not everyone's logic is based on truth. That is why imagination and questioning are wise.

"When dealing with people, remember you are not dealing with creatures of logic, but with creatures of emotion." - Dale Carnegie.

323
"Self-Esteem"

High or low? Which is it? Lots of confidence or no confidence? Shy, bashful, put yourself down, or are you out there with boldness and more guts than three rows of teeth? "Who is the best-looking person here, and why am I?" Or is it "O dear, I feel useless."

Either way there are reasons for our self-esteem. I am no doctor, but there are always reasons for where we put ourselves on the "self-esteem" meter. It could be a series of events or a single event that puts us where we are. In addition, we could have great self-esteem in some situations and low self-esteem in other situations. We all know popular and talented people who suffer from low self-esteem and real jerks who have high self-esteem. Sometimes, it's hard to tell because people have clever ways to hide on who they are.

I had a group of employees rank themselves in certain categories from 1-5, with 5 being excellent. They were all close except for two people. One rated himself with all 5's. The other with all 2's. They were both way off. The one who rated himself 5's would have been 2's at best. The one who rated himself 2's was definitely 5's. Interesting indeed. Do you relate?

Life has told me, "When we feel low, just keep going; when high, be quiet."

Being honest helps. Sometimes we take ourselves too seriously. We need to laugh at ourselves more and focus more on encouraging others and helping them with their self-esteem.

I am long-waisted, so I have a hard time keeping my shirt tails tucked inside my belt. The answer is to buy longer shirts or keep them outside my belt.

<u>Consider this:</u> Maybe we shouldn't be looking to build this thing called self-esteem. Jordan Peterson suggests *"focusing on personal responsibility, facing challenges, and striving for competence and improvement."*

Instead of worrying about how we feel about ourselves, let's focus on being the best we can be with what we have.

See Humility.

324
"Judge Not – Who Says?"

Does the Bible really say we are not to judge? How could we possibly get by if we didn't judge? Without judging, we would be choosing the wrong friends, speaking out of turn and wearing clothes that didn't match, or heaven forbid, burning the roast. We have to judge and discern in order to make decisions.

Should we go around openly criticizing people because we don't particularly like their character or behavior? That's a whole different issue.

Those who hide the phrase "You shouldn't judge" are misreading the part in the Bible which says:

"Judge not, that you be not judged. [2] For with what judgment you judge, you will be judged; and with the measure you use, it will be measured back to you. [3] And why do you look at the speck in your brother's eye but do not consider the plank in your own eye? [4] Or how can you say to your brother, 'Let me remove the speck from your eye'; and look a plank is in your own eye? [5] Hypocrite! First remove the plank from your own eye, and then you will see clearly to remove the speck from your brother's eye. Matthew 7:1-5

This is more of a caution than an instruction. It is saying if you are going to give an opinion or criticize someone else, you need to look at yourself first. Who am I to say someone is overweight if I am also overweight? Who am I to say someone has faults if I have similar ones? Do we see the faults in others? Of course, we do. The scripture doesn't tell us not to be wise, aware, and discerning. In fact, to the contrary,1 it says in John 7:24, *"Do not judge by appearance but judge with right judgment?*

We all judge every day to make decisions and take action. How can we discern right from wrong if we do not observe and judge? The big deal is the opinions we cast on others without paying attention to our own shortfalls.

325
"Lost and Found"

Joe was visiting the city for the first time. He had never been on a bus. For a number of consecutive days, Joe would board the bus, light up his pipe, take in the sights, and observe the city folks as they got on and off the bus.

One day, a lady with a big dog came and sat by him. They greeted each other as Joe continued puffing on his pipe. The lady was annoyed with his smoking.

"Would you mind putting out your pipe and stop smoking?"

"Well, I rather like my pipe. I do this every day, and no one complains."

"But it bothers my dog."

"And your dog bothers me. You put off your dog, and I will stop smoking."

The back and forth continued. Finally, they made a deal. Joe was coming close to his stop, so he agreed to put out his pipe, and the lady decided to put her dog off the bus. One stop later, Joe got off and walked towards his home. He saw the dog running towards him. Guess what was in the dog's mouth.

The missing brick from the other story is on page 309.

326

"Man"

Is there a template for a man?
We have heard the expression, "He is a man's man."
What does that mean? Men are different, to say the least.
Is there a model to be copied, or have real men already ceased?
Tough, rugged, and strong was a trend.
A provider and protector to the end.
A loving family man was admired.
A strong work ethic and never tired.
A man of his word you could trust.
Truth, logic, and common sense were a must.
Where have all the real men gone
The ones with the brains and the brawn?
 A man should be on top of everything
Yet they are trying to make him feminine
He can still be sensitive, caring, and kind
But that doesn't mean he has to be blind
 To what is happening in the world
And show respect to all and every girl.
If you are a girl, maybe you are not
Get over that, don't give it a thought.
Men, get out and work and pay your way.
Your parents love you but don't want you to stay.
Don't listen to the brainwashing you get from the school.
Search for the truth so you won't be a fool.
Don't worry if you feel alone
Have courage and be strong to the bone.
Raise your kids properly; don't abuse or confuse them.
They may turn out like you, a real gem.
Don't be the standard bump on a log
Get off your behind and pay attention to God.

327
"Resurrection"

"Were you there at the resurrection?"

"No"

"Then how do you know it happened?"

"Were you there when the Titanic sank? Were you there when Caesar was emperor? Were you there when Columbus discovered America."

"No"

"Then how do you know they happened?"

"We have history books and reports from first-hand witnesses."

"Same thing."

"Same thing, what?"

"We have history books and reports from first-hand witnesses."

"Oh, like what?"

"Ten documented times for sure. Tradition says even more. At least three women at the tomb. Two men on the road. Ten disciples in a room. Eleven disciples again in a room. Seven on a fishing trip and had breakfast with Him. Appeared to His brother James. Over 500 people at one time."

'Where are you getting all of this?"

"Recorded history from credible authors. Also, the Roman guards at the tomb were bribed to lie about the empty tomb and the moved stone. Oh yes, the tomb was empty. And there are literally thousands of manuscripts written in the first 50 years after the death confirming their stories. Would you die to defend a lie?"

"Wow, I didn't know all of that."

"I know. Many smart, brilliant people have set out to prove it false but ended up believing it."

Good talk!

328
"Science vs. Bible"

<u>Round earth.</u>

"It is He who sits above the circle of the earth." Isaiah 40:22

The ancient Greeks, Egyptians, Babylonians, and more confirmed this.

<u>Circumcision on the eighth day.</u>

"And on the eighth day, the flesh of his foreskin shall be circumcised." (Leviticus 12:3).

Dr. Armand James Quick: "It is not a coincidence that the religion of Moses sets its ceremony for circumcision on the eighth day." In other words, only on the eighth day of life do blood clotting substances reach their all-time high – well beyond the amount that will accompany a normal human being for the rest of his life.

<u>The Water Cycle</u>

Water evaporates and comes back as rain, as indicated by the scripture, which says:

"All the rivers run into the sea, Yet the sea is not full;
To the place from which the rivers come, there they return again."
Ecclesiastes 1:7

<u>Worldwide Flood</u>

Evidence of the flood is all around us. Various fossils, including fish, are all over the earth, even in high mountains.

"Now, the flood was on the earth for forty days. The waters increased and lifted up the ark, and it rose high above the earth. [18] The waters prevailed and greatly increased on the earth, and the ark moved about on the surface of the waters. [19] And the waters prevailed exceedingly on the earth, and all the high hills under the whole heaven were covered. [20] The waters prevailed fifteen cubits upward, and the mountains were covered. Genesis 7:17-20

"Employees On Bosses"

This is what I have heard from employees:

Networker should read Get people on your side.

<u>Good qualities</u>	<u>Poor Qualities</u>
Good mood, easy-going	Moody and unpredictable
Encouraging	Ignorant, rude
Future-oriented	Don't know, don't care
Objective	Won't admit mistakes
Dependable, Honest	No backbone
Trusting and Trustworthy	Poor communicators
Responsive	Takes all the credit
Keeps promises Courageous	Doesn't give feedback
Great Delegator	Unapproachable
Good Time Manager	Self-centered
Mentors	Doesn't follow through
Appreciates	Breaks promises

"Success Qualities"

These are a few of the qualities I have noted in successful people.

<u>A positive winning attitude</u> – if you don't believe you can do it, you likely won't. Chances are you won't even try. By thinking and saying, "I can do it," opens up the possibilities and causes you to be resourceful, innovated, and determined.

<u>Action and results-oriented</u> – waiting and pussyfooting around is not an option. Get to it today. Plan it and do it.

<u>Do what it takes</u> – face and deal with obstacles and challenges as they come. Allow for them as much as you can. You are not easily deterred. Make good use of time.

<u>Purpose and vision-focused</u> – Be on a mission. Know what you want or what has to be done, and you won't be distracted. Have a plan and stick to it.

<u>Aware of strengths and weakness</u> – know your limits and when you have reached a point that is beyond your capacity. Be willing to say, "I need help." Don't let your pride get in the way. Call on someone who can help. It doesn't mean giving up. It just means you are wise and humble enough to get assistance.

<u>Big picture thinker but sees the details</u> – vision is obvious but don't have tunnel vision to the point of missing little things that can creep up.

<u>Networker</u> – Get connected and stay connected. Get people on the side. Build good relationships and unity. Know how and when you can use each other. Develop and help others.

<u>Don't complain or brag</u> - put things in perspective. Be willing. Be teachable. Take advice.

<u>Have High standards</u> – aim high and hit high

<u>Credible</u> -Decisive, flexible, responsive, prioritized, organized, empathetic, patient, and impatient - firm but fair, determined, courageous. Be who you claim to be. Have integrity.

331
"Challenges"

Nobody is going to go through life without challenges. We will all face challenging and difficult times, as well as challenging and difficult people. Shucks! We may well be the challenge and difficulty that others have to face.

"Every challenge is an opportunity to grow and improve."

Challenges are opportunities. People who are looking out for opportunities and ignoring challenges are missing the big picture.

"I have never had an opportunity that didn't make me better off in some way." Who said that? I just did. Can you say it?

We are living in a society that expects and wants the road to be easy. It is one thing to want it but don't expect it. If everything was easy, we likely wouldn't have jobs. That is not to say we don't seek ways to improve things.

The world will not end for us when we have a bad day. That's not really the case-it could end or at least slow down if we choose to throw a tantrum or panic. Challenges affect us, no doubt.

A manager writes: *"My boss hired me because he heard that I was capable in certain areas. Being into the job a few years after experiencing great growth and success, the economy took a downturn., We incurred heavy losses from customers who either closed or went bankrupt. We were in trouble financially. I showed the boss the details. He looked at me and said, "Well, that's why I hired you. I know you can get us through this. It was tough to take, but it was also encouraging. We got through it."*

The crew of Apollo 13 could have given up when they faced their challenges when they were well on their way to the moon. They did what they had to do to get back. Watch the movie. There are many lessons there.

Every athlete and sports team that ever won a championship faced challenges. They face them, grow, and learn. That's why they won, and even if they lost, they still grew. Every family has its challenges too. They faced them, grew, and learned.

Oh, and by the way, we may have to change our attitude and our ways to deal with our challenges.

332

"Employees"

We are not hired because we need a job, even if we do need a job. We are hired because there is work to be done, and we will be paid to do it. We are hired to produce.

We are expected:

- To do our best at all times
- To take instructions from our bosses at all times.
- To get along with fellow employees
- To serve our clients and fellow employees
- To treat other employees as clients
- To be honest
- To be polite
- To be on time
- To follow company policy and the law
- To be professional
- TO NOT BE A COMPLAINER

Management has much the same job descriptions as we do, in addition to seeing that we do our jobs and help us to grow and get promoted within our company. Managers have the same responsibilities as us, except they get paid a bit more to see that we do our jobs.

Our salary is dependent primarily on four things:

- Our performance *(This is the one you have the most control over)*
- The company's performance *(That depends a lot on us too)*
- The supply and demand of someone with our skills and talents
- Industry standards
- The economy
- Government guidelines.

Our attitude and efforts pay off.

Be patient. Be helpful. Be willing. Be teachable.

Don't be defensive, negative, or a pain in the butt.

We are entitled to nothing. Earn what you get.

333

"In Charge"

(See also136 - Management, Bosses -167) Employees on Bosses -329).

Are you in charge at work or in any organization, even at home?

Here are some things bosses should keep in mind:

The relationship you have with people will be the biggest factor in your success. People come and go depending on how you treat them and how you get along with each other. This has been proven over and over, and quite often, people will stick with you for less money. (Don't take advantage.). Years ago, Gallop did a poll, which, from my experience, holds true today.

> *"85% of employees change jobs because of their relationship with their immediate bosses."*
> *"More than two-thirds leave because of the manager's incompetence or ineffectiveness."*

Many bosses/managers do not understand their role as managers. They are not working hard or wise enough to become better managers. The primary role of all managers is:

To Serve: Your Customers – Your Company- Your Employees – Your Families - Yourselves

Note the emphasis of the word "your," i.e., they are all your responsibilities.

> The serving managers understand that if they give people more of what they need, they will give you more of what they need. This is called the law of the harvest- reaping and sowing.

Note also the order. We should also emphasize that needs are not always wants.

One more thing: Managers have an obligation and duty to set and maintain standards. That means they have to confront and hold people accountable when those standards are not met. If not, then the standards have changed.

> *"The standard you accept is the standard you will get."*
> This applies to all aspects of our lives - yes, even at home.

334

"Disaster"

What do we do when a disaster hits? Do we panic, get depressed, give up, or step back and say, "Um, let's think about this?"

Most of us will never know what we would do because we have never had a real disaster or a catastrophe that is beyond our control and leaves us with severe consequences that may change our lives forever. Oh, we have faced some tough times that we may well call disasters. Heaven forbid that our hydropower would go out, our cell phone would go missing or we didn't get our way in something.

But I mean a real catastrophic occurrence like what is going on now in Ukraine or what happened in Israel on October 7, 2024, or the destruction of the Twin Towers in New York on 911. Remember the earthquake and tidal wave in Japan on March 11, 2011, that took the lives of over 18,000 people and wiped out whole towns? Those are all disasters that we all dread or certainly wouldn't want to experience.

Disasters and catastrophes come in different forms, and what is a disaster to some may be a normal day for others. Real disasters mean a major loss of life, property, wealth, or even relationship and status.

Reactions vary. In the famous 1929 stock market crash, many people committed suicide. They just couldn't face it. Some were in denial, while others, though with great difficulty, did what they had to do to get through it and survive, and some eventually flourished.

No one is really prepared for disasters. That's why they are called disasters.

We all hope we never have to face one, but if we do and if we are among the fortunate ones who do survive, we must, as the old expression goes, "Take the bull by the horns and do what we have to do" and not allow our reactions make the disaster worse. We have to face the facts, put on our adult hats, get our emotions and attitudes in order, roll up our sleeves, and look forward to a full recovery by working with others and being truthful. Don't allow the media to increase your panic.

The biggest disaster for the world is not acknowledging who made the world.

"Bible Quiz 3" (Answers)

1. Who was born first, John the Baptist or Jesus? **John the Baptist**

2. Who were the parents of John the Baptist? **Elizabeth and Zechariah**

3. Where was Jesus born? **Bethlehem (means House of Bread)**

4. First openly recorded miracle by Jesus? **Turn water into wine.**

5. Baskets left over after Jesus fed the 5000?   **12** *(Mark 8:19)*

6. What Gospel was written by a doctor? **Luke** *(Colossians 4:14)*

7. Who is said to be the last disciple to die? **Said to be John**

8. John wrote **5 books (John, 1, 2 & 3 John, Revelation.**

9. Who did Moses drown with the closing of the Red Sea? **Roman Army**

10. How many? Name them. **Don't know their names or how many.**

336
"Passive Aggressive"

We looked at Aggressive (146), Passive (230), and Assertive (270). There's one more. This is the one that attempts to allow others to think they are passive, but they are actually aggressive. Hence, they are known as passive-aggressive. They may avoid having a conversation but express aggressive behavior either directly or indirectly, in spite of their silence. Deep down, they may be angry or upset, but rather than expressing themselves directly, they respond with what some say to be sneaky, backhanded, or childish. *(Just quoting)*

Behaviors vary but may include:

- Silence- "I'll fix you. I won't say anything."
- Avoiding – "I just won't talk to you. I won't even answer your calls."
- Sarcasm – "I didn't know you were so smart."
- Condescending – "I am sure you can do anything."
- Insulting compliments – "Your outfits finally suit you."
- Using jokes but being serious
- Agree to do something but don't do it.
- Moodiness – sulking, etc., or pretending to be. How do we handle this?

- Don't take the bait.
- Confront it head-on
- Encourage them
- Be assertive
- Be passive-aggressive – "Oh, you are so good at being passive-aggressive." Then, laugh and wait for the fight. Just kidding!

337
"Tree Shortage?"

What happened to the tree shortage? All we heard in the 80's and 90's was how we were running out of trees. Remember when the grocery stores switched from paper bags to plastic bags? "We have to save the forest." (Oops - plastic is dangerous now!) Lumber prices went up. Paper prices went up.

However, reforestation and better management went a long way to making lots of trees available.

Didn't hear much about it until Covid. The price of lumber soared but not because of a shortage of trees, but due to the supply chain and between you and me, there might have been a bit of price gouging in there. I can't prove it.

Climate change has been blamed for supply shortages as well. Forest fires take a lot of trees every year. We may as well increase the cutting, especially where fires happen a lot. Why don't they do that? Forest fires produce a lot of carbon, don't they?

I have driven from coast to coast. Our forests are vast both in Canada and the US.

I am sure it is a little complicated. But I have a feeling it is about money and control again.

Just me. I don't think there is a shortage of trees. Shortage of honesty, for sure. Trees generally grow when and where they are planted.

338
"King David"

What we know about this historical figure:

A shepherd boy, the youngest of seven sons of Jesse.

Lived around 1000 BC

Chosen by the prophet Samuel under God's direction to be king to replace the first failed king of Israel, Saul.

Defeated Goliath, the giant of the Philistines, with a sling and one stone. He then cut off the giant's head with the giant's own sword.

Became advisor to King Saul.

Hunted by Saul for years, having to hide in caves and live under terrible conditions.

Could have killed his enemy Saul, but didn't.

Became one of, if not the best, king of Israel.

Led his military to capture Jerusalem and make it the capital of Israel.

Established a strong government, caring for the people and making Israel a Godly nation.

Messed up by committing adultery and murder.

Was forgiven by God when he confessed. (Psalm 51)

Known as a man after God's own heart.

Known for his famous quotes about God and prophesies and for writing most of the Psalms in the Bible.

Famous Psalm 23.

339
"Designed for Life – "Earth"

Dr. Jonathan Corrado *(as per his published bio),* B.S., M.S., M. Div., Th.M., Ph.D, who has more qualifications and degrees than Kellogg has corn flakes, also has extensive experience, including at management level, in systems engineering, nuclear engineering (including enrichment), nuclear safety, as well as research and development. Some of his professional years were spent working in the defense industry as well as serving in the US Navy which included several years as a nuclear engineering officer on the aircraft carrier USS Dwight D. Eisenhower. He is currently a senior officer in the US Naval Reserve, and his reserve career has included a breadth of assignments and command roles on several occasions. And he has been awarded many personal, campaign, and unit-level awards. He has authored a number of technical and research papers in his field and much more. His quotes include:

"System Earth has all the tailor-made features researchers have determined are necessary for a planet to be capable of supporting living things. Scientists have long identified more than 250 optimized design requirements a planet must have for this. These include a robust and customized atmosphere, appropriate quantities of water in its various phased states (ice, liquid, and vapor), an ideal range of surface temperatures, and a period of rotation on its axis that is finely tuned."

"The fact that System Earth has these (and more!) design elements essential for life suggests it is a systems engineering marvel, one that shows all the hallmarks of incredible intelligence."

"The earth's distance from the sun also appears precisely measured for a stable water cycle. If the earth were too far away, most water would freeze. If the earth were too close, most water would boil. Furthermore, the earth's rotation period, axial tilt, magnetic field, crust thickness, and the amounts and proportions of atmospheric oxygen, nitrogen, and carbon dioxide all show signs of conforming to the appropriate specifications set in advance. So too does the system that ensures that high in the atmosphere, the balance between ozone's formation and its destruction ends up with the amount needed to protect life on the surface from destructive ultraviolet rays."

**The above quotes are directly copied by permission from Dr. Corrado's article in Creation.com*

340
"Equality vs Equity"

There is lots of talk going around these days about equity in a number of different contexts. As usual it is being misrepresented and confused by its proponents.

We like equality which means equal opportunity and fairness. No problem. I am by no means a grammar expert but there is something intentional going around that is promoting equity under the guise that it is the same as equality.

Dictionaries (Mariam) states that *"Equality refers to the quality or state of having the same rights and opportunities as in "women struggle for equality."*

We all likely agree with that definition of equality, DON'T WE? Let's stick to the woman's rights and opportunities for a moment. (Meriams dictionary used it, so I can use it.) Equity is saying, regardless of what spin is being put on it, that women should have the same outcome. Yes, I am stepping on dangerous ground with some readers here. Women or any other group should have equality of rights and opportunities but to guarantee the same outcome, i.e., "equity," is a different story.

My 45 years in business saw the push to be fair to women, which I supported. But, some companies went out of their way to place and promote women in positions just because they were women and not because of their qualifications. They had the same opportunity. Good. But that doesn't mean they should be given priority treatment. Opportunities in the workplace for sure - that's Equality. But meeting those opportunities should be based on qualifications and performance and not gender, social status or anything else. Doing so is upsetting the apple cart.

<u>Examples to upset the equity promoters:</u>

If I had a physical handicap, equality says I should have equal opportunity to try out for any part in a school play. Fair. Extreme Equity says I should get the part of the dancer.

Equality says we all have the same opportunity to an education. Fair. Equity says we should all get the same grades.

Equality says we should all have the opportunity to work for more pay. Fair. Equity says we should all get the same pay.

341
"Practice, Practise"

FYI – Practice is the noun. Practise is the verb. My "Grammarly" wife taught me that.

Perfection, excellence, or even average and acceptable is difficult to achieve without lots of practice. We have all discovered that and quite often the hard way.

In judo, we were instructed to do our "uchikomi." This is a Japanese term meaning "repetition training." We would take our favorite technique or any other technique and practice it. In the case of a throwing technique, we would go in and out to the point of contact and throw our opponent every so often. There were sessions when the instructor would make us practice the technique a minimum of 25 times, 50 times quite often up to 200 times. Why would we have to do this?

He not only wanted us to get it right, but he wanted it to be so natural that we didn't have to think about it. It just happened.

Too many people are not willing to be in practice to train and prepare themselves for their particular sport, trade, career, or, better still, life. Have you ever noticed professional guitar players, athletes, speakers, and singers perform flawlessly on stage? It doesn't just apply to entertainment and sport. The same applies to business, communication, and interpersonal skills. People get good at what they do because they practice. It is the requirement, discipline, and desire to practice that enables people to be good at what they do. It is also the unwillingness to practice that prevents people from improving and essentially causes them to give up or be mediocre at best in their performance.

You have heard the expression "practice makes perfect," which is essentially true, but we need to take it further and say that "perfect practice makes perfect." Obviously, we don't become perfect at the beginning, but we need to practice what works and not keep repeating old habits and things that don't work. We begin slow, work on the basics, and gradually speed up, continually fine-tuning. In the case of Judo and other sports, we work on the technique first, then the speed and, of course, power. And yes, speed often defeats power.

The quote, "Don't just practice until you get it right. Practise until you can't do it wrong," has been requoted by many to follow the principle of practice.

"I fear not the man who has practiced 10,000 kicks once, but I fear the man who has practiced one kick 10,000 times." Bruce Lee

342

"Omnipotent - Omniscient - Omnipresent"

The word Omni means "All".

Wouldn't it be something if you and I were omni? We could know all, be all, and be everywhere all at the same time. To have all the power there is to have, would be neat. There would be no one greater. There would be no one or nothing we could not control if we wanted to. We could command traffic, be the perfect chef, control the weather, and heal ourselves or anyone else. Determine who gets what. Answer requests. Settle everybody's quarrels.

"I would give my right arm just to be ambidextrous." (If you don't get this one-look up ambidextrous.)

Omnipotent means all power or unlimited power. Wouldn't it be something if you or I had all the power there is to have? We could win all kinds of powerlifting tournaments. We could move our house to the country. We could control all governments. Amazing!

Omniscient means all-knowing - knows everything. Wouldn't it be something to know everything there is to know? We all know something. We all know something that nobody else knows. But we don't know everything. We would know the ins and outs of science, technology, the earth, the universe, our human bodies, everybody's thoughts, how tall is the tallest tree in British Columbia and, how tall it will become before it is cut, and what it will be used for. Imagine what that would be like.

Omnipresent – everywhere present, all at the same time. Wouldn't it be something to be at work and home with our family all at the same time? Would it be something to watch a movie with the kids and be in the garage fixing the car at the same time while you are still taking a shower and maybe having a nap all at the same time. You could be with your golfing buddies while holding a meeting with your community organization. You could be celebrating your 50th birthday while at the same time enjoying your high school graduation.

You would have to be special to have any one of these but to have all three of these, you would have to be really special.

You would have to be God.

343

"Addictions"

I don't claim to be an expert on addictions. I get a taste of it *(pardon the pun)* when it comes to my eating habits. It is nearly impossible for me to pass a piece of chocolate that my wife is saving. I have difficulty eating only one cookie if there is an open box in front of me.

All joking aside, this is a serious issue. Lives are being ruined, families broken up, and the ripple effect is endless, including financial issues, crime, and even suicide.

My friend, Tom (not his real name), is an expert. He was an alcoholic for more than twenty years. He would correct that statement and say, "I am an alcoholic." He tells me these are some of the typical characteristics of a person with addictions:

- Good con artists
- Lie
- Fun at a party
- Blames everyone else for their problems – doesn't take responsibility.
- Has to drink or use drugs over any other priority
- Unable to stop drinking
- Will spend their last cent on drinking
- Will stop at nothing to have access to the addiction
- They are manipulative, secretive, impatient and impulsive

Tom tells me they are difficult to help.

However, Tom has not had a drink in over thirty-five years. He attends AA several times a week and spends a lot of time helping others. Tom's research and his own experience have told him that there is no medical cure for alcoholism and that alcoholism is a spiritual sickness and can only be helped with a spiritual cure. He goes on to say that many medical doctors dread having to deal with those in addiction because of their inability to cure them. He says Alcoholics Anonymous (AA) works. It does work for one main reason, which is confirmed by the medical association, which has gone on record to state: "Outside of a spiritual awakening, there is no cure for addiction such as alcoholism.".

344
"Sympathy – Empathy- Apathy"

They rhyme, don't they? But are they the same?

Do you feel sorry for people who don't know the difference?

Do you relate to those who don't know the difference?

Do you care about the difference?

There, we just defined all three emotions.

You should now have some notions.

Sympathy is feeling pity or sad for some who has it bad.

Empathy is understanding why they feel the way they do.

Even though you may not condone what they are going through.

Apathy is caring less about their stress.

You are concerned only about yourself.

Everyone else's needs you put on the shelf.

Sympathy is caring, though you may not understand.

Empathy is relating, on the other hand.

With apathy, you have no feeling and just bury your head in the sand.

Do you get it now that there is a time and place for each

But now you know when you make your speech.

Some you will care for, and some you will be just there for

The rest, you are not concerned about why they are even there for.

345

"Love Again"

There is a saying going around that says. "Love is Love." Do you really believe that?

Loving chocolate is not the same as loving a game of golf or loving a sunny day on the beach. They are all love, but not the same kind of love. We love our kids, but we love our sweethearts in a different way. They are not all the same kinds of love, are they? We eat chocolate, we play golf, and we care for our children. Eat, play, and care are different. Therefore, all love is not love. If we loved our children, we wouldn't give them too much chocolate. If we loved our children, we wouldn't leave them to be playing golf all day long.

Loving chocolate and loving golf are the kinds of love when we receive something or do something that gives us pleasure. But loving our kids or our sweetheart is giving love. Yes, they give us pleasure as well. We enjoy all of them, but if we had to choose between chocolate and our kids, we would hopefully choose our kids.

The Greeks talk about their six different categories as "eros," or sexual passion. They say that "philia" is a deep friendship and "ludus" or playful love, which is the kind between children and can drift into eros in adults. Their "Pragma" is the kind of love that is longstanding between long-married couples. Their word for self-love is "Philautia." Then they have "Agape" love which they call love for everyone. This is a giving love and is often translated as charity, or the kind the bible states when it refers to the love of God.

This agape love is distinguished from the others in that it is focused on others rather than on oneself. With more of this kind of love, we would have less greed and fewer people asking, "What's in for me?". Instead, they would be asking, "What can I do for you?"

Sure, we love and enjoy things and find pleasure in things for ourselves. While that is natural, true love is action-oriented toward thinking of others first and less of ourselves.

How is your love working? Is it selfless or selfish? Do you love enough to give and forgive? Do you love enough to sacrifice?

IMPORTANT POINT: Loving someone, regardless of the meaning we use, doesn't mean we have to agree with or accept everything they do or say.

346
"Earth's Age"

The earth is now 4,000,000,004 years old. I know that because 4 years ago, I read that some scientists said it was four billion years old. Plus, a calendar was unearthed showing the year 4 billion BC. It had a picture on the front of the Statue of Liberty. No, that's not right because the Statue of Liberty wasn't built then. It was another picture, maybe the Mona Lisa or a caveman.

I love scientific research. But I get disgusted with information that cannot be proven and is just put forward to promote an agenda or make somebody famous for writing a paper based primarily on their own wishful thinking or misinterpretation of the facts.

There are two schools of thought about the age of the earth: It is old, or it is young. For those who believe in evolution, it has to be old. For those who believe everything was created by God, then it should be young.

There is another school of thought, and that is "we really don't know for sure." The young earthers and the old earthers have the same information and evidence. However, they interpret it differently. There are qualified scientists on both sides of the argument who give their respective reasons for what they believe.

No scientific method can *prove* the age of the earth and the universe since all dating methods use unproven assumptions about the past.

For greater incite in the age of the earth as well as aging methods, google creation.com and search "age of the earth." Have fun.

347

"Woman"

What is a woman?
Now there's a question that has been asked.
But to give an answer, many people will pass.
Why, I wonder, is it difficult to see?
The difference between she and he
What about what used to be taught in school?
We know the facts; we are no fools.
The biology is there for all for sure
It is so obvious when they come through the door
The feminine traits are hard to cover up
One thing for sure is the size of her cup
Sexual organs are facts of life
And yet, there are plans to change them with a knife
The science is there in all the discoveries
Men just don't have ovaries
The body structure is plain to all
Women are generally physically smaller, weaker, and not as tall.
Men and women are equal but different
In emotions, intuition, and even their scent.
Why are they bothering to change the world?
Everyone knows a boy is not a girl.
We should all pitch in and defend her rights,
But it has nothing at all to do with her rights.
Women, we love you, and this is from a man.
Who sees you for who you are whenever we can
You are smart and beautiful and deserve lots of respect
That should happen whenever we connect
You have been used and abused and treated unkind
Have been taken advantage of in body and mind
You don't need to change who you are
We can tell who you are even from afar.

348

"Fun"

I love fun, don't you? Have we gotten away from it? Seems that way all too often. We know there are times to be serious, but we can have fun even when times are tough. We have covered a lot of serious, important, and sometimes negative topics in this book, but that doesn't mean we can't have fun. In fact, we need to have fun to be able to deal with them.

Albert Einstein said, "Having fun is the best way to learn." Look at all he accomplished.
Everybody knows "time flies when you are having fun."

I was often criticized for saying work should be fun, but most of the time, I still got everything done. Sure, there is a time to dig in and get to work, but we can do that without being a jerk.

Fun is good therapy. We sure need a lot of that, don't we?
We all want to succeed and get to the top, but there is nothing to say we can't have fun on the way.

Fun can be planned, but I find it is generally an attitude of who we are, and we often take ourselves too seriously. I got laughed at yesterday for wearing my green army fatigue shorts with a blue and red plaid shirt. They didn't match, but I changed quickly when I came home from being caught in a downpour. I was the brunt of the jokes all night. My wife and son had a lot of fun. I pretended I didn't, but it was a laugh. I let on that I was a fashion statement.

"What's the point in life if you can't have fun?" So says actor Paul Walker. He is actually not far out from what the half-brother of Jesus said, *"Consider it all joy when you fall into various kinds of trials."* James 1:2

Having fun is a choice. We can have fun and still get a lot done.

349

"Government"

Oh no, we just talked about fun, and now we are on to government. Why do we have to spoil the fun? Hold on, that is part of the fun. Don't you have a lot of fun making government jokes?

"The difference between death and taxes is that government doesn't meet every year to make death worse."

"What should we do about people who rely on handouts and refuse to work? Vote them out of office."

There is one thing worse than bad government, and that is people who elect them and keep them in power.".We need government. It is a great institution that was actually instituted by God. It has a very important role in society to ensure that justice and fairness are done. And yes, there is lots to be done, and yes, they need some of, not all, of our money in the form of taxes. While we would like to keep all of our money and pay no tax, we should be responsible and not cheat on our taxes. Doing so is very unfair to those who do.

I am a big supporter of government but as you could likely tell from some other pages in this book, I am not a fan of some of the things that certain political parties and their politicians do when they are in government. I won't repeat them here. But we need to be able to differentiate our views on the institution of government from some politicians and how they run government. I know that can be difficult to do. *"Politics is supposed to be the second-oldest profession. I have come to realize that it bears a very close resemblance to the first." —Ronald Reagan.*

Often, depending on the party in power, one of the biggest downfalls in government is their controlling of the media and the misrepresentation by the media.

Let's take an interest in our government. It is there to represent us and work in our best interest.

350
"Drugs"

Your typical internet search will show statistics such as:

"More than four (4) times as many people died from drug overdose (OD) than from homicide in the first month of 2021."

"The annual death rate in the US has gone from 6 per 100,000 to over 21 per 100,000 between 1999 and 2019."

"Opioids (pain relieving medicine) contribute to the majority of these deaths."

These few internet stats have drastically changed for the worse since Covid and open border policies.

Can we change it? How? Stricter laws or more law enforcement simply treat the systems and not the cause.

Why are so many people hooked on drugs? A better question would be, why are they so set on taking drugs of any kind?

Is there a bigger problem than the use of drugs that is causing people to resort to them? Is drug use a symptom of our society that has lost its way?

It doesn't seem to be addressed. Is it a health problem? Is it a financial problem? Is it a spiritual problem? What do you think?

I have to admit I have more questions than answers here.

351
"Signs"

Some great signs from various Facebook posts:

"Open 24 hours, 7 days a week. Closed between 2 am and 5 am Friday to

Sunday." Notice: The patio is currently not open because it is closed.

Sign on washroom floor: The toilet is out of order. Please use the floor below.

The billboard read, 'I started out with nothing. I still have most of it."

The seminar leader showed on a screen, "Remember, you can't use logic on someone who can't tell the difference between a boy and a girl."

Church display: "The inventor of autocorrect died. The funnel will be a tomato."

Restaurant sign reads, "Do not eat metal, or you will sheet aluminum."

"Give me a coffee to change the things I can. Give me wine to accept the things I can't change."

"I am taking steps to overcome my hiking addiction. I am not out of the woods yet."

"Inspecting mirrors is a job I can see myself doing."

Church sign says: "We are still open between Christmas and Easter."

352
"Perfectionists"

Dictionary meaning: "a person who refuses to accept any standard short of perfection."

If I were going on a space rocket to the moon, I want a perfectionist on staff. If I am going in for open heart surgery, I pray the doctor is a perfectionist. I think we would all go along with those two examples.

But

Do we need to be a perfectionist in everything we do? Will you settle for excellence? Or how about "good enough"? When is "good enough" good enough?

Attention to detail is admired. We can be detailed in some things but could care less about other things, especially when it comes to satisfying ourselves. If we do something for someone else, we tend to be more particular, or at least should be.

The upside of perfectionists is the wonderful detail. Their downside (so they tell me) is they run the risk of not finishing something on time, and sadly, they are never happy, i.e., they worry a lot. Of course, the extreme perfectionist is labeled as OCD or Obsessive Compulsive Disorder. If you are reading my book, you are likely already dissatisfied, upset, and frustrated at the way I have expressed things. Sorry!

My rule of thumb for the level between carelessness and perfection is to ask questions like:

- Who am I doing this for?
- How important is the quality?
- Will it make a difference if it is a little better or a little worse?
- What does the client want?
- Do I need to impress someone?
- Can I live with it?
- Am I being unrealistic?
- Am I missing the whole point?
- Will they really care?

353

"Conspiracy"

"They are coming to get you. You know that, don't you?"
"They didn't really land on the moon. All does pictures were fake, and all the space pictures you see from space are fake too."
"Elvis is still alive, and he lives in Tweed, Ontario."
"Aliens built the pyramids"

Get the idea? There is a saying that 'conspiracy theorists have strong legs because they jump to conclusions.'

There are many conspiracy theories going around that are crazy. On the other hand, there is so much corruption in our world today we can hardly blame some people for being conspiracy theorists.

How is this for a conspiracy theory? Some people are calling other people conspiracy theorists just so they won't question them and discover their conspiracy. Yep! Happens all the time in politics and political and social agendas. It happened during COVID, Big time. Does that make me a conspiracy theorist to say that?

Liberals say that conservatives are bigger conspiracy theorists than liberals. Is that a conspiracy theory, or do liberals say about conservatives what they are themselves? Both sides have conspiracy theories. Which one is the worse?

Just because we question a story does not mean we are conspiracy theorists. It just means we want to know the truth. But when people don't reveal the truth, then there is reason to question motives.

"Hundreds of people got stuck in an elevator between floors. Don't believe it. They made it up."

354

"Water"

Water is such a unique liquid. Here are some qualities of water that may not be commonly known:

- Pure water is tasteless and colorless
- Natural water has salt minerals, giving it a taste
- We drink it, wash in it, swim in it, cook in it, and sail in it
- Our bodies are 65% water
- We would die in about 3 days without water
- Earth is said to be the only place in the universe with liquid water
- Water boils at 212 degrees Fahrenheit (100 degrees Celsius)
- Water has a good surface tension, making it easy for bugs to walk on it
- Water is a super solvent, making it suitable for dissolving things

According to Healthline.com

- Water helps us create saliva – regulates our body temperature – protects our tissues helps digestion and constipation – improves circulation, and helps us lose weight.

Water can exist as a solid(ice), liquid or gas(steam)

It is used to generate electricity and is vital in numerous industries.

Water expands when frozen – hence, ice floats on water since it is less dense than water.

Water also expands when heated.

Water has its highest density at 4 degrees C. It will then expand if it goes higher or lower in temperature.

Water freezes at the top of a pond.

The word water appears in the Bible over 400 times.

355
"Thermodynamics Laws"

These three laws have to do with heat and energy.

The first law is known as the <u>Law of Conservation of Energy</u>. It states the energy of a system may change forms, but it is neither created nor destroyed. The total of kinetic energy (energy in motion) and potential energy is always the same.

The second law of thermodynamics states the entropy of a system not in thermal equilibrium increases. In plain language, this means things wear out. They get worse. Things go from good to bad, not bad to good. Things degenerate.

The third law states the entropy of a system approaches a constant value as the temperature approaches absolute zero. Absolute zero is the lowest theoretically possible temperature (0K or zero Kelvin).

The entropy of a system at absolute zero is nearly zero but not necessarily exactly zero. Entropy depends on how many ground states a system has. Pure crystalline matter attains perfect order. It has one minimum ground state and has zero entropy at absolute zero. However, most matter never quite attains zero entropy.

Confused? Me too. Zeroing in on the second one means that our bodies will not improve with age; they will wear out. Life in any form doesn't gain function; it loses function. It doesn't evolve. It devolves. The universe is not improving; it is getting worse.

356
"Christmas"

Goosebumps, excitement, presents, decorations, food, meals, family, food, time off work, visits, friends, parties, shopping, rushing. Is this what it is all about?

For sure, if you don't know the real meaning of Christmas, and even if you do know what it is all about, you can enjoy all the things on the list, but it is not what it is all about. It is about how we do things and why.

Christmas is celebrated, or at least should be, for the simple reason that Christ is in Christmas. It is the celebration of the birth of Jesus Christ. Everybody knows that…you would think, but not so. For many, the birth of Jesus is hardly, if ever, thought of during the Christmas season.

Jesus was promised for thousands of years, all through the Old Testament. The words are there to tell us that He would come, why He would come, how He would come, where He would come, and what would happen to Him when he did come.

He came. Jesus God in the flesh as described in John 1:1-4 and 14:

"In the beginning was the Word, and the Word was with God, and the Word was God. 2 He was in the beginning with God. 3 All things were made through Him, and without Him, nothing was made that was made. 4 In Him was life, and the life was the light of men."

14 And the Word became flesh and dwelt among us, and we beheld His glory, the glory as of the only begotten of the Father, full of grace and truth." Pretty clear, isn't it?

Jesus wasn't really born on December 25. But that is the day it is celebrated. It is the tradition in many places in North America to celebrate Christmas from December 25 to January 6.

Merry Christmas!

"Fredbits"

For more than 25 years in my career, I have used frequent newsletters to maintain contact with employees and give them relevant and sometimes irrelevant information just for fun.

Some of it was original and some were requotes.

Did you know?

"There is nothing that is more certain sign of insanity than to do the same thing over and over and expect the results to be different" — Albert Einstein.

Insanity is hereditary. You get it from your kids.

Many people worry too much about facing death and not enough about facing life.

"Double standard" – Doesn't it annoy you when people insist on correcting the faults in you that they don't correct in themselves?

Just heard this one yesterday: "Knowledge is knowing that a tomato is a fruit. Wisdom is not putting a tomato in a fruit salad."

Some people who try so hard to get attention don't understand why they don't get attention.

My buddy Bill sipped his coffee when working on his sermons. He began doodling around his coffee stains and ended up with beautiful doodles based on his sermon topics. He called his doodles "doodleonomy".

"Little Bo-Peep has lost her sheep and can't tell where to find them. Leave them alone, and they'll come home, wagging their tails behind them." Did you really think their tails would wag in front of them?

A human can lift an average of twice its body weight. An ant can lift 20 times its body weight.

The parable of the prodigal son in the Bible portrayed a young man rebelling. He left home to find out the hard way how good he had it. He returned to his father, who gladly took him back.

358
"Tough"

I grew up admiring tough people, especially physically tough people. I wanted to be strong and tough like my father. His physical strength was amazing. (I know I am bragging- I wrote a book about my parents. It is called "Skipper Ches - As Tough As It Gets." Go get it if you don't already have it.

He and other people in that era and that location understood what it was to be tough, yet they just took it for granted. They did what they had to do to survive, live and yes, they had fun.

They just weren't only tough physically. They had the whole package of tough, which included courage and bravery. They didn't have time to be "namby pampy" and "whimpish". They were strong and tough both physically and mentally.

Are people tough today? Have we trained people to be weak? Do we have it too easy?

The pioneers had to be tough when they ploughed across North America. Famous inventors like Edison had to be tough to be successful in their endeavors.

Do we have a society that has too many people who give up too easily at first sight of a difficult challenge? Have we created a culture of handouts and entitlements? What happened to those of us who had to walk 10 miles uphill to school both ways? Joking, of course, but you get the point. We close schools for the first flake of snow. We remove playground equipment for fear of injury. We can't speak our minds anymore. Everyone is offended, and we dare not offend anyone. They take away tests in school. Everybody becomes a winner in sports. Discipline in schools is non-existent. While encouragement is wonderful, kids need to be prepared for the world.

Don't get me going. Too late! Sure, there are still lots of tough people. I know lots of them. Maybe some tough times will make us tougher. Who do you know that is tough?

"If you fell down yesterday, stand up today." H.G. Wells

"Life is rough, so you gotta be tough." Johhny Cash

359
"Politics" *(not again)*

I paid no attention to it as a kid, not even as a teenager. Nothing was spoken of it in school. I didn't know and didn't care. As I aged, I just assumed that government people knew what they were doing and were doing the right thing for our country. I took note of the occasional comment and noticed that opinions varied as to who was better or worse.

In my university I could tell politics was an issue. It seemed really important to some that you followed certain candidates in elections. But I didn't understand it and I didn't know that the candidates followed an agenda depending on their party. I volunteered once in a campaign having no idea what I was doing. I was in my early 30s before I really started paying attention. I listened to the words of one candidate, and it made sense. I voted for him. He was a disappointment.

As years went by, I began to tell the difference between two main sides of politics- Right vs left- conservatism vs liberalism.

According to Wikipedia: *"**Conservatism** is a cultural, social, and political philosophy that seeks to promote and to preserve traditional institutions, customs, and values."*

According to Wikipedia: *"**Liberalism** is a political and moral philosophy based on the rights of the individual, liberty, consent of the governed, political equality, right to private property and equality before the law."*

I question both of these definitions.

Conservatism is labeled "Right." Liberalism is labeled "Left." When we hear far right or far left, that would certainly indicate the extreme of the respective side.

It seems that in North America, we are divided, and the division is getting to the point that each side is intolerant of the other.

How does one choose? It seems pointless to vote based on a candidate because the party platform will outvote him/her. Could it be that candidates are more interested in staying in power than what is right for the country? Could it be that money is swaying politicians? Could it be that people are confused, mistrusting, misled, and way-led? Is it a game, or is it a battle? Are we taking politics too seriously or not serious enough?

Just asking.

360
"Nice"

When I like something, I tend to say that four-letter word "Nice." I have been criticized for it. A client let me have it once when I complimented something by saying, "That's nice." He said, "Can't you think of something more exciting than nice?" I shocked him and said, "I am sorry, that's really nice." We both laughed.

There are lots of beautiful and flamboyant words for complimenting and behaving, but I still like nice. If we could just get people to be nice to each other. Wouldn't it be nice?

Nice means pleasant. That's a good start to a conversation and a good way to conduct a conversation and end a conversation.

People remember nice. They will say, "Well, isn't he or she a nice person?" It is enjoyable and satisfactory. It is kind, friendly and polite. Yes, we can be more exciting, effervescent and have flair. But most people will settle for nice.

Nice is better than abrupt, crude, rude, quick, and insulting.

Did you have a nice visit? Yes, I had a nice visit. But did you mean it? Did you just say nice because you have a poor vocabulary, or were you sincere? If you were sincere, then that's nice.

Nice is not hard. It doesn't cost a lot. It's better than nasty.

Jimmy Durante said, *"We should be nice to people on the way up because you may meet them on the way down."*

Being nice doesn't have to be phony. It's a great way to be for all ages and all types of people and in all situations. It doesn't matter our status or position in life. We can even be nice in bad situations. Who knows, the person you are nice to may be going through a rough time, and your nice was just what they needed to get through the day.

If we can't be nice, maybe we should be quiet. That may not be nice though.

Were you nice today? Was someone nice to you today?

Sure, we can be wonderful, beautiful, exquisite, amazing, far-out, and cool, but let's at least be nice.

It was really nice writing his page. I hope it was nice for you to read it.

361
"Grief"

The words below have been taken by permission from the inside cover of a book entitled "Grieving Room," published by Broadleaf Books, and written by Leanne Friesen. Leanne is an author, speaker, grief educator, ordained minister, and curator of the popular Grieving Room Instagram account. She has pastored for 20 years and serves as a conference and retreat speaker across Canada. She holds a Master of Divinity degree from McMaster University as well as a postgraduate degree certificate in death and bereavement from
Wilfred Lauier University. She is currently the Executive Minister of "The Canadian Baptist of Ontario and Quebec."

"People long to reduce the enormity of our grief. "Time heals all wounds," they tell us, or at least "she isn't in pain anymore." Yet, no matter how hard others try to stuff our grief into a process or a plan, grief cannot be willed away.

Leanne Freisen thought she knew a lot about bereavement. She had studied in school and preached it at memorial services. But only when her own sister died from cancer did she learn, in her very own bones, what grieving people don't need – and what they do. In *Grieving Room*, Friesen writes with vulnerability, wisdom, and somehow wit about the stark and sacred lessons learned at deathbeds and funerals. When someone dies, we need room for imperfect goodbyes, she writes, and room for a changing faith. We need room for regret and room to rage at the world, Room for hard holidays, and room in our schedules. We need room for redemption and room for resurrection – and we also need room to never "get over it."

In this poignant account of a sister's mourning and a pastor's journey, Friesen pushes back against a world that wants to minimize our sorrow and avoid our despair. She helps those of us walking with the grieving figure out what to say and what not to say, and she offers practical ways to create ample space for every emotion and experience. Reflection, questions, practices, and prayers at the end of this book offer guidance and ideas for individuals and groups.

In a world that wants to rush forward with closure and healing, Grieving Room gives us permission to let loss linger. When the very worst happens, we can learn to give ourselves and others grieving room."

362
"Bible Books - Title Meanings"

Ever wonder what some of the titles of the various Bible books mean? I used to. Here are some original meanings, along with a few synonyms of books that are not titled with the authors' names.

<u>Genesis:</u> The book of Beginnings – Origin – Birth - to be born. Gives the story of creation and more.

<u>Exodus:</u> Departure – Emigration in large numbers – Original word means to leave. Over two million Hebrews left Egypt after 400 years of captivity.

<u>Leviticus</u> Comes from the Hebrew word for 'law of the priests. The tribe of Levi (son of Jacob) were designated as priests. They were given laws and guidelines to live by in the book of Leviticus.

<u>Numbers</u> – The obvious has to do with facts and records. It was a roll call and census of those in the wilderness.

<u>Deuteronomy:</u> Derived from the Greek "copy' or 'repetition.' In this book, Moses sums up much of the previous four books of history, laws and teaching.

<u>Psalms:</u> From the Greek word songs. Most of the Psalms were written to be sung

<u>Proverbs:</u> The original meaning was 'to be like' or 'parable' conveying self-evident truths.

<u>Ecclesiastes:</u> Preacher or "one who calls an assembly," Solomon speaks and preaches about wisdom and his lessons from life.

<u>Revelation:</u> The full title is "The Revelation Of Jesus Christ." Jesus reveals many mysteries about Himself and the future.

363
"Advice"

"Dangerous ground" that is giving advice.

Before we give it, we should think twice.

Who are we to think we know it all

Enough to cause others to rise and maybe fall?

True, we may know more than some.

Do we have facts or are there more to come?

Should we tell them what to do or help them figure out

Their own solutions, without a doubt?

But advice is good, and listen we should.

But we need to consider if it works for us

Instead of just giving them in a rush.

We all need help, so let's seek it where we can

But in the end, it is our decision on the other hand.

We all know something with which we can help others

But we are not everyone's fathers and mothers.

One piece of advice we should all heed

Is to take the advice we offer and apply it to our own need.

364
"Help"

That's the opening chorus from a Beatles song. A lot of us need help. Everybody needs help. But is everybody seeking help, and will we accept the help that is offered?

Too many people hesitate to ask for help for fear that people will think less of them. Asking for help doesn't have to mean we are weak and dumb. Asking for help can be wise. It also means we are honest about our own abilities.

"There's no shame in asking for help. The real shame is in refusing it when you know you need it." – Unknown.

The key to that quote is recognizing when we need help.

"We all need help. Don't be afraid to ask for it." – Steve Harvey

<u>Qualifier:</u> Let's distinguish between needing genuine help vs. not wanting to do anything for ourselves.

Back to help. I have to get over the vulnerability of asking for help. I have to admit I still have flashbacks of thinking, "If I can't do it, it ' be done." That attitude borders on stubbornness and pride. Let's be brave and seek help when we genuinely need it. Every successful person has received help somewhere along the line.

Asking for help takes courage, and it also adds to our knowledge, strengths, and skills. I can't imagine where I would be if I didn't ask for help or use the help I received.

There is another side of help which is helping others. Many of us could do a lot more in that area. As we need help, we also should be willing to offer and provide help where it is needed.

"Life's most persistent and urgent question is, 'What are you doing for others?'" – Martin Luther King Jr

365
"Answers"

We began with questions on the first page

Questions that will change a lot with age.

You got more questions through the book

But for all the answers, we still do need to look.

We just skimmed the surface of the things to know

None of us have all the answers. That is easy to show.

But we all have experiences to talk about.

You have received some of them is this book throughout.

I don't claim to be right in everything I've said.

They should get you thinking if you carefully read.

Don't take everything as absolutely true.

Doing your research is now up to you.

I hope I have challenged your thinking. I hope you have been

informed. I hope I inspired your emotions and hope you

laughed up a storm.

We will run out of answers when we run out of questions,

But let me leave you with one more suggestion

It is good to have the answers you sought

But now, what will you do with the answers you got?

About The Author

Born on a small Island community off the east coast of Canada in 1950, Fred's experiences in his early teenage years included being in partnership with two friends as lobster fishermen. His summers also saw him working at the local fish plant. After graduating from university in 1971 as a Physics major, he taught school for a year before spending 13 years in the banking industry, accepting multiple transfers whereby he ended up in the greater Toronto area of Ontario. Fred's experience with management and finance opened doors to other opportunities that led him to success for 12 years in the printing industry.

In 1998, he founded Dyman Management Inc., consulting for various businesses, conducting seminars on leadership and management across Canada, the US and even Scotland and Russia. During this time, he wrote and self-published "That Book About Management."

While his working career kept him busy, he continued with his two favorite interests. He took up both Judo and wrestling in his second year of university. He continues to teach Judo as a sixth-degree black belt, having competed provincially and nationally for 15 years, winning numerous provincial titles, and regional titles.

Parallel to his working career and Judo, Fred's spiritual life and work with churches opened the door in 2015 for him and his wife, Judee, to be full-time pastors of a church.

In 2023, he authored a biography of his parents, entitled "Skipper Ches, As Tough As It Gets".

Fred and Judee live in a small town one hour north of Toronto. They have seven children, 14 grandchildren and nine great-grandchildren.

www.FredDykeBooks.com

www.ingramcontent.com/pod-product-compliance
Lightning Source LLC
Chambersburg PA
CBHW080600300726
48975CB00010B/2742